## PLEASURE'S TORMENT

"My God, you are beautiful," Ram whispered as his hand drew circles over the taunting peaks.

Joy bit her lip with a muted cry and closed her eyes tight. "Please—"

He countered her bewildered torment with another chuckle. "Please what, I wonder? A cry for mercy?" he asked as his lips and tongue teased the rosy tips to shameless desire. Never had she imagined anything like this! She flushed with tumultuous sensations rippling through her. "Mercy you shall get," he said softly as he gently massaged the swollen peaks. "A slow, sweet and blessed mercy, indeed . . ."

# Passion's Joy

### Jennifer Horsman

**ZEBRA BOOKS**
**KENSINGTON PUBLISHING CORP.**

ZEBRA BOOKS

are published by

Kensington Publishing Corp.
475 Park Avenue South
New York, NY 10016

First  printing: November 1987

Printed in the United States of America

# Part I

# The Girl Who Loved Freedom

# *Chapter One*

The light of a single candle flickered in the small room, casting dark shadows over the neat white page where Joy Claret sat writing. She wore naught but a thin cotton night dress which, taken with her dark unbounded hair falling past the small of her back and the soft light illuminating the delicate features of her face, gave her a deceptively angelic appearance.

Fine blue eyes—eyes perfectly illustrating Shakespeare's observation that this feature was the window to the soul—were presently much absorbed in task; she was lost to the wealth of ideas and feelings that flowed into words as she wrote:

February eighteenth, the year of our Lord, eighteen eighteen

Dear Diary,

Dawn awaits, so do our three passengers hidden in the cellar of the infirmary, cloistered like so many before them in the cool holding cell beneath the floor. Oh, my dearest friend! I feel the excitement and fear common to all freedom seekers, and as I write this, my heart pounds and my pulse races at a pace befitting a chased pickpocket!

Chased we shall be! The two male passengers, both young and strong, worth much at the marketplace I think, have a bounty of fifteen hundred between them. The reverend learned of it yesterday. That sum alone is sure to be of a size attracting the most infernal of bounty hunters. But that is not all dear diary, we also carry a woman passenger this time, and her bounty is an unprecedented one thousand dollars gold! I feel compelled to explain—

The sound of a regretfully familiar cough came from the room down the hall and it stopped her. She waited, knowing exactly how bad the cough must be to wake her ailing guardian, her Uncle Joshua, and when it was mild enough to let him keep sleeping. It subsided quickly and the tension left her face.

The interruption made her aware of the sounds of the city, drifting in through the open window. She heard the boisterous noise of taverns that never closed: drunken laughter, talk and music, all sounding distant and faint like the echo of a dream upon waking. The brick bell-tower atop the Ursuline Convent suddenly sounded thrice. A carriage clamored down the street, and as she listened very closely, she heard the first faint bustles of the marketplace signaling the start of yet another new day. From her own room came the soft sound of Cory's slumber.

Time was of the essence, and she returned to her writing.

—this matter at length, my explanation not merited by the incredible sum of the woman's bounty but by the passenger's uncommon circumstances. She goes by the common name of Mary and could be no more than my own seven and ten years, and my but she is as pretty as a storybook princess. The characteristic most uncommon is her coloring. She is blue-eyed and fair, many generations removed from her Negro blood, and

8

this—even Joshua concedes—will allow her to pass in a cooler climate, thereby providing her with the ultimate ticket to freedom. She was obviously a house servant, her smooth-skinned hands show no signs of arduous toil, and her speech and manners are polite and refined. For what lascivious practice her master put her to use—a practice worth $1000 to him—I dare not contemplate in my blissful innocence.

Danger shadows the day and my apprehension grows as I write, for Mary is also ill and weak. She has passed too much blood, even for a late monthly, and the good doctor's potion did little to ease her discomfort. The reverend tried to postpone the run, but the receiving end said nay to this—today or the next month following. So I had Cory give Mary extra dowsing strips, and Sammy lined the cart with extra peat moss and hay. This, I pray, will suffice.

I offer to God's ear my traditional prayer for safe deliverance of our three passengers on to the blessed shore of freedom. The bright light of the North Star shines in my heart and I leave you as always, my friend, with the fervent hope for the freedom of all God's children—

Cory rose with a start, bolting up in the small feather bed. Dolls lined the shelves of the room, and though each childhood treasure was by light of day familiar and cherished, the masked faces took on a demonic and ghostlike vision in her sleepy haze. Soft brown eyes immediately searched and found Joy Claret at her desk, and relieved, Cory eased her skinny frame back against the pillows.

She always woke like that on the mornings before a run, as though her anxieties and fears built through the night into a crescendo upon waking. She yawned and stretched, throwing back the covers to slip silently from the bed. The floor board gave a small creak as she lifted it to remove the small bundle of clothes hidden there. Holding the bundle, she came around the other side of the bed, and with disapproval in her gaze, she watched Joy Claret close the leather bound book and lock it with the tiny gold key before returning it to the drawer.

"Dat book's gonna send us all to the grave."

"Honestly Cory!" Joy gasped in a whisper, "you move like a savage stalking deer!"

While Cory smiled, she was hardly deferred. "I'se a piece of mind to tell Massa Joshua 'bout it, I do."

"You wouldn't!"

"No, but I should," she said softly. "I knows I should. Come on, you'se should be dressed by now."

Cory referred to the two commandments of conducting: never ask a passenger's name, their former master's name or from where they came, and secondly, never but never keep a written record of the runs.

"Of course, you're right," Joy admitted as she rose without token tribute to that coveted virtue of modesty, pulled off her night dress and stood in her bare skin.

Joy lacked self-awareness and did not realize the beauty of her unclad state. Hard work and exercise—far too much for a lady in the clerical class—kept her trim and slender. Nature had done the rest, endowing her with alluring feminine proportions. Of course, those few times she took stock of such things, she found fault with her shoulders. Even when she practiced in front of Cory, her shoulders steadfastly refused even a conscious effort to slope prettily in the fashionable way—a way that made a woman look somewhat whimsical and delicate. As though her dignity were fixed and unalterable, straight narrow lines drew her shoulders and the proud arch of her small straight back. Nature's gifts showed elsewhere though: in full and rounded breasts that tapered to a small waist and in the shapely lines drawing her slender hips and long legs. This was fortunate, for Joy possessed little patience for feminine fussing, and like many other women in hot and humid Louisiana, she could never imagine submitting to an hour long arduous tug of war with stays, huffing and puffing and feeling faint, all to get the slenderness she already had due to the rigors of hard work, the family's worsening means and quite literally not having adequate food stuff.

Presently though, danger and its close companion, excitement, were felt as a nearly tangible force in the room, and the tension brought an unnatural silence to the two as Joy stepped into the potato sack breeches, then pulled a red frayed shirt over that. The small unloaded pistol slipped into her shoulder harness and a worn vest fit over it. Cory worked Joy's hair into long braids, a task made difficult by what she called the jitters.

"Mercy," Cory's whisper finally broke the silence, "I'm as skittish as a fresh born colt. Dat Mary girl's given me a might big pause fo' worry."

With her costume in place, Joy strongly felt Cory's nervousness, but she replied with feeling, "We must pray for her safety."

"One thousand dollars gold! Lawd, but it don' do a soul a lick of good to 'magin' why a man would consider a woman worth such a 'rageously high 'mount."

"No, it doesn't," she agreed as Cory placed the strawlike blond wig attached to a wide straw hat over the loose crown of braids to top the picture. "All I can think is she must have suffered terribly to risk running—"

The horses and cart pulled up outside interrupting Joy mid-sentence, and Cory, already holding an old jar of dirt, hurriedly smeared grime on Joy's pale face, then wiped her hands clean on the boys' breeches. With a kiss they quickly bid each other goodbye, but as Joy turned to leave, she stopped suddenly.

"Joshua had a good night. He should be better today."

Cory heard the familiar hope lift in Joy's voice and knew

11

what was being asked. "Don't worry, I'll take special good care of him."

Joy Claret nodded. "The medicine's low again. On the morrow, I'll try to work out our next scheme to get the money for the next round."

"You'll think of somethin', you always do."

The vote of confidence brought a smile and Joy slipped through the door. Cory then blew out the candle and fell inelegantly into the desk chair. Sometimes life seemed filled from one day to the next with naught but worries: worries over medicine and money, worry over Joshua and bounty hunters. "Mercy but there sure is a passel of worries to fret over . . ."


Pulled by two matching bays, the rickety looking peddler's cart made slow progress down the well-traveled river road. Piled clumsily atop the cart, the wares jostled in a continuous rattle; there were pots and pans, brooms, horse brushes and mops, a pile of nearly new carpets, along with bonnets and combs for the ladies, work shirts and belts for the men, slop jars and one pair of children's boots. There were Indian artifacts, none of these genuine, and an array of pocket and hunting knives. A whole cabinet full of medicines stood against one side. Inside this were cherry cough lozenges, vegetable tonics, headache and rheumatoid cures, a bottle of Fay's Female Elixir and unnamed potions for whatever ailment the ailing named. A pretty mare pranced in back, but a rain canvas and a tall pile of weightless bundles hid the mare's fine lines, leading the outside observer to think Libertine was naught but an old plow nag.

Seated in the driver's seat with reins in hand, the reverend was dressed as a peddler. The old Irishman's short, five-foot two frame was clad in black, tattered and moth eaten shanks, frock coat and boots two sizes too large. A frayed, black top hat covered the strings that held an unkempt beard in place.

Thick spectacles hid lively dark eyes, eyes too sharp for the poverty stricken scoundrel he pretended to be.

Joy smiled, affectionately patting the reverend's knee as they rode along. If there was any one thing she had learned in her five years as an adventuress, it was that folks rarely bothered to look past the surface of things, and this worked to their favor time and again.

So long as she kept her mouth shut, she could fool everyone. With her eyes lowered beneath her hat in a convincing look of dull apathy common to poor whites and a quick swipe of a dirty sleeve to her nose, she fooled the most observant. No one could ever suspect the dirty peddler's brat of being the good doctor Joshua Reubens's lovely young charge, Joy Claret Reubens.

The river road paralleled the great waterway for hundreds of miles, and one could not pass an hour anywhere on the Mississippi without seeing at least one or more boats passing on their way to New Orleans. Hundreds of back river flatboats cluttered the waterway for miles north of the city and its marketplace. To the south of the city on their present course, docked in rank order roughly according to size, sat the larger boats: houseboats, fishing vessels and medium sized cargo flats. The boats grew in size and importance until miles farther downstream rose the tall masts of the proud ocean-going vessels.

The river road south of New Orleans bustled with activity as these great ships were forever in the process of loading and unloading cargo, setting sail and docking. It was somewhat quieter now in the early morning hours. Taverns and houses—the small farming parcels that forever battled the encroaching claim of the forest—became increasingly rare, at least until Carlisle. The cart's destination lay a few miles past Carlisle, another eight to ten miles down the road where a small ship, the *Nirvana,* would be waiting. The ship's master and captain, Mr. Fairbanks, was the paid conductor. Although trustworthy, it irked Joy's keen sense of justice to

13

have to pay Mr. Fairbanks for the passenger's safe deliverance into the good hands of the famed abolitionist Mr. Archibald Cox in Boston.

God's will should be done for honor alone, she thought.

Thinking of money and Joshua's medicine and all, Joy waited as two young boys with fishing poles passed before asking in a whisper, "Can I talk?"

The reverend normally forbid her to speak. He usually explained to those few people who stopped them that his lad was mute, for Joy's voice gave her away quickly.

"Clear back here," Sammy called from the pile of carpets where he kept watch on the back road.

"Go ahead, darlin'."

"I was just wondering how much the good Captain Fairbanks wanted this time?"

"Ten dollars a head."

Joy Claret's face registered quick shock. "Oh dear! Do you have it or will we have to beg a debt?"

"No, I got it." The old man smiled, patting his coat pocket.

"Where did you get it?" she asked too quickly, letting curiosity get the better of experience. Unless one wanted to hear a scandalous tale, one never asked the reverend how his pockets came to hold coins.

"Why darlin', it was simple."

"It always is for you, you unscrupulous fraud."

The old man laughed, pleased with this apt description of his character. "I arranged a small—tiny, really—cockfight at the Hampton's barn. Bunch of green seamen just stepped on land, and the lads seemed mighty anxious to part with their hard won earnings."

Intimately familiar with the reverend's mendacity, Joy Claret knew that "arranged" meant "fixed," and she laughed. The reverend had only been caught once or twice at one of his numerous swindles. Back on the merry shores of England, fortune arranged the good doctor's presence at the reverend's sentencing. Joshua had just testified in a hearing

14

involving an old man's untimely death. When lingering on the unpleasant outcome, he chanced to overhear the reverend's pleading—and so convincingly—for his fate. The magistrate thought the reverend's face was familiar, and he was not as persuaded by the fine speech as Joshua who always nourished an unquenchable faith in the ultimate goodness of many undeserving human beings. Taxing his meager savings and convinced he could reform the reverend's petty criminal proclivities, Joshua bought his contract and, only then, found himself saddled with the most unlikely indentured servant, one whose presence in his life brought blessings and curses in turns.

Of course, the reverend claimed he simply couldn't help parting fools with their monies, and if someone was looking to be taken, it was his job to see the business done. There was little doubt that the reverend had a heart of gold; it seemed he took money from one pocket and put it into someone else's—a more deserving someone according to some odd sense of justice he alone knew. The reverend never viewed his mendacity as inconsistent with the doctor's high falutin principles of justice, liberty and freedom for all—the famed abolitionist cry, all of which the reverend enthusiastically embraced. It was Joy, though, who harbored the unkind suspicion that the reverend viewed the underground railroad as yet one of many ways to part people with their property.

Adding to his duplicity, unbelievably, the reverend was known throughout Orleans Parish and beyond as the hellfire and brimstone Reverend Doddered. All manner of people called on him to strike the fear of God's wrath into the minds of the most indolent, idle and uppity Negroes with his Negro sermonizing. On the pulpit, the Reverend Doddered would tell the sea of Negro faces that, while their bodies belonged to their masters, their souls belonged to God. If they had any hope of finding God's freedom in heaven, rather than Satan's eternal chains in hell, they must repent their idleness and indolence; they must work harder for their good

15

masters. And as the reverend helped the planter class with never ending Negro problems, Sammy crept around whispering to a carefully selected few just how a Negro might find God's freedom a bit before Judgement Day.

Joy was waiting as a chain gang of longshoremen passed. Led by an overseer on a mount, each man carried a huge bale of cotton on his dark-skinned back. Once the group was out of sight, she asked, "Is there enough left for Joshua's medicine?"

"Aye, and I believe a mite bit more for a new dress."

"A new dress!" She could hardly believe it, for it had been over two years since she had had a new dress. The thought of having one as well as not having to worry about Joshua's medicine sent her arms around the old man's neck in a demonstration of her gratitude. "Oh, Reverend! Whatever would we do without you?"

Sammy answered with a deep chuckle. "'Bout da same, I'se figure—only minus a load o' troubles."

As their easy laughter calmed, the reverend cautioned against any further talking. Since the runaway slaves had been on the run a good two weeks or more and had not been caught, the bounty hunters would know the escape was aided by the loosely knit band of abolitionists that stretched from one end of the country to the other—the network of the underground railroad. They'd be watching this road like hawks, knowing water was the only viable means to escape.

Still, there was no sign of danger. After they were already a good two miles from the marketplace, Joy felt her tension ease a bit as the landscape filled her senses with happier thoughts.

The great river widened slowly. For miles on either side of the water stretched dense forests of live oaks and water sycamores, berry briars and vines, all draped in dark Spanish moss and ivy. In the first blush of day, the dense foliage looked lush, dark and shadowy. The noisy chatter of birds filled the warm morning air which was pushed by an ever-present southern breeze. It was lovely; her senses rejoiced.

The huge towering masts of a great ship rose in the distance, and as the peddler cart approached, Joy caught her breath at the sight of the largest, sleekest and most magnificent ship she had ever seen. Little wonder why ships were referred to with feminine pronouns! As they came closer, she made out the bold name: *The Ram's Head.* "Of all the names." Joy laughed out loud. A group of seamen splashed in the water off the ship's side. They must have just docked this morning, she realized, for the men boisterously made use of the suddenly unlimited fresh water.

An audible snore rose from the passenger's hold. Sammy's rich voice answered with one of those haunting songs common to field hands, songs that blended the despair of long days of endless turmoil with religious hope of redemption. It was a timely play, for suddenly, coming up from behind rode the most arresting group of men.

Blue eyes widened enormously, as Joy turned to stare. Wild looking and dangerous, three mounted men led a larger group of men on foot. A huge half-naked Negro walked amidst the cluster of men as an equal. Another man, with a large barrel stomach and a bald head to match, displayed more gold chains around his neck than were in the front window of Ponce Fredrico's jewelry store. A tall, mean looking man had hair as long as her own. More remarkable for its color of angry fire, it was braided and worn like a rope wrapped around impressive biceps. Their clothes, mixed, matched and no doubt stolen from the four corners of the world, were a fashion ensemble representing many different countries. One wore fancy, blue velvet breeches and a matching coat of an aristocratic Englishman, torn at the sleeves to fit larger shoulders. Another two wore garb she recognized from a book she had once read about an English gentleman's travels to India, and another wore red silk pants that spoke—like the small dark eyes of the owner—of oriental origins. There was another rope of long hair, hanging from a man's belt like a trophy, and Joy, in a breath, prayed the woman had parted with her fine tresses willingly.

It required only the space of two minutes for them to overtake and pass the peddler's cart, but she took in everything. The leader—he must be a leader—rode ahead on a large, white stallion. He was a remarkably big man and looked even larger atop that white horse. His long, golden hair fell like a mane to wide shoulders, and his face was long and lean, almost handsome if his appearance weren't somehow so frightening. He wore plain, gray breeches, moccasin boots and a cotton vest. She witnessed the laughter rising clear in his fine, hazel eyes, and this more than anything surprised her.

"Who were they?" Joy asked in a breathless and awed whisper.

"Don't have a farthing, lass." The old man chuckled. "But from the worldly looks of 'em, seems 'ole LaFitte is in for even more trouble."

The famed pirate was presently being pursued by relentless American authorities, who—unlike their French predecessors—nourished no fondness for lawless sea crimes.

"Pirates!" she exclaimed. "Well, my word, I never have seen—"

"Hit's dem!" Sammy's whispered cry sounded the alarm. "Two comin' from the Nawth! Move it, chile!"

Tension burst into action. With a practiced motion, Sammy pulled the bundles from Libertine's back and untied her lead as Joy hopped from the moving cart and ran back. Sammy boosted her onto the mare's back, handed her the reins and then jumped back to assume his seat. Horse and rider disappeared into the forest only a split second before the two riders rounded the bend.

Sammy hit the plank board three times to warn the passengers, then resumed singing. Joy's absence gave the reverend freedom to remove a whiskey cask and enjoy a

18

long draught.

Joy, trailing the cart through the forest, saw this, and instantly her mouth pressed to a hard frown. Drinking! Already he was drinking! Lord, but was there no end to his gall! It was a cry too late to scold him though, and the reverend's grin told her he was well aware of the fact.

"Hold up thar, ole man!"

The reverend brought the bays to a slow halt and turned around. As he and Sammy had anticipated, they were in for trouble, for these were not local boys parading for the day as paddyrollers. Hired professionals, no doubt. He took another long sip from an ever-handy cask.

Jimmy Cochran stopped his mount in front of the reverend and leaned casually forward in his saddle, scrutinizing the reverend with a cool dark stare and watching as the old man fumbled with the cask, nervously taking another draught while mumbling unintelligibly. Short and not large for a man, Cochran's even blond features were shaded, nearly hidden by a wide brown hat. A red kerchief was tied around his neck. "Well, well," he first said. "What have we here, Davey?"

The other man, who had been circling, finally came around to face the wagon. "Looks like a peddler man, don't it?" The opposite in appearance, this man looked big, ungainly and dark and, as the reverend engaged in his own scrutiny, about as ugly as they came. Unsightly pock marks scarred the large boned face, and his nose looked like it had been hit once too often. The sleeves of a frayed, once white work shirt were rolled over his forearms. A notably unimaginative tattoo showed on his left arm, the name Ann circled by flowers.

"A good day to ye gents," the reverend offered a greeting in his most affable Irish lilt while tipping his hat. "What can I get fer ye? Got some fine English work shirts, just off the boat ... or mayhaps a shawl for ye misses?" He then chuckled. "Cause nothin' warms a lass's heart like a pretty new rag, and when 'er little heart gets warmed, the heat's bound to spill over to your bed. Men like women and women like rags and—tell ye what I'll do, seein' 'ows thar be two of ye. I'll give you—"

"Hold that tongue, ole man. We ain't interested in any new rags—" Cochran stopped and spit, but the reverend never gave him a chance to resume.

"Oh? Well then, mayhaps you'd like to see me brand new line of the finest boots this side of the 'lantic. Last a lifetime, they will—"

"Shut the trap, ole man," the small man snapped more in exasperation than anger, then had to steady his mount. "The name's Jimmy Cochran and this here's Davey. We've been hired to track us down some runaway niggers."

"Darky hunters, are ye?"

"Sure are. You seen any suspicious niggers in these parts?"

"Can't say as I have." The reverend replied in a marked tone of disinterest and took another long draught.

Suspicion remained, but after an uncomfortable pause, Cochran suddenly chuckled. "Why Davey boy, don't this ole man look like that Yankee scoundrel folks been talking about?"

"You mean that fellow who's been swindlin' poor old widows?" Davey grinned hugely. "Come to think of it, he does."

"I'll have you know," the reverend pretended great affront, "I've never, not once, been called a yeller Yankee. I be Irish! And you do me grave dishonor to think otherwise."

"Then tell me, ole peddler man, what's the likes of you doin' in these parts, so close to the Orleans' market?"

"I picked up a few goods, that's what, and now me and my boy Sam is headed for Carlisle to visit me mate before headin' north to escape the infernal heat of your upcoming summer."

"What's this friend's name?"

"Grady O'Neill, not that it's any of your concern."

The two men exchanged glances, their suspicions still plain. Davey suddenly fixed his gaze on Sammy and then led his mount to the back. Cochran followed.

They were on to them, and there was only one thing that could give the charade away, and Cochran, with a parrotlike cock of his head, asked, "What's a piss poor peddler doin' with this young buck?"

"Sammy? Oh, had him fer years now. Bought him from an old lady when he was just a young pup, knee high to the ground, up thar in Beinville Parish. Been with me ever since."

Sammy only stared at the ground.

A calloused hand reached down to jerk Sammy's head up, a thumb pushed open his mouth. Teeth were examined. "Just look at them gleamers," Davey whispered and withdrew his hand, wiping it on his pants as he appraised Sammy's impressive build. "Hell, a buck like this could go stud on a pickaninny farm. How old are you boy?"

"I'se nineteen, massa, twenty come summer," he replied with a meekness common to a beaten field hand. "Das de truth, massa," he added in feigned simplicity.

"Why haven't you sold him?" Cochran asked. "Worth more than your whole wagon load of crap."

"Sell him? Hell no! My boy is worth his weight in gold! Aye, come summer in the Carolinas, I have the only darky in the whole town of Sommerville. I lend him out fer fifty cents a day, sometimes seventy-five, depending on the work, meals included of course, and—"

"Jesus, if you don't run on worse than a coyote at the moon!" Cochran laughed, amused and oddly not angry. He then proceeded to make a long ceremony out of finding a tobacco pouch in his saddle bag, working it into a chew. "You seen any runaway niggers back here boy?" he asked Sammy.

"Naw massa!" Sammy shook his head. "I'se don' seed no niggers, naw suh."

"Davey here." Cochran motioned to his companion. "Well, he hates all niggers, but you know what kind of niggers he hates most?"

With the malleable docility and fear common to any Negro confronting a white man's malice, Sammy shook his head. "Naw suh!"

"He hates lying niggers most."

Davey grunted assent and pulled a knife from his boot for the next part.

"Know what Davey does to a lying nigger, boy?"

"Naw suh," Sammy said in feigned alarm.

Davey rested the point of his knife over his abdomen in a not-so-subtle indication of a cruel practice.

"You ain't lyin' boy, are you?"

"Naw massa, I sho ain't."

"Well now"—the reverend had had quite enough—"if you gents don't mind, we'll be on our way. Gotta reach Carlisle by noon, I do. Unless mayhaps I can interest you in those medicines I was speaking of? As a matter of fact," he stated, flashing his most convincing smile, "I have one bottle left of Dr. Kent's gentleman's tonic, guaranteed to put the old spirit back in a man's vitals—"

"Oh hell! Go on, git old man." Cochran laughed suddenly, shaking his head. "Don't reckon I could stomach much more of your bull. Come on Davey"—he reined his mount around—"we got us some niggers to catch."

"No cause to be nasty," the reverend muttered as he gave a slash to the reins.

The two bays jumped, and the cart moved forward.

It was over, and Joy breathed a heavy sigh of relief until the seconds wore on, and Davey had yet to move. He remained mounted, staring after the cart. Impending danger consumed the air; she stopped breathing as her gaze followed his. A small pool of fresh blood marked the middle of the road.

Davey spurred his mount to the spot, and looking down,

22

he laughed loud and clear as a long pistol was withdrawn and then cocked. A shot shattered the calm morning air, and Libertine bolted, throwing Joy Claret hard to the ground. Cochran raced back in a gallop, took one long look at the ground, and within minutes, the cart had been stopped, and the reverend was staring at the long barrels of two ivory handled pistols.

"Why, peddler man." Cochran was grinning now. "I do believe blood is dripping from your cart." Like barnyard cats, they would play with the mice before the mercy of a kill. "Looks like nigger blood, too, don't it Davey?"

"It sure as hell does."

"Blood ye say?" The reverend pretended surprise and turned to look incredulously at the road. Now, the trick was to buy Joy time while trying to get another shot fired. There were two shots to a pistol, and they had only to get Davey to fire again to disarm him completely. "Well, I'll be a son of a gun! You hear that Sammy? The horses boy! Get down and check the horses."

Sammy knew his part well, and as the men watched the reverend, he found his own pistol in the pile of carpets. "Massa, I'se mighty 'fraid of de horses, you'se knows hit."

"Are you lookin' fer trouble now?"

"Naw suh, I sho ain't." The pistol slipped beneath his breeches; the cold sting of the metal felt like a dip in ice water, tensing the long length of his muscled back. "I'se just mighty fearful of dem beasts. Don' make me massa, please!"

"Why you insolent guttersnipe!" the reverend yelled back. "You get the hell down here and check out the horses, or I'll give you something to be fearful about!"

Joy Claret finally calmed Libertine enough to vault onto her back. She made painfully slow progress to the spot where the cart was stopped ahead, maneuvering slowly through the trees and brush with Libertine's each step sounding to her like a trumpet announcing her presence.

"Massa, I'se beg you—"

A shot fired, whizzing close enough to the reverend's ear for him to understand George Washington's famed remark comparing bullets passing his ear to the sound of music.

"Git off your seat, peddler man!"

The reverend slowly eased to the ground.

"Boy! Down!"

Careful to keep his back to the cart, Sammy's bare feet touched the cool earth. He slowly made his way to the reverend's side, looking as scared as a child awakening from a nightmare. With hands behind his back, he kept the great width of his shoulders hunched and his gaze lowered. Yet Sammy caught Joy's movement in the forest behind them, and the two men's horses danced nervously, sensing what the riders did not.

Sammy suddenly dropped to his knees before Davey. "Don' a shoot me, massa, don' a shoot me!" He pointed an accusing finger at the reverend. "I'se didn' do hit! I'se a beggin' mercy, don' a shoot me!"

Catching on, the reverend kicked Sammy good and hard. "Why you miserable, ungrateful black arse! I'll teach you to turn belly up on me! I suppose you think I—"

The third shot fired, and the reverend bolted back and fell to the ground. He was unhit, but his frail bones were shaken nearly out of their sockets. In the flash of the moment's distraction, Joy moved. Cochran heard her horse; but it took one too many seconds to crash into his consciousness, and a barrel of a pistol nudged hard into his back. "Drop it, bastard! Drop it or I'll blow your innards sky high!"

In the same instant, Sammy drew on Davey, bracing for the possible cross fire.

Mercifully, none came.

Joy controlled her half wild horse with two chin knees and answered Cochran's hesitation with another hard nudge. "Drop it Mister! I won't waste air tellin' you again!"

Pistols dropped to the ground, and the reverend struggled up to recover his dazed wits. He was just getting too damn

24

old for this kind of scam, good as it was to play. Joy backed up a few safe paces, then gathered her reins back in hand to stop Libertine's nervous prance. Cochran turned to see that the queer voice belonged to a pipsqueak of a boy. Size showed only in the width of the boy's grin.

It was Sammy's and the reverend's show now. The bounty hunters were first ordered off their horses, then into the cover of the forest and onto the ground, stomachs down and faces to the dirt. From the cart, Sammy produced ankle chains to secure their feet together, then tied their arms behind their backs with a rope.

Back on the road, Joy quickly tended to their horses, removing saddle and tack to set them free. Haste urged a fast pace, for there was no telling when someone would come along. Only luck had kept the road deserted so far. Uppermost in all three captors' minds was the small pool of blood lying in the road. Mary must be brought to the ship's surgeon as fast as possible.

The whole thing was managed in minutes. Joy remained to watch the road, while the two men were forced farther into the forest, falling hard every few steps due to the indignity of the chains. A small clearing appeared not far from the road, and here, Sammy began tying the two together to the base of a huge oak.

"I don't believe you two gents had the benefit of proper introduction to my man Sammy," the reverend said, as Sammy secured the ropes as tight as his great strength permitted. "As your dim wits might have allowed, Sammy here is not your average nigger."

"Naw suh, I sho ain't." Sammy grinned.

"Know what kind of nigger Sammy is?"

Sammy stood before them, his huge frame bellowing with unmasked amusement like a sail with winds. He held Davey's dagger in his hands now, fondling it with a lover's caress.

"You see, Sammy here is a nigger who hates white men."

25

"Yes siree! I sho do."

"Know what kind of white men Sammy hates most?"

Bright red fury mixed evenly with fear, but neither man would play this game, at least until the reverend kicked Davey hard in the face. "I asked you a question."

"No!"

"Well, Sammy here, he hates bounty hunters most of all."

"I'se sho as hell do! Yes suh!"

"Know what Sammy does to the bounty hunters we catch?"

Sammy positioned the knife over Davey's abdomen, smiling a grin of pure madness. Cochran's gaze burned with furious rage, but Davey's nervously darted with sudden fear, as the inconceivable became suddenly feasible.

Abruptly though, the reverend found an objection to that particular form of torture, complaining of the hours it took the last time to wash the blood from his clothes. Other forms of torture were discussed in detail but were discarded one by one until Davey fell into incoherent mumblings for mercy, and even the cocksure Cochran twitched some with fear. Finally, it was Sammy who decided to leave them as crow bait, despite the reverend's objection that the death took too long and they always seemed to die of thirst long before the birds even got to their eyes.

---

Joy knocked on the side of the cart thrice. Her heart pounded furiously, and her breathing was hard as she anxiously watched the road. "Are you well?"

"Yes, maam." The voice was soft and unmistakably frightened.

"All's well, but Mary, is she all right?" asked Joy.

"She's been out cold fer de longest spell, but I'se feel her breathin' regular."

"Hang on. It won't be long now."

Glancing in both directions, she nervously petted Libertine's neck, far more to calm herself than her horse. She could never stay for the final violence, for she could not abide it, even when it was necessary. Despite her proclivities for these noble but wild missions and though she never discussed it, violence still frightened her to the depth of her soul. Even the chicken slaughter at the marketplace easily brought her to her knees. Tender hearted she was, and though she loathed this feminine pretension, try as she might, she simply could not bare to witness suffering of any kind.

This was the reason she refused to let Sammy load her pistol. She would more easily shoot herself than another person, even bounty hunters—who surely were the lowest and most undeserving of all God's creatures. Besides, threatening men with an empty pistol worked just as well as a loaded one.

The reverend and Sammy finally returned.

"Are they out?" she asked.

"Out cold." Sammy's huge hands rested on his hips and he smiled. "Joy Claret, chile, you did good, real good. But hit's a sho thing dat ya gotta stay, girl."

She nodded as she had expected it. Someone had to watch until the passengers were safe and the peddler cart hidden to make sure the men didn't wake and try to alert a passerby.

"How's the girl?" the reverend asked as he quickly ascended to the driver's seat.

"Unconscious but still breathing." Anxiety marked Joy's features. "Surely she needs a doctor; you must make all haste!"

"I'll have her to the ship surgeon inside of two hours. Don't worry darlin'. Now lass, I want to see you perched up in some branch and remember, if thar's any trouble, any trouble at all, you're to—"

"Fly with the wind," she and Sammy both finished the familiar warning and then laughed at their synchronicity. She watched as the old cart disappeared down the deserted road. Taking hold of Libby's reins, she turned to lead her mare into the forest.

The sun's position announced a ten o'clock hour. Shadows shifted and shortened by the minute. The moist air filled with the rich scents of spring growth: trees, ferns, shrubs and always that putrid, though hardly unpleasant, smell of the river nearby. Birds called distant and near, and the flight of unseen creatures gave the familiar landscape a lush exotic feel.

She might have been lost on a deserted island.

In a small clearing the size of a decent parlor, Joy Claret found the two men unconscious beneath a wide oak tree, safely bound, tied and gagged, looking far more like drunken fools than the nefarious devil-doers they were. She kept at a distance. Close inspection of the surrounding trees led to many possibilities. She finally chose another old oak, one with a fairly low hanging branch, directly across from her charges. She positioned her mount beneath the chosen branch, and with a remarkable agility few of her sex possessed, she swung onto the branch. "Stay close, my pet, stay close," she whispered the soft spoken command to her horse.

Libertine tossed her head in agreement and wandered nearby to graze. Joy settled against the upturned and moss-covered branch, and after a careful inspection for spiders, ants and any other unwanted companions that might think to share her space, she settled her gaze on the prisoners for the long wait.

A narrow hunting path led into the small clearing, and as she noticed it, her fanciful imagination flew down the escapeway it presented. She was soon lost in a pleasant daydream:

She was an Indian maiden, separated from her tribe and family, and through a quick succession of unlikely events, she was in perilous need of rescue. Always the same boy would magically appear to rescue her. He was blond, blue-eyed and handsome. Like Joshua, he was not as strong of build as he was clever. A series of more unlikely events followed in her mind's eye, until this unnamed boy, by virtue of wits alone, rescued her, declared his affection and ended the dream with a kiss.

She woke from her dreamy haze with a blush, an inexplicable warmth moving through her limbs. She could not make sense of it. Lately, as she lay in bed at night or during the family reading time and once right in the middle of old Miss St. Ivy's tea, these silly school girl dreams would take hold of her mind!

What in heaven's name was wrong with her! The daydreams were bad enough in themselves, but after a conscious review of the content, it irked her to realize she was always in need of rescuing, instead of doing the rescuing. Yet, whenever she changed the circumstances to suit her well-defined character and became the rescuer, the dream suddenly had as much appeal as a slice of wet angel food cake.

A low groan interrupted her musings, and as she sat up, a shrewd cautious gaze instantly replaced the dreamy one. The dark-haired devil lifted his head but with a great effort, then it fell back with another low muffled growl.

Alertness fixed in her large, blue eyes.

A dog barked in the far distance. The sound came from the forest rather than the road. A quick glance behind reassured her that Libertine was near, but the mare's ears were pricked with sudden caution. The sound drew closer still, and as her gaze riveted to the hunting path, she withdrew her pistol.

It was the habit of Ram Barrington to run for no other reason than the sheer joy and exhilaration of physically exhausting himself. He'd developed this odd habit as a young boy; it helped him escape the pain and terror of a troubled childhood long forgotten. Later, running had eased the accumulated tension and restlessness of many long sea voyages taken as a young boy aboard his great uncle Sir Admiral Byron's English man-of-war. Then, as a young man, it helped ease the tedium, his impatience with the slow peaceful pace of India's eternal summers. The habit carried over into adulthood, and he sometimes chuckled to himself with a vision of an old eighty-year-old man, cane in hand, still passing an early morning hour or so trying to run.

He had cleared a good six or seven miles, with another mile or two left in his legs, when Rake, his great mastiff dog, caught scent of something and dashed on ahead, barking. The narrow path ran alongside a fair-sized stream. Ram spotted the pond, dammed by two large fallen trunks, and after a quick inspection, the cool depth could not be resisted.

As he rested, drying in the sun, he suddenly realized Rake had not returned or stopped barking. Not particularly wanting a dead rabbit dropped at his feet, he set off in pursuit.

The path led abruptly to a small clearing. Agitated and still barking, Rake held an attack stance in front of two bound, gagged and apparently quite unconscious men.

"What the devil is this?"

Joy Claret was asking herself that exact question as she stared in great alarm. She could not explain the threat she felt from this man's inexplicable presence, but he was like no other man the innocence of her eyes had ever beheld. She felt the danger—danger that moved as a physical force through her frame, causing her breath to catch and a cold numbness to seep into her hands as she clutched the pistol tightly.

The blatant masculinity of his imposing form as he stood there, hands on hips, staring at the bounty hunters, seemed at once more dangerous than . . . than even those pirates she watched pass on the road! Half naked and bootless—this did seem the day for affronts to her sensibilities—the bronze frame was tall, taller even than Sammy, and he wore only sun-washed white breeches, cut at the knees, and a black belt. His bare form radiated a threatening and well-exercised strength. Muscles, he seemed nothing but muscles. Numerous scars marked the wide breadth of his bare muscled chest—testament to what could only be too many battles fought and won. Thick, raven-black curls crowned markedly aristocratic features. As if an artist painted the square cut to his jaw, his wide firm mouth, fine large nose and markedly prominent forehead, his features were all drawn with clean strong strokes. Yet the final stroke, she saw with a small gasp, was a black patch that covered one eye.

Alarm rose not from any one of the recklessly handsome features but by the complete impression. She had no strength, depended solely on her wits, and what frightened her the most was the sense that he also had an intelligence so quick and sharp it could swallow hers in a bite.

She had yet to take a breath when he moved toward the captives. The pounding of her heart produced the idea of remaining silent and not alerting him to her presence. It was no use; surely he'd spot Libertine and then her. And oh God, where had her senses fled? If he should be allowed to rouse the captives, all would be lost.

A long jeweled dagger, pearl inlaid and sparkling with rubies and emeralds, appeared in his hand, and when she saw this, she found her voice. "Hold it right there, mister! Or I'll blow you to bits!"

Ram stopped and froze, his normally quick mind requiring several long seconds to give reality to the squeakiest, queer voice he had ever chanced to hear. He turned slowly and found the owner of this voice perched in the tree like a parrot. Surprised by so unlikely an event as being held at gunpoint by a small brat not yet in his teens and out in the middle of nowhere, his amusement took some seconds to overcome his incredulity.

"What mischief is this?"

31

Joy Claret knew the exact moment laughter warmed the coldest, dark gaze she had ever endured. The man's amusement, to say nothing of the arrogance of his demand, spoke wagon loads for her trouble. "Whatever it is, mister, it is not your concern!"

Simultaneously, both their gazes turned to Rake. The huge monstrosity of a dog maintained an attack stance on the two bound men, completely ignoring what anyone else might think a real threat to his master. This brought Ram's gaze back to the tree, and with sudden renewed interest, he started toward her.

"Hold it!"

He stopped, now only four paces from her.

"That's right, just stand still while I reason out your fate."

A dark brow lifted. "Indeed!" He chuckled. "Well, no insult to your reasoning capabilities intended, but I hardly intend to rest my fate in your ah, trembling hands." He watched her sky-blue eyes look to his hands as Joy desperately attempted to steady her gaze. "I'll tell you once, brat," he said more gently. "You'll fare far better if you drop to the ground now and start explaining this mishap."

Anger flushed her cheeks. She couldn't believe it, him, his unequaled arrogance! "News to you—you nefarious scoundrel—I have a pistol pointed at you!"

Nefarious scoundrel? he mused. Hardly the curse words of a backwoods brat. Damn that voice too, so curiously feminine, as though the lad was a recent audition for the Vienna Boys' Choir—

The thought brought a quick appraisal of the lad's hands. In all his years he had yet to see a boy—any boy—with clean and manicured nails, let alone fingers so obviously thin and feminine.

He stared long and hard at the delicate and lovely features that were suddenly far too feminine, even for a pretty boy. Quick anger arrived, controlled only by a sudden—and for him, rare—curiosity. He would play her game only long

32

enough to know where it led.

"Now—" she desperately attempted a gruff, mean and male tone that remained infuriatingly out of reach. "You just sit where you stand, while we wait."

"Wait for what?"

"For my friends. I can't very well keep a pistol to you and tie you up at the same time, can I?" she began to explain. "So, we'll just have to wait for my friends."

"And how many, ah, friends are we expecting?"

"Two—I mean twenty!" She quickly changed her mind. She had to sound meaner, much meaner. "So sit, mister!"

"You shouldn't threaten a person with a gun if you don't have the necessary inclination to use it."

Her gaze narrowed. "What makes you think I won't use it?"

"Had you or your, ah, *twenty* friends been murderers, no doubt those two fools there"—he motioned—"would have bullet holes where only bruises show."

Disarmed by his quick reasoning, Joy tried to dissuade him from his belief. "I assure you, sir, I'd be just as pleased to shoot you as to look at you!" She misread plain malice as tension, and ridiculously, before she thought better of her natural inclination, she said, "Oh, don't worry, I truly won't shoot if you just do as I say."

"Thank you kindly, brat. I suppose this means I can stop my quivering," Ram replied.

A small smile tugged at the corner of his mouth, and his wit disarmed her, though she quickly decided his charm was best ignored. His hand still held a dagger, and she saw this as her first exercise in authority. "You can drop your dagger first off."

"My thought exactly." He lifted the dagger as though to drop it, but with a casual flick of his wrist, it sliced through the air in a flash, expertly hitting its mark right between her open legs. Joy gasped, tried to catch her balance, but fell backward and landed with an ugly thud to the ground.

33

Although the wind was knocked out of her, she quickly scrambled to her feet with a speed that impressed Ram. He let her run a few paces to satisfy a desire to see her backside before he tackled her to the ground in three easy strides. Strong arms braced her, and she cried out as, curiously, those same arms cushioned her fall, allowing an impact no more jarring than a tumble to hay.

Then his weight came upon her.

Joy had the good sense to be frightened at a distance, but now she knew terror as his hard weight pressed intimately upon her form, stifling any thought of a struggle. He pinned her arms to the blanket of moss, and her terror grew as his gaze raked over her in unsurpassed scrutiny.

"God, girl"—his gaze finally returned to her face— "there's enough femininity in this package to arouse a blind man. I don't know how you thought to disguise it."

Until that moment she hadn't known he had guessed her sex. A maiden's fear sprang quickly in her enchanting eyes, real, tremendous and forever alien to him. Why this bothered him, he couldn't say; she at least deserved the fear.

"Your explanation had better be good, brat. That a young girl mustered the audacity to behave so is only slightly less infuriating than the thought of the man who put you up to it."

He saw she could barely comprehend, let alone venture a reply, the enormity of her fear was so great. Her breath came in huge gulps, and she looked as though she fully expected a blow to her face. "Rest easy, brat," he said slowly. "I have not the inclination to molest young girls by the roadside." She remained perfectly still, and her apparent disbelief at his assertion suddenly caused some amusement. "Even if I had though, you'd have naught to worry. You're pretty enough, I suppose," he ventured, lifting partially from her to again review her assets, "provided one had the imaginative facilities necessary to see through this garb. But this skinny slip of a figure hardly offers a temptation."

34

Comprehension sank through her fear, very slowly and then only partially, the terror of being caught, held and helpless, left her nearly deaf and certainly dumb. All she gathered from his speech was the subject of molestation. "Please don't hurt me . . ."

The frightened plea disarmed him, doing more for her case than a hundred jurists, not just because it accurately revealed the extent of her desperation, so markedly incongruent with the boldness of her behavior, but because of the tone. Her voice sounded frightened, altogether feminine, and held an alluring blend of accents—an English lilt mixed with soft Southern lyricism.

"After I turn you over my knee for a well-deserved thrashing, I won't hurt you. Probably."

She frantically searched the devilishly fine features to finally discern his amusement.

She suddenly realized that he thought of her as nothing but a misbehaving child, and huge relief swept over her small form. Once released from the burden of that fear, she was suddenly, acutely conscious of the great inexplicable warmth of his body pressed on hers, the shocking intimacy and feel of his hard muscled strength. "What then shall you do?" she asked rather breathlessly.

"That depends wholly on your story," he said, glancing up at the two bound men. "Now, what has happened here?"

One coherent thought rose through the waves of her pounding temples. Sammy and the reverend would not return for over an hour, and somewhere in that time she must escape from this man to warn them. Libertine neighed angrily nearby, making plain her displeasure with her mistress' situation. "Please, loose me—"

"Not in your wildest dreams," he said simply.

"Oh but"—she squirmed to give credence to the complaint—"you're hurting me so."

"What an inconsistent little fool!" he chuckled. "After holding me at gun point, you would now beg privileges of your sex?"

"But I can't talk like this! Truly!"

"You better try because I've already mentioned the only other position you're likely to get from me."

This confirmed the growing suspicion that he was hard-nosed and mean, cruel in the extreme. She had not lived with the reverend's mendacity without picking up a few tricks. "I know what this must look like," she began dramatically. "But honestly, you mistake the circumstances! You see," her tone lifted higher as the lie came to her. "My uncle, Sammy and I are the victims here! We were traveling to Carlisle when these two . . . bandits over there tried to rob us. Well! Few men can best Sammy—our Negro—or my uncle. And I can assure you—and you can see for yourself—they soon reversed the situation. They tied the highwaymen up and knocked them out, as you see there, and left me to guard them while they went to fetch the proper authorities."

Nothing in all her life, even in these last awful minutes, scared her as much as the changed emotion on his face, and all he said was: "The next lie you tell will be your last; I will make you regret the breath it was uttered in."

She waited for her next breath, which would not come. The silence filled with the sound of rushing water and the ever present cries of birds, flying with a freedom she had cause to envy.

"I'm growing impatient with you." The hard lines of his face gave credibility to the statement.

Joy in no way wanted to discover what happened when his small patience wore thin, yet all she could think of was "I can't tell you."

"Only slightly better than a lie. Why not?" Now his tone suggested the casual interest of tea time chatter, and his apparent capriciousness left her stunned.

"It could risk the lives of many innocent people," she replied.

"Innocent?" He chuckled. "I've seen more innocence in the

36

spread of a whore's thighs."

Unbelievably, the metaphor brought quick color to her cheeks, and this, more than any one thing, surprised him. He stared in sudden wonder. Try as he would, he could not reconcile that single blush with the girl's behavior. This added dangerously to both his curiosity and impatience, and he was just about to make his threats explicit when suddenly one of the bound men groaned and tried to lift his head again.

Still maintaining the lowered attack stance, Rake barked angrily, and Ram glanced up, for a moment distracted. Joy Claret saw the chance—her only chance—and before her fear could caution her, she stiffened purposely, cast her gaze behind her captor and screamed, "No! Don't shoot him!"

She never wasted a moment to marvel at the speed of Ram's reflexes. The words had not left her mouth, and Ram was off her, standing in his own attack stance at an invisible perpetrator. Alerted and barking, Rake dashed to his master's side, adding confusion to the startling few seconds it took Ram to search the surroundings and see that no one was there. Just as he turned back around to catch her, Joy vaulted her nervous mount with an agility that gave lift to Ram's brow. Libertine leaped into the air, and the last thing Joy heard—the only thing she heard—was the fine sound of Ram Barrington's laughter.

# *Chapter Two*

Startled, Libertine leaped in the air, and not having bothered with the superfluity of reins, Joy clung to the frightened animal's neck as if it was a life line. Through the pounding of her heart and the rush of wind, she was too panicked to contemplate just what that laughter meant. She could only keep to her horse as the great creature dashed through brush and forest. Once on the freedom of the road, Libertine broke into a crazed run, slicing through the air at a dizzying speed, knowing only to carry her mistress away as fast and far as her four strong legs were capable.

Tears of intense relief and fear blinded her along with the wind, and it was four or five miles later before she swallowed her frightened panic and attempted to gain control of the reins. Libertine's fear could have easily fueled another five miles, and mastering it proved a hard struggle. She finally grasped the reins, and with a hard tug of all her strength, she called, "Whoa, whoa! Easy girl . . . easy. . . ." Libertine gradually slowed to a quick trot, and Joy dug tight with her knees, matching her movement to her horse's with the skill of a seasoned rider. Once she had full control, she came to a complete stop to take stock of her situation.

No one chased her, though as she wiped her tears and drew her first even breath, she found herself the recipient of more than one interested stare. She was dangerously close to the marketplace. A tall Negress, with a huge basket of apples on her head and two wide-eyed children hanging on her apron string, watched warily from off the road where she had obviously retreated to in fear of life and limb. An old Cajun fisherman stood nearby with the same expression, and from down the road she caught sight of a band of seamen approaching.

She slipped from Libertine's back and led her into the safety of the forest as her mind raced over the situation. As soon as that pirate man roused the bounty hunters, the whole world would be looking for her, an old peddler and a tall, strong, young Negro. Hopefully, by this point, Sammy and the reverend would have gotten the passengers off, hidden the cart and changed back into their respectable unassuming selves. They would probably be riding the bays back at this very moment to fetch her. She must warn them still, for if the bounty hunters were released prematurely—as no doubt they would be—it would not be safe to return until dark, even minus their disguises. Then too, there was no telling what that pirate man would do once he had the real story.

Joy clutched her sides tightly, trying to quiet the rage of her emotions long enough to think. What to do? The trouble was that he—that pirate man—stood between her and Sammy and the reverend.

The large, blue eyes darted over the surrounding forest. The only option was to ride Libertine south on a back trail and avoid him. Then she'd head back on to the road a couple of miles south of where he had held her—as close as she dared—and keep on south, praying she ran into her comrades as they were riding north to fetch her. It was the best she could think to do, and if it didn't work, if she could not find them to give warning, she'd simply hide in the forest until it was safe to return home.

If Joshua ever heard of this one . . .

40

With a little effort she found the back road through the forest that paralleled the main road. She pushed Libertine to a trot, keeping her head down now to avoid the overhanging vines, branches and occasional blankets of moss. The path cut a narrow line through the dense brush, following a stream off and on.

She had traveled a good distance when, quite suddenly, the path opened to the familiar clearing, and just as panic coursed through her small frame causing Libertine to lift to the air in response, she saw that no one remained.

The pirate man was gone! As were the two bound and tied bounty hunters! Her gaze flew to where her pistol had fallen, but that too was gone. All that remained was an imagined terror, and the tension of this brought a sudden kick of heels to her mount. Horse and rider flew onto the main road once again.

A midday sun lifted over the zenith as she kept Libertine at a fast lope, once again letting the landscape fly past her. A familiar bundle of clouds waited on the far horizon, stopping to gather strength for an evening battle to capture the springtime sky with the certain triumph of rain. Never far from sight, the great river flowed lazily south, adding the illusion of greater speed to her flight. The warm wind splashed her face, drying the nervous moisture as it appeared.

A few wanderers spiced the road here and there: passersby, more fishermen, a few farmers who worked the rich farmland surrounding Carlisle, the farmers' Negroes and the Cajun people. She slowed a little with each encounter, half expecting arms to be raised with voices crying: "There she is! Catch her!" No such alarm sounded though. She seemed to solicit nothing more than a curious stare or two.

There was no sign of her comrades, and she stopped about a mile out of Carlisle, as close as she would dare. She'd have to wait. She reined Libertine to the side and fixed an anxious stare down the deserted road.

She waited and waited.

A carriage rounded the bend in the distance, and as it drew nearer, she recognized the familiar faces of the Baxter family of Rose Hill. The driver was Hark, an elderly Negro, affable and friendly, but one of the many house servants of whom Sammy warned, "Dat man ever 'spects what's goin' down 'round his nose at dese sermons, he a gonna run right straight for de massa and drop to his knees, all a blabberin'."

Seated in the carriage was Madame Baxter, wearing all the plume and finery of her class, and a plumper version of this lady, her young daughter Margaret. Opposite them sat Clyde and Tom, the two youngest Baxter boys. Joy knew them all quite well. She had had tea at Rose Hill many times during the days when Joshua had been well enough to enjoy society and had danced between times with both young men at various parties.

Joy pulled her mount farther into the forest, knowing they were far more likely to recognize Libertine than herself. The carriage passed in front, and Joy met Madame Baxter's unkind stare with her own: a perfect replica of the po' white trash look of scorn and antipathy toward their betters.

"Hmmph!" Madame Baxter seemed to ruffle her plumage. "This road gets worse each day. The hoodlums begin to appear in alarming numbers—even worse than free darkies! You must remind me to mention it to your father."

Another time Joy might have laughed, but impending disaster, which she could feel, left no room for the natural humor she normally found when confronting the startling duplicity of her life. All she felt was an ever increasing anxiety as she returned at once to study the road.

Good Lord, where were they?

The answer came with a quick prayer for the reverend's unlikely salvation. The only possible thing that could explain this wait was that the reverend must be bent over his cups in some seedy tavern down the road, already inebriated, leaving her to stay perched in that tree for eternity.

Oh Sammy, how could you let him?

Sammy would have left him to fetch her, of course, but what would he do when he found her and the bounty hunters gone? Race home to see if she had made it safe? Yes! Yet when he found her not home, he would panic and a search would be on.

Realizing what must have happened, she turned her horse back, but Libertine had not kicked dust to the road before she heard the familiar voice from behind call, "Joy!"

"Sammy!" Relief once again swept through her in a wild rush, and she turned her mount back around and raced to him. Her relief was so tremendous that, as the two horses met, she fell from her seat and into the security of Sammy's strong arms.

Sammy, for his part, cast a quick glance in both directions before, holding her small weight with one arm, he pulled her and the mounts off the road. Only thing worse than nigger freein' was miscegenation—hanging would not be enough for a Negro caught in an embrace with a white girl.

"Sakes alive girl! What's a happened? I'se jest gwina to git yo—"

The story gushed out in bucketfuls of superlatives: Colossal size and herculean strength, bigger than Sammy, meaner than a rabid dog and madder than a wet hen, cold as New England frost! The pirate man had become so huge in the eyes of retrospect that all Sammy could think was either they were dealing with the very devil himself, or his girl's wits had finally collapsed under the great weight of God's work.

"Hold on girl!" He finally grasped the point and placed a gentle finger on her lips to silence her. "Yo' paintin' one fanciful picture. Ain't lak you'se at all to fall 'part on me," he gently scolded. "Nows, slow down some to think on what we're gwina do."

The reprimand hurt coming from Sammy, whose complaints about anyone or anything were as rare as desert snow, but he was right. She must gather her wits to form a plan.

"The reverend's down yonder in the Red Barn."

"I knew it!"

"Ain't nothin' new 'bout the reverend drinkin'. Now lookie here, I'll head back up the road and sees if'n hit's safe—"

"But what if there's a road block? What if they're already looking for you?"

"Do I'se look anythin' lak dat ole peddler's nigger dey's lookin' fer?"

Nothing remained of the peddler's boy but Sammy's height and build. The Negro wig had been removed, and Sammy's large, dark head gleamed in the magnificence of its baldness. The powder used to lighten his skin had been washed away by a quick dip in the Mississippi, and now his skin shined as dark as night. He wore the well-cut, clean clothes, not just of a free darky, but of the tradesman he was. The Reverend Doddered's man stood well above reproach. Everyone knew that. Besides, he had pass papers folded neatly in his pocket. These alone would answer most any suspicion.

"No," she had to admit. "Though your size Sammy, and they did look at your teeth."

"I'se plan to keep my mouth shut tight as fox teeth on a rabbit's foot. Now, if'n I'se don' return in de hour, den you can knows hit's safe. Still, when you'se head back, you'se be sure to keep to the back roads, all right?"

She nodded.

"Now whil'se you wait, you gotta head down to the Red Barn an' pass warnin' to the reverend. Try to sober him up some. You'se got any money to bribe the barman?" he asked checking his pockets. "What's wrong, Joy chile? Your face looks lak 'twas struck with a bolt of lightnin'?"

"I can't go into the Red Barn! That place is filled with

44

nothing but backwoodsmen, criminals and pirates. Why, I bet LaFitte himself would tread warily in that water, and Lord, Joshua would hit the ceiling if he ever found—"

"Somebody's got to warn the reverend dey's lookin' for him, and you'se dat somebody!" he interrupted. "Lawd, I don' reckon I'se gwina understand white women if'n I live to be a hundred! Here you'se is, dressed up lak a boy, ridin' round on dat hoss laks you'se a boy, barefoot to boot and breakin' half de laws of de state by stealin' folks' niggers, and yet yo' sen'bilities is taxed by settin' foot in a tavern? Even if'n it might mean savin' de ole man's life? Boy, you sho is somethin' girl, and if I didn' love you as my own, I—"

"Oh, very well!" she snapped, properly embarrassed by this verbal attack on her inconsistencies. The duel sense of propriety that Joshua had raised her to know would never amount to more than confusion.

"Okie dokie den, here's what to do. You wait outside the Red Barn after you warn de ole man. Hell, I ain't sayin' it's gwina do any good; the reverend don' care a passel of yams whose chasin' him, 'specially when he's drinkin', but seems to me we gotta at least warn him dey's gwina be out thar. So's you jest run in thar real quick like an' come out to wait to hear from me. After an hour or so, you start wanderin' home and, lak I'se says, keep to the back roads. If anythin's amiss, I'll high-tail back to warn you." He stared down at the anxiety in the pretty blue eyes. "Now what in tarnation's ailin' you, girl?"

"It's just that I—" She could still feel the ever so disturbing imprint and warmth of that hard muscled body, and she shivered. "Nothing. Just you take care and hurry. Oh, please do hurry!"

Sammy's hand reached down to affectionately brush her cheek, and then he winked. She smiled back, pretending to be reassured, and watched him once again, as he mounted and rode off, disappearing down the road.

The ribald sounds of drunken merry-making and the

45

noxious fumes of liquor greeted her well before she turned Libertine off the main road. True to its name, the Red Barn stood as an immense brick structure in the shape of a barn, lifted on huge thick stilts to protect the establishment from seasonal floods. Four large houses might be placed inside its walls, with room left over. A wood veranda circled round the front, and wide steps led to the front door, though no windows shed light in the devil's den. She noticed an impressive number of fine horses among the otherwise common stock, and this she took as proof that in these dark days pirates and criminals could afford the best.

After allowing Libertine a long drink, Joy tied the reins and took a deep breath to gather courage enough to march up the worn steps. Her pulse quickened, and the sounds grew louder with each step, culminating in an assault on her sensibilities. With the final step, she went through the door.

The sheer size of the place overwhelmed her, making her feel both small and mercifully unnoticed. It was crowded. Hay covered the floor, soaking the odor of spilled drinks, food and other imagined substances she did not find it worthwhile to consider. Fifty or more tables and four times as many chairs cluttered the room in an apparent design of chaos.

Loud cheers and cat-calls rose from one corner of the room. On a table, its top covered with coins, two huge and red-faced men arm wrestled to the excited cries of the betters. Cards were being played at two other tables as well, though the vast majority of men contented themselves with mere talk and drink. She stepped quickly away from the door to escape notice, hay tickling her bare feet as she did so.

Then she saw them; the pirates they had seen pass on the road that morning were separated from the others by a respectful distance. The great blond leader sat prominently among the dangerous group. She searched for the reverend; the sooner this was over, the better.

Kegs of ale, stacked in pyramid shapes, marked opposing

ends of a long counter. Bottles of finer stuff were behind the bar. One sign insisted coin must be shown before serving, and another offered hard-boiled eggs, pone or apples for a penny. Two gruff looking men tended the bar. The place was noticeably devoid of bar maids, indeed any female with less than four legs.

The reverend sat right in the middle of the two opposing pyramids of kegs. His head lay in his arms on the counter. No doubt resting precariously on this side of oblivion, she thought as she started toward him.

Joy's gaze darted nervously to and fro, but no one gave her any notice, for after all she looked a sight less than common. Even the bartender gave the appearance of an unkempt river rat as she stepped behind the reverend's back. He now wore clerical black, the beard, hat and spectacles had been discarded, replaced by the ruddy cheeks and reddened nose of a religious man who had indulged in one too many drinks.

"Reverend! Reverend!" she whispered urgently, shaking his thin shoulders. "It's me! Wake up!"

At the sound of the familiar voice, and with great effort, the old man lifted his head. "Lord of mercy," he cried, seeming neither surprised nor alarmed by her presence, which told her he was not halfway to oblivion, but there. "It's too sad . . . too sad."

"What's too sad?"

"Didn't Sammy tell ye?" he asked in a thick slur.

"Tell me what?" She stared with incomprehension at the genuine tears in his eyes.

"The girl. Lord, 'tis a cryin' shame, 'tis. Right on the threshold of freedom and the good Lord sees fit to take her."

"Take who? What are you mumbling about?"

"Mary. We lost her lass." And with the burden of these genuine tears, only slightly affected by four cups of ale, he laid his head down again and promptly passed out.

Joy stood staring in shock, seeing nothing as the tragedy of it filled her young heart. It worked swiftly and completely, overwhelming her with a familiar sadness, a sadness she once described in her diary as the sound of a thousand silent tears shed . . .

"Hey, you thar boy!" a voice called from her side. So numb had this news left her, Joy did not realize she was being addressed until the man asked, "What the hell is wrong with you boy? Yeah, you! I kin see plain that ye be dumb but are ye deaf as well?"

This rude comment solicited a chuckle or two from the patrons hanging out at the bar. Joy lifted clear blue eyes to the man speaking. He was a common seaman—one could tell by the worn cotton uniform—a good sized, crude looking man, one who would pick on the only small person in the place. Malice, plain and simple, appeared in unremarkable brown eyes, and with great alarm she realized he saw her as sport.

"Boy, you look like you been up to no good. Is that the truth or what?"

The real doer of no good approached, and Joy leaned hard into the reverend.

"Yes sir," the man grinned meanly, displaying a mouth where the only teeth that were not missing were yellow and rotting from tobacco stains. "Am I right boy? Tell the God's honest truth now—ye've been up to no good, haven't ye?"

Alarm increased ten-fold, and Joy shook her head, desperately trying to jostle the reverend awake.

"Why, I bet that dollar ye got in ye pocket that ye got a dollar there from all the no good ye been up to!"

The logic of this assertion brought more laughter from the patrons as they watched in amusement. Joy could only shake her head again, casting a quick glance at the door.

"Don't be lookin' to that thar door, boy. That ain't gonna save ye. What's gonna save ye is handin' that dollar of yours over to Jack here."

Never had Joy Claret wanted a dollar more than this moment.

"Well then, if ye won't hand it to me, I see I'll jest have to shake it from ye."

Joy gasped, stopping herself just short of a telling scream as, with a chuckle, the man's hands fitted round her, and with some exertion, he turned her upside down. The onlookers roared with pleasure as he shook her senseless. She grabbed her hat; it was all she could do, all she could think to do as her brain rattled inside her skull, for every ounce of her energy and strength went to stop the scream in her throat.

Suddenly, like a cold fresh wind, a great hush rippled over the crowded room. One by one, voices dropped, then ceased altogether. Activities stopped and in this ominous silence came only the tiny clinks of cups being brought slowly to the tables. Even Jack, who still held her upside down, fell silent and still like everyone else, his gaze held fast the person who just walked through the doors.

The huge room seemed suddenly to grow small by nearly all accounts, and even those few persons who did not know this man were wisely cautioned by the silence of those who did. A small handful of the Red Barn's patrons would at this moment have gladly parted with a handsome sum to quit the place if only the very act of getting up and leaving wouldn't draw this man's attention to their desire to escape.

Attention was not what one wanted from Ram Barrington.

The man's reputation proceeded his every appearance, and he and the twelve or so men behind him were quite used to the effect their entrance caused. A cool intelligent gaze surveyed the room and spotted immediately the table he sought. He headed for it with long sure strides. His men followed, with the noted exception of two who remained on either side of the door to further caution all those who found that sudden need to flee.

Only one person remained unaware of this silence and its threat. All she knew was that she was going to be sick, very sick if this man did not—"Git your cotton pickin' hands off me, mister!"

The horrifying sound of her small voice against the larger silence shocked her as she instantly realized she had just made herself the sudden interest of every living soul in the room.

The sound of the familiar voice brought Ram to an abrupt stop, and he was laughing even before he turned round to confront the sight of her, in all the ridiculousness of her precarious upside down position. If there was any surprise at finding her in a place like the Red Barn and in the unusual position, it showed only in the sound of his amusement.

"What's your name, my good fellow?"

"Who me?" Jack could hardly believe he was being addressed.

Ram nodded.

"Jack. 'Tis Jack, gov'ner," he answered back.

"Well Jack, I believe that's my baggage you're handling there."

"Yours, gov'ner?"

"Mine," Ram made the simple pronouncement. "And you'll do me honor if you drop it where you stand."

"Well, certainly gov'ner." Jack dropped Joy, and because he sensed Ram Barrington's animosity toward this baggage, he did so unceremoniously. Joy fell in a heap on the floor. Gasping for breath and fighting dizziness, she found the way to her hands and knees. Only because she had to know if her worst nightmare had become a reality, she ventured a bold glance up and across the room.

How he looked taller, meaner and far more threatening than before, she could not for her life imagine, but he did, standing there with his hands resting on his hips and staring at her with all the respect due a naughty child not yet out of swaddling clothes. As her gaze traveled up from the shiny black boots and over the tailored black breeches and open, white silk shirt—gentlemen's garb notably minus any

50

fashionable foppish adornments of nicety—her emotions were best represented by the urgency with which she scrambled to her feet and made a mad dash to the door.

Ram motioned to a man, and with no further interest in the matter, he turned and approached the table where the other pirates were congregating. Joy had not gotten as far as the door when, from behind, a man's merciless strong hands put a quick halt to her flight. She cried out as the man tossed her over his shoulder like the baggage she was named and headed in the opposite direction she would have chosen. Small, white-knuckled fists pounded furiously on the large back, and though she tried, she could not catch enough breath to give voice to the screams in her throat.

Ram stopped before the table and locked his gaze with the giant blond leader. Had anyone besides their men cared to notice, they would have been surprised, even shocked, by the plain, unmasked affection in both gazes.

"Such a dramatic entrance, my lord," the pirate said in dispassionate exasperation and in a voice that rang with clear evidence of English aristocratic breeding. "It gets worse each time I've a chance to witness."

Ram chuckled, then shrugged. "I can't seem to stop it. Although, much as I hate theatrics, I must admit it does wonders for business." Knowing they would talk later, Ram surveyed the group of men, nodded to the familiar faces and saw nothing or no one amiss. "My man said you already had something Sean?"

It was half question, half demand, and Sean motioned two men up to see to it. While they waited, Ram turned his attention to the frantic cries and desperate struggle of the baggage draped over Derrick's shoulder.

Derrick set Joy Claret on her feet. Panic molded her pale, fear-stricken features, and her breath came in those huge uneven gulps Ram was getting used to seeing in her. So frightened by him, she could not even think to know it was her absolute end. She stepped back, shaking her head, and

Derrick, not wanting to chase again, grabbed her shoulders and asked, "Where do you want it, Ram?"

Ram lifted one long leg over a bench and indicated his bent knee. "Why, right here Derrick." He smiled.

Odd how quickly his intention crashed into her scared wits. The frantic cry "Nooo!" sounded with Derrick's chuckle as he lifted her again, only to drop her over the place Ram had indicated and this, to the chorus of amusement that rose from the crowd.

The sting from Ram's hand spread like hot bolts of lightning through her small form, and though she struggled for all she was worth, he held her with maddening ease.

Turning a brat over one's knee apparently was not unusual or mean enough to solicit more than perfunctory notice from this crowd, notice expressed in some mild amusement and at least one comment: "That little tyke doesn't look more than a stone's throw from apron strings but hell, look at the fight in him!"

Sean watched with mild interest, too, far more curious about what the brat had done to earn Ram's interest. "Dear me, Ram," he asked in mocking sarcasm, "has your benevolence extended to the reformation of delinquents, or can we hope this is an isolated incident?"

Ram laughed, and without missing a beat, he advised, "I know one brat who better be praying it's an isolated incident."

Joy was praying all right; fervently praying that she would not let herself cry, but when she finally exhausted her small strength and felt his last hard slap, the tears were plain in her eyes.

Ram brought her up to sit on his lap. So consumed with the rage of her emotions, she failed to notice that her hat and wig had fallen. An interested gaze stared at the beauty thus revealed to him: the bright flush of humiliation in her cheeks, the large, translucent blue eyes filled with tears and fury—

eyes that seemed like openings to a summer sky. And that hair!

Ram withdrew two visible pins, and the thick, long ropes of light, auburn hair swung down past her waist to curl on his lap.

"Bloody Mary, it's a lass!" was heard from at least ten men. Even Sean's brow lifted with interest.

Ram ignored most of the comments and exclamations, and perhaps only Sean could guess at his emotions: anger, anger at how terribly young she was, at the innocence etched so plainly in the lovely features and innocence so at odds with her behavior that it begged destruction.

Joy could not think to save herself. Not a thought could rise beyond the helpless humiliation and blind fury that raised a trembling hand to give a hard slap to his face.

"That sweetheart"—he caught her arm well before it hit its mark—"will only get you more of the same."

For the first time in her life, she understood the base fury that led to violence; her rage demanded revenge, immediate, quick and merciless. She wanted to hit, pound and hurt him, but he held her hands, making her helplessness clear with an all consuming strength that left her trembling. Then abruptly she lost his interest, and it only vaguely penetrated her thoughts but somehow added to her rage; it was grossly unfair that her emotions toward him could be so enormous, while his toward her were naught but passing.

Sean's men returned with a chained and bound man. The man was led directly in front of Ram, and she forgot her own rage as she listened in horror to this man's violent curses and threats. Humiliation and rage shook his much larger frame, but his straight back and squared shoulders spoke of a great pride, despite his unenviable circumstances. He had aging and rather distinguished features; he looked past forty, with graying, dark hair, a new beard and markedly intelligent eyes. Cory always claimed that the lord wrote a person's deeds on his face—especially white folks—and Joy thought of this as she stared at this bound man. There was something in the lines and creases of the man's eyes and mouth that suggested cruelty—not the small common meanness of men like Jack or indeed, even the bounty hunters—but larger somehow, revealing itself most in the shrewd glare of his gaze.

Joy would have been alarmed to know that what she read as pride, the far more experienced men of the crowd read only as the ignorance of a man too stupid to be afraid.

Abruptly she sensed Ram's gaze—she could actually feel it! She took one quick look of confirmation and lowered her eyes quickly, embarrassed by the shocking intimacy of being held like this, on his lap with his arms wrapped securely around her, confused by the inexplicable warmth of his body pressed against her, and so afraid, she could not for her life stop trembling.

Ram was acutely conscious of her fear, a fear he'd see increased two-fold before he was through with her. He gently brushed loose tendrils of her hair from her face, and because she could no longer manage to meet his gaze, he lifted her face to his. "I still don't know your story. Indeed, I don't even know your Christian name."

She refused to lift her eyes. "I'll not tell you," she whispered in the passion of her fury. "Never! You can beat me ten times and you still won't hear it from me!"

This boldness lifting through her fear brought an amused light to his eyes. "Fortunately, I'm not depending on you for the information. Because sweetheart," he whispered against her ear, "your small strength is not impressive even for one of your sex, and I don't think you'd survive one more thrashing, let alone ten."

All waited for Ram, and in a single fluid motion, he stood, lifting her to set her back on the bench alone. "Since you seem bent on playing in a man's world, you might enjoy witnessing a man's game. Sit tight and behave yourself."

Cold fear battled with rage, and as her mind spun with the danger, her wits returned at once. He didn't know yet, but when he discovered she had helped to free slaves, all was lost: the reverend, Sammy and herself. Perhaps even Joshua would be implicated in the felony crime of the highest order. Yet she was far less afraid of the fines and jail term than the knowledge that Southern justice was not often dealt in a court of law.

Hanging might only be the merciful end!

In all her years as a conductor, never had her mind conjured the risks in such graphic detail. Added to this was the frightening attempt to guess what he might personally do to her. This contemplation could not be borne, for whatever it was, it seemed bound to be worse than the worst.

Her whole body screamed one word—Run!—and this was tempered only by the crystal clear understanding of just how far she would get. She cast a quick glance back to where the reverend slept at the bar, deciding that no help would be coming from that direction. She found two exits, the front and a hallway, surely leading to the back door. Nervous, still trembling with fear, she could barely contain herself as she saw she must to wait for her chance.

Ram stood near the bound man, conferring with two of his men. His attention finally turned to Sean, and for the first time, the large crowd of men joined in the deathly quiet with the rest of the room. Even the bound man, whose voice had been raised with vicious threats and curses, all at once fell silent.

"Allow me to present Captain Willis." Sean began in that dispassionate air of boredom of his, as though, like the great blond Viking God he resembled, these mere mortal surroundings thoroughly taxed him. The impression was completely situational, rising from the knowledge of the bound man's chains. "We followed the foul stench of his ship—the *Blue Crest*—from the Caribbean Isles, allowing her some wind to see where she'd go. We caught her less than

55

a hundred miles directly due east from here."

A dark brow lifted; this information interested Ram, and the prisoner received another appraisal.

"Who the hell do you think you are?" Captain Willis interrupted to demand of Ram, no longer able to contain his indignation, bewilderment and rage. "The bloody green gall of taking my ship—I still cannot believe it happened and in New Orleans to boot!—why, I'll be damned if I don't see every last one of you cutthroats hanged before the day is through! And if you think for a moment you bloody bastards can get away with it—"

Ram had set down his cup and motioning for silence, said simply, "You will not speak until asked."

"The bloody hell I—"

With no warning, Ram brought the bunt end of a pistol against the man's face with an untaxed strength that even few in this room could match. The impact threw Captain Willis hard against the floor, and Joy screamed as her hands flew to her mouth with the shock of his demonstration showing the terrifying difference between how he treated a man as opposed to herself. The man struggled to lift himself up but collapsed with the effort. As though he had done nothing more than swat a bothersome mosquito, Ram's gaze returned to Sean.

"The cargo was what one might expect." Sean continued with matched dispassion. "Though I suppose certain details bare mentioning. The *Blue Crest* was rigged as a brig and small at that—less than three hundred tons—but with a burden any seaman would find too large for a thousand ton schooner."

"The exact number, Sean," Ram demanded.

"Two hundred and eleven."

The number hung in the air, seemingly more damning than God almighty's fingers, and Joy tried to understand what it meant.

"Needless to say"—Sean shrugged—"this forced our good captain here to position his passengers back to back lengthwise, stacked like oh so many flapjacks in a small four-foot hold. And apparently either the crew was particularly lazy or the rations particularly bad, for there was one dead man to every one still managing to breathe in that stench."

A slaver! Joy's eyes widened enormously, then dropped to the man lying on the floor. If even half of what Sean claimed was true, then it was not cruelty etched in the hard features of his face but evil. The unconscionable evil, Joshua often said, of running a slaver was the first, most awful step in the long journey to hell.

Uncertainty added to her fear as she looked at Ram anew. So many thoughts clamored for her attention, she could hardly make sense of it beyond the single pressing question. What part does he play in this evil?

"The crew?" Ram asked next.

"Ah, we dealt with them," Sean sighed, smiling. "You know how hard it is to control my men in these situations."

The men's grunts, nods and amusement lent credibility to Sean's assertion, but Ram answered with: "I only know how little you try."

Sean smiled with a shrug. "Don't worry, my lord, I did manage to save you this captain, and in the event he perishes before he breaks, I have two of his, ah, officers in wait."

"Oh, he'll break all right," Ram said, looking at the fallen man. "I wager it won't even be hard."

"About that," Sean said with the barest hint of disgust lifting through his dispassionate interest, "we also found two wenches tied and beaten in the captain's cabin. The man's obvious fondness for whips bares mentioning only as it might enhance your much deserved reputation for dealing justice poetically."

The meaning of this was not lost on Ram, and he chuckled lightly as he motioned to two of his men waiting on the sidelines. Missing not a word or implication, Joy watched as the fallen man was lifted to his feet by two of Ram's men. One of these men drew a clean shiny saber. The sword sliced through the ropes that bound the captain's hands, but before he had even shaken blood back to his numb limbs, his arms were forced over his head and bound again.

An ugly swollen welt already marred his face, and his nose was broken. Fear finally found its way into his face as, with smooth practiced motions, Ram's man tossed the rope over an overhanging beam and then secured the tail to the table, which was held down by the elbows of over ten of the strong and able-bodied men watching.

Joy's attention was riveted on the scene before her, and she did not see the man enter the tavern, quickly making his way to Ram's side. He was middle-aged, in his forties, with a magnificent mane of silver and white hair and bright blue eyes. The quickness with which he approached Ram seemed in defiance with his immense stocky frame, for one might think his muscles far too large and cumbersome to allow the apparent ease of his movements.

As the man spoke, Ram's attention returned to her, his eyes filled with surprise. "Bounty hunters?"

Bart quickly gave the details, and Joy would have felt more alarmed if she had witnessed Ram's appraisal of the men in the bar. Based on the briefest description, Ram's gaze rested on none other than the reverend. He mentioned something inaudible to Bart, who nodded in turn, and after exchanging a few hearty greetings with Seanessy's men, Bart turned away.

Joy had determined for a fact that she could not, would not, ever, no matter what, bear witness to a hanging, and as she began to deliver a fervent prayer to her pounding heart to make her faint, she saw with ever-increasing horror that hanging was not the intent.

It was worse.

Ram's man ripped the shirt from Captain Willis's back, and his first scream sounded pure fury as the sharp blade of the saber cut a neat red cross on his back in blood like some large illiterate signature. One of Seanessy's men stood up, sporting a long black whip in his hands, the common tool of overseers. With easy flicks of his wrist, he sent the whip cracking over the captain's bare feet. The captain's muscles jerked and tensed, sweat laced his brow in an effort to stop the cry in his throat. Sean's man mercilessly waited for each breath to ease his pain, bringing feeling back again, before cracking the whip another time. Amidst sudden grunts and growls, many of the other men abruptly found displeasure with the quality of the tavern's rum and tossed the hot liquid over the fresh bloodied back.

Joy covered her eyes and turned away, shaking and sick, jolted visibly by each gasp of the man's pain.

Ram waited impatiently for the man to gain some semblance of control, then finally explained, "Your life hangs precariously on my small mercy. Do you understand that?"

The man was breathing so hard now it was mistaken by all as a nod.

"I want to know the numbers first. How many slavers are running from Orleans?"

Ugly hatred flared in Willis's eyes, and he spit, missing Ram by inches. "That's to your numbers!"

The whip cracked, a fiery snake coiling around his neck, searing it with a blazing hot pain that arched his back, and Joy's gasp was drown in his scream. The whip cracked twice more in quick succession before suddenly, he cried, "Five!"

Leaning arms on his bent knee, Ram interrupted the motion of bringing his cup to his lips. Apparently it was the wrong number, for he gave it but brief consideration. He nodded slightly to his man with the saber, and the blade had only to lightly run across the open wounds of the captain's back before he screamed, "Eight!"

"Ah, that's more like it. Now I'll have the names of those financing these ships."

Horror lifted through the man's pain, as though he had not expected this question. "Oh, no." He shook his head, throwing large drops of perspiration to the bloodied straw at his feet. "You'll have to kill me first, 'cause I'll not—"

He never finished, for the whip cracked angrily, the sound crashing through Joy's terror despite the hands held tight over her ears. She did not know she had bolted from her seat until Ram's arms were on her, forcing her still with her backside against his long length.

"Something wrong, sweetheart?" he whispered against her ear. "I had thought you'd be good for a while longer—it has, after all, only begun."

Panic kept her mute, but her eyes, filled with fresh tears, terror and desperation, pleaded her case. When the man's next scream jolted her small frame with a physical force, Ram knew she had indeed reached her end. She was hardly conscious of those arms lifting her to the air, carrying her down the hall and through the back door, until the blessed fresh air filled her lungs, and she opened her eyes to the bright sunlight.

She trembled still, and Ram set her to her feet, cursing when her knees gave way like a paper doll's. He caught her back into his arms and brought her beneath the shade of a willow tree. He sat down against the trunk, fitting her beneath his outstretched legs, and for a long while he just stared. The dramatic evidence of just how shaken it left her only fueled his anger.

"That show obviously has upset your, ah, delicacies is it?" he asked.

Joy glanced up to meet the anger in his cold gaze. Now, all her fear rose from the single dread that he would force her to return to that nightmare. It was all she could do not to beg.

"If that scene reduced you to tears and trembling, sweetheart, imagine this," he said evenly. "Imagine a young girl on some ill-conceived mission of charity, donning boys' clothes in a ridiculous attempt to disguise her . . . oh so obvious sex. Imagine that girl entering an establishment like this." He motioned to the Red Barn.

"Now, sweetheart," he almost whispered, catching her

thin arm in his hand, as if he needed more of her wide-eyed attention. "Imagine the patron's delight, nay excitement, upon discovering this young girl's sex. Imagine this girl being thrown backside to a foul smelling floor—"

She covered her ears, "Nooo . . ."

"Yes." He caught both her arms to force her to hear the rest. "Imagine the line forming, a line that would not stop when the girl finally, mercifully passed out. A line that would only stop when there was enough blood between your thighs to convince the most dull-witted among them that you were indeed quite dead!"

She tried desperately to deny this vision, and while she shook her head almost frantically, the graphic details he drew could neither be escaped nor ignored. It was the straw that broke the camel's back, seeing not what could have happened but what probably would have happened. That nightmare was the last awful end to the worst day of her life. Emotionally and physically exhausted, she collapsed with the last tears, now drained even of the burden of caring what he would do.

Exhaustion was her only explanation for what happened next. She didn't know how it happened; perhaps she had collapsed into his arms or perhaps those arms had guided her there, but suddenly she was folded in his embrace with her face buried in his chest, crying softly.

She had never before experienced the comfort of a man's arms, save for Joshua, the reverend and Sammy. It was even more odd that he—a man who had dealt her nothing but the most punishing blows—was the one providing her comfort. Yet, even through her dazed wits, she intuitively grasped that he was no longer going to harm her, that while she still had reason for fear and uncertainty, his anger had diminished as she had broken.

She felt her emotions quiet somewhat, and her thoughts struggled to answer the most pressing question: Who was he? He sat like a king on a totalitarian throne with a stream of men at his beck and call: huge, mean, terrifying men that included a whole band of hardened sea pirates. He even had the attentive deference of their leader. She had witnessed his great strength and aura of command when dealing cruel and harsh justice to the evil of running a slaver. This demonstrated such an unlikely and unexpected nobility of purpose, the thought sent her into a quick tumult of confusion.

To say he was not like anyone she had ever known or heard of or even read about was an understatement. He seemed ten thousand times stronger than most men, not just physically but also of will, and at least that much as sharp. She did not think he would be received in any house she knew; yet he had an aristocratic bearing that made Louisiana's grandest look as dull and impoverished as the reverend's peddler's hat.

These thoughts registered but dimly on her mind, waiting to crystallize and grow with the mystery of Ram Barrington. What was not so vague was the gentle stroke of his hand through her hair, that inexplicable warmth of his touch and his scent: clean, fresh and masculine. The increasingly disturbing effect of these things caused her pulse to quicken, as a heat spread physically through her limp limbs.

"There's something about you," he finally said after a long study of an innocence so blatantly plain, "something past the breeding in your voice, that makes me truly believe you never considered this." He looked at the boys' clothes as he wiped the last tear from her cheek, his hand traveling all the way down the long rope of hair. He loved braided hair, long braids as Mary once wore. "You are a curious, if not alluring, mix. Tell me, how old are you?"

Like his touch, his stare was casual, yet assuming an intimacy that would have brought a blush to her cheeks with any other man. "Ten and seven," she finally whispered.

He would have guessed even younger, but then it was hard to tell with her in this costume. "What's your name?"

Panic lifted quickly to her eyes. "I can't say."

"Why is that? Do you think I'm unenlightened as to the activities that brought bounty hunters after you?"

She gasped in surprise, "You know?"

He nodded.

Running slave ships was no more illegal than stealing slaves to freedom, and she saw how he had dealt with the former. On the heels of a frightened pause, she asked, "Are you going to turn me in?"

"Why should I? Is there a reward posted for you?"

The answer appeared in quick renewed panic. There was indeed a reward, not specifically for her by name but for the information leading to or the capture of anyone aiding and abetting runaway slaves. The sum of the reward was monstrously huge from her estimation, and as she thought of it, Ram felt her small form tense, then watched those lovely blue eyes dart to the horses.

"Easy sweetheart," he warned. "You're not going anywhere, not until my . . . ah, curiosity is at least partially satisfied, and besides," he said to put her back at ease long enough to answer his questions, "whatever that reward is, I'd wager I spend more on a pair of boots. I'm not the pernicious type, nor am I motivated by want of coin; but even if I were, I can't fathom the sum that would be worth seeing a noose around this neck."

He reached out to trace a finger there, and she shivered lightly, then caught his hand to stop him. For a moment time seemed to stop as she studied the size and strength of his hand, the dark bronze color contrasting sharply in the paleness of hers. The effect of his touch was disarming and she was confused by it. Still feeling an odd lingering heat from the line he drew, she dropped his hand and covered the place on her neck.

This was not lost on Ram, and a small hint of amusement lifted on the handsome features. "Rest assured, I won't turn you into the ah, so called proper authorities."

"What will you do with me, then?"

"Not," he assured her, "what I might want. I'll send you home. You do have a home?"

She nodded.

"And parents?"

"No, but I've a guardian, an uncle who's as good and kind to me as any parent might be."

"I'm not convinced. What kind of guardian would permit this?" He indicated her clothes.

"Oh, but he doesn't know!"

To his relief, this told Ram that her guardian was not the old drunk at the bar. Still, he said, "Ignorance is hardly an excuse."

"Well, no it's not, of course." She looked down. "But you see, Jos—my uncle—" she thought better than to name him—"is not well and his illness, I'm afraid naturally consumes his energies and attentions."

He noted the sadness springing quickly into the enchanting eyes as she spoke of this. "What kind of illness?"

Joy stared at the ground and hesitated, always finding the subject difficult to face. "He has consumption and the affliction leaves him weak and often bedridden. He's recovering, of course"—her tone lifted slightly, then dropped—"though it does seem to be taking a very long time. I'm told that such is often the case."

The intensity of the young girl's love for the man—whatever he was—as well as her concern over his health were plain to Ram, not just from her words but by her tone, softened with trepidation and fear. "So," he said gently, "he remains unaware of what you're up to?"

"Sometimes I think he suspects but then—" She looked away again, studying the distance as though to discover something. "Cory provides excuses for my absence, while the reverend—" Instantly, her gaze shot to his face to see his reaction.

"I thought I already established I'm not going to turn you

in," he replied easily. "Which brings me back to my original question in all this. Tell me your name."

"Joy Claret."

"Ah, Joy Claret. I might have guessed you'd have an unusual name." He laughed. "I can easily imagine why a woman would name her daughter that. Joy upon birth, yet all from a single night of passion, one owing to a bottle of claret."

He was right of course and she blushed. She had yet to decide if she liked her name or not. Her mother had been a language teacher at a prominent English girls' school, her father—Joshua's older brother—a language teacher at Cambridge. Her mother, like so many women, died at her birth; her father died two years later in London's worst cholera epidemic to date.

Joshua told her many stories about them. He painted a picture of two hot-headed and eccentric people who, like all members of the Reubens family, were fanatics on the subject of religion—Methodist—and slavery. Joy was inordinately proud of her mother's role as a founding member of the prestigious anti-slavery society, the English Christian Women's Society of Abolitionists. She had also fought hard for the rights of women to speak publicly. There were no children from the ill-conceived union until the twenty-third year of marriage. Her parents went from one argument to the next without stopping to catch breath and her name told her the rest.

Ram marveled at the emotions playing in her eyes. "So," he continued, wanting to know more. "Tell me what your relationship is to that old drunk at the bar?"

Joy stared in sudden alarm. "You do know!"

When he nodded, she shocked him by throwing herself against him with clenched fists and begging, "Oh, please tell me you won't hurt him! He's done you no harm—"

Ram caught her arms to hold her still and said with tempered anger, "That man does not deserve your concern, which I can only surmise comes from some undeserved affection. Your guardian is bad enough, but I shudder to think how that man would come to your defense in there, drunk as he was. And he obviously has quite a lot to do with your very presence in there—as well as in the forest."

Each angry word lashed at her, causing a slight jerk of her head, obviously scaring her witless. Yet each time he witnessed her blatant femininity, the obvious fragility and vulnerability, his anger rose. He simply could not reconcile it with her previous actions.

His anger merely reduced her to sputtering imbecility, yet anger was not the cause of her fear. Her body melted against his with a treacherous enthusiasm that sent shock waves through her. His hands pressed the small of her arched back, holding her softer form against the hard muscles of his. The startling sensations that swept through her—vaguely reminiscent of the sweet warmth brought by her silly school-girl fantasies—caused a tensing, not at all unpleasant. At the points where their bodies touched, a quivering of tingling excitement spread through her abdomen. Her reaction alarmed her with an instinctual, primitive force, a gasp. "Loose me," she begged breathlessly, attempting to pull away only to hear his capricious chuckle, warm, yet menacing as he caught her hands, holding them captive behind her back.

"I believe you insisted on the position. In turn I'll insist on the outcome."

Instantly, she tried squirming loose only to realize that this was absolutely the wrong thing to do. The shock of sensations, no less than his sharp intake of breath, stopped her instantly.

Ram had as many ways of kissing a woman as the sun had of shining. All depended on his mood, his inclination, his interest. His mood was dangerous and always capricious; there had been little inclination until the moment her small body fitted against him, giving an arresting hint of the curves hidden in the baggy boys' clothes. His interest had been only mildly intrigued, until the moment he touched her lips.

Fear molded her lips with a maddening vulnerability, while her sudden stillness said this was her first kiss. These two things, combined with the sweet moist taste of her mouth, formed an unexpected urge.

As his tongue swept skillfully in her mouth, she froze with panic and fear natural to a young lady with plenty of worldly, unchaste knowledge, but not a real kiss to her experience. Yet as his mouth molded to hers with the play of his tongue, she was stricken with a tremor, a warmth in its wake, making her dizzy, weak knees and limp again. Then she was melting as the kiss suddenly deepened.

He broke the kiss at last and stared for a long moment. She was unaware he had granted her freedom, so she remained intimately positioned in his arms, dazed by the kiss, the heat of his body, the roar in her ears and the pounding of her heart. Then, with a warm chuckle against her ear, he whispered, "Joy Claret, my surprising vixen, would you have me—a virtual stranger—lay you beneath this tree to take your virtue?"

Some small part of her mind that was still working managed an uncertain shake of her head, and warm, wonderful humor lifted into his gaze as he laughed.

Only then did she realize she was free. Gathering her dazed wits, she slowly stood to her feet and backed away. As long as he lived, he'd not forget the small hand touching her lips, the eyes wide with wonder and incredulity.

She backed right into Derrick.

"Yes? What is it?" Ram asked, as he stood brushing off his pants.

"You're not going to believe it, Ram." Derrick caught her at the shoulders. "'Twas little wonder the bastard didn't break with a whip given what he knew. Sean finally said we seemed to just be making a mess of the floor, and he put Cane on it, with that Oriental thing he does. That always works, but lord," Derrick laughed, "the bastard didn't have to give us all five names. One would have done it."

"Get to the point."

Derrick passed a meaningful glance down at the girl. "You better come inside, Ram. Suffice to say, this favor you're doing for your uncle has suddenly grown larger, even for you, as it seems to shed considerable doubt on the integrity of some of Orleans' finest families."

"Well," Ram chuckled. "I'll be damned. A day full of surprises." The worst day of her life ended as he ordered Derrick to fetch Bart to escort the lady home, then gently caught Joy's arm and whispered into her ear just what he was likely to do if he ever found a girl dressed as a boy out without an escort. Color raced to her cheeks, and she was quite speechless, helplessly humiliated and immobile again. With plenty of laughter, Ram returned to the Red Barn.

## Chapter Three

The hot Louisiana sun glistened in a bright ribbon of light on the river nearby as Bart and Joy rode along. The humidity covered her with a thin sheen of perspiration, and Joy was as acutely conscious of this as she was of the dirt and grime covering her body. She looked ridiculous and felt confused, never having known vanity as she did now, and somehow the uncomfortable thoughts of her disheveled appearance were paired distressingly with the memory of Ram Barrington's gaze. To make matters worse, every time she thought of his threat, which was every ten paces it seemed, she felt herself blushing, rosy embarrassment traveling from the roots of her hair to the tips of her toes.

Bart was proving to be an amicable and talkative companion. She might add sweet-like, if his very size didn't preclude such niceties. He claimed to be Ram Barrington's personal valet, which was yet another surprise. The thought of Ram Barrington needing help getting his boots on in the morning seemed patently absurd, though nonetheless here Bart was in all his glory.

"Well, just who is he?" she asked in a whisper of wonder.

Bart, furiously engaged in a futile battle with gnats, chuckled at this and relaxed a bit. "Unless ye've got time for a book the size of the good one lass, ye'll find the man kin not

69

be summed by words."

She believed it, yet she was also quite determined to discover all the reasons why she should dislike Ram Barrington. "Well, where's he from, then?" she pursued.

"England, but 'e was raised for a long spell in me own country, on the Irish coast there in Kilerian. 'Is family's titled to a piece of me island, ye see."

She couldn't believe this. "He's titled?"

What Bart couldn't believe was the creature crossing the road, and he gasped, reining his mount to a halt, while simultaneously withdrawing a long-barrelled, ivory-handled pistol. "What the hell—"

"Oh 'tis only an armadillo." Joy stopped Libertine as well. "They're quite harmless really."

Bart was hardly convinced as he watched the creature move slowly across the road. He simply could not get used to this dark swampy land, a place where steam rose from its very bowels as though it was that close to Satan's own hell. This place was full of fist sized insects, gnats and mosquitoes—creatures not seen in his worst nightmare— dark skinned Negroes and girls dressed in boys' clothes— sweet as the last might be. He felt a good deal safer in England, even with the intrigue threatening Ram's very life and the assassins sent to kill him.

"'Tis only the snakes one has to worry about," Joy explained as they started forward again.

"Snakes!" Bart turned to the water, expecting to see slithering horrors there. Just that morning he had been swimming with the others— "What?" He realized she asked him something.

"You say he's titled?" she repeated in a question, trying to sound nonchalant.

"Aye, indeed he is: Lord Ramsey Edward Barrington III, Lord and Regent of Dreisbury, Compton and Cornington." Bart forgot to be afraid as he named the endless list of Ram Barrington's titles. "Ah." He smiled when he at last finished.

"I see ye are properly surprised by it!"

Shocked might be a better word, for she simply could not imagine how Ram Barrington could possibly be a product of England's titled and privileged class. The reverend had imparted many of his thoughts on the English aristocracy. For hundreds of years, he oft explained, England's been spawning her blue bloods, men who never 'ad to lift anything heavier than a tea cup, men whose major concern was the quality of their tailoring, fops whose lives are oceans removed from their fellow countrymen . . .

"Indeed I am," she admitted. "'Tis hard to imagine how the parlors and sitting rooms of the great English houses could have created such a . . . a formidable man."

"Ah, very insightful of ye, lass." Bart continued the battle with the damned gnats, trying to figure out how the tiny beasts kept up with the horses. "The truth of it 'tis, Ram has seen precious few parlor rooms. 'E was removed from 'is class at birth."

"Why was that?"

"Oh"—he waved his hand and a marked bitterness sprang in his gaze as he remembered something—"I don't suppose 'tis me place to say, except that thar were trouble between father and son. Lady Alisha, Ram's mum, died at his birth. No one—not me own da even—no one in the whole entire 'ouse'old could do anythin' fer the lad. Oh 'tis a sad tale; strong and willful as Ram be, I don't think 'e would of survived to 'is fifth birthday if 'tweren't fer the sweet blessed Mary."

"He's religious?" Now she was shocked.

"Oh, 'eavens no! I mean Mary Seanessy, Sean's mother—ye know, the captain ye saw back in the tavern. Sean and Ram are as close as brothers, raised as such. Mary was jest common village folk, poor and strugglin', but Mary—she owned a 'eart as big and brave as the best. She raised the lad! Imagine it! To this day, no one knows why she took it upon 'erself—not even Ram—save for her goodness. And oh,

71

Mary were not atall afraid of Ram's father. Once I remember 'er givin' the man a tongue lashin', unmindful she was of the consequences. Anyway, 'twas Mary Seanessy who raised Ram with her own Sean durin' the years that Ram's father tried to forget 'is boy lived. Lord," he chuckled dreamily, remembering, "ye never saw two such wild and unmanageable lads. Oh, but they were a terror fer miles around! And poor Mary aged a good twenty years to the day, trying to chase the two of 'em down."

Joy smiled at this, despite herself, imagining the unenviable task of trying to raise two wild hellions. As her curiosity peaked, and with but a tiny prod, Bart provided a brief outline of Ram Barrington's startling history.

He said Ram Barrington was ten and four years old when his great uncle, Admiral Byron, finally discovered how his sister's daughter's son was being raised, and assumed the responsibility for his welfare. This information held an unnerving coincidence for Joy, though she wisely kept it to herself. The admiral had Ram removed to the proper schools but only to find he was far too late.

"The lad never even stayed long enough to be expelled, and after three tries, the great admiral took 'is charge directly under 'is wing and onto 'is ships that sailed the waters of the dark continent in the bloody effort of tryin' to control this God forsaken slave trade of yours . . ." Bart's voice trailed off. That was yet another horror in this place!

Joy quickly assured Bart that she had naught to do with her adopted country's great evil, though this part of Ram's history brought a flurry of questions. Here Bart disappointed her, for he had not been with Ram upon his voyages, nor afterward, when the Admiral was called to India and they stayed there for two long years. "But that heathen pot put the queerest notion in 'is 'ead, I don't mind tellin' ye. Ram struck up friendships among these Muslims and Hindu sepoys—ferocious men indeed!—and to this very day, Ram keeps a friendship with an Indian king." He shook his head,

"Imagine Muslim and Hindu friends! We got some as crew, too!"

Joy never met a Muslim or a Hindu and was not at all sure she wanted to. The road was gradually becoming busier as Bart went on to tell of how Ram's father died and Ram finally came into his inheritance. "He returned to England, or rather Ireland, reunited with Sean. Somehow he got it in 'is 'ead that Sean and 'imself were in need of polishin'. So," Bart laughed, "'E bribed Sean into spendin' four years with 'im at Oxford; Ram's position provided admittance of course, while 'is fortune was more than enough ta keep the promise that if Sean completed the polishin', Ram would give him 'is very own ship." Bart chuckled heartily, slapped his thigh and made his mount dance as he recounted this tale. "Sean stayed, while to nobody's surprise, Ram lasted five minutes into the headmaster's first indoctrination speech afore, 'e ups and heads fer the nearest bawdy 'ouse and got 'imself drunk with two pretty loves—" Bart stopped suddenly, remembering who he was talking to, but Joy had been so engrossed in the details of Ram Barrington's life that, to her further embarrassment—as though she hadn't enough—she forgot to be properly shocked by this. If the truth were known, she was far more shocked by how quickly they had reached the outskirts of New Orleans.

No more of Ram's history was offered, as Bart thought it necessary to impart his wisdom on the matter of wild young ladies during the short time they had left together, not realizing Joy was of an age where advice went in one ear and out the other, never stopping in between. Besides, after this most awful day of her life, she had far more weighty matters to consider.


After already writing late into the night, Joy skipped her morning chores to again seek the solace found only in the pages of her diary.

Dear Diary,

My dearest friend! I am even more distressed now. Every few minutes my panic pushes me to my feet for a fast furious pacing, but finding no outlet, I turn in desperation to these pages.

Finally, the reverend has returned. Never before have I seen the reverend turned belly up—like a cowardly mutt—humbled and meek, and from naught but Lord Ramsey Edward Barrington III's tongue lashing! I begged, pleaded and finally threatened to no avail, for the reverend insists on confessing to Joshua, which he is doing at this very minute!

How much will he tell? Surely not all! Dear God, please don't let him tell all! Joshua couldn't bare it; the discovery of my duplicity would distress him endlessly, and his health—

I shall not think of that.

Nor shall I think of Ram Barrington's threat to me, the threat that made explicit just what he would do if he ever caught me leaving the house without an escort, let alone dressed as a boy—what business is it of his!— for every time I think of that threat, I flush, jump back to my feet with embarrassment, more indignation and no small amount of alarm.

The one thing I cannot seem to stop thinking about is his kiss. Why oh why did I let him kiss me so? As you well know my dearest friend, it was not my first kiss. Not really. The night of the Beauchamp's soiree, when Joe Campbell's spurs tore my dress as we danced, he kissed me in the garden as he apologized. Yet that chaste kiss was in no way similar to Ram Barrington's!

And why oh why, with everything else that happened, can I think of nothing else? I am beset with embarrassment as I remember that kiss: My face flushes, I feel this queer tingling that forms a knot at the bottom of my stomach and the emotions! Emotions and emotions, I cannot think through them!

That kiss put me on the edge of a knowledge that in my innocence I never really knew. It is the difference between putting the words of a poem to heart and grasping the poetic beauty. The poetic beauty is wonder. I wonder if this is what fuels the physical aspect between men and women—the sweep of sensation that banishes thoughts, morals, virtue! I wonder if that's why women, especially girl's mothers, make it sound so wicked. I wonder if I have at last discovered why escorts and chaperons are so necessary, if this is why there are such sad creatures as fallen women. For it occurs to me that I would not just have fallen, rather I would have dived into the sweeping currents his lips pressed—

A knock at the door interrupted Joy's fanciful, always dramatic words. The reverend opened it and stepped inside her small room. She calmly set her quill down and looked up. Still not able to meet her gaze, the reverend motioned with a nod for her to attend her guardian.

Joy anxiously searched his face for a clue of what to expect. The search revealed nothing but the same uncharacteristic humbled and meak countenance. She rose nervously and walked softly down the stairs into the dark light of the study.

Joshua was sitting up on the divan, his thin arms rested—shakily, she saw—on his knees. His hands held a cup of the expensive medicinal potion. She met his eyes but briefly, for the disappointment there was punishment enough.

Dr. Joshua Reubens had never been a handsome man. Fairly tall and lean—a man who routinely forgot to eat, his mind pressed so by infinitely more important things—his long thin face, wild red hair, large thin nose and most of all the frightening intensity in the bright blue eyes absolutely forbid handsomeness. One realized at once, though, this was a man of consequence.

He was a rare man indeed. Even as a young boy, he—with some horror and alarm—confronted his vast ocean of ignorance and subsequently developed the desperate need to learn, which his father, a well to do country parson, bookish by nature, encouraged. Knowledge had been the first guiding principle of his life and, over the years of study, there sprung a deep rational belief in man and his science. Just as his older brother turned to the study of languages, he turned to the study of medicine. Yet both his father and his brother imparted a deeper sense of moral purpose, one naked without the guidance of their religious faith, that is until the abolitionist cause.

All this was before the insidious ravishment of the disease. Though he had only met his forty-second year, the affliction had aged him at least ten more long years. Frail and as weak as a kitten most days, his hair was thinned and flattened, his face drawn, weary and tired, and the most telling sign was his color. There were days like today, when he had a faint grayish pallor—as though the darkness of the beyond hovered hearby. Joy absolutely refused to see this; she only saw his unchanged eyes, eyes that were alert, serious, intelligent and filled with love for her.

Joshua cleared his throat to speak, coughing weakly as a result. "What do you have to say for yourself, young lady?"

She shook her head, nervously twisting a handkerchief in her hands.

"I have lived too long with the reverend's mendacity to be surprised by it, Sammy more so, but you, Joy Claret," he said gravely, "I don't know which is more distressing: the fact that you behaved with such great wanting of discretion, propriety and plain sense or the fact of your deception."

A long awkward pause followed.

"Doesn't it matter that my indiscretion helped lead souls to their freedom?" she finally asked in her defense. "Does not the moral purpose negate such a small, insignificant thing as the want of propriety? And Joshua"—her gaze finally lifted—"I did not deceive you—I meant only to spare you worry and concern, thinking of your health—"

"How dare you use my health as your excuse, young lady!" His gaze intensified as his face reddened, and the sudden emotion sent him coughing again. "You did not consult me because you knew I would forbid the undertaking! How far has your own mendacity grown? My God girl, have you learned more from the reverend than from me?"

She had never seen him so angry, and it frightened her, bringing home the magnitude of her crime as nothing else could. Tears sprang in her eyes, and with a rush of skirts, she fell before him on her knees.

"Joshua, I didn't mean to—"

With a heavy sigh, his arms came around her, and for a long tender moment he held her. "My anger rises from my fear, Joy Claret." He lifted the tear-streaked and lovely young face. "Do you know how many deaths I would have to face if you had been hurt? Can you imagine how a man feels when he is too weak to extend protection to those who he loves and cherishes most?"

"But . . . my absolute safety seems a small price to pay for the good I have done. The reverend and Sammy need me, and so long as I have Libertine near me, I can always escape. Joshua," she pleaded, "two people are now on their way to Boston because of it! And obviously, I am not harmed!"

"Yes, but thanks only to the most advantageous appearance of one Lord Barrington. The coincidence seems too great to comprehend. Admiral Byron often mentioned his nephew in the long years of our correspondence, and the idea that it was him who rescued you from that place is both a source of great gladness and, admittedly, embarrassment. I can only hope his own correspondence with his uncle does not include amusing anecdotes about a wild, young

77

American abolitionist."

Joy Claret paled, mute with the shock of Joshua's full knowledge; the reverend had not even spared names and titles! She had of course learned of the connection between Ram Barrington's uncle and her own guardian from the unknowing Bart, but this she had fervently prayed to keep from Joshua.

Would the horror of that day never end?

"The reverend has already dispatched a note from me to Lord Barrington that naturally cannot express the full extent of my gratitude. I can only hope he'll accept the invitation accompanying it so that I might have the chance to personally express—" A sudden coughing fit interrupted him, and he missed the growing alarm lifting over Joy's pale features as he spoke. "Naturally, you will send your own note of thanks—" Again he coughed.

Each cough brought her quick pain.

She would not dare tell him why his request was impossible. If not for Ram Barrington's interference, she would not now be the source of Joshua's distress, nor would she now be begging for his forgiveness.

"That however, is the minor point." He recovered somewhat. "The main point is your promise to never take on the danger of actually leading people to their freedom again."

He recognized the familiar spark of rebellion in her widening eyes and it alarmed him. He had seen the exact same spark three short years ago when he had tried to send her back to the finishing school in Virginia, which she had run away from.

"Joy Claret," he said slowly. "I will hear your promise that you will never do this or anything like this again, that you will from this day forward confine your abolitionist practice to that which can be accomplished with quill, ink and paper."

Joy's nod came on the heels of a long hesitation, and

78

Joshua, fortunately, was too tired to notice that the rebellion had hardly left her face. All she knew was it wasn't enough to write long letters to editors that nobody read, even longer letters to congressmen, or to give speeches at garden parties to ladies who were far more concerned with their neighbor's dress than they ever would be with a Negro's suffering. It was in no way comparable to the thrill and joy of loosening a Negro's chains directly. Joshua could not expect so much of her.

Joshua's growing weakness gave rise to another coughing fit, and he was unable to deliver the stern lecture he intended. Joy left quickly to heat his potion, and Joshua lay back in an attempt to catch his breath. A great weakness settled over him, and with it memories suddenly spun clear and vivid in his mind's eye: memories of Joy, the single light in his life.

Joy might have been his brother's daughter by birth, but she had always been his daughter at heart. He thought of her as such. After all, he had raised her from the time she was two years old, a feat that had been anything but easy. Heavens no!

What a bittersweet mix of joy and worry she brought to his life! She had never been perfectly sweet, at least not with any consistency. She was four when she announced she would be a boy, simply because she noticed they had far more fun. That was also when it became apparent she had inherited her parents' gift for languages, picking up one maid's French by the time she mastered English. There had been the endless stream of nursemaids; each one tiring in turn from the perpetual chasing of their irrepressible young lady, each one alternately cursed and blessed his girl: "Oh, I cannot tell ye the 'eaven of holdin' the little girl on me lap and singin' until those blue eyes finally—at last!—close, but they always open again. That's it, I can't turn me back for a blink of an eye and she's gone! Trouble, she's naught but trouble. Wild and rambunctious like a lad, can't sit still for a minute—not even a second! And those questions of the little miss. Where do they come from? Oh, she's a wild thing, she is, and I would stay on if, truly, if . . ."

Always if.

Hoping a mother's love would help, he took and subsequently survived not one but two wives—fine ladies each. Henrietta had died after only three months of marriage and Maria, sweet young Maria, had died with Joshua's own child in childbirth. Yet Henrietta and Maria both had expressed the exact same attitude, complaints and praise for his extraordinary charge.

Two events had exasperated the problem. While he could not seem to keep a wife, the reverend had joined the family keeping to them with a most tenacious bond. Then they had moved to this new wild country, for the better, warmer climate—he had already succumbed to the first stage of the consumption—and to do what they could for the abolitionist cause which by then, as for many of his English countrymen, had become his moral passion. Joy Claret had even less guidance as he became weaker and though she had a startling, quick mind for her studies—the classics, history, and even figures—this also went too far. She was just as likely to find entertainment in the swamps, swimming in a lake or riding that infernal horse of hers bareback, with a skill that even the most liberal would consider indecent for a woman.

Add to this the abolitionist cause. The very first day of their arrival in Louisiana, Joy, a child of ten, had witnessed the unmatched horror of human beings chained and led past their modest carriage by the threat of a whip. Until then, she had only known the evil of slavery from her uncle's long pontifications and lectures. Through the endless garden parties and church meetings, slavery was a thing her young maid connected to fairy tales, stories of princes and princesses, far away distant lands where strange and magical things happened. The harsh reality presented to her innocent eyes had been felt, known, encompassed even then; she had cried that very first day.

Living in an abolitionist household further separated her from the conventions of the surrounding society, though Joy did experience a popularity among the predominantly French community unknown to any other English or American young lady. The French forgot the Napoleonic wars, the battle of New Orleans, even the much hated immigration of so many Americans the moment she displayed her command of their language. Her acts of charity were as well known as they were widespread, and few could forget the young girl in the clean, white smock with a helping hand who followed the doctor into rich and poor houses alike, before his consumption had settled completely.

It was odd, too, how her moral superiority finally developed; she looked at her neighbors and friends, not with contempt or scorn for their support of the peculiar institution, but rather with pity for their lack of vision, understanding and compassion, for trading morals for wealth and justice for comfort. Indeed, she seemed to treat slave owners the same way they treated their slaves—as small ignorant children.

The thought brought a worried frown.

Where would it end? Could Joshua possibly live long enough to move to another place where she might have the chance to meet her equals? No, he knew; the end steadfastly approached. He would be hard pressed to see her into a loveless marriage in any case; moreover, it would be absolutely impossible to give her to a man who violated the principles she was taught to hold as dear and sacred as the good lord's very breath. Thus, he had turned down the two gentlemen who had already asked for her hand; both had been from good families, but both had been wealthy and with that had come slave holdings.

What was to become of Joy?

A last prayer closed his eyes and he fell into a restless sleep. Joy returned and set the glass on the table. With a gentle touch, she eased the worried lines from his brow and kissed him. She then spun around, leaving to find the traitorous reverend.

She would give him a piece of her mind!

After a long, drawn-out and tedious meeting with the bankers, Ram Barrington stepped into the warm morning air. The bank faced the far end of the marketplace, and though the street bustled with people and activity, he immediately discerned Bart had yet to return with the horses. With the unexpected few minutes of leisure, he strolled through the crowded marketplace down to the levee.

Ram had seen dozens of ports around the world, and yet as he stood there staring in the midst of the Orleans' marketplace, even his experienced and knowledgeable gaze was dazzled by it. Every language and nationality, every color and creed of people seemed to be represented. The sheer abundance of merchandise and goods astonished him. He stopped for a moment, detached, watching the endless stream of sailors load and unload cargo at a frantic pace. In the ribald exchange of their greetings and pleasantries many languages were spoken: French, English, Spanish, Creole, Portuguese, Greek, Italian and, to his amusement, a group of small golden skinned men at the far end were speaking an oriental tongue.

He smiled at the sight.

Mounds of coal, bales of cotton, barrels of tobacco and sugar filled the levee, mixed among case after case of merchandise stretching as far as the eye could see. Merchants ran back and forth, desperately shouting orders in a futile effort to be heard above the incessant noise. Longshoremen, their strong black and nearly naked bodies glistening with sweat as they rolled barrels or lifted bales, sang songs in strange African dialects, songs that blended into a garbled English or Creole patois. Gracefully and effortlessly, Negro women carried huge baskets of goods on their heads, calling out wares for sale.

A few paces away, the marketplace looked even more exotic. Rows of canvas-shaded stands spilled out in every direction from the long brick structure resting beneath the Palace D'Arms. Over half of the marketplace seemed to be taken up by food stands, offering every palatable item imaginable along with many unimaginable and unrecognizable. The produce area alone occupied two rows, selling every type of greenery known to the world. Alongside the produce stands sat a long row of fish and meat stands. Small Negro children obediently fanned flies from the fresh meat and fish; a signal from their master sent them dashing to the river with a bucket—a dark streak in the glaring sun— returning to dump cool water over the fish. The stench was overwhelming, but oddly Ram felt he was the only person among the multitudes who even noticed it.

Every other kind of ware was for sale, too: clothes, fabric, housing goods and wares, even one book stand. The far side offered livestock: pens of cows, sheep, chickens and goats, other pet pens of dogs, kittens, birds and even monkeys.

Proprietors shouted unceasingly for the attention of the jostling crowds of buyers. Grand Dames, dressed in silks and twirling brightly colored parasols, walked alongside peasants, beggars, Negroes and even savages. He never would have believed it, without seeing it.

Eventually he found himself seated at a table in a small cafe, his back to the bank to watch for Bart. With a colorful blue and white striped awning, the cafe provided pleasant shade as well as a panoramic view of all the many activities. Waiting for his meal and coffee, he leaned back and sighed with satisfaction.

The first part of his plan was set in action. He hired two agents to look for a prime piece of rich delta land. The land would be cleared and a manor would be built, all to create the impression that he planned to make Louisiana his home.

Which he would have to do for a while.

The information his agents had gathered left no doubt that the five men he would see ruined were close to the wealthiest, if not the wealthiest, in the state. Though these men certainly deserved to be hanged, he was not going to give them the mercy of a hanging—that was too easy. Their atrocities sprang from simple greed; therefore it was their fortunes he'd see ruined. The whole endeavor was a favor to his uncle, and while he certainly didn't mind the effort this favor required, to say nothing of the results the favor would reap, the time required bothered him. Time was the enemy of life, especially his life. There would never be enough time for all he wanted to accomplish.

A friendly mulatto, serving wench placed a huge plate of gumbo, honey-baked rolls, a glass of claret and a fresh cup of coffee in front of him. Ram thanked her with a more than generous tip. He was enjoying his meal as much as the sights, sounds and bustle of the marketplace, and he took no notice of the carriage that stopped in front of the bank he had just quit. Two older women descended and entered the bank, while three fairly young ladies made their way across the muddied street, clacking, giggling and fussing over their skirts. They stepped into the cafe with a dazzling burst of pale color and spent at least three minutes trying to decide where they ought to sit in the nearly deserted place, drawing but brief attention from the newspaper Ram read.

Ram took no more notice of them, though each of the three young ladies was of the age where she noticed him. They fell into hushed whispers, bursts of giggles and blushes, quick sideways glances at his table. Ambrosia went so far as to drop a pretty pink lace handkerchief, one that matched perfectly her cotton day dress. The prompt serving woman quickly picked it up, shook it, and folded it neatly in front of the girl with a smile.

"Well, this is a first," Ambrosia assured her two friends.

"Oh my!" Katie cried happily, "Look, it's Joy! Yoo-hoo,

darling!" She waved, jumping up. "Joy Claret!"

The name instantly solicited Ram's attention, and he looked up and over the street, held by the unexpectedness of it. She looked both lovely and magnificent; he knew no other way to describe how she appeared atop that beast, controlling the fine mare beautifully. He smiled—thank God she rode side-saddle. A young colored girl sat astride behind her, skirt hiked over bare legs, hanging on to her mistress's waist for her life.

Joy Claret reined Libertine around, and seeing who called to her, she smiled and kicked Libertine to a pretty trot. She pulled up alongside the platform of the cafe, coming to a stop. "Why Katie, Ambrosia, how do you do!"

"Joy darling." Katie introduced the third unknown young lady, "This is Melissa, my cousin, all the way from Memphis for a visit!"

"Pleased to make your acquaintance. This here's Cory." Joy smiled, pointing to her fellow passenger.

Comprehension was slow to follow confusion. Melissa managed to nod but remained so shocked that the young lady introduced her darky to her, she hardly heard the rest of the conversation.

All it would take was a quick glance to the back to see who else sat there, but Joy's eyes never left her friends. Ram was able to enjoy the uninterrupted pleasure, and he missed nothing of this first view of her in feminine apparel, nor did he miss the surprising and ever so admirable proportions of her slender figure which were noted with a highly appreciative raise of brow. She wore a wine-colored skirt and a plain, white cotton shirt, the dark color, like the homespun quality of the skirt's material marking her family's poor financial situation. A matching maroon scarf held back her long unbound hair—hair that matched the dark roan-colored mare. She held with a light hand the wide, straw sun hat that crowned her head.

"Have you come to town for shopping?" Joy was asking.

"Yes! Slippers and shawls for our party next week. Oh, you are coming Joy, aren't you?"

"Oh, yes!"

"And tell me, darling, how is the good doctor faring of late?"

The question quickly subdued her gaiety. "Oh, better I think," she answered quietly. "Though goodness, his recovery is filled with . . . well, occasional setbacks."

Katie reached a hand to Joy's and squeezed it affectionately. "Well, my word"—she knew to change the subject—"where are the two of you off to today?"

"You all won't believe it when I tell," Joy brightened with an excited laugh. "Cory and I are aiming to travel down river to where that old witch lives, the Negros' medicine woman."

This drew the wide-eyed attention of all three young ladies. Ambrosia even gasped with shock, while Katie exclaimed, "Why, I don't believe it!"

"Oh, but we are! I'm going to ask her for a potion for Joshua." She bit her lip and looked briefly away to add, "Dr. Morson seems able to do little good these days."

"But aren't you afraid?" Katie pursued. "To hear our darkies talk of that woman, I half suspect she's as much myth as Methuselah. And not one of their tales doesn't lift my hair from my neck!"

"I'm not afraid at all. She might have something to help Joshua, and besides, the worst she could do is turn us away. Honestly, I'd march through Hades with a banner if it could help Joshua."

"But what if she puts a hex on you?" This was Ambrosia.

"Oh, I don't believe in that silly voodoo nonsense." Joy dismissed this with a wave of her hand. "And if one doesn't believe, one is perfectly safe."

Ram smiled at his young lady's fearlessness.

The logic of this was lost on Ambrosia, who was quite stricken with the entire idea, while Katie found Joy's courage remarkable. "Well, who's escorting you on this adventure?"

she asked, looking around for Sammy or the reverend.

"Escort?" Joy questioned with a glance at Cory.

Ram thought he could actually see her mischievous mind forming the lie, and sure enough she announced: "Sammy's joining us at the crossroads."

"Even with him, I'll be praying for you," Katie said, but then was suddenly struck with a thought. "Joy darling! If you're really going to see that woman, I mean if you're quite determined, then could you ask her something for me?" She rose from her seat to whisper something, and Joy leaned over to hear it. The whispered conference lasted a minute, finishing with "It's so bad that I find I spend two days every month in bed. Will you ask her for me?"

Joy smiled, assured her she most certainly would and, after bidding them good day, was off and gone. Katie watched her ride off and predictably, as was always the case whenever she chanced to meet Joy Claret in the company of others, especially Ambrosia, she faced an argument.

"I hardly believe my ears!" Ambrosia exclaimed. "Why, my mama's so right! She is the wildest thing! If she doesn't catch a husband real soon, she's as good as ruined!"

"Well, she has had two proposals—"

Ambrosia never let her finish, "Doctor Reubens had the nerve to turn them down, too, as though she's going to get a better offer!"

"She introduced her darky." Melissa still didn't quite understand.

Katie addressed this first. "She doesn't think of Cory May as a darky. Not really. Why, they're more like friends or even sisters."

The contempt on Ambrosia's pretty face suggested this was beneath contemplation.

"And Joy Claret's too good and charitable to ever be ruined!" Katie then addressed Ambrosia's criticism.

"My mama says all her charity's for naught but to detract from her wildness. Visiting sick houses, sending those boring books to the infirmed and imagine, volunteering services at the Negro infirmary! The Negro infirmary!" She still couldn't believe this. "She just does it so folks will feel bad when they talk about her, but I refuse to be a hypocrite, and"—she leaned forward conspiratorially—"did you see her skirt? Our field darkies wear better homespun than that!"

Katie blushed at her friend's cattiness, always embarrassed by such things. She hardly knew where to begin to defend Joy. Yet Melissa, with a far softer temperament, perceived Katie's difficulty and tried to ease between the two. "Is her family very poor?"

"Yes, I'm afraid so," Katie replied. "You see, her guardian, Dr. Joshua Reubens, is quite ill with consumption. It leaves him bedridden most of the time. Oh, but Joy Claret is so devoted to him! Their household is quite small, but still, they have almost no earnings to support it. They do have the Reverend Doddered with them, but his earnings are from Negro sermonizing and I'm afraid not very much. You see," she whispered, "the doctor refuses to lend their darkies out. Somehow he even came up with enough money to send their man Sammy to trade school!"

They each knew what a pretty sum this generosity cost. Sending a darky to trade school was the ultimate reward for good service. Even the best and most wealthy families reserved the honor for precious few, maybe one Negro each generation.

"I suppose she didn't have the benefit of a finishin' school, then?" Melissa asked curiously, this being the distinguishing mark of a lady—one separating the clerical class from the menial.

It was the worst question possible; Katie braced herself for what came next.

"Did she ever!" Ambrosia met the question as a warrior meets battle—fiercely. "She was at my finishing school, Prinkley's Girls' College of Virginia, and how Dr. Reubens ever found the tuition for the best, no one knows! Joy was hopelessly in trouble from the start, and she didn't last but months. I was a year older than she, but I can assure you, the entire school knew all about her. First, she insisted on showing she knew far more than the teachers, and as you might imagine, this didn't set right, not at all. For a while the teachers tried placing her with the upper class girls—my class—but then finally, she was just such a know it all, the head mistress was forced to personally take over her instruction. Why, she has a mind for figurin' and books like . . . like a man!"

"She is very smart," Katie added. "Why she's always at the library and her French is perfect! Even the most stuffy French families here like her, for she speaks so beautifully and fluently. The Arcadians, too, and you know how much they isolate themselves—"

"That was not all though," Ambrosia quickly interrupted. "She was always exposin' the most disturbing niggerite notions one ever did hear. She wouldn't even be quiet about it after repeated thrashin's! And she would do outrageous things, like, like once she took her boots off, unlaced them and set them under her desk, right in the middle of class!"

"Really!" Melissa exclaimed in a wonder tinged with horror.

"Some say she was dismissed, but I heard a rumor that she actually ran away! I was there when it happened—the last straw so to speak. It all came about with this booklet the upper class girls were given to read: *Every Christian Wife's Duty*. Did you all read that in Memphis?"

Melissa felt a hot blush at the mere mentioning of it but determined to maturely meet this flirting with impropriety, she calmly replied, "Why, hasn't everyone?"

"Indeed, well," Ambrosia continued, "the next day we were all standin' around discussin' it in a circle. Seems everyone knew that the book discussed somethin' unpleasant in the extreme, somethin' that required a lady's good Christian fortitude and forbearance, but not one of us could put our finger on exactly what this duty was. Well, Joy Claret overheard us and she stepped right into our circle and said, 'Why you silly ninnies, the book is discussing—'" Ambrosia leaned forward to spell in a whisper, "'f-o-r-n-i-c-a-t-i-o-n with your husbands!'"

All three heads turned at the sound of the devastatingly handsome man's sudden laughter. He rose, still laughing, thankful for Bart's arrival just in time to spare him the ending of this story, no doubt filled with young ladies fainting at his wild young girl's frank explanation of their wifely duty. Besides, he had to rush if he was going to catch Joy at the crossroads.

Joy Claret thought the lovely day a great portent of fortune, and she and Cory raised their voices in pretty song as they made their way down the long river road. They had traveled less than two miles from town when Joy reined Libertine to a sudden stop and stared in apprehension down the road.

"What's wrong?" Cory asked in whispered alarm.

"His ship is docked down there a ways."

"Yo' mean dat man?"

She nodded. "Cory, let's head back and catch the back bayou. I don't want to risk seeing him again! Ever!"

"Lawd, to hear you tell of him, de man's meaner than a mad dog and stronger and taller than a Injun."

"I wasn't exaggerating," she reiterated and not for the first time.

"No matter," Cory replied, leaning her head against Joy. "The back road's a long haul safer all 'round."

Joy turned her horse around, but then, just fifty paces from the turn off, she looked up and gasped, seeing who rode in her direction.

Curse the blasted luck!

She suffered a paralyzing minute of indecision, first questioning if he had spotted her yet, then wondering why it mattered, for every fiber of her body shouted the one word—run! What stopped her though—admittedly it was not the thought of Cory's precarious position for such a flight—was that she discerned the expression on Ram's handsome face as he and his man approached. He wanted her to run! He knew her predicament—somehow, he knew—and it was the source of his amusement that dared her to try.

She wisely held Libertine at bay, trying to steady her heart and breathing—how he affected her! Why it irked her that he kept his own beige stallion at a nicely controlled walk, as though he had all the time in the world, she could not say.

"Oh, no!" Though Cory really did not want to know, she found herself asking in a whisper, "Don' a tell me—dat's him?"

"Yes, that is indeed Ram Barrington."

The two men stopped in front of them, and Libertine, much like her mistress, danced nervously at the sheer force of the masculine threat suddenly surrounding them. Joy tightened the bite, while simultaneously petting and calming her frightened mount.

"What a pleasant surprise," Ram offered first, though there was no mistaking his sarcasm. "Bart, you remember our young lad, Joy Claret?"

"Don't see how I could forget." Bart dipped his head with a smile.

Joy did not know which angered her more: the condescension in his sarcastic amusement—oh, how she'd love to slap it from his face!—or the questions pressing foremost in her mind as she glared at him. Why, oh why, did he have to be so terribly, terribly, handsome? Wasn't it enough that he was rich, titled, smart, strong and the ten other superlatives she attached to his person? And how could that small scar, the patch, be the final stroke to complete the devastating picture?

91

She bit her lip; do not think of his kiss now!

Ram did not bother to hide an interested appraisal of unsurpassed thoroughness. She abruptly felt the heat of it raking her; she might have been bare skinned and naked. She bit her lip again, blushing, resisting the ridiculous impulse to cover herself. Trying to recover, feeling an odd comfort as Cory tightened her arms around her waist, Joy forced a stilted greeting. "Good day to you both."

"A lovely day for a pleasant ride, is it not, Bart?"

"Oh aye, very pleasant."

"How far do you ladies plan on going?" Ram asked, not seeing Joy's efforts to calm her horse, he reached into his saddle bag then out to Libertine. He rubbed the horse's nose, and Joy felt a sharp pang of betrayal and some small wonder as Libertine threw her head back, danced a bit and then returned to nudge Ram's hand and steal the treat offered.

"Not far," she said, passing a meaningful glance to Cory. "Not far at all." She forced a smile.

"Just where are you two headed?"

"Oh, just out and about, you know."

"I do indeed know—out and about. Of course, I also know that after last week you wouldn't dream of traveling out and about without an escort."

"Oh, no Ram." Bart vigorously shook his head. "I've never had much faith in a woman's sense—fair as the fairer sex be—but no lass could be that dim-witted!"

All Joy could think of was his threat, and while she fancied herself an honest person, she admittedly knew the virtue's opposite and when best to use it. "But we do have an escort!"

"Oh?" Ram said, enjoying the apprehension lifting on both young ladies' faces. "And where is this person?"

"Where? Why we're meeting him."

"Where?"

"At the . . . crossroads."

"You mean that crossroad?"

There was no other she knew of, and so she looked where

92

he pointed and nodded.

"Odd, I don't see anyone."

"Well, he'll be here any minute, I'm sure. Don't worry. Sammy will be here any minute now and well . . . as I'm sure you have things to do and—"

"Nonsense. We'll wait with you, won't we Bart?"

"Aye, wouldn't be right at all leavin' two defenseless young ladies on the road without a proper escort."

"I assure you that won't be necessary—"

"I assure you, it is," Ram promptly returned.

The trap was perfectly clear. What was much less clear was how she could get out of it. Her anxiety was hardly appeased when Bart inquired with feigned politeness, "How long a wait are you expectin', lass? I don't inquire for meself, but for Ram here. I know how he hates a wait. Don't ye, me lord?"

"Indeed."

"Well." She glanced meaningfully at him. "I can't say. Exactly. He said he would meet us by the midday sun." She was pleased with the credibility the specification lent her cause, and she felt suddenly brave; she had only to pretend and stick to her lie. "That was all."

Ram did not bother to look at the sun's position but pointed out. "Any dim witted person might realize the sun is well past the midday point."

"So it is. Well honestly, I don't know what could be keeping him. Cory? Do you have any idea? Oh yes, please may I introduce Cory May." She remembered. "Cory, this here is Mr. Barrington and Mr. Bart."

Why did it bother her that it didn't bother him that she neglected to give him his title?

Cory was too frightened to speak, much less pass a friendly "pleased to meet you." She turned shyly from the two polite nods.

"Well, no matter. I suppose you're determined to wait?" Bart asked Ram and received an affirmative nod and a smile. "Let's say we dismount and spread a blanket. I've a bit of

93

cheese and a bag of apples. We can pretend the water's wine and have a picnic while we wait."

"An imaginative idea!" Ram declared. "Unless—speaking of imagination—the lady doesn't think her ah, escort will ever manifest?"

This seemed to leave her absolutely no choice, and soon she and Cory were sitting on a red plaid blanket spread over a thick cushion of dark green moss beneath the pleasant shade of an ancient oak. The river rolled lazily nearby, providing the pleasant sound of rushing water. After Bart attended to the mounts, he assumed a seat at the trunk of the tree, watching her and Ram with curious bemusement.

Ram lay lengthwise on the blanket, resting on his side. His crossed legs in a casually disarming pose, he expertly sliced apples and cheese with the jeweled dagger Joy remembered well. She felt so acutely conscious of him, every detail of his person pressed like a poet's word to her mind. He wore tall brown boots, tight-fitting brown breeches and a white cotton shirt. The sleeves were rolled over strong muscled forearms, forearms marked with an athletic show of veins, rippling ever so slightly as he swiftly flicked his wrist in task. A small scar cut directly across his right hand. The gold belt buckle was an expression of the finest craftsmanship: a magnificent Ram's head over two crossed swords. This same symbol appeared on a gold ring he wore on his right hand, and as she studied these details offered by his nearness, her mind swam with a hundred questions she would like to ask of him.

Yet the first and most pressing question was whispered in defeat: "I don't suppose there's any chance of Cory and I leaving without an escort?"

Smiling, Ram shook his head as he offered a napkin of sliced apples and cheese. Joy and Cory exchanged glances, resigning themselves to their thwarted mission, while noting the quality of the cheese. It was of a kind they had not had on their table since the doctor took ill and neither could resist.

"Thank you kindly," Cory said softly with lowered eyes that made Ram aware of her shyness.

"You're more than welcome." He enjoyed the food himself, as his gaze returned to Joy. "I received the two notes of gratitude from your house. I found the doctor's note most gracious. Your note, however, lacked a certain sincerity. If I were capable of unkind thoughts, I might think you were forced to write it."

Cory turned to hide her smile.

"Why, how could you possibly question my sincerity!" Joy's indignation rose in an instant. "I only owe you the worst day I've ever had the misfortune to know! Joshua's still distressed over it, the reverend treats me now with the infuriating solicitousness one might best use for picking a fragile flower, to say nothing of the terror of it, a terror that still haunts my sleep and, oh!" she cried as her hands fitted to her backside, ignoring Ram's plain amusement at her outburst. "I'm still sore, and the humiliation—" She stopped, as her hands lifted to cover her cheeks, where indeed that emotion showed as she remembered his thrashing and somehow paired it in her mind with his kiss.

"Ah," he chuckled with a suggestive lift of brow, "but I understand you're quite familiar with the common practice administered to misbehaving children."

"What do you mean?"

"Tell me, were you dismissed from Prinkley's Girls' College or did you run away?"

She suffered a long minute of shock. "How could you know of it?"

"I was under the impression it was common knowledge."

"Yes," she finally, reluctantly admitted, "I suppose it is."

"What happened to you there?"

Ram was slicing another apple and more cheese, and she stared at him, surprised by his genuine curiosity. Somehow this was not a conversation she had ever imagined having with him.

95

"I don't really know," she replied after a pause. "I don't think I belonged there."

"Was it that bad?"

"Oh, it was," she assured him with sudden feeling. "Every hour of every day assigned to the most tedious, monotonous tasks, all of which seemed to center on needlework and stitchery and prayers, endless prayers! Why, I often thought it might be a good deal easier if we all just died and took our stitchery to heaven for direct communication with the maker!"

Ram and Bart both chuckled at this, and she watched in amazement at how wonderfully laughter transformed his features. He wasn't threatening her, she saw then, and though he was preventing her from the day's task, this truly was quite suddenly a pleasant afternoon picnic.

A tiny lizard darted onto the blanket, and she watched as Ram lifted the little creature off to send him on his way. Such a small gesture, yet it somehow said much, and suddenly the conversation shifted as she began to ask the hundred or so questions she had of him.

It was their first discovery of each other, and Bart's surprise increased as each minute followed the last, filled with a conversation that traveled to talk of England, what it was like now, then of Ram's boyhood past on the ships patrolling the dark continent, Ram's amusing and wild anecdotes that purposely stayed clear of the horrors. They spoke of horses, of polo and racing, and Joy talked of Libertine, of how she got her and how much she loved her. Oh lord, he knew how Ram could charm the ladies when he liked; the man had almost as many mistresses as the number of simpler, single night tumbles. Never though, had he witnessed Ram giving a lady so much attention, at least not in an upright position. Added to this was the obvious fact she was not his type, physically or otherwise, far from his normal preference for older, sophisticated and well, larger women. Yet then again, the young lady was not anyone's type; one

96

might lose his mind trying to squeeze the lass's curious mix of charms into any classification.

The vast majority of Joy's conversations began, ended, and had their middles filled with the abolitionist cause, and here she met her first disappointment with Ram. He refused the abolitionist title.

"I don't understand." She pressed. "You're not for slavery are you?"

"No, I'm not. Slavery is antithetical to man's nature, but while the abolitionists in your country and mine are quick to fill the air with hot bellows of self-righteous moral outrage, they are noticeably mute when it comes to the practical issues."

"What do you mean?"

"By practical issues? I do hope you've at least considered some of the many questions like what will over a million Negroes do with themselves once they are freed?"

"Celebrate," she said simply. "They shall celebrate their freedom as people have done from the beginning."

"Men have a great deal of trouble celebrating when women and children are starving."

"Well, they shall have to work, of course—"

"Where? Who will pay them? Their former masters?"

"Well, in some cases, of course."

"You are startlingly naive, love. Reduce it to simple economics. The vast majority of slave owners are the small farmers, men who sweat from dawn to dusk right alongside their Negroes in a pitiful effort just to put food on the table. The number of slave owners who have a cash crop large enough to pay over one or two field hands numbers less than one or two hundred. Subtract that from the half a million men who will be looking for work and one begins to see the trouble. If there's any one thing I've learned in my twenty-eight years—and as the French so dramatically demonstrated—it's that the most dangerous creature in the world is a man without means."

97

This simple exercise in mathematics and logic visibly upset her, showing Ram just how naive and idealistic she was. Still, he had to admire her when she finally rejoined with: "The difficulties involved in freeing the oppressed Negro race do indeed seem large, even insurmountable put your way, but still we must do it! We must have faith that eventually the good will emerge to triumph from the pain and struggle."

"I wish I could believe that," he said honestly.

"But you do agree the people must be free?" She pressed.

"Must is not the word I would use, but yes, it seems inevitable that someday the Negro race will be freed."

This satisfied her immensely, though she had to ask, "How long before congress sees the reason? How long do you think before it ends?"

"Reason?" Now he laughed meanly, this laughter rising from another side of his nature, a cruel and hardened side that frightened her to the depth of her soul. Without knowing why, she found the black patch the sudden focus of her study as he said, "I assure you, freedom has never sprung from reason."

"But then, what shall it spring from?"

"Blood, and enough to soak in. When enough blood covers the land—from Boston to the Florida straits and probably beyond—then and only then will you see your precious freedom."

Ram watched as the large blue eyes searched his face, focused still on the patch of which he was so rarely conscious. He could almost see her thoughts spin in an effort to deny his statements. The frighteningly solemn note might have ended the lovely day, but in the familiar role as a rescuer and mischief-maker, Seanessy made a sudden timely arrival.

All heads turned to the sound of galloping hooves. The great white stallion raced toward them at wind's speed, and just as Joy and Cory screamed and jumped to their feet to avoid being trampled, Seanessy reined the mount to a quick halt. In the same moment, he lifted to a handstand in the saddle and sprung round to land on his feet paces from the blanket.

"And you chide me for my dramatic entrances," Ram laughed, never having bothered to move a muscle, watching with naught but amused disinterest. Bart however, with less faith in Sean's shenanigans, had also risen quickly to his feet with a curse.

"Ah, I'll do anything to impress the ladies." Sean turned a keen eye toward Joy and Cory. After introductions, Joy, laughing and just a little shy, assured him that they were indeed impressed. The handsome pirate surveyed the whole scene. "But of course, you're picnicking, Ram; I don't know why I'm surprised really. The world is falling apart, but the blue bloods must have their picnics."

"Is the world falling apart, Sean?"

"Yes, but nothing takes precedence over these lovely ladies. Though Bart, it might help if you see to the long line formed outside our lordship's chambers."

Bart bid the ladies a pleasant good day and departed.

Seanessy, with show and humor, feigned horror at the discovery they were without wine. He whistled to his horse, which pranced quickly to him, and he withdrew a wine cask from his bag. Then he did indeed join the party.

Sean and Ram turned a magic trick and banished thoughts of time again. Ram was perfectly aware of Sean's purpose in drawing Joy Claret out—to discover what beyond the lovely surface attracted him—and he enjoyed Sean's show the short time it lasted.

Sean moved in the circle of his choice; Ram had witnessed his friend, when it suited Sean's purpose, dazzle and impress everyone from the Prince Regent himself to a blind beggar on the street. Capturing Joy's respect and admiration was easy; Sean merely directed as many questions to Cory as Joy. While Joy was pleased and surprised by this, Cory felt at first shy, more than a little embarrassed by such unlikely attention. Nonetheless, Sean effortlessly worked his great natural charm, and like Ram, he soon had both ladies laughing from the enormous generosity of his wit.

Ram did not have to wait long for Sean's conclusion. At the end of an engaging story—telling of Sean's initial impression of her city—a story which caused Joy's eyes to widen in stages, Sean finally sent her falling back, holding onto her sides with laughter. "No, I don't believe it!"

Ram stared at the sight of her prone position but briefly before laying back himself with a meaningful groan and chuckled, too.

"It's perfectly plain now." Sean presented his conclusion. "Though no doubt you were aware of the difference between her backside in breeches and this." He motioned to Joy as she struggled to recover and make sense of this new twist in the conversation. "I do hope you've also noticed how young she is?"

"Ah, I am acutely aware of the sad fact."

"Still," Sean observed with a grin, "I've not seen that look on your face since you were thirteen and discovered the upstairs' maid."

Ram laughed at this, supposing it was probably true. "I'll not deny the unthumbed fruit is tempting—though it is a first for me—but I'll be damned if I do the picking."

"Why?"

"Christ Sean, it's as you say—look at her." Ram stared, his look part amusement, part something else that alarmed her senseless, confusing her even more so that she was but vaguely aware they now found her the subject of some inexplicable criticism. "Why," he chuckled, "a man might wager better than even odds that she has yet to take the dolls off her shelves."

Sean cast an affectionate look at her, then laughed. "No, no dear, don't blush; it only makes matters so much worse." He turned then to Cory, mischief ever present. "Cory May, you must shed light on this issue; I assume you're familiar with the lady's bed chambers?"

Smiling, Cory nodded.

"Cory, I swear to heaven, if you say one—" It was as far as Joy got, for Ram's arms suddenly held her still and his hand gently covered her mouth as he waited with an anticipatory smile. Everything changed in that instant for Joy. Consciousness existed only where she felt his arms, his body on hers, his hold as inexplicably gentle as it was strong. A disturbing warmth swept into her, and she blushed profusely, this having nothing to do with the painful embarrassment of Ram guessing what still sat on her bed chamber shelves.

"Tell us Cory." Sean pressed eagerly. "Are there dolls still on her shelves?"

Cory could not betray Joy, at least not directly. "I can' rightly say." She giggled. "'Ceptin' hit's a chore to dust the shelves with all the what nots sittin' up thar."

The two men roared with laughter. Cory laughed too and laughed even harder when, after Ram and Sean finally saw them home, the first thing Joy did was march upstairs and furiously remove each and every one of their childhood treasures from their long held throne atop the shelves.


Dear Diary:

I met him again! This time I suspect he knew more than happy chance put me at the library at the same time as he, for when he came upon me sitting in the hard wood chair, book in hand, that amused light sprang in his remarkable gaze, a knowing smile played on his lips. Oh, how I tried not to blush as I stammered through my hastily prepared explanation of my presence there again. He listened politely, too politely, and I kept stammering until he said, "Joy, you don't have to explain to me. I know why you're here."

He stared at me so intently, yet still with amusement, and my heart and pulse raced, imagining he would put words to my real reason. Then he simply picked up my book and read the title. "You came to get Aristotle's Politics. Don't tell me Prinkley's Girls' College neglected Aristotle?"

Then, as before, he asked me how I liked it and what I thought. How he baits me with those questions that follow! How he makes my mind stretch and reach for comprehension that I should never have arrived at alone! Those times when I am confused, not understanding the high and noble ideas I read, he ends my confusion with an explanation that is as clear, simple and brilliant as Aristotle's own logic.

How can I say what happens to me when I am with him? It is a ravishing, strange tropical illness that leaves me trembling and weak in its wake. The feelings and feelings! When he laughs at something I say, when he draws near to point something out, when he speaks and his hand strays to my hair or arm with that touch so casual yet not! I get this warm rush of nervous butterflies deep inside me—as though he is kissing me again—and I am all a blush and smiling and cannot seem to stop. There is no longer a blond boy in my dreams, only him. I can hardly think of anything else. Sometimes, I imagine—

Yet Joy stopped, for she could not write the things she had been imagining of late.

The sun began its long descent as Ram and Sean turned their mounts back to the ship. The cool twilight felt pleasant, momentarily peaceful with its quiet, and they kept their mounts to a slow pace, as much to enjoy the dusk as to discuss their business.

Ram was explaining what his agent discovered of their five victims' finances: "It's a good deal better than I expected; three of the families are living on the edge of their wealth already, depending on the season's cotton price to see them through. I'll be buying their debts this week. The fourth is only slightly better off, but the congressman—well, he presents a slight problem."

"How's that?" Sean asked with a pretense of shock. "Don't tell me the good congressman has used his position to increase his fortune?"

"Actually, the deals rising from his status are petty compared to the tricks he's used in the dark of night. About five years ago, fires were set to both Mississippi's and Louisiana's cotton warehouses simultaneously; no one discovered the arsonists. A number of people died in the blaze; still more families were ruined with the loss. Oddly," he dryly drawled, "Simone made his fortune that year as the market adjusted and the cotton price soared. He has a good deal of money; not enough to stand up to my concerted attack of course, except that I'll probably have to extend my stay here, travelling back and forth between here and England until things are settled over there."

Sean of course knew what Ram referred to—the problem Ram's immense fortune presented to the crown. It was a blooming intrigue, one with danger woven into ever increasingly complex twists. When Ram was younger, he had thought he could keep it from society, but nothing excited English society more than an unmarried lordship with a sizeable and magnificently growing fortune. They never knew how it happened, only that it did; and so everyone from the crown prince to the lowest chamber maid knew that Lord Ramsey Edward Barrington III would not take a wife; there would be no heir to his title or his fortune.

Soon afterward, Ram learned through his infinite web of connections that the crown had drawn a document to be implemented on the day he died. Based on outdated church law and neatly added on to an attractive tax measure, it fled through the house of commons with no dissent. The Barrington estates—including Barrington Hall—and his fortune were to be divided among certain select members of the aristocracy by default. This could not be borne, and Sean, as long as he lived, would never forget the weeks of Ram's sustained rage that had followed this discovery.

Drastic measures had to be taken. Ram had to disown the country of generations of his ancestors and adopt this new young republic as his own. It was the only country where law superseded the will of individuals, the only country that would recognize his own will and testament. His fortune and properties had to be liquidated and transferred to the states piece meal, and ever so slowly to avoid discovery.

Here lay the danger. As soon as the crown and the named aristocracy discovered he was leaving his country and taking everything except the Barrington estates, Ram's own life would be worth less than a farthing. One of them, probably all of them, would see him assassinated.

Sean would have gladly shot the crown prince. Sean was Irish after all, and despite the prince's catholic princess, the crown prince was even worse than his father, the ailing King George III. The tyrannical northern protestant rule was nothing but a puppet government for the prince. Between the threat to Ram and his much loved country, he certainly had good reason to shoot him. Yet Ram protested, "Violence begets violence and it would take more than one assassination to see me out of this. What good is all that killing Sean? Let us work the other way."

So Ram lived on the razor's edge, they all did, waiting for the day when so little would be gained by his death that they'd leave him be. Of course the situation led to many intrigues, lines separating those who knew and those who didn't; there were numerous bribes and payoffs. It was a bloody mess; no other man could even begin to pull it off.

More than Ram knew, Sean questioned if even Ram could succeed.

Sean lived with this fear, and as Ram was as dear to him as his own life, he could not passively sit and watch. He had his own plan, and though he had waited for years to meet the lady who would play the crucial part, it occurred to him that he might have met her the day of a picnic beneath an old oak tree. Now with these amusing book meetings his intuition— and his was great—told him the young lady had finally been found, though it would take many interviews to know for certain. It was with this thought that Sean pursued the rest of the conversation.

"Well, I don't mind staying here awhile," Sean first said. "I rather like Orleans, though I'm aware of your trouble. Two months and you've already been through the entire stock of wenches in the place, and by the way, my men tell me you've made quite a spectacle of yourself."

"Are you referring to last night?" Ram asked with some small interest.

"Yes, and every other night since we made port. Honestly, I wonder how your mistresses survive your homecoming," he laughed. "I think it must be all this running you do; it must somehow stimulate the appetite."

Ram sighed in sudden irritation. Just as weary of the turn in conversation as he was tired of managing the half-wild stallion that needed a good long run. "Sean," he said, dismounting and taking the playful stallion by the reins, "I don't recall you ever being a candidate for celibacy."

"It's a matter of degree, my lord," Sean explained, and following Ram's lead, he dismounted to fall in stride alongside his friend. "And speaking of extremes, what book has our young lady read this week?"

Instantly the reference softened Ram's features with amusement. "Machiavelli." He laughed. "Needless to say, she failed to comprehend his brilliance."

Ram proceeded to amuse Sean with a brief retelling of his rendezvous in the library. He had never meant for these meetings to continue. His connection with Joshua was bad enough, a connection that so often put him in her house, though he arranged the visits for those times when she was out or late at night when she slept. Yet somehow he could not seem to resist the library meetings.

What he could not resist was the play with that mind of hers, so fresh and lively, sparkling with rare intelligence, yet in desperate need of guidance and direction, which her guardian refused to give. Joshua feared she was already too different, her education already too excessive for what anyone thought decent for a young lady. Joshua was right of course—even women of society were taught to read and write only well enough to follow scripture during family bible readings. Then too, his own Greek scholarship and his mechanical work, being separated from his library at Barrington Hall, made him a frequent visitor to the library. At first it was chance, then clearly not, he was enjoying the encounters with Joy tremendously.

Admittedly it was a sad fact that this was the first time he had ever been attracted to a woman's mind. He could hardly reconcile that such a mind existed in a girl: a girl with the infuriatingly naive passion for the word freedom, a girl he had first seen perched in a tree, wearing boys' breeches and aiming a pistol at him, a girl with long brown hair and lovely sky-blue eyes, a girl with a maddening innocence in her every manner and gesture. "Aye," he finished the telling, as he thought of those things. "I am courting disaster. That will be the last time I meet her."

"Surely you don't imagine resisting that temptation?"

"Ah, but I do."

"And I've yet to see you resist anything you've wanted for less reason. After all," Sean smiled, unalarmed at Ram's reservations. "The dolls must come down sometime, and a maidenhead is such a small obstruction really."

Ram chuckled but rejoined with: "For such a small thing, it brings a man a good deal of trouble."

"The only good is in the taking." Sean pursued as if explaining to a young child. "The trouble comes only if virtue remains too long, and then, it's considered a woman's greatest misfortune."

"Somehow," Ram sighed with a boyish grin, "I don't think Joy is in the risk of suffering that particular misfortune."

"Which is my exact point. The girl is far too lovely and far too poor. She will no doubt be married by the year's end; indeed, I'm surprised it has not already happened. Why not spare her the inevitable wedding night, when her clumsy fool of a husband—so overwhelmed by what his fortune bought him—embarrasses himself before he has taken her clothes off? Why not bed her good and proper?"

To Ram's amusement, this was asked in all seriousness.

"At the very least"—Sean's grin widened—"she'd have a few things to show the poor fellow."

Why Sean's picture of Joy's inevitable future bothered him, he couldn't say. It was all too true; precious few men were good lovers, lacking either the experience or inclination, usually both, and it was no mystery why many women never learned to enjoy the pleasure to be had from love. He supposed this was the trouble. There was more sensuality hidden in that girl's innocence, her misguided passions and ridiculous wildness, than he knew wise to contemplate, and while he never took Sean seriously on the subject of women, it was indeed true. If any woman was made for a man's love, it was Joy Claret.

For these very reasons he would resist the temptation. He knew with inexplicable certainty she would give her love only once; her passion would be final and complete. This seemed as obvious as the very promise hidden in her innocence; perhaps it was part of it. No doubt it was a lucky man indeed who came to share her love, but he'd be damned if it would be him. The tragedy of her love not returned would match any Greek tale, and though he was capable of many nefarious things, that would not be one of them.

Sean studied Ram with incredulity, humor and mischief, knowing him better than anyone and seeing the thoughts even through the near complete darkness. "I see you will try to resist the temptation of our, ah, unthumbed fruit?"

"Sean," Ram said with plain regret, "I would ruin her; it might be a good deal easier to put a bullet to her head. So yes, unlike Adam, I will resist."

Sean laughed, and the very devil shined in his eyes as he stopped to draw Ram's full attention. "And I, my lord, wager you don't succeed. My Vermeer for your Rembrandt."

Sean referred to their paintings, for both their fortunes were of a size that made money meaningless. For a number of years now they wagered with their art collections.

Ram met the challenge directly with his laughter. "I'll warn you now, Sean, you'll lose."

"Not if you'll be seeing her again. With the connection between you and her guardian and with your prolonged stay, you will be forced to at least occasionally move in her circles."

Ram shook his head, chuckling still as he removed his shirt and then his boots, for like his mount, he suddenly needed a good long run. He packed these into his saddle bag and said, "Time can't be unlimited; name the date I hang your picture."

"Eight months or until she's married, whichever comes first."

"Sean, I've seen you capable of a good deal of foolhardiness, but never until now have I seen you play the fool." With this, Ram handed Sean the reins and ran off, quickly disappearing into the darkness with a song on his lips.

Sean laughed loud and long, too. If he was right about Joy Claret, he would not be playing the fool but rather the serpent. It would not even be hard; he need only to present the forbidden fruit in a different light. Though Ram's bite would indeed be sweet, the benefits he imagined went much further than hanging Ram's coveted Rembrandt.

## Chapter Four

Joy needed to escape the sickness threatening their house, the sickness in the Negro infirmary she usually visited on the Sabbath, to escape her family's financial troubles and the frantic pace of the city growing too large, too fast, to escape everything, if only for a couple of hours. Cory and she worked all week to have their chores done by Sunday—the house cleaning, the wood gathering, the privy dump—so that the only thing left was the marketing.

The night was broken by two cats fighting in the alley, incessant howls indistinguishable from the screeching cries of babies. Still, Cory and she had risen by the fourth bell to fix a meal and see the reverend and Sammy off to their day of sermonizing at Garden Court, one of the largest plantations in Louisiana. Cory went back to bed, promising to take care of Joshua and meet her later. Joy went out the door, heading for the stables.

Moving south, Joy turned Libertine out of the city. Dawn spread in a violet light, shading everything with an enchanting color, and she let her thoughts rest peacefully on the awakening of the day. She found her way onto the back road, then lead Libertine onto the old, Indian hunting path,

111

winding to the lake. Of course, there was an unlikely chance of meeting him on one of his queer runs but this, she told herself, was not the reason she chose the old hunting path. No one woke at this early hour, certainly not when Ram's burgeoning reputation put him in Orleans' finest houses, reputable and not, at all hours of the night.

"One doesn't have to be a mental genius," she told Libertine as she brushed away the overhanging Spanish moss and vines, "to know the odds are astronomically against a chance encounter."

The narrow path wound through the bayous and eventually led to an open tree-shaded clearing, opening out from the shady banks of a small lake—a lake many less imaginative people would call a pond. A stream ran in and out of it, keeping the water fairly clear and clean. Libertine pranced into the open space, and Joy stopped her, momentarily dazzled by the splendid colors of the water hyacinths and lilies, blooming in magnificent profusion in the first light of day. A recent rain had washed the land, and the sweet scents of wild flowers filled the fragrant air. In the early morning light, within the shade of tall oaks, the colors appeared darker and muted, painted with an enchanting mysterious air.

A garden of paradise she thought.

In all its great beauty, nature reminded her of the fundamental loneliness of the human condition; each breath told her no one had ever used it before, no one would use it after. She was alone and with this came freedom.

Joy slipped from Libertine's back, removed her things and let Libertine roam to graze freely. She spread a blanket, arranged her things upon it and stood to remove her skirt and blouse. In just her chemise, she stepped to the edge of the water. Not timid in many things, she gracefully dove out and into the cool depth.

Water offers the ultimate freedom and she made use of it. Throwing a rock and then diving for it became a playful divergence. She stayed clear of the menacing area where the rush of the stream created hidden whirlpools, which some said could catch and hold the very strongest swimmers. She had no thought of water moccasins, the rarer but more deadly coral snake, or even of the painful pinch of a crawfish. She knew only the play of water, morning light and gulps of sweet tasting air.

The day dawned bright and lovely, not a cloud in the sky. She came out of the water as oblivious to her nakedness as Eve in the garden. She removed her wet undergarments and hung them on a strawberry bush to dry in the sun. In the meantime, she stepped into her skirt, pulled her blouse on and tucked it in, before sitting comfortably on the blanket.

She created a fetching picture. A wide-rimmed, straw sun hat with a pretty red ribbon covered her head. The long wet hair trailed over her arm and off the blanket as she lay on her stomach with her bare feet in the air. Her diary lay open before her. She ate an apple. One hand held the Frenchman's new and remarkable invention, the pencil. As was her habit before starting a new entry in her diary, she read the last. It had to do with the Simone's soiree, her last encounter with Ram Barrington.


April 21, the year of our Lord eighteen, eighteen.
Dear Diary,
   Katie swears he will be there, that he has arranged a meeting with her father and other prominent members of the community to take place at Monsieur Simone's soiree. I should not leave Joshua, I know, and I feel ill at ease doing so; but the thought of seeing him again could not be long resisted. In this way I am no different from anyone else in Orleans' parish. All people talk of is Ram Barrington this, Ram Barrington that. Even the French! I confess I am filled with tingling nervousness, a heady excitement fringed with apprehension even now, as I wait for Madame Beauchamp's

carriage so thoughtfully offered to me.

Cory has been teasing me about my new found vanity, and I confess she is right. I know not to be ashamed of our poverty, and yet when I look down at my blue, cotton party dress, my best dress simply because it is my only good one, and I think of all the ladies who shall be there in silks, with flowing crepe overcoats, their hair fashionably dressed in pretty ringlets, I cannot help but know I shall look pale in comparison. Why or why won't Joshua let me cut my hair until I am married? He only ventures that young ladies do not cut their hair until their wedding day, smiling so strangely when he adds: "Then the matter will be decided by your husband." He is not dissuaded when Cory points out I shall never have a husband if I don't do something proper with this unmanageable hair of mine! The best we can do is braid it and wrap it around my head as in the olden days. It looks foolish and I feel so awkward! I know this is but silly ramblings, yet—

She had been interrupted then, returning that very night to write what had happened at the soiree.

Dear Diary,

The great gold clock struck eight o'clock, and I pretended to be the only person not to notice he had yet to honor the house with his presence. The music was the best to be found in New Orleans, indeed in all of Louisiana, and as my dance card was full, I was having a gay time of it. In the upstairs ballroom, in the midst of the music, I never heard the great flutter of whispers, which Katie laughingly told me about later, when Ram bore the hundred—it seemed to her—excited introductions as he finally honored the house with his presence.

Katie said he bore the endless introductions with a

noted indifference that bordered on the uncivil. Of course this could only excite the society further. The ladies—even some of the men—found him more handsome than rumor had it, what with his impressive height donned in the finely tailored clothes, noticeably without a waistcoat or jacket, and his neck cloth recklessly loosened. "Was that how they were wearing 'em in England?" I heard Mr. Avton ask at one point, then "one of his mistresses was Josephine's confidant in the French Court of old?" "No!" came another. "Yes indeed, he cuts a devastating form! How did he get that patch?" "Did Lord Barrington really buy the entire Dubois estate outright? Even the town mansion?"

Society's interest in him is insatiable!

Well, as Craig Knowles twirled me across the crowded polished floor, and just as I was laughing gaily, blushing at his flattery, I felt a sudden tingling down my spine. I glanced up instinctively, and the world—my world—stopped. There he stood on the balcony, in the center of a large group of men that included Mr. Simone, Governor Claighborne, Mr. Beauchamp among many others. He stared at me, and in the instant my eyes met his gaze, the world came to its sudden stop and I stumbled clumsily.

Craig caught me in his arms and held me steady; embarrassed, feeling the fool I was, I looked back at Ram, fully expecting to see him laughing at me. Oh, I saw amusement all right, but something else, something that made me instantly aware of the impropriety of the way Craig was holding me. I gathered my wits, apologized and pleaded a sudden thirst, which Craig immediately set off to remedy.

Then I stood for a moment alone, flustered, wondering how he could affect me so by a mere glance. The dance ended prettily and a great shuffle of feet followed, pleasantries were exchanged as people looked for and found their next dance partners. The noise was deafening. I remember solicitously commenting on old Widow Cosell's pretty new gown and glancing at my dance card to see Tom Henry's fine signature, just as the shiny black boots stepped in front of me.

"In the desperate hopes that I might be the next gentleman you stumble into, may I have your next dance?"

This was what he said to me!

I looked up and could only think: Why oh god why was I blushing, my heart pounding so? And how did he manage to make a request into a demand, insult me as he begged a favor? I lowered my gaze. This bothered me, but it seemed the only way I could reply. "I'm sorry," I was glad to tell him, "but my dance card is full."

"Dance cards?" He looked down at my hand. "Why, how charmingly archaic."

"Doesn't England have them?" I naturally inquired.

"Not for so many years. Well"—he lifted my hand—"let's see to whom I owe my misfortune. Mr. Henry, is it? He wouldn't be a dark-haired fellow, would he?"

"Why, yes, tall and thin—"

"That's the fellow. I hate to be the bearer of bad news, but I believe Mr. Henry is at the moment quite indisposed."

"Oh my." I looked around. "What's wrong?"

"Nothing a lady would care to hear about, I assure you. In any case, do permit me to take the poor chap's place, hmmm?"

Without waiting for an answer, he swept me onto the dance floor, and then for all I knew, we were suddenly alone in the world. Never have I danced like that! I could not meet the intensity of his stare, yet my senses filled and flew as he expertly carried me through the waltz. What a magnificent dancer! My slippers never touched the ground. I felt that warmth of his, the pleasant and disturbing scent of him, the effect of his gaze, of being held in his arms, twirled on a cloud of dreams, and I was lost!

Abruptly, he laughed and drew my gaze to him. "What brought you amusement?" I asked.

"I laughed at how dim my memory of a very fine painting has suddenly become."

This made no sense, and I first thought I must have heard wrong.

"This will never do," he stopped dancing, though he still kept me close. "I want to take you from this place. Will you go for a stroll in the garden?"

"Oh . . ." I cast a conspiratorial glance to both sides, thinking he had something to tell me. "You wish to speak to me in private?"

"Something like that." He only smiled and led me through the doors.

I was conscious of the strong hand on the small of my back, a tingling dart of sensation racing from the spot. I ventured a blushing glance up and around to discover we were the subject of many people's interest. One of these, Tom Henry, was glaring furiously at Ram!

"Why, that was Tom Henry!" I said.

"Who?" He didn't know him!

I lifted my skirt to descend the stairs and bit my lips to stop my laughter. "I know what you did. You lied just so I would dance with you!"

"Ah," he chuckled then, "what a clever girl! Not only do you read Greek philosophy but you've managed to discover my small intrigue."

His teasing made me laugh as we passed through the entrance hall and out the doors, stepping into the only slightly cooler night air. Bright stars danced in the clear night sky, and though the moon was absent, it was not needed, for festive lanterns lit the pleasant garden path where we strolled.

"You are not a gentleman," I first said.

"So I've been told. But if you humor my pretenses, I'll humor yours."

"But what pretenses have I?"

"Here you are, moving among friends and neighbors—the people you routinely steal from."

"Oh, that. Well yes, it's sometimes difficult for me here, but I try not to think of it."

"What happens when you do?"

"I try to forgive them."

He laughed then. "How very kind of you!"

"Oh, you're mocking me again!"

"I can hardly help it. Tell me though, how do you manage the duplicity of it?"

The sincerity of the request bade an honest answer, and I found myself sharing the difficulty of living these two separate lives, how it often alienated me from others and made me feel different, and the worst part, how I feel lonely sometimes because of it—if not for my family. As always he listened attentively. The questions he put to me demonstrated both his understanding and sympathy; each insightful question seemed to lead to realizations I might not have reached on my own.

Oddly, one of these realizations was the very contrast in my honesty with him and my relations with others. He demands my honesty; his questions allowed nothing less, and I was startled by the depth of feeling this brought. The leisurely stroll must have lasted well over an hour, and I often found myself forgetting the acute physical consciousness of him for long stretches of time as he shared his own life situations and anecdotes in turn. His stories have an arresting way of holding me with bated breath, waiting for the con-

clusion, and when this comes, it inevitably solicits
my laughter . . .

Joy read no more. She closed her eyes to remember his
kiss, and lost in a dreamy haze, she soon fell asleep. Sleep
owing to a sleepless night, a long swim, the warm touch of
the morning sun and the lure of running water.

Rake never barked, finding nothing in the sleeping girl to
warn his master about, and as though anticipating his
master's wishes, he settled happily beneath the shade of a
nearby tree to rest. White against the lush, dark-green
landscape, the undergarments warned Ram when Rake did
not, and he was smiling even before he spotted the familiar
horse. As he came upon her sleeping form, his gaze absorbed
the full impact of the innocent beauty before him.

She lay on her stomach with her head resting on her thin
arms. A sun hat shielded her face from the sun; the long wet
hair spread off to the side told him what he had just
missed. She was covered but not, for the colorful Spanish-
style peasant skirt molded to her form, and the white blouse
was all but transparent. He studied the slender lines drawing
the small proud back, the small waist—had he ever seen a
waist so small on a woman or was it the pairing of smallness
with the soft flow of the blatantly beckoning curves
elsewhere?—then the curve of her hips, the long lines of her
legs, even the cross of her bare feet. Never had a woman's
backside been so damnably alluring.

Ram never thought of waking her. Not yet. With not a
sound to his movement, he joined her on the blanket. Never
thinking of propriety, knowing full well what it was, he
picked up the book and began reading, eating one of the two
apples she had brought as he enjoyed himself.

The diary was written with a delicately flowing yet
confident hand, the words were not without impact. He
expected the innocent musing of a young lady, talk of friends
and parties, reflections of the past and hope for the future,

and indeed he found these. Yet there was more, so much more. He could not read all of it but only skimmed. Much of the diary concerned family relations, most of which concerned Joshua and much of that on concerns for his ailing health. Yet she also wrote at length about the wisdom Joshua imparted, his ideas, thoughts and reflections that became the poetry of her own mind, a poetry shrouded in her love for her uncle.

With amused interest, Ram read his first entrance on the pages and chuckled at the enormity of her impression of his kiss. He passed quickly through this. Needless to say, the long hard paths of his life strayed far from anything close to the matters of a young girl's heart. Tender amusement sustained him as he continued skimming through the impressions of their library meetings until the last meeting.

The sudden emergence of vanity brought a soft chuckle, the hope that her future husband had Joshua's good sense about that hair of hers. Yet he remembered the night well, remembered how her poverty could not touch her beauty. All the other ladies looked pale by comparison. He remembered all too well the taste of those soft lips and how close he had come to losing a bet.

He closed the book and placed it in its former position. Twirling a strand of straw in his mouth, he traced the tip of the straw along the line of her thin arm. She stirred with a soft sigh and turned over, still sleeping.

Ram drew a sharp breath. A vision spun by the gods to torment him. She lay with one arm raised over her head, the other at her side. The blouse was all but transparent, and as his gaze rested on the delicious curves of her breasts, he knew he courted disaster.

She awoke to his kiss. Yet, still dazed with sleep, she remained unaware of landing on this very real shore of her dreams. His lips first teased, barely touching. She gasped slightly, and her lips parted with an innocent invitation. One not neglected. He lay on his side, leaning over, partially resting his weight over her. The feel of her soft curves was madness itself. He wanted more and brought the small of her back against him just as his tongue swept into her mouth to drink deeper.

Warm languid heat lifted through her, sending her into a soft swoon, melting and helpless. As though reaching for a lifeline, her arms curved around his neck, and her fingers ran through the thick, dark curls of his hair. Oddly, it was the band of his patch that jolted her with sudden alarm.

She pulled away. "Ram!"

He chuckled at her surprise. "Were you imagining another?"

A hand went to her flushed cheek, and she drew a shaky uneven breath as her eyes travelled over the surroundings and she remembered her circumstances. "You watched me as I slept!"

Leaning back, he returned the straw to his mouth and nodded with amusement.

"How long have you been here?"

"I have no watch to mark the time."

Indeed, no watch and precious little else. He was exactly as she had first seen him: half naked and like a savage, that muscled bronze frame clad in sun-washed white breeches, a belt with a jeweled dagger hanging from its side. He looked the very pirate of her imagination. There was also something alarming behind the menacing amusement in his gaze as he stared at her, something that made her eyes abruptly rivet to her diary.

"My diary!"

"That's what that is?" he asked evenly, his gaze dropping briefly to the book too.

The statement itself brought relief, though she still reached to take the book safely in her hands. She would die, that was all, she'd simply load her pistol and shoot herself if he had read it. "You didn't—" she couldn't even say it.

"Read it?" he asked with an inquiring lift of brow. "Joy,"

121

he scolded, "what nature of character do you assign to me?"

With her relief came the awareness of where his gaze rested—the cause of his amusement—and she crossed her arms over herself as heat rose in her face. "I'm hardly dressed—"

"So I've noticed."

She didn't know how to explain what happened next. He purposely put a silence between them, one broken only by the babbling stream, the distant cry of birds and dragonflies dancing in the still morning air. Yes, he was threatening her. Without a word of warning, she was afraid to get up, afraid of the loneliness of their surroundings and the position she had put herself into. Afraid of the look in his gaze.

Afraid, without reason of the black patch.

She felt her heart and pulse take flight as her nerves stretched taut like tuned strings of a musical instrument. She knew instinctively that he not only understood the emotion in her eyes, but he had put it there with intent.

Quite suddenly her thoughts changed as she met the source of her fear: the ominous black patch, the signature to his devastating handsomeness. Owing to her nature, concern shadowed her fear. She leaned forward on hands and knees in a pose so unknowingly seductive it jolted him with quick, hard and hot desire. A timid hand trembled ever so slightly as she reached to his face, a finger gently ran over the patch and scar. "How did this happen?"

The softly whispered question, the concern sparkling with fear in her eyes drew some emotion from him that he absolutely refused to consider. He caught her hand, brought her backside to the blanket and came partially over her, pinning her small hands to the earth and said what she simply could not believe: "You draw too close, girl; you play with fire."

She touched the strange and awful thing that was the mystery of him, and more than a virgin's fear, the shocking heat of his hard muscled body straining against hers brought a rush of panic. "Then, let me go."

Time stretched endlessly. It was a kaleidoscope of moments in which he saw many things in a crystal clear form. She was and would be his first and only battle against the dark streak that fate wove into his life. He knew it then; he was fighting a battle he had already lost to the force of desire coursing through him.

His desire was hauntingly primitive, far transcending the lure of her physical beauty and the tease of her sensual innocence. It was a desire woven by fate, and though the consequences were conceivably grave—

"It's too late," he whispered as his lips brushed over her face. "It's far too late."

"No." She shook her head. "Please—"

"Don't fight me. Not now." His lips hovered closely over her mouth. "I think I've fought enough for both of us."

He stopped her protest by possessing her mouth, a kiss given with force yet marked with a strange tenderness. She tasted of warmth and sunshine, a promise called to the very center of her being. She felt herself succumb to the sensual press of his mouth, and she stopped writhing, which only served to make her aware of the hard muscled maleness of him. His desire radiated a warm energy into her, and she went limp, pliant beneath him again, her body answering his call against her will.

Then he broke the kiss with a soft victorious chuckle. "Ah, I was enjoying your struggle the brief time it lasted. But you, Joy Claret"—his lips trailed slowly down her neck, pleasing him with the shivers this caused—"have not the armor with which to fight a man."

A hot slap of shame competed briefly with desire, and on cue, her struggle renewed but briefly again, for the shame washed over her in a heated rush so closely connected with desire it stopped her instantly. His next warm chuckle told her he was well aware of it. "Shall I show you more, Joy Claret?"

"No," she said weakly.

"Yes." He laughed and she saw he was teasing her, unbelievably and mercilessly he teased her. He was teasing; she was dying. He was a playful lover, though the next kiss was anything but amusing. He forced her lips apart for a deeper invasion, one slow, hot and tantalizing. She could not fight her desire to surrender, did not want to fight it, as her lips welcomed his, seeking in turn.

His hands came over her form, and his touch felt like fire. She was alive only where his hands caressed her, and all of it was somehow connected to a tightening knot deep inside her. With wild alarm, she realized the tingling she felt rose from her breasts which were pressing against his chest. Her whole body strained to meet his.

Ram's lips finally left hers, and Joy opened her eyes to see clouded desire mixed with tender amusement still in his gaze. "Aye, I tease you my love"—his lips brushed her face and ear, and wild shivers raced from the spot—"but know why torment is returned tenfold with a desire as new to me as it is to you."

He lifted partially from her, only one hand holding both of hers as his free hand pressed the thin material of her blouse against the maddening tease of her breast, then stopped to draw the shirt up to finally unveil the beauty tormenting him. He pulled the blouse over her head but kept it entwined around her arms. She forgot to breathe. The heat of his gaze was no less than that of his body, and she twisted, not understanding the small warm rushes between her thighs, pulsating now . . .

"My god, you are beautiful," he whispered as his hand drew circles over the taut peaks.

She bit her lip with a muted cry and closed her eyes tight. "Please—"

He encountered her bewildered torment with another chuckle. "Please what, I wonder? A cry for mercy?" he asked, as his lips and tongue teased the rosy tips to shameless desire.

124

Never had she imagined anything like this! She flushed with tumultuous sensations rippling through her. "Mercy you shall get," he said softly as he gently massaged the swollen peaks. "A slow, sweet and blessed mercy indeed, yet not with impunity."

The rich timbre of his voice brought her eyes open only to close as his lips took hers again and her bare flesh was brought against his. Just as desire might have at last overridden her innocence, his hand lifted her skirt over her hips. The sensation of his hands caressing her hips, the naked skin of her abdomen, put her on the edge of sudden fear, a fear mixed with heated anticipation, another gush of warmth and then—

Rake barked, and instantly Ram stopped, his muscles rigid with anticipatory mobilization just moments before Seanessy's voice, raised with an old Irish song, was heard in the distance. Ram collapsed all at once, and through her thick daze, the first thing Joy was aware of was his laughter, laughter filled with relief and regret both.

"Seanessy, Seanessy," he laughed. "I bless and curse you in turns. Ah my love," he said to her, quickly bringing the blouse back over her head, "it seems you've been granted impunity after all."

As he lifted her to her feet, she felt a disappointment that might have been pain and heard herself ask stupidly, "I'm safe?"

He finished tucking in her shirt, then took her chin to lift her face. "Joy Claret," he chuckled warmly, "you would not be safe in a convent with a habit over your head." He kissed her lips lightly. "Certainly you are not safe from me. I think we would do well to remember it."

The great white stallion emerged in the glen, and Seanessy's song ended. Cory, seated behind him and, unlike Sean, oblivious to the scene they interrupted, clapped with merry applause for his song.

"I am sorry, my lord!"

125

"Not, I can assure you, half as sorry as I."

"Quite the contrary, it is my loss after all. I lay the blame at Cory's feet though. Of course, when you did not return, I, imagining assassins lurking the woods, set off in pursuit, but nothing—" he laughed—"nothing could have made me interrupt. Cory had not my same inducement. When I found her along the way, very determined to find her mistress with news she swears is of immediate import, I, alas, had no choice."

"I figured as much."

Joy hardly heard the banter between them. She was still lost in a flushed haze of this first taste of his love. Her whole body, indeed her entire being, seemed ready, flushed and feverish, waiting for something that wasn't going to happen, a promise unfulfilled. It confused her, bringing an enormity of emotions, all of which were velvet mixed with stark naked disappointment. Then, too, how could she possibly make sense of the apparent capriciousness of his emotions: the streak of cruelty, his baiting and teasing, all of which were mixed with tenderness. Now, one might never know there was something between them!

"Joy." He turned back to her, purposely standing in front of her as he stared down at the bewilderment of her face. "The pleasure has been mine, but it is not one I would share. Go and find the rest of your clothes, love."

The words brought back the awareness of the indecency of her dress, and she hurried away, needing no more warning. Sean lowered Cory to the ground as he commented on how inviting the cool depths of the pond must look to those wallowing away their time beneath the heat of a Louisiana sun. The comment was greeted with laughter as Ram indeed dove in. Cory, however, swiftly found Joy behind the bushes putting her clothes back on. The fear and excitement on Cory's face had nothing to do with Joy having been in an apparent state of undress at the lake with Ram.

"Yo'se ain't gonna believe—"

Joy's attention abruptly snapped back to earth. "What's wrong? Joshua?"

"No, no, he's doin' fine, jest fine. I left him asleep to meet you for fishin'. Dis is hit—" she rushed on. "I was stashin' our poles in our hidin' place, and I came out of the woods to see the Baxter carriage comin' up the road. Miss Katie's father was with dem. De carriage stops when dey's seen me, and Madame Beauchamp pass greetin's, inquirin' after Joshua and yo' and all. Well, yo' knows how she can talk! She kept me standin' dere for quite a spell, goin' on 'bout dis and dat, and all de while, I'se listen to de Massas and der boys talkin' 'bout dis meetin' tonight."

"A meeting? So?"

"Seems dey's all bandin' together to work on somethin' to do 'bout these niggerites hidin' in dese parts, stealin' darkies from under der noses."

"Oh my word! . . . Where Cory? Did you hear where?"

She nodded as she spoke, "At de Rowe's Palace, tonight. Dat place men's always talkin' up."

"Oh my goodness—"

"Hit ain't all," Cory whispered lower, drawing Joy closer with a dark skinny hand on her arm. "De meetin'—" she glanced behind her through the bushes, where a certain someone swam in their lake—"gots somethin' to do with him, Massa high and mighty hisself."

The air was filled with the heady perfume of over six hundred hot perspiring bodies jammed into the wide space of the tree-lined meadow. The reverend's voice thundered from the pulpit. Babies wailed, jiggled in their mother's arms. Coughs erupted and rippled through the crowd as though by some prearranged consensus. A dog fight broke out on the side, and the five armed overseers nearby quickly placed bets on the outcome.

Standing on a bench to see over the heads, Sammy

127

watched from the back. Some of the people sat, others stood but all listened with rapt attention to the reverend's crock of bull. He could smell the collective fear brought about by the hellish pontifications, and he wondered again what if? What if someone rose and shouted, "Dis is bull! I say bull! Ain't no snow-white lawd sittin' in heaven sayin' to all de niggers dat make hit: 'you thar boy—need some spick and span round de throne room! Hop to wid de mop, boy!'"

Or what if someone rose and said: "Lookie here! Thar's only five mens wid guns! Dey can stop one but dey can't stop all de peoples! We can take 'em and run! Run for freedom!"

What if all the people got up and ran?

Anger filled his chest and he looked away, disgusted. It would never happen. Not as long as fear and submission and ignorance were beaten into the people at their first breath. No sir!

Where the hell was Delilah?

He searched the crowd of women bustling frantically to and fro around the four long tables off to the side in an effort to prepare the Sunday meal for six hundred people. He spotted her immediately, shouting orders to two other women. No one could miss Delilah—not with her great bulk, and the wide straw hat that never left her head.

Delilah was the black mammy of white folks' imagination: dark as night, a big woman to start and round as a barrel, twice as wide with a hundred or so extra pounds. Delilah held the unenviable position of head slave cook for the Simone plantation, but she had once, a long time ago, been mammy for a well-known Virginia family. The family sold her down stream when the barest whisper of suspicion said it was Delilah, the family's mammy of nearly two generations, who had been putting arsenic in the youngest master's food, killing him slowly each day.

Sammy and the reverend—unbeknownst to Joy at the time—had once got Delilah drunk, and that memorable night Delilah had told her story. This was how they knew

128

that plump ol' Delilah nursed enough white folk hate to fuel a massacre.

Sammy finally spotted her, watching as she made her way to his side. Looking out over the crowd, she shook her head, clacked her tongue and muttered, "Look at all dese snivelin' bootlickin' scum!"

"Amen," Sammy said.

"I got a live one." She got to the point of business. "Name is Jim Boy . . ."


The Palace Rowe dominated the entire west section of town. Strategically centered on the corner of an intersection that neatly divided the decent houses and businesses from the not so decent houses and businesses, the grand building towered three stories high, built of common brick but, like all fine houses, plastered with white-washed stucco. The windows all had the same shocking, red-velvet drapes, fringed with gold tassels, matched perfectly by the uniformed grooms and doormen who lined the wide veranda. Except for the curtains, it might have been the Palace D'Arms for all the stately and well dressed stream of gentlemen who went through the huge, mahogany doors.

Joy was acutely conscious of the fact that it was not guarded, as she waited and watched, hidden in an alleyway across the street. This was one of Orleans' most famous gaming houses. The only thing distinguishing Rowe's Palace from the taverns, bawdy houses, gaming halls and wine shops down the street was the wealth of the gentlemen inside there. These were not backwoods men, river boat men or idle sailors with a season's pay or a pocket full of monies to waste. Oh no! She watched as Monsieur Baxter and Hughes, so distinguished in their tailored suits, arriving atop fine mounts, were quickly taken by two waiting grooms then ushered with familiar greetings by the doormen; this alone was more than enough evidence to know the Palace catered to Orleans' wealthiest and most prominent citizens.

Shrewd blue eyes watched from under an unkempt wig and old straw hat as Mr. Beauchamp arrived. He was shown the same solicitous treatment. Soon afterward, a buggy arrived and Monsieur Simone alighted. The distinguished planter snapped quick orders to the waiting grooms and ignored the doorman's greeting with the hauteur, and arrogant reserve of the very rich.

Joy knew the man and his family well, not just from various social functions, but because she, the reverend and Sammy had seen seven of his people to freedom. The reverend and Sammy were at Garden Court, his plantation, this very moment. Unlike most planters, he treated his six hundred field hands with a particularly harsh hand, working them extra hard. Food was said to be bad there, too, and while that might not seem an overly damning complaint, Joy knew better. If one works at arduous toil twelve hours a day, every day except the Sabbath, living a life stripped of every small comfort and luxury, the only thing left to look forward to was meals. If the food was bad, life was bad and that simply was that. Yet, there were other complaints as well. Though Louisiana had laws regulating when and how punishment of slaves was administered, these laws were not enforced. At Garden Court, indolence was punished by beatings, and this was almost unheard of elsewhere.

Obviously, she scowled, Charles Simone had reason to participate in the proceedings of this meeting.

Restless and tired of standing, Joy crouched to bent knees, waiting still. The street vendors, market shoppers and carriages disappeared as darkness settled in the night. Bright lights appeared in the windows, music and laughter, boisterous noise, came from inside. The streets filled with an increasingly rowdy sort. It occurred to her that no lady she knew would venture on these streets after dark, even with an escort, and the thought made her smile.

Of course she had no way to gain entrance into the

establishment, but she saw she didn't have to. She did not long contemplate the purpose to which the upper floors were put, and it seemed logical to assume the men would not be holding their meeting amidst scantily clad women. The activities dominating the lower floor were gaming and drinking. The meeting was bound to be held in a smaller room off to the side. It seemed only a matter of circling the building, hoping a window was left open to clear out the tobacco smoke. Men, she knew, smoked when ladies were absent and business was discussed. With any luck—

Ram Barrington finally appeared, and she might have known, with a flourish. The clamor of horses' hooves first warned her. She pressed herself flat against the closed wine-shop wall in the alley where she hid. Ram, Seanessy and two other men raced their horses galloping at a breakneck speed through the city. A race! Followed closely by another two men, Sean and Ram appeared first, Sean's white stallion winning by a hair's breadth. As they reined to a clamorous stop, laughing, she saw why. Ram rode the most magnificent black stallion, and as he pulled the reins, the great beast reared high in the air. No one else she knew could have kept to his seat! He was an adept and skillful rider, but the horse was only greenbroke at best, what with his wild prance and the manner by which Ram controlled the beast.

People did say Englishmen learned how to ride before they could walk.

How handsome he looked! Her heart thudded wildly as though a meter of his proximity. Without knowing it, her hand reached to her mouth, and she blushed, thinking for the hundredth time of the shocking things that had transpired only hours before. It was not just that she could have been ruined, rescue provided so unexpectedly at the last moment, but it was that she would have been happily ruined. She could not delude herself. She was of a nature she had not known and didn't understand. She welcomed his kisses as the petals of a flower welcomes rain, as green leaves of a plant welcome the sun.

Was she in love? Was she unbelievably and most unwillingly in love? Could she fall in love with a man who frightened her to the very depth of her soul? He was unlike anyone she knew, ever dreamed of or imagined. He had everything, title and fortune, a wit and charm that sprang from a deep intelligence, an ability to move with ease and command in all circles. The lightest touch of his hand could start a tumultuous revolution in her body! She was certain, too, he courted hundreds of the most beautiful and desirable women in the world. He had not mentioned either love or marriage, and a great part of her fear was knowing he never would.

What was the mystery of that black patch, the scar?

Ram bantered with Seanessy and the other two men as he dismounted with agility and grace, handing the reins to the groom. Seanessy and the others rode off. Ram strode up the stairs. He stopped suddenly, frozen. He swung around, his gaze sweeping the intersection as Joy pressed herself hard against the wall. Just in time! He turned back, said something that made the doorman laugh, and the doors were thrown open for him.

The black patch rose in her mind's eye, and she relived that awful moment. "You draw too close girl; you play with fire."

Was it too late?

She did not know what he had to do with this meeting, but with the thought of finding out, she slipped out of the alley and into the darkness of the night.

Music sounded from the distant rooms as Joy stopped beneath each window, waiting and listening for a moment, before moving on. It was dark in the narrow alley. The only light shone directly from the windows above her. Governor Claighborne's recent innovation of street lanterns, in hope of stopping crime, did naught but attract hundreds of fire flies, mosquitoes and moths. No light that she could discern entered the alley from those poles.

The ground floor was used for house servants and the preparation of food; the next level was about eight feet above. Quick of mind, Joy already carried two discarded liquor crates she had found in back, one held awkwardly in each hand, trembling as she neared the onset of her noble purpose.

She had almost rounded the house when from the next to the last window came the faint but familiar sound of Mr. Beauchamp's voice. Freezing with the instincts of a wild animal, then taking a deep breath, she silently positioned the crates and climbed up. The thick, red curtains were drawn. A dim yellowish light emanated from the edges and as she had imagined, the window was open, a stream of billowing smoke pouring forth. With one hand braced against the wall, the other actually resting lightly on the window, she started listening.

"My God," Monsieur Simone exclaimed. "We would be supplying the entire South!"

"And the Caribbean." Ram pointed out. "The English might have moral objections to slavery, but their planters have no qualms about indentured servitude. Where," he wondered out loud, "would their plantations go without the renewed ship loads of precious black ivory?" Then he chuckled and launched into an engaging story drawn from his considerable experience with his uncle, Admiral Byron.

Joy listened with heightened attention. The crown had placed Admiral Byron in charge of the British ships patrolling the dark continent in an effort to stop slavers. This was popular knowledge, Ram explained. Upon capturing a slaver, the cargo was inevitably dumped on the Caribbean and the poor wretches—naked savages, starved and homeless, with no means to return—had no choice but to sign up for twenty years indentured servitude to some British planter. "Hell," Ram concluded. "The poor bastards are grateful to their captors. And while the Caribbean planters might only pay half as much a head—if we can supply them these numbers here—well gentlemen, as you can see, half as much is still an arresting number. Yes it will cost you each a sizable sum to buy shares in the thirty ships—no doubt, most of you will have to sign your properties over to the banks for a year or more to get the loan—but I can practically guarantee ten times the return."

"Yes, yes," Mr. Hughes and Mr. Baxter agreed simultaneously, impressed.

A long pause followed of which she could not fathom the meaning, unless they were studying papers.

"Mr. Barrington, it does seem too good to be true. I have to wonder why we merit your selection for this venture? It must be more than . . . ah, neighborly kindness?"

"There are indeed other reasons besides the fact that I'm moving my ventures into Orleans. I'll be frank, gentlemen. My connections are in Boston and England, places known for their abolitionist sentiments, and as you know, being Admiral Byron's nephew, I am naturally associated with the abolitionist cause. I could find no willing investors among my associates and friends, or even their connections. They're hypocrites all," he said with masculine scorn. "What with the northern and English textile mills running full steam on southern cotton."

Agreement abounded.

"It is a rather large investment," Ram finally continued. "It will take over half a year to build and buy the ships, another year or so to deliver the black ivory, but eventually," his speech slowed with dramatic effect, "I'll make your fortunes and mine triple."

Monsieur Simone waited, then seeing Ram was through, he asked, "But you haven't answered: Why us?"

"Simply." Ram smiled unseen. "Because I've learned you have each made the investment before."

"Not in these numbers though!" Mr. Beauchamp exclaimed. "If something went wrong, it would ruin me! It would ruin all of us."

There was another long silence before Ram finally said, "Mr. Beauchamp, fortune and risk might be synonyms; a man can't have one without the other."

Another long pause.

Suddenly Mr. Simone laughed. "Well, I'm in," he announced simply. "Mr. Barrington, welcome to Louisiana." One by one, amidst hearty chuckles, the others followed until only Mr. Beauchamp remained.

"Mr. Beauchamp?"

He shifted nervously, turning it over and over in his mind. "I can't turn it down," he finally said in a tone of pained reluctance. "It is too good to be true. Hell, if I got just half the return I could buy out the Taylor's bottom acres sittin' next to mine . . ." He paused yet again, then in a lowered voice that only partially revealed his thoughts said, "Though God knows, my wife—" He looked up. "Can you assure us that you'll run decent ships, Mr. Barrington?"

Ram stared hard at Mr. Beauchamp, seeing the man's concern as the trouble: a man's greed or ambition or plain self-interest watering down the human concern, pushing it a comfortable distance away until the terror of a slave ship was considered in a simple question of decency. Evil made into banality.

"A decent slave ship?" Ram questioned, as his shadow dominated the window. "Is there such a thing? And do you really care, Mr. Beauchamp? Which matters more, the ah, discomfort of a few people of color or the return of your investment?"

"Hell, those stories are exaggerated, Tom. You know that," Mr. Hughes broke the uncomfortable silence of Mr. Beauchamp's contemplation.

Ram would waste no more time, for he had somewhere to go, and leaving Mr. Beauchamp ample time to answer the question, he concluded with: "Gentlemen, I'll give you till Tuesday next to present your bank statements. But with what might be premature anticipation"—his gaze returned to Mr. Beauchamp—"I do believe this calls for a toast."

Joy Claret had not yet moved her head. The world seemed suddenly to recede; her hand trembled slightly and she pressed it harder to the window to halt the slight clatter it caused. She forced herself to wait, to keep listening and waiting for the one word, any word, that would make the discovery go away.

She knew these men, knew their wives and children. The Baxters, Simones and Beauchamps belonged to her congregation. Katie Beauchamp was even her friend. Yet it was not that these five men would invest in slavers, that they would just condone and passively allow that evil to exist on the earth, or even that they would actually cause it, make it happen. No, she told herself, she should not really be surprised.

It was Ram Barrington's duplicity. The pain of her disillusionment engulfed her with cold hard shock. She had just overheard words that reduced him to the vilest creature of contempt, someone she could not even pity but could easily hate. The pain of it overwhelmed her; it felt like a dagger thrust into her heart. Yet, even as she stood there trembling, it took second place in her heart to another.

Ram Barrington was on their side. She tried to tell herself he was but one man, that one man cannot matter. But somehow, by some trick of her mind that constantly weighed, measured and balanced these things, by removing Ram Barrington from her side and placing him on the other, the scales tipped overwhelmingly to the side of evil. The angle seemed so severe it removed the single strength that fueled her struggle: Hope.

She could not live without it.

"What are they saying now?" Ram asked, casually watching from the side.

Joy Claret first thought the familiar voice came from inside; she pressed her ear to the window even harder. It took several seconds for the alarm to register, turning her to the culprit.

She gasped with a start, and her foot slipped on its precarious balance; but Ram, having known this would happen and always willing to rescue this damsel forever in distress, caught her fall. Strong hands circled her waist as he gently lowered her to the ground.

Ram wondered if she had ever looked more beautiful. The ridiculous costume aside, it was the blinding fury in her eyes that caused his breath to catch, a tension seizing the whole of his body, one jolted from him with her soft spoken but fierce command: "Don't touch me!"

The pain marring her lovely face only told him how far the untried attraction had travelled: too far, much too far. His hands left her reluctantly. She backed away, her eyes blazing with an intensity of emotion that pierced his very soul. "Joy," he said slowly as a warning, "appearances are deceptive."

A light bitter laugh followed her gasp. "How true! And you are obviously well versed in the art of it. I just can't believe it . . . any of it!" Tears were quickly forming as trembling hands came to her cheeks. "You're not like the others; I can't even pity you. I hate you . . . I hate you! And I'm going to stop you! I don't know how but I swear, I'm going to stop you—" She turned and ran from the spot.

Ram made no move to stop her. No doubt enlightenment would dawn by morning light, if not sooner, even if she didn't speak with Joshua, who of course knew the whole plan. These things he dismissed. What he had more trouble dismissing was her passion and his desire to own it.

## Chapter Five

Ram had designed the captain's quarters on the *Ram's Head* himself, solely for comfort on voyages marked only by the tedium of the rise and fall of waves. Few people could enter the magnificent room without a gasp or drop of mouth. Practicality and function marked the spacious room, yet excellent and expensive taste colored any and all impressions. Ram's desk, the large dining table and chairs that often sat twelve for dinner, a huge over-stuffed bookcase and the bed's headboard were all made of the finest dark rosewood. A dark maroon and rich blue tapestry rug—a fine piece of art work in itself—threw lush color into the room. Dark maroon, velvet curtains hung on either side of the bed, which Sean often commented was an indecent size for a ship. Ancient maps adorned the walls. An eight foot whittling of rosewood, carved by seven carefully selected wood sculptors, rose prominently in the far corner.

After a long run and swim, Ram stood at the gold-framed shaving mirror telling Sean and Derrick of the night's meeting and how the bastards had taken his bait. Bart entered and set the coffee tray on the long, hand-carved rosewood table. Bart's gaze immediately found Rake, who sat on his haunches, devouring a huge femur bone on the floor he had just seen polished. Ram, he knew, cared far more about animals than he did about floors, but after seeing dog and bone out, Bart was still going to complain when he realized the topic of the talk and knew better than to interrupt. After a splash of cologne on his face, Ram sat at the end of the table to enjoy his morning coffee, while updating Sean and Derrick on the plan's progress.

After tethering Libertine to a nearby tree, Joy Claret hesitated as she stared at the proud oceangoing ship before her. She felt quite the fool. Joshua and the reverend explained of course. Everyone was entitled to mistakes though, weren't they? If the truth were known, she felt far worse about having left before overhearing what those men were going to do about the niggerites stealing their darkies—the second topic on the agenda—than she did about not trusting Ram enough to know he, despite his ruthlessness and dangerous strength, was by far and away incapable of the nefarious evil she had imagined.

She had one purpose and one purpose only in seeking Ram out. Joshua said Ram would not be persuaded to keep Mr. Beauchamp out of his plot, but still she felt she must try. Joshua had understood this and granted permission for this trip. After all, Katie and her mother were friends and had shown Joshua and herself nothing but kindness and charity ever since the day long ago when Joshua had saved Madame Beauchamp from a breach birth. Even if Mr. Beauchamp deserved ruin, Katie and her mother did not. Then, too, it was not that Mr. Beauchamp was really a bad man, just morally ignorant. This was the case she would put before Ram.

She tried for a brief moment to compose herself, but it was of no use. Her composure and Ram Barrington's proximity were like night and day; one chased the other away. She felt the meter of her heart and pulse fluttering more frantically with each bold step up the plank, and her blush, she knew, was not from the interested stares of his men or the humor of their masculine comments as they all but stopped their work.

A man knocked and opened the door, but before he could announce the arrival of the timid though nonetheless insistent young lady, let alone tell of her beauty that had interrupted the work of his men—bets were already being placed on how long her stay would be—the young lady herself came through the door.

Upon seeing him, Joy stopped instantly. Never had he looked so handsome! He seemed to dominate the room with his long legs resting on the table as he leaned back in the chair, returning her stare. He wore black boots and clean white breeches, no shirt but an open white vest over the smooth bronze skin of the wide expanse of his chest. "Oh Ram, I'm sorry . . . I had thought you were alone—"

"Ram's misfortune, no doubt," Seanessy said, proceeding to exchange greetings with her, but those blue eyes abruptly swept over the room in unabashed interest in the magnificence of the room. Due to the angle of the door, she thankfully missed the bed off to the side. While Seanessy bantered good-naturedly about her beguiling spy trick of the previous night, Ram still had not said a word, for his only thought was his desire must cloud his judgment. She could not be that lovely.

She wore the same Spanish peasant skirt of bright crimson, green and gold that outlined the slender curves of her hips, while the plain white blouse, gathered at the sleeves, was covered by a light cotton shawl. Like a peasant girl, too, her long dark hair was braided, the ropes of hair falling beneath a matching crimson scarf to drop past her small waist.

Recovering sufficiently from the blatant masculine personification of him in his quarters, she stumbled through an explanation. "I am sorry to interrupt, truly. I'll come back later," she whispered, turning to leave, but even before he could stop her, she swung around. "Oh Ram! I must speak to

141

you about it—"

"No doubt," he interrupted, "you've come to apologize."

"Well no," she said softly, and gathering courage from Sean's smile somehow, she added more boldly, "Why should I? You were horrible to let me believe it."

"I don't recall you giving me a chance to explain."

"And I don't recall you asking for one."

"Joy Claret"—a smile lifted to his gaze—"It's very difficult to beg favors from a young lady dressed ridiculously as a boy in a dark alley, who is telling you how much she hates you."

"Oh but I did hate you!" she said and told him about her night spent plotting his murder, how she was stopped only by the moral consequences of it, this related with several examples from the Shakespearean tragedies. Just as her dramatic speech won her the prize of four men's amusement, a sound came from the immense bed that she had yet to notice.

Joy's eyes widened enormously. There was a lady sleeping in his bed! The woman's face was turned toward them, and she was so beautiful and naked—naked!—beneath the sheets, naked in front of men and so unconcerned that she managed to sleep. Asleep in his bed—

She turned back to Ram, who watched her with that infuriating and ever present amusement.

"Your impetuousness has not gone unnoticed," Ram said easily enough. "I can only guess that the next time you burst into what is essentially a man's bed chambers, unannounced and uninvited, you might be better prepared for what to expect."

Propriety, any semblance of it, demanded her immediate withdrawal, but this was not on her mind. What was came in a shocked whisper. "But . . . but you were kissing me just—"

The unfinished accusation solicited a quick round of sudden laughter, and Sean almost lost the sip of coffee in his mouth. "Ram! How could you betray our lady like that?

Kissing her and bedding another—with but one day's passing! Why, it's too horrible to contemplate. I suggest we refrain from doing so at once."

She wished the floor would open and swallow her up, so great was her embarrassment. When no such merciful thing happened, she knew to heed the dictates of propriety, and she turned and ran out of the door.

Ram made no move to stop her, but he turned to Derrick. "Derrick, see which way she rides. If it's south, then get some men out to follow her. I may not be the one to ruin that innocence, but I'll be damned if someone else will either. And Bart, let's get some breakfast in here. At least I'll get one appetite satisfied."

The two men left, still chuckling as Sean turned to Ram. "I posted a letter to our servants on our last ship bound home, mentioning to make space in my study for your Rembrandt." He grinned, ignoring Ram's sigh, chuckle, the shake of his head. He picked an apple from the fruit bowl. "A bite my lord? The taste is sweet indeed."

Ram laughed heartily and tossed another apple in the air, catching it in his mouth with a healthy bite. "Sweet indeed," he laughed.


Joy battled furiously with herself not to cry. This was not worth crying over! Yet the humiliation of the scene she just quit threatened to overwhelm her. This was mounted on top of the crushing discovery that she was not special to him. His attentions had made her feel special, their auspicious first meeting, his connection with Joshua to say nothing of how they shared the same utilitarian principles, the intimacies in the library; all these things had been deceptive. His kiss, the awakening to his touch had been deceptive! That lady casually sleeping in his bed brought home the fact that he considered intimacies with women with an infuriating masculine callousness. It frightened her—frightened

143

her senseless.

Humiliation gave way to indignation at last. She decided if she ever made a fool of herself again in his presence, she would hang herself. That was it; she would simply hang herself. At the same moment she looked up to notice she had passed the turnoff to the small shanty town where the medicine woman was said to live.

Joy reined Libertine around and pressed her into a lively trot, but not more than ten hundred paces gone, she stopped again, practically running into the two men following her.

Libertine danced nervously, and Joy skillfully calmed her, while glaring furiously at the two mounted men she recognized from his ship. "Did he send you after me?" she asked.

"Aye miss," one man replied. "He did indeed."

Joy did not know Ram's men nearly as well as they knew her. Nor did she know that Joshua had asked Ram to extend his protection to her, a request Ram took seriously. Between Sean and himself, they had over a hundred and fifty men in Orleans alone, and for the last three weeks Joy had been watched everywhere she went. Had she known, she would have considered shooting the two where they sat as a clear message of what she thought of Ram Barrington's protection.

"Tell Mr. Barrington that he can go to the devil!"

"Believe me, he's been there and back." The other man laughed. "Though we'll be sure to relate your sentiments."

Oh, it was infuriating; he was infuriating. "Well, I'll not have his men follow me." She came to the point. "I'll lose you each and every time and yes," she said the exact moment she raised the riding crop, "that is a challenge!"

Libertine leapt in the air and was off. For a long moment, the two men sat stunned by her brash boldness. Joy pressed her horse into a gallop, loosening the reins to permit the speed for which Libertine forever strived. She was one with the wind, and with the exhilaration of a winged flight, she lost them by the first bend in the road.

Still, she barely managed the rein necessary to slow and turn Libertine onto the narrow path winding alongside the tributary leading to the shanty town. She recognized the path only because it came after a wooden bridge. Libertine trotted east, disappearing in the bayou forest, and when she heard the thunderous clamor of the two men's mounts pass on the wooden bridge, she had cause to wonder at the enormity of her thoughts and emotions that had made her pass by the turn in the first place.

About two miles later, the narrow path led to the tiny fishing village. A great wall of earthen dikes separated the wood houses from the river, for times of seasonal swells. The houses were small but neat, modest homes of Cajun fishermen and freed people of color. There were well tended gardens in front of each house, pretty potted plants and flowers on the porches. Though she searched the surroundings, there was nothing that suggested a voodoo witch.

Joy slipped from Libertine's back and stretched to draw the reins over her horse's head, then stood back and looked about again. The place was completely deserted at this hour; it was profoundly quiet save for the rush of the river and the ever present distant cry of birds. A butterfly circled her thrice and made her smile, just as the sweet sound of a song broke through the forest.

Joy followed the sound to the edge of the trees on the wide bank, as her eyes discovered the path that led into the forest again. She felt a curious tingling, a prelude to an adventure. The sound was not from far away. She tethered Libertine to a tree and slipped down the path on foot, entering the wilderness of the forest.

The sound of a babbling brook nearby, yet unseen through the dense foliage, seemed to mirror the very song she followed. Bright sunlight burst through the shade of the towering, gnarled water oaks and the play of light, with the song, created an air of mystery and magic. She quickened her pace.

Two hundred or so paces away, the path made a sharp turn through the trees, and Joy rounded a bend at the exact moment the song stopped. She stopped, too, staring for a long moment in delight.

The old stone house was lovely and startling so, a refuge from the surrounding wildness and surely drawn from the pages of a fairy tale. It was a small stone house, stone being uncommon enough in the moist muddied land to be a miracle in itself. A blood-red waterfall of bougainvillaea spilled down one whole side of the house. A dazzling array of colorful flowers surrounded the area, all with waist-high blossoms tamed into rows distinguished only by the color of the blossoms: pansies and daisies, trumpets and marigolds of orange and red and gold, and wild red cannas, alongside rows and rows of pale pastel roses.

Smiling, Joy practically skipped through the garden path but quickly came to another abrupt stop. Seated in a rocking chair beneath the shade of a tree was the old woman. A dog lay at her feet, lazily thumping his tail without a lift of head. Two goats wandered nearby. An old, white tom cat slept in a potted plant on the only window sill. A hummingbird's house hung from an old oak shading the house, and many tiny creatures were noisily visiting it.

"Well, hit's 'bout time," the old woman said. "Have a seat and sit a spell. I have many things to tell."

Joy's gaze locked with the old woman, and for several long seconds it seemed someone threw away the key. Old yet ageless, many lines marked the passing years, and the old woman grinned toothlessly. Yet the thin face presented a perfect symmetry of features that suggested a profound serenity.

This could not be the voodoo witch people spoke of with terror!

Joy felt an inexplicable warmth as she studied the puzzle presented in the old woman's eyes. The dark pools shined with a bright light and seemed to be the source of the warmth she felt, yet for all this, there was mischief in those eyes, too. She decided in the instant she liked her a lot.

The old woman was shucking peas into a wooden bin; her hands worked without interruption. An empty chair seemed to be waiting for Joy, and on the small wooden table between the two chairs, sat two tall glasses of lemonade. Placed next to these was a coconut shell, oddly with a black ribbon tied around it.

"Do you know where I might find the medicine woman in these parts?"

The old woman chuckled, "Dis is me, chile. Don't you knows hit?"

"Ohhh!" Joy was pleased. "Well." She got to the point. "I came in the hope you might help me," she first said, setting her boots down to pet the small shepherd dog. "I'm told you have knowledge of herbs and medicines, and well, you see, my guardian has consumption. I hoped you might have a potion to help him."

"Nothin'll help him but the maker, chile."

Joy felt a sudden warmth wrap around, spiraling from her bare toes upward, enclosing her being in consolation and security. As quickly as the heat spiraled up, it spiraled down, then vanished completely.

"I made him up some medicine though." Her gaze moved to the coconut jar. "I ain't sayin' hit'll cure him, but hit should ease the worse of his time."

Joy slowly touched the jar with a question. The old woman must have kept potions ever ready for the many ailing people who came to her, but the fact that the concoction was used for all ailments made her question its value. She had a half dollar to pay, but she did not want to spend it for a potion of no worth.

"Ain't no charge," the old woman said. "I don' charge folks worse off dan meself."

With some alarm, Joy glanced at her clothes wondering if

147

her poverty showed there like a sign, only afterward realizing that the woman had guessed her thoughts.

"Sit down a spell and taste the best lemonade in de whole world. You can help me shod dese here peas. Name is Tetelle—little star, dat's what I is."

Joy took the seat offered, and after one sip, she agreed it was indeed the best lemonade she ever tasted. Quite suddenly and unexpectedly, they fell into an easy conversation. The old woman talked of many things: of her garden and her green thumb, of her creatures and of life out in the middle of a forest swamp. Joy could not help but inquire about her reputation mixed with voodoo.

"Oh dat. Well I'se been taught by a high sittin' voodoo queen, mainly cause I'se got sight, dat's for sure but I don' practice none. Folks, I suspect, get practice and knowin' all mixed up . . ." Then the old woman began telling her of her many visitors, of medicine cures that were easy and those that were not. Joy learned of many helpful treatments; some were highly unlikely and certainly unconventional, many she would discuss with Joshua at length.

There came a pause, the peas were done and the old woman leaned back in her chair. "'Course," she said, "my best talent is for fortune tellin'."

Like any well-bred and educated young lady, Joy received this with disbelief and delight in equal shares. "Ah." She smiled. "Will you tell mine?"

"Yours, well now, hit's what you're here for. I suppose, I should start by sayin' yours ain't a common fortune, as yo' don' have a common soul."

Joy had not the vanity to entertain the truth of this, but she smiled indulgently. She would humor her new friend, as she no doubt would hear of how she would marry well, have many fine and healthy children and live to a ripe old age.

"To tell truth, I ain't never—in all my born days—seen such a light as yours chile. Lawd, hit be bright to start, but now hit shines with da lives yo' touched. What gives me

148

pause is, if'n your light is such, what must his be lak? Even stronger, I knows from my dreams."

Confused, Joy hardly knew what to make of this. What light? She shifted uncomfortably and looked across the field of flowers where the sun marked mid-afternoon. That light? What light?

"An' de babe sittin' on your shoulder," she continued calmly, "is as familiar as my own hand now. He, too, visits my dreams so often."

Joy glanced in alarm at her shoulder. Of course there was nothing there, and she blushed, embarrassed by this sudden nonsensical turn of the old woman's mind. Oh dear, was the old woman mad? Perhaps senile?

"Sown with the seed of his father," she continued, "he will have dat man's great strength but with your very own goodness. His light is brighter dan de both of yourn—" she shook her head—"I can't 'magin' hit. Hit's a gonna spread over de earth lak a great river quenching de thirst of misery everywhere. Yes, everywhere! Lawd a mercy, everythin's depended on his birth"—she stared hard at Joy—"even de other lights in your womb, and dat all depends on you fightin' de one man you'se not able to fight."

The old woman leaned forward and said in a distant and soft voice, "If'n I squint my eyes just so an' look out yonder"—she stared off into the distance—"I kin see 'em— There!" she said with an enormous grin.

Joy looked in the direction to see a dark forest background of flowers. Dragonflies and butterflies danced on the blossoms and bees—

"There dey's all gathered. Lawd a mercy, each light is so bright, special and distinct; de only thing dey have in common is de joy of your name. Dere's de second one with his visions, a mind filled with numbers and figurin', and he's a gonna build great things dat is admired long after our bodies is ashes in earth; an' dere's de poet, words touched by God but shaded with the devil's own wit, and oh de ladies"—

149

she chuckled to herself—"de ladies flock to him like bees to a hive! An' dere's de one dat you favor, so serious and dedicated to his medicine like de love past; dere's de other one and oh he be a handful lak his father, wild and rebellious, and well, he's gonna surprise everyone; and den de last. Yes! Dere she is, I'se see her! De little girl who's gonna make her father swear she's more trouble dan all his sons, as much trouble as her mother, but yes, she too is gonna surprise everyone with her life's path."

Joy was staring at an empty field of flowers washed in gold shades of late afternoon. She glanced back at the old woman, who stared with a distant bliss at things that simply were not there. Joshua said the best way to deal with insanity was with calm—

Joy started, as the old woman suddenly collapsed. "Oh Lawd," she cried in her hands. "I see 'em all so clear! Why, oh why do you let me see 'em so plain when dey's nothin' but what might be! When dey's not real lak other visions?"

Absolutely unnerved by this point, Joy was about to jump from her seat and bid a quick goodbye and good day, but suddenly, the air warmed, thickening with a hushed stillness that warned her to be still.

"You'se in fer trouble, chile. A great darkness lies ahead."

Joy gasped slightly. Though she thought this poor old woman to be stark raving mad, and what little of the strange mutterings of the insane mind she had understood, she didn't believe, a small broken voice still had to ask: "Is it Joshua?"

The old woman shook her head, and strangely the madness seemed gone vanished with the visions. "The curse of my fortune tellin' is dat I can most never name things lak dis, 'cause hit's might hard for me to see into de darkness. I tell you dis dough, darkness don' come from him."

What worried Joy most was Joshua. So this brought a great relief, for Joshua's worsening health was by far her worst fear. She could handle anything else. The very relief was silly though; it made no sense because, of course, she didn't believe any of this.

"So much is at stake, chile." Ole Tetelle shook her head. "So much. Let me start with dis."

The old woman rose and searched the ground until she found a small stick. Upon returning to the chair, she drew a circle with three points on the circumference and one in the middle.

"Dese are de three lights shinin' on you. Dey each is men. Dis one is dim and fadin' in 'de here and now, but chile, you'se got to 'member dat hit'll be shinin' in your life forever after."

Staring intently, Joy wanted to ask who this was. Now that her fears concerning Joshua were relieved, she naturally wondered whose light was "dim and fadin'"? Though of course, it was all so silly. She didn't believe a word of it.

"Now dis one is mischief." She pointed and laughed at what she saw. "Or hit was at first. His light just startin' to shine on you, but da more he touches you, da more serious it becomes. And so, dis is de man who starts de whole thing. One way or de other, he is responsible.

"Dis is de one, chile." She pointed and drew the top point larger and larger. "Here is your life. Everything rests on him. His light is de brightest lak I say, brighter even den yours. But hit's streaked with black. Dis is part of his great strength, and dis is the part you will fight. Dis is de source of de darkness ahead."

Joy struggled to make sense of it, of any of it. "Who is he that is my life, who will I fight and for what?" As soon as she asked this question, she regretted it, for it sounded like she actually believed the turn of the old woman's mind!

"You will be fighting for de gift de lawd gives you and for de world, and against him for de life. And dis is de help I can give: you must not doubt dis gift, de goodness of your blessing, for hit's upon de doubt dat all rests. Your strength will come if'n you know, if'n yo' remember what I'se said. An' child, you will need all dis strength to fight him."

Suddenly forgetting she didn't believe it, Joy waited with heightened attention for the old woman to explain those words. No explanation was forthcoming and it was over. The hushed stillness was gone; she heard the unseen brook running nearby, the birds chirping, moving through the trees, the hummingbirds darting in and out of the little house burgeoning from the tree and the goats grazing at the side.

"Yes chile." Tetelle mirrored her thoughts yet again. "I will leave you with dis." The old woman took Joy's hand in hers and pressed her thumb in Joy's palm, closing Joy's fingers around it.

A heat suddenly burned there, spreading up her arm throughout her whole body, and Joy looked to Tetelle with shock, an unspoken demand for an explanation.

"You'll feel dis when hit comes. Hit'll help you heed a foolish ole woman's words." She withdrew her hand but gently brushed Joy's face with her fingertips, and Joy was staring at unmasked sympathy in the startling depth of her eyes. "No matter what, chile, you'll have a good life, even if'n you are not strong 'nough to win. No," she whispered, "you won't be happy, but you already know happiness is but a small price for goodness."

Dear Diary,

Joshua woke early, and the greeting and smile he bestowed on Cory and I spoke of good spirits, despite the increasingly raspy sound to his cough. He breakfasted on an orange and melon—not knowing I stole this in our increasingly desperate financial straits—and fell into deep slumber. Doctor Morson claims the affliction often takes a turn for the worse, just before a period of recovery. Recovery, my dearest friend, that you know I await eagerly with all my heart.

Sometimes I wonder if Joshua knows. Of course he must, for he's known forever this was the year his small

152

inheritance ends. It would not have mattered so much, I think, if he was still able to practice his medicine. Still, he never mentions it, and needless to say, neither the reverend, Sammy, Cory or myself ever mention to him the increasingly desperate situation in which we find ourselves. My, but the money begins to worry me! I think of it nearly all the time.

Sammy works six days a week, the Sabbath saved for sermons and the chores Cory and I simply can't complete for want of sheer strength. Though Sammy rises at dawn and works till dusk—Mr. Farnsworth granting no more than a privy break in between—and exhaustion wears hard on him, the few paying jobs he manages at night—repairing storm shutters, a table leg, helping erect a new barn—barely manage to keep us from debtor's prison. We owe three merchants, the pharmacist and the stables, and our landlord grows tired of our excuses.

What to do? What to do? Sammy has six months left apprenticed to Mr. Farnsworth, six months that never shrink, for every time Sammy borrows a dollar here, a dollar there, Mr. Farnsworth adds weeks to his servitude. At this rate he will never be free! I have long suspected Mr. Farnsworth of racial hatred, unkind I know, but how else can one explain his treatment of Sammy, except that Mr. Farnsworth by some cruel trick of his mind resents Sammy's freeman status?

How vainly my efforts to secure a position are received. You know I have posted hundreds of letters, answered every ad and to naught! I rarely get a reply in return. This, I am told oft enough, is owing to my unmarried status, my age and lack of experience. So desperate, I would gladly condescend to the menial work of a kitchen maid if my placement in the clerical class did not strictly forbid such undertakings, and if this work was not already absorbed entirely by the slave class.

As each day passes and we have but a month or so to our name, even I cannot be upset by the desperate shame the reverend plans as soon this night's run is through.

Tonight is the night . . .

Unable to rid herself of her worries and turn to the subject of the night's adventure, Joy set her pencil down with a sigh. For long minutes she stared at the hundred or so tiny prisms of raindrops stuck to the window. The warning came unbidden to her mind "A great darkness lies ahead."

Was this what the old woman meant? Financial ruin? She had given considerable consideration to the meeting with the old woman; she even considered going back for a clarification of the strange words, the ominous warning that made absolutely no sense to her, especially in retrospect. Thinking back, the impression became naught but a jumble in her mind. She realized this as soon as she had left and unexpectedly met Seanessy on her way back. Atop his white stallion, Sean escorted her the entire way home, and as she had tried to relate what had just happened to him, it occurred to her just how little it all made sense. She had then dismissed the whole incident by making fun of it.

Yet, every time her mind unwillingly encountered the warning, it was paired with a small scar, a black patch, the mystery of Ram Barrington. Presently, it was no different and she shook her head, forcing the thought to leave her as she returned to the matter at hand.

We leave by noon. Joshua was told I shall be staying the night at the Beauchamp's (who, by the way, I've abandoned all hope of saving, leaving Katie and her good mother in God's knowing hands). Joshua mercifully greeted the idea without suspicion. How I loath our deception; but freedom's call, so loud and clear in my heart, demands my rebellion, and I cannot, in good conscience, abandon its cry.

Jim Boy is not an unusual case. Among the multitudes of slaves, he is one of the many who simply refuses to accept fate's bondage, and lured by campfire tales that sing freedom's song, stories of daring Negroes who made it, he had set out on his own twice. Only to discover hope had woven lies into these freedom tales—freedom was not forty miles north past two small towns and "there it is! The land of milk and honey, where peoples of color is freed! I swear it! I knows 'cause once, I overhear . . ." or even "just two night trucks through the swamps and lo an' behold, there it is!"

No, freedom is hundreds of miles away, and the only passage to it is on the underground railroad. Since Jim Boy had tried twice on his own, caught within hours each time and whipped twice for it—so the reverend said Delilah said—Jim Boy is now branded a perpetual runaway and malcontent. Word has it that Simone's plantation manager—a man I don't know—is going to see him sold next week to the living hell of the turpentine fields. So, now it's imperative Jim Boy escapes, and the reverend, Sammy and I myself, with the help of Delilah, our only connect at Garden Court, will see it happen.

I leave you as always my friend, with the fervent hope . . .


As the rim of the sun touched the horizon, washing the rich land with a splendor of golden colors, the evening horn blew. It came as a long onerous sound but a sound as welcomed as Gabriel's trumpet. Moving as a collective whole, the fifty-three dark-skinned men working the far eastern fields laid down their short handled hoes and straightened slowly to ease the pain of the long day's labor from their backs. Some smiled and sighed, others groaned as they stretched to work out the worst of the dull ache in their backs and shoulders.

The men formed a loose line, and all eyes turned to Massa Cain, the overseer, in wait of his signal to move along. Riding atop a horse, Cain partook in a long draught from a silver rum cask, wiped his thick moustache with a dirty sleeve and then, with a motion of his hand yelled, "All right boys move it!"

The long two miles march back to the slave quarters began. Talk and laughter, more than one complaint sprang up and down the long line as each man looked forward to the three or so hours before sleep as their own, a precious time filled with camp talk, songs and of course the evening meal.

For long weeks since the last whipping, Jim Boy could hardly pass words with anyone. There was less than a week left till the day he would be sold. He was afraid. No one, not even his long time friend Peter, who tried the hardest, could engage him in anything. He walked to the fields alone, walked back alone and was the last in line for everything. Tonight was no different.

It was no different except for a bright red ribbon on Delilah's hat recently passed to her from the reverend. Jim Boy stared blankly at his huge hands holding his supper bowl. A long handled cup poured pork and beans into his bowl. He glanced up, saw the ribbon and stared in shock. His hands started trembling before he even heard the words.

"Tonight's de night, boy," Delilah said. "Getcha on to de main road. Wait. A cart'll stop and take you'se away. Take you'se to freedom, boy—an' dis time you'se gonna make hit."

Jim Boy stared for a long moment. The old woman might not have passed a word. She stirred the big pot, wiped her thick fingers on her worn apron and started fussing with the baked loaves nearby. He realized abruptly the pounding in his ears was his heart. Then the last thing he heard was "Don' be so skeered." Delilah whispered, "Mercy boy, ain't lak you's got somethin' to lose no how."

He stared blankly ahead; the tremble in his hands revealed the violence of his emotions. It was not true. He had his life to lose. The God given gift had always meant something to him; a good deal more than it did to others, for it was in truth all he ever had.

He knew enough to pretend everything was normal; although his heart pounded like a savage drum, breathing felt labored and his food was as edible as wood, certainly that hard to swallow. The overseers rotated night watch and through the encroaching darkness and the dim light of the campfire, he saw it was Massa Cain and Lockhorn on watch. Good. They could both be counted on to get half a heat on by the time the fire died.

Cain and Lockhorn stood a dozen paces away, shootin' the breeze and listening to the supper time chatter. No one liked pork and beans night. Too many beans and not enough pork.

"Hey, how's that distillery of yours coming?" Cain asked, working the tobacco into a chaw.

Lockhorn chuckled, spit. "Hell, just about done. Know what I found inside this morning?" He didn't wait for a reply. "A God damn rabbit."

"Geez." Cain laughed.

"Can't figure on how it got up top, but hell, it took one whiff of my moonshine, done died and went to heaven."

The two men laughed until Cain suggested Lockhorn fetch some to pass the night away. "It's a bit early, but like women, I'll like it hot just fine."

"Hot? Hell, it's liable to burn right through our innards! But I am game, my man."

Overhearing this, Jim Boy could not believe his luck. The two hour wait until lights out felt like a whole season's passing, slow as a snail's crossing. Finally, he lay on the mat, listening with heightened sensitivity to the sounds of the night. Snoring rose from all sides, ole man Hoss the loudest. A night owl screeched in the distance. Crickets sounded like a thunderous roar. He could hear the brook in the distance. Cain and Lockhorn were settled round the dying embers of the fire. He heard the slosh of the jug passed back and forth, their distant talk grew progressively louder, filled with white man's humor—horse stories and whores, that was it.

Minutes ticked on, collecting into an hour. He no longer heard Lockhorn, and Cain took to singing a song about the sea. Finally that died, too. Now was the time. Jim Boy sat up, arranged the bed covers and stalked silently to the door.

Thus, his longest night began.


"For a moment there, I thought Mrs. Beauchamp was going to force me to stay the night by locking me in a room," Joy complained.

"Aye, she did everything but cough up the crown jewels," the reverend replied. They had just dropped some apples off at the Beauchamp's for the Church charity bake. Charles Simone had been kind enough to provide the apples, while unknowingly providing the opportunity to get word to Jim Boy. It had been hard to get away from him as well. Seems Madame Beauchamp wasn't the only one who wanted the lass, the reverend sighed.

The cart now headed back south, toward the city, and the next stop was to pick up Jim Boy as they passed the Simone plantation again. It was night now; the moonless night offered the security of darkness. The lanterns, swinging on each side of the driver's seat, cast queer eerie shadows onto the woods surrounding the northern river road. It seemed unnaturally quiet, too, as though night creatures and insects alike stood on the sidelines watching in mute horror the daring of the mission.

Joy shivered despite the warmth of the late spring night.

Nerve wracking business to be sure, but as always, her major fear was that Joshua would find out. There would be no getting out of it this time. It would take years of sweet talk before he forgave her, if then.

"Just around this bend, darlin'," he said in a hushed whisper, feeling on edge, too, despite his normally cool reserve. Joy focused on the darkness that was the road ahead. The reverend took up a whistle as though Jim Boy, wherever he was, needed more sound than the racket of the cart to know they were coming.

Jim Boy pressed his muscled frame against the tree so hard he scraped his skin. The terror of his wait could not be imagined. A thousand times he convinced himself he should turn back. There was no cart, no reverend, no freedom. It was all some cruel trick by the master or God to catch him again. Then his mind would snap and he'd hear Cain and Lockhorn comin' after him, sober as the night was long and ready to shoot, only to realize the stomping, so loud in his mind, was but a small unseen night creature scurrying over the dark road.

Relief swept over him in hot sweat.

When he first heard the distant sound of the cart, he knew he was mad. The steady sound grew progressively louder and louder still, and he never knew he was crying, that choked sobs shook his chest and his throat. He only knew he was saved.

Saved Lord! He was saved!

Jim Boy stepped into the dead center of the road, appearing suddenly in the light, and Joy and the reverend started, instinctively grasping one another as the horses reared and neighed. The cart came to an abrupt halt. The reverend jumped down, and without even taking a moment to look around, he moved into action.

"We got nearly twenty miles to the ship. We'll be stopping in about an hour to disguise ourselves and the wagon. That's it. Won't stop again till daybreak, if then. You ready?"

In the wavering lamp light, the reverend discerned the shadow of tears, and he stared in an unusual moment of reflection. This was not a scam, not some game created to swindle folk from what never really belonged to them in the first place. No, the stakes were higher, much higher . . .

The reverend smiled wide, gave the young man a reassuring pat on the back and helped him inside the hidden compartment.

An hour or more passed uneventfully as the cart moved steadily south until finally they came to the narrow, shallow creek crossing over the road on its way to the Mississippi. This was their meeting place. Sammy waited a few paces off the road, already decked out in his field hand garb, powdered light skin and wig, holding Libertine's reins. The reverend forced the cart off the road. The lanterns were extinguished as whispered greetings were exchanged.

Sammy had already brought up the peddler wagon disguise left hidden nearby for over a month now. As he quickly set about arranging it onto the cart, Joy grabbed her sack of clothes and slipped into the darkness to change.

The entire operation took less than fifteen minutes. The lanterns were lit again. All in their respective seats, the reverend cracked the whip lightly over the nags' backs, and the cart lurched forward and then around, clumsily and noisily rolling over wood boards placed over the muddied creek for all carriages to pass.

"How long do you think before we reach the city?" Joy asked.

"Oh, about three-and-a-half, maybe four hours." He patted his lap. "You can try to sleep if you want."

"As likely as a leprechaun's song on a moonless night!"

A cry broke the night time peace in the field hand quarters. There came a sputtering, a sick gasping sound, and then as old man Hoss sucked in his last breath, he released it in a scream. Not just any scream but one Peter, like everyone else, woke to and swore was straight from the bowels of hell.

Peter, who always took matters in hand, rose and was the first at old man Hoss's bedside. Others followed. For a while they remained mute, staring dumfounded.

"You all right ole man?" Peter asked cautiously. No answer. He placed his hand on the old man's chest, and when he felt nothing, his hand moved to the old man's ridiculously wide open mouth.

"Lawd have mercy! De ole man up and died on us." He stared for a moment with the others, then suddenly turned to one of the boys. "Hey you—go rouse Cain up! And you"— he pointed to another—"get some torch light in here."

Within the next half-hour's confusion, close to a dozen men knew Jim Boy had run. No one said a word. They just, each in turn, wandered to the bunk and felt the pile of bedclothes to verify the reality of the rumor. With all the hustle and bustle to get the dead man out and buried in the middle of the night, Cain and Lockhorn might not have noticed anything amiss or anyone gone, except that Jim Boy was the only soul managing to sleep through the ruckus.

"Hey, look at that." Lockhorn pointed to the mat. "How the hell can that boy sleep through this ruckus." He chuckled, shaking his head. "Wager that boy there's got himself—" Lockhorn stopped, suddenly catching two nearby men's nervous shift of gaze.

Cain was pretending he didn't notice, battling furiously with himself to keep on pretending. He didn't want to notice, but Lockhorn nudged him. "Check that boy out, will ya?"

Cain moved slowly to the bunk and lifted the blanket bunched in a pile. Of all the ill-begotten luck. The boy picks the one night to run when ole man Hoss up and dies. Beggar's luck for sure.

Well, hell, they would have caught him by noon anyway.

"Looks like we got a live one," Cain said out loud.

Sammy heard it first. "Stop de cart," he called up.

"What?" the reverend said.

"Stop de cart!" he practically screamed.

The reverend reined the cart to an abrupt halt. He and Joy tensed, twisting around to see what Sammy was about. Sammy's board-straight back was to them, and he cupped his ear, straining to listen. Neither Joy or the reverend heard it, no not then, but they knew when Sammy cursed under his breath and announced, "Dey got de dogs out. Hell and damnation, dey's on to us!"

The reverend grabbed Joy's shoulders so fast and hard, her mind spun like a child's toy. An odd distortion sprang on the familiar face. It was fear! The reverend panicked, and this was the first time she had ever seen it. "Listen up, lass." He stopped just short of shaking her. "This has never happened to us before. It's bad, real bad. We've got to split the pack. You're going to ride that horse of yours like you've never ridden and as far away as she'll carry you. Can you do that?"

"Yes, but—"

He silenced her quickly, then jumped down, bringing her with him. Sammy had already untied Libertine and was now opening the passenger's compartment. "Come on man— we'se got us trouble."

Jim Boy froze.

"Come on! Please to God, we'se got troubles!"

Looking scared witless, but no more than either Sammy or the reverend, Jim Boy slowly slipped out and then onto the ground.

Sammy could not mince words; he got right to the point. "You'se got to piss on the hoss, Jim Boy! Dey's called the dogs out and our only chance of seein' daylight is if'n you'se got some piss for dis here hoss's legs!"

Jim Boy looked as though Sammy just said his time was up and he was going to hell for being such a sinner. Joy herself had felt no fear until the very moment she heard it. In the farthest distance and gaining fast came the frantic yelps of dogs hot on a trail. "Oh God hurry! They're coming!"

The words penetrated his confusion; he suddenly understood. Sammy and the reverend watched in silence the several long seconds it required for Jim Boy to comply. Libertine danced nervously, not liking this kind of abuse at all and making her sentiments plain.

"Joy, Joy." The reverend grabbed her again, and all the instructions he could think of tumbled out in the space of seconds. "Ride east for about two miles. Stop until you hear them pick up your trail, then turn circles until they start gaining. Head back to the river road and then ride her for all she's worth lass. Don't stop till she drops. That horse can go a hell of a lot faster for a spell, but those dogs will be forever gaining. Once she's spent, let her go. You head back home but keep to the water. If ever those dogs come after you, then start swimming. You got it?"

"What about you?" she asked frantically as Sammy lifted her onto the saddle.

"There's a triple split about a mile down the road. If the pack splits and the lead follows you, we've run a good chance of confusin' 'em more, and then we'll just have to keep movin' till we find somewhere that's safe. Now go lass, go!"

Libertine leaped into the air at the tap of Joy's feet, disappearing in the darkness. Jim Boy was back in the compartment, now a coffin in his mind's eye, and seconds later the cart moved forward. Sammy and the reverend in the driver's seat pressed the old bays for all they were worth. The dogs sounded much closer, less than two miles now.

"You ain't never told her that thar ain't no place safe in heaven or on earth when you'se got a pack o' hungry dogs on you!" Sammy shouted above the frantic rattle.

"Have I ever let you down?" the reverend shouted back.

"No, but I'se mighty afraid I'se about to see de day."

"Not on your life Sammy!"

"Dis is what I'm a sayin', my man!"

The reverend laughed, unbelievably he laughed and that

163

made Sammy laugh, too. The old man's finally gonna meet his maker in hell and he's jest such a fool he's a laughin'.

The old cart was ill-suited for speed as was the reverend. His bone-thin frame bounced painfully, rattling miserably in the hard wood seat. He had reason to abruptly realize how loose two of his teeth were, but still, with one hand holding his hat and another the reins, a miracle occurred. He managed to remove the rum cask in his pocket, get the cap off and enjoy a gulp or two. After all, it might be his last. Holding on for his life, Sammy was far too scared to appreciate the trick, all seconds before they rounded the bend and came abruptly on the triple cross.

Sammy jumped down from the still moving cart with the large canister of turpentine. The river road kept to the right; less than four miles ahead it would pass the front of the city at the levee and continue on south. The middle road would head to the city as well, but around the back way. The third road offered the best bet; it led northwest twenty or so miles to Gainsport, eventually all the way to Georgia and beyond, supposin' some desperate fools like themselves wanted to quit Orleans and fast.

The dogs sounded in the far distance. "Hear that?" the reverend called as he, too, took one of their three canisters of turpentine to splash it down the Gainsport road.

Two hundred paces down the river road, Sammy stopped and listened. The distant yelping sounded chaotic, scattered; the dogs were confused! He ran another hundred or so paces down the road, splattering turpentine, then crossed through the woods to the middle cross, the city's back road, and still splattering turpentine, he raced back to the cart.

The reverend just returned from the Gainsport road. Nothing confused a dog's scent like turpentine, or so said this old hound man to whom the reverend once had purposely lost three good card hands, all to discover what in tarnation would throw off a pack of hounds on a trail. He and Sammy jumped back on the cart, and with a hard slash of the reins, they were off.

"Gainsport and the likes of me get on fine. Did I ever tell you Sammy 'bout this card play I pulled up there?" he yelled against the wind.


Breathless and surrounded by darkness, Joy crouched low on Libertine's back and with her own heightened senses listened. Nervous and frightened, too, Libertine kept tossing her head, neighing and dancing, fighting for more rein that Joy absolutely refused to give. "Easy my pet . . . easy . . . listen up! Are they coming?"

Libertine quieted somewhat, and Joy heard the dogs in the distance but could not isolate their direction. It sounded like they were going in all directions at once. Alarmed by the dogs, cries and screeches of night birds added to these sounds, and Libertine's hooves cracked loudly as she danced nervously over the leaves and twigs. The darkness was nearly impenetrable, only the darker outline of trees, moss and bushes showed in the night. Suddenly, yes—she heard it!— the barking drew together as the dogs finally found the scent.

Joy reined Libertine back toward the river but only gently nudged her side, while holding the reins tight to control the speed. Still, even a slow lope through the dark forest was sheer madness; a rabbit hole or a stump would send Libertine crashing to the ground. She held her breath and kept low, digging her knees in tight, praying only to see the road that would give them the freedom to run.

The dogs sounded closer and closer. Joy gasped with a pained cry as a sharp branch slashed across her arm, tearing her shirt. With the dogs and that one small cry, Libertine panicked, fought the bit and won. Joy grabbed Libertine's neck and held on for her life as her horse thundered through the forest. It was like hanging on the edge of a cliff, looking into the certain abyss of death! Die! She was going to die!

Abruptly sounds came from ahead! Horses, men and dogs

in the back and dogs ahead! Confusion crashed into her consciousness a split second before Libertine leaped back onto the river road.

"Catch him! Catch him!"

A pistol fired! Another and another! Joy couldn't think to know what was happening. Libertine had instinctively turned south, running now as she never had, and all she could do was keep the horses, men and pistols behind her, but the dogs! The dogs were ahead of them!

"Run Libertine! Run!" she screamed, and as the words sounded to the wind, the miracle happened. High strung to start and now crazed, Libertine never stopped or reared or even slowed. She crashed straight through the pack of dogs.

And then, with the dogs, pistols and horses behind, Libertine became the wind; she had wings, and they were flying.

Tears blinded Joy as she desperately clung to her horse through the dizzying whirl of speed. Thoughts crashed into her consciousness. The pack had split, one pack had followed her into the forest, while the pack and riders she just met on the road were following the cart. The other pack, including the lead dogs, would soon catch up to the others, yet they would all be following her now. The reverend, Sammy, and Jim Boy would be safe. Had she a breath to spare, she would have laughed at the unplanned and unbelievable perfection of their escape.

Libertine raced past the triple cross and ever onward toward the city. A brief whiff of turpentine brought a sudden wave of nausea to her but it passed quickly. Still keeping low and holding to her horse with her knees, Joy managed to get back the reins, though she did not even attempt to regain control. Libertine flew by herself.

The gallop was wild still, the night flew past, minutes flew past and all with the speed of the wind. The dogs sounded farther and farther away as Libertine lost them.

The danger had only just begun.

The city lay about a mile ahead. It was probably an hour or so to midnight, and the streets would be nearly deserted. She decided to risk the run through the levee. The thought of slowing for safety seemed more risky; the dogs would not be put to rest tonight.

Libertine pressed onward, panicked still, able to hear the dogs when Joy could not. The night lanterns of the city appeared ahead. The marketplace and levee would be empty of all but the night watchmen, who would surely be telling of the runaway horse and rider on a suicide run on the morrow. Joy lifted her head a scant few inches, tears and wind blurring her vision.

A neat stack of cotton bales lay smack in the center of the levee road. An empty stand, with its poles and awning, sat on one side of this, the river on the other. The cotton bales rose five feet if an inch. These facts were assimilated in an instant, along with the last fact that it was too late to stop.

"Stop! You're gonna hit—" an idle sailor jumped up from nearby, his hands flying to his head as he anticipated the inevitable.

Flatboats, barrels, lights flew, created in one long blur in her mind as Joy braced for certain death. Consciousness heightened. She felt a loosening as though Libertine's great strength gave out but knew it was the opposite—Libertine would try to clear it! She felt the muscles of the huge beast lift into the air, and she knew magic. Joy soared; Libertine's back hooves caught the top bail, sending it crashing back, as she glided back to earth with a wondrous fluid motion.

Libertine raced out of the city. The lights fell behind them. The river rushed to the side. A darkness stretched ahead like a velvet glove over her eyes, and her heartbeat, indeed her whole body, matched the rhythm of Libertine's hooves.

The fall was as smooth as the winged flight over the cotton bales. Unlike grapes, miracles do not occur in bunches and luck does run out. It happened so fast that Joy never knew what caused it. Libertine just suddenly tripped, crashing

167

forward to her knees, throwing Joy into the air and onto the ground as she rolled with the impact. Her head hit the ground so hard that an instant darkness swirled in her mind, spreading then stopping.

Joy felt Libertine's hard nose nudging her awake. Pain shot through various points of her body—her buttocks, neck and a finger—but she bolted upright. Nothing but the dark night met her wide blue eyes, and it was perfectly quiet except for—

"The dogs!" She jumped to her feet, panic overriding any and all pain. She was struck with a wave of dizziness, then nausea, yet she grabbed Libertine's reins, stepped back a pace and vaulted. Only to feel a sharp stabbing pain shoot up her arm that sent her falling back to the ground.

Closer, they were gaining!

She jumped up and tried again, careful not to use her right hand. Once on Libertine's back they were off and running, but she felt the difference immediately. Libertine had not the same speed, and the dogs sounded so near now if she dared look back she would see them! She panicked, tried to think of what the reverend said to do. Ride her till she's spent, then loose her and keep to the water. She'd swim if she had to but—

But Libertine would never leave her! Libertine would keep to her and the dogs would keep to Libertine!

The darkened landscape flew past. The dogs were falling a bit behind but Libertine was slowing, too, her breathing unnaturally labored, sweat gathering into foam on her coat.

What to do? What to do?

A million unlikely schemes filled her mind as she raced along the road. Tie Libertine up and run on foot! Yet once they found the abandoned horse, they'd put the dogs on her trail! Could they do that? She didn't know; she didn't know!

Lather, a thick and white foam covered Libertine's coat and her breathing grew so labored, Joy feared she would drop any minute. Then it happened, abruptly, like the snap of fingers, Libertine broke to a trot. Spent, she was spent! The dogs sounded close in the distance. A choked sob escaped Joy, and hot panic swept in. Just as she was about to jump her horse and throw herself into the cold mercy of the river, she looked up to see providence's sweet salvation.

Ram was not narrow minded; he believed in coincidence to a point, a generous point, but then it became something else. Having felt an unusual restlessness that night, not appeased by his long run and swim, the thought of the meeting with the bankers, their wives and company was unendurable. He cancelled, and with the unusual free evening, he sat in his desk chair, a book spread on his lap and his legs on his desk. A single lamp shone from above. A pitcher and glass of water, another of brandy, sat on his desk.

Rake pricked his ears and started barking. The huge dog stood up, suddenly agitated. He pranced back and forth, barking. There was some kind of commotion outside, dogs barking in the distance. "Settle down, Rake," he ordered indifferently.

The dog lowered with a whimper, but as Ram returned to his book, his man suddenly called alarm. Rising, Ram went to the door. His hand had only touched the knob when the door burst open and Joy Claret flew into his arms.

She was flushed and breathless, looking as though she had wandered onto a battlefield and lost. A small bruise showed on her cheek, and there was a bloodied cut on her arm where her shirt had ripped. An enormous fear shone like madness in her eyes, and all this was grasped in the instant she gasped, "Help me . . . please—"

While he didn't know the details of the story, he could easily guess—disastrously involved in freedom fighting.

"Here they come! They're after her Ram!" one of his men shouted down from his watch atop the quarter deck.

"Get out boy," Ram told his dog. Rake never hesitated,

169

racing out the door. The dog was no longer barking, for true to his nature, he would not even warn of his protective attack. "Hold them off for a minute, Eric."

"Hell, we'll pick 'em off if you want!" another man said with a chuckle.

"Don't be an ass!" Ram shouted back, yet an appreciative grin betrayed him. "Absolutely no shooting!"

He slammed the door shut. Joy fought desperately for some control. The mere sight of him, let alone the feel of his arms around her, brought an overwhelming surge of emotions. Desperate and panicked, she had looked up to see his ship moored, to see the only absolute refuge for her, and she had known he would be there. Tonight he would be there!

Inexplicably her emotional swell crashed, changing in the short seconds it took Ram to advance with an unwavering amused look of a predator catching a trapped and helpless animal. He raised a hand, and she instinctively cowered as though about to receive a blow, but he only swiped her hat and wig from her head. Hair pins fell to the floor, and her long braids swung free. "What are you—"

He moved with swift speed and assurance, so fast she never had a chance to react. His hands were upon her, everywhere it seemed, ripping her shirt open, pulling it from her. She cried, trying to twist backward and away from the assault, but he caught her hands and trapped them behind her back as a dagger appeared from nowhere. The dark gaze never left her terror stricken face as, not bothering with the buttons or the cord used as a belt, he simply sliced diagonally across her abdomen and her pants dropped in a heap to the floor.

She stood naked before him, so shocked, mute and confused that her mouth opened to cry out but no sound was forthcoming. Ignoring her, Ram moved with such quick sure strides, one might reasonably assume he had rehearsed what he did next a hundred times. He swept the pile of clothes up into his hand but separated the hat with the wig glued in it. He smiled as he placed this on the top shelf of his bookcase. "I think I'll save this as memorabilia but these"—he held the remaining boys' clothes as he moved next to the lantern—"I will see in hell."

Dogs barked, horses neighed and men shouted outside. Ram lifted the glass from the lantern and caught the clothes under the fire while simultaneously opening a desk drawer and finding a long cigar. He lit the cigar by the fire of the clothes, puffing till a sweet scented cloud of smoke rose in the air mixing and covering the smoke from the clothes. Holding the flaming clothes, he calmly walked to the dressing water, waited till the flames touched his hand, and doused them.

Still stunned and quite speechless, she watched as he turned back to her. A smile lifted on the handsome features, a strange light appearing in his gaze as he stood directly in front of her, staring down. The startling beauty of her unclad state did not pass unnoticed. Her arms crossed over her breasts with a maiden's modesty, taunting maddeningly as he stared; the small flattened waist, the beckoning curves of her slender hips and the long lines of her legs were swept with the heat of his gaze. Yes indeed, she was carved for a man's love.

"Joy Claret," her name was whispered against her ear, as his hands drew hers behind her again, bringing her against him. "You have come to fulfill my fantasy. Do you know, my love"—his finger traced a line over her mouth—"how often I have dreamt of these lips?"

She shivered but with warmth, her body knowing what was being said and done to her, but her mind was somehow firmly fixed on the danger, the burning clothes, the men outside who would be hanging her. Ram held her chin in his hand and chuckled briefly at her obvious state of distress before taking her lips in his.

It was like a dam bursting. Despite the fear shaking her

knees or because of it, heat surged so swiftly into her limbs she half thought he had lifted her under the fire of the lantern. Deep and devastating, the kiss lasted but a minute before the door burst open and two men stepped inside with pistols drawn.

Ram broke the kiss with a feigned start, turning around but careful to keep her figure concealed from the intruders' view. Pistols lowered as shock lifted into the expression of each man. Cain stood next to none other than the Orleans' constable, who had been roused from bed by the chase.

"What the hell is this?" Ram demanded in a tone marked with a clear and natural authority.

Embarrassment quickly replaced shock and Cain stumbled back.

"Monsieur Barrington!" the constable exclaimed. "Sorry . . . Mercy Madonna, we did not know you were in here with a—"

"We're chasing a boy." Cain recovered first. He of course knew Lord Barrington, and his only thoughts now were that they absolve themselves from certain disaster. "Nigger runnin' and his horse is out there—he ran onto your ship!"

"A boy? Well gentlemen," Ram said, "I can assure you there's no boy in here."

"No, no, of course not. We're checking the rest of the ship but—" The constable retreated to call out to his men, "Find him?"

"Not yet" came a quick reply.

"Well, we'll get the boy yet. Sorry to disturb you. Very—"

"And how has a mere boy managed to be running Negroes?" Ram could not help but ask.

"Ah, it's the damnedest thing an' to hades if I know," the constable's words quickly burst into a string of fluent French curses.

"Sweetheart, this should only take a minute," Ram said, motioning the constable out before he moved.

"So, what happened?" he asked as he, too, stepped outside

172

and shut the door.

Cain explained as they stood on deck waiting for the others to return from the search, his voice raised to be heard above the yelps of the dogs, which Rake saw were kept on the road.

"We're from Garden Court—"

"Simone's place?"

"Aye, and we're missing a man and set the dogs out. Picked up the scent real quick, they did, and we were off. Three or so miles toward town the pack split. I was following the dogs on the road, and suddenly this boy leaps out from the forest. Ain't never in all my days seen a horse and rider like this, no sir. Well, we fired on him but missed. That horse runs right through the pack! Can you believe it?"

Ram assured him he could not. "Well, the chase was on. Then we come to the triple cross and hell, but turpentine's been spilt! Don't know how the boy spilt it when he's riding so hard and we're so close, but there it was. Then, finally the dogs pick up his scent again and we're on the road to town."

"Now"—Cain motioned with his pistol—"I didn't see it, but to hear it told, that horse went through town like bullet fire! Took a jump over cotton bales that I did see. Five feet if it's an inch!"

"Is that right?" Ram appeared but mildly interested, a dark brow lifting.

"Cleared the jump if you can believe it but fell about two miles after that. Came on him as he was jumping back on that horse. Chased him to here. Saw him go up the plank with my own eyes."

The men returned empty-handed. The constable swore and ordered them back. "He's on this ship somewhere! Find him!" And with more cursing, he left to search, too.

"What we can't figure," Cain said, "is what the boy has to do with our nigger? Must have given him a ride somewhere, but still, for the dogs to be this hot on his trail, you'd swear the horse was Jim Boy."

173

"I'd like to see that horse."

"Got away," Cain said. "That horse was lathered up real good but still got some fight left and reared up, then tore off."

"I see." And he did. He saw that to keep her safe he'd have to cast her neck in bronze so no one else could break it, least of all herself.

Joy waited nearly an hour before the door opened and Ram returned. She was so fraught with anxiety, she practically jumped him. "What happened?"

"What happened?" He leaned casually against the door. "Well, not finding a boy on board, they finally reasoned he'd jumped into the water and drowned. They're going to look for your body on the morrow. Right now they're headed back to where the pack originally split to start again. The dim wits abruptly realized a boy," he drawled, "could not have caused such mischief alone, so I sent some of my men with them to make certain their efforts are fruitless. Then I sent another group of men off on the Gainsport road, where I assume the good reverend and Sammy, along with this Jim Boy, will be found."

"Oh Ram—"

"No!" He held up a hand. "Don't thank me. I did it only to get the reverend's hide before the dogs do, which I will, for there's no excuse for idiocy, the unprecedented—" and on and on he went, swearing and cursing the reverend up one side and down the other, then turning on her. His voice rose with aristocratic viciousness, his arms waved violently as he stomped back and forth, stopping only to shake an accusing finger at her.

No one could listen to such a tirade and remain unaffected. Joy was no different. He was furious, yet the violence of his anger was not likely to be as deadly as a wild chase with pistols, men and dogs. So, while her head snapped at each thrash of his tongue and she was held mute and helpless, perhaps spellbound by the violence of his furious eruption, the increasingly gruesome nature of his threats, she nonetheless felt oddly relieved.

He stopped abruptly in the middle of his worst threat and seemed to lose wind all at once, mercifully finishing the sentence with a shake of his head. Then he sighed, leaned back against the wall and just stared at her.

Why couldn't she be like other women? Why couldn't she keep to her home, sitting about a fire, reading a book or engaged in embroidery, local gossip or music, or any of a hundred other pleasant, tranquil domestic activities? Why did she have to be running in and out of infirmaries where disease was rampant, writing those hell rising anonymous articles in the paper—he had recognized her words as easily as he would have recognized his own—and, the very worst, why does she have to ride at neck breaking speeds through the dark night, chased by dogs and men with pistols? A stunt few men would dare to save their own lives and yet here she stood, this small slip of a female, out to change the entire plight of the Negro race!

The rhetorical questions remained unanswered, fading slowly save one: Why did she have to be so lovely, standing there wrapped in a sheet? Each detail was studied: the long hair bound in pigtails that made her look so young, too young; the arch of thin brows over the wild, yet somehow bewildered, look in the large blue eyes with a shadow of thick lashes beneath; that small pointed nose, the tiny white teeth nervously biting the sweetest lips it was ever his misfortune to taste; the delicately pointed chin, the long neck leading to straight slender shoulders and the damnable sheet that now hid the beckoning curves of her small body, the startling beauty of which he had only moments to know.

The minutes ticked away in silence until suddenly, not understanding exactly why, she blurted, "I need some clothes—I have to go! The reverend will need me and—"

Ram did not respond past the barest hint of amusement that fought briefly with the intensity of his gaze. My God, the vixen would tempt the celibacy of the pope! Yet he could not, would not have her. He would not be her first, for it would mean being her only, and he had not the freedom to take that binding role. The day at the lake had been a mistake; he would not make another, at least if his feet could find the way to the door. The two steps felt like a climb to the highest peak of Mount Everest.

"Where are you going?" she asked as he turned away.

There never was an answer, just a lingering look of the dark mystery of his gaze. Then he was gone. She flung herself after him, reaching the door just as she heard it lock behind him. Locked! Trapped! She cried out, then screamed bloody murder, pounding furiously.

It was after a long hour of this, that she finally gave up and collapsed on his bed.

She'd kill him for this! Nay, murder was too good for the likes of—

She stopped suddenly as the maddening sweet scent of him filled her senses. She turned her face into the pillows, drinking the intoxicating scent. Like a potion, within minutes exhaustion claimed her as swiftly and surely as darkness had hit after her fall, and she was asleep.

# Chapter Six

Seanessy met Joy many times in the following weeks, always unexpectedly and usually when she was out riding. She delighted in his company, and for all his attention, it amounted to naught but a growing friendship and distraction from the ever mounting worries at home. He dropped his air of arrogant reserve, amusing her with his wit, charm and humor. They talked of many, many things—everything from the volatile politics of the day to thoroughbred racing spurs—yet it was the anecdotes from his and Ram's life she enjoyed the most. She learned a good deal more about Ram, refused to believe many of these tales but was entertained and amused nonetheless. Yet for all of Sean's unexpected friendship, she always felt as if she was the subject of his study, as though he watched her responses and measured her words much as a biologist might study little beasties under a microscope. She once questioned him about this, but all he said was: "But of course I study you, my dear. Each life is a piece of art, each person an artist. Your art is as delightful as it is interesting."

Oh how she thought and dreamt of Ram with the unceasing vigor of a young girl's first love, but for all of it, Sean explained Ram's avoidance of her with only those infuriating metaphors that forever strayed from her grasp.

She had not seen Ram since that night. The morning after, Bart had appeared with her clothes and the happy news that Ram had caught up with the reverend and Sammy, Jim Boy was put in a flatboat and brought safely to the ship and it was over. She didn't understand why Ram avoided her; her heart was burdened with it, and her diary was filled with alternate pages of sad guesses and wishful excuses.

Soon though, these things were only a backdrop for far more pressing events. Trouble grew and developed, finally shadowing their small dwelling like a dark cloud. She could not spare Ram, or indeed anyone, a thought. Joshua's health was worse still; Joy would not leave his side, not even as he slept, which seemed to be most of the time now. His shallow breathing continued to hold a raspy edge, and he no longer seemed to cough much. Doctor Morson began sidestepping her questions, leaving her only with the hope the bad period would end with recovery.

Joy thought of this as she watched his fitful rest, interrupted by those weak gasps for breath that one could no longer call a cough. She sat in a chair by his side. The dim light of a single lantern shone on an open book laying on her lap, though she could no more entertain herself with this favorite pastime than she could sing. Worry lined her brow as she stared anxiously at her loved one, thinking of the trouble mounting from another direction as well.

They were to be evicted in one week unless they came up with the three months' rent owed. Their landlord could afford no more excuses; his heart was hardened to their misfortune. They had no place to go, except to ask the charity of their friends, but even if they could take such a drastic position, they all agreed that to uproot Joshua at this time begged certain disaster. Besides this, there was medicine and food to buy. The food they could afford was meager indeed, and most of it, Cory, Joy and the reverend unanimously agreed, had to go to Sammy.

Two of the reverend's scams failed! None of them could

believe the ill-begotten luck of it! It seemed folks in the county were becoming suspicious of Reverend Doddered and his gambling. Gambling was the gentlemen's pastime of choice, especially among the French, and though a few ladies minded, most people accepted it as a fact that drinking went side by side with this famous pastime. However, once people realized the reverend combined the two vices with excessive regularity—mercy, but in a man of the cloth!—they began to talk. Quietly at first, as Mr. Reginald Templeton merely mentioned what he observed the good Reverend Doddered doing on a protestant Sunday—and after such a fine sermon!—but he made this observation to his wife, who had the inclination and nature to pass it along at her bridge club. Then, just as the sterling silver of his reputation was tarnished, many men began to notice that gambling with the fast talking reverend was as fruitful as betting on a lame horse.

The reverend was not discouraged, or if he was he didn't show it. "Oh hell and blazes—it was bound to happen sooner or later," he said as he discussed his plans to leave. "I've never stayed in one place long enough to find out. Don't worry darlin', all I got to do is head up fer the next parish, er . . . mayhaps the next one after that. I'll be back in time to shove the rent money in that greedy bastard's face. I promise."

So now the reverend was gone. It seemed like weeks but—

Cory knocked softly and opened the door to step inside. As soon as Joy met her eyes, she knew something horrible had happened. She rose, and the two stepped outside.

The fear and alarm in Cory's eyes said everything, and Joy almost didn't have to read the note just received at the door. The constable of Jefferson Parish got directly to the point: Two hundred dollars' bail or a seven year prison sentence after a week of public humiliation in the stocks. Immediate delivery or the sentence would be initiated no later than the first Monday next.

Tears filled Cory's eyes as Joy stared numbly at the note. Orleans Parish had banished the cruel injustice of the stockade many years ago, and it came as a shock to discover this low form of retribution existed elsewhere in her young progressive country. The bail must be got.

The bail might have been a thousand for the sum seemed that far from their reach. The back rent was due; the stables, pharmacist and practically every marketer in town was owed now. No further credit would be extended; they had not a penny. Mr. Farnsworth would never lend them two hundred dollars. One might beg charity from friends in the form of shelter and food, this was difficult enough, but one simply could not ask for the sum of money the letter demanded. Three days ago, in an act of desperation, Joy had lifted a chicken and some apples from the marketplace, all of which went to Sammy. They were living day to day on the small fish Cory and she occasionally caught and potatoes, and there were only a dozen of those left.

So, what to do? They had no credit, no income, no job. That left one thing; they must sell something. Joy had already parted with the last of Joshua's books and pictures, receiving only a quarter of their value. Oh God, what else did they have worth at least two hundred dollars?

"What we gonna do?" Cory asked in a frightened whisper. She first tried to stop herself; but the sting of tears filled her eyes, and without a thought, she fell into Joy's arms for comfort.

Joy stood there trying to comfort Cory, and it was then that the image emerged in her mind. Her thoughts spun, approaching the oh so obvious solution, hesitantly at first, with trepidation and then with shock. Shock that it had not come to her before this time!

Twilight settled over the landscape as Joy led Libertine past the stables, barn, kitchen and cold house and finally into the circular tree-lined drive leading to the Baxter's plantation house. Shells cracked beneath Libertine's hooves. The garden was neat and well tended by a dozen hands at least. The magnificent manor, two stories high, shaped in a rectangle, plastered and white washed with attractive green trim, so clean, grand and large, stood as a monument to the wealth of the planter class. This did not escape her, as a growing numbness settled in her heart, one allowing her to proceed. She dismounted and slowly marched up the wide steps to the door. The brass knocker fell twice. She heard footsteps, and Saul, their house man, swung open the door to greet her with surprise.

"Why Miss Reubens!" He looked behind her into the growing dusk, searching for an escort. "Missus Baxter and the chiluns are away visitin'. Dey won't be back for a spell an'—"

"I've come to call on Mr. Baxter," she said simply, finding it oddly difficult to say that much.

"Ohhh! Well dat's different, you'se step right in, Miss Reubens."

The whole proceeding took precious few minutes, most of this was spent in a shaky plea for cash rather than a bank statement. "Young lady, I simply cannot send you home with a purse holding this sum!"

"Please don't worry, sir," she whispered, just these few words cost her much. "Sammy's waiting outside and . . . and he is very competent with a pistol, you know."

Mr. Baxter hesitated a moment, then reluctantly stood to withdraw his cash box from behind the doors of a lovely hand-carved cedar cabinet.

Joy painfully enumerated many conditions, none of these were negotiable, but thankfully, Mr. Baxter made no argument. His was by no means the best offer she'd ever received, but she knew how he treated his stock and knew he wanted Libertine only to breed. She could trust him to keep the promise never to race her.

The last favor she asked was to see Libertine to the stables herself. Outside again, Joy took the reins and held the harness so tight it brought a dull ache up her arm. She would not cry. No matter what she would not cry.

Memories betrayed her though, spinning clear and vivid in her mind. She remembered the young thirteen-year-old girl presented with the green-broke colt on her birthday; she remembered crying then, somehow not able to stop. Of course the reverend had swindled the colt, but the owner had hardly cared. The ungainly beast was obviously an awkward creature: legs too long and shaky for its time, an ugly head size, an infuriating stubbornness to boot. She never knew enough about horses to perceive those damning faults; she only saw the wonder of a beautiful creature who would give wings to her dreams. No one believed that she, ignorant and so small, could train such a wild creature, but she had and effortless, for Libertine knew from the start that she belonged to Joy and Joy alone, the young girl with the gentle touch and the beckoning call of her laughter.

Wings to dreams . . .

Libertine sensed something amiss, and she tossed her head with agitation, neighing meanly as Joy led her into a clean stall. This was too much. The great horse bucked and reared, crying displeasure or for help, Joy did not know which, did not even wonder at how a creature could know what was happening. She didn't know anything but Libertine's pain, breaking through her numbness, bringing her own heartache rushing to the surface. She was suddenly clinging to Libertine's neck, and the great horse calmed and held still, as a hundred too many tears fell against the silken surface of her coat.

Libertine's frightened wails followed Joy onto the main road, and she walked over a mile before she realized her hands still covered her ears. She took a deep shaky breath, lifted her shawl over her head like a hood and slowly began home. Tears fell unheeded to the ground, where each step on the cold earth reminded her of whom she left behind.

Three miles later, after passing only one lone rider and two Cajun fishermen who gave her no notice, she heard the sound of riders coming from the north. The six mounted men were loud and boisterous, filled with the night's success and shenanigans, and more than one brandy cask was passed between them. With her head lowered in sadness, she never ventured a glance up, even as she stepped to the far side of the road to let them pass.

Ram reined his mount to a halt, and Seanessy stopped at his side while the five others stopped behind. Ram would not normally notice women on the road, especially as her face was lowered and hidden in the darkness. Any one would assume that the woman was a serving wench or worse, a woman ruined long ago, stripped of virtue and caring so as to have nothing to lose by venturing a lonely walk on a deserted road.

Yet what alerted him was the very smallness of her waist, a close enough approximation of her height. "Seanessy, Seanessy," he chuckled meanly, "tell me it isn't her, not on this of all nights, out walking on this deserted road, alone when I'm feeling the devil's own—" Ram handed the brandy cask back and said with another laugh. "Well, you know what I'm feeling."

The familiar voice brought her eyes up, but they lowered quickly again. She felt a tremor of fear, yet nothing that could ride over the numbness in her heart. Her sadness was personal; she wanted only to be left alone with it.

Accepting the cask and after a long draught, Seanessy's laughter filled the night air, too. "My dear lord, while it is my life's single wish to serve you, I'm afraid that small lovely creature standing there inhibits my time honored duty. Alas, I can offer no assurance it is not she."

Laughing, Ram pressed his horse to her side, and without bothering to dismount, he leaned over and reached gloved hands around her waist, lifting her easily to his saddle.

Unwilling or unable to look up, she stumbled ineptly through the start of a greeting. "Oh Ram . . . I—" before her voice dropped with the effort.

His body tensed, stiffened, and with a previously unknown fear, he saw the tears in the dim light of the half-moon. A cold blade sliced quickly and too easily into his heart; the pain was searing as he brought her face up. He'd kill them, that was all. Whoever hurt her would pay, and it was all he could do to control his voice to ask, "Has someone hurt you?"

Seanessy was at his side, and he, too, felt every fiber of his body tense to await her answer.

"No, no." She shook her head. "I'm fine. I—"

"Why then are you crying, sweetheart?"

His hand gently wiped her cheeks, then returned to surround her as both hands gathered the reins to check his horse. Those arms, his nearness threatened her with a promise of comfort, and she struggled to resist, to control her tears. She shook her head again. "Oh, it's . . . nothing, really . . . I—" She bit her lip hard enough to draw blood, unable and unwilling to say more.

Something had broken her heart, and he would know what it was. "What are you doing out here alone? And where is that horse of yours?"

She stared up at him, alarmed. She could not venture the explanation, though her eyes dropped to the purse clutched tightly in her hands. Ram took the purse and opened it to see the contents, then with a soft curse he brought her un-resisting form against his chest.

"Who'd you sell her to?" he finally asked. "The Baxters down there?"

She nodded, and as though she needed to justify her choice, she whispered, "He promised me he'd never abuse her or put spurs to her, and that . . . that he would never see her in a race."

Still holding her, he turned to Sean. "You will do me

the favor?"

"Ah." Sean smiled. "But of course. Should there be a limit?"

"I don't know why you even bother to ask me that."

"Only because the bastard does not deserve to profit. But as you wish." Sean smiled and motioned to the men to follow as he rode off.

Lost to him in the warmth and comfort of his arms, Joy hardly listened to the conversation that did not concern her. "I'll take you home," Ram said, "and you will tell me what has happened to make you part with that creature you love so much."

Unconsciously having taken to toying with a button on his shirt, she looked up. "I thought you would think me silly and childish—"

"For what? Attaching such soft sentiments to an animal?" He smiled down at the tears and said in a voice of fond tenderness, "Joy, I have only to think of Rake to know. How can one wonder at our attachment to animals? It's not just how they depend on us, soliciting any and all propensity we have to care for things, but unlike humans, animals give their devotion unconditionally; they give everything and ask for so little in return." He had stopped his mount again so that his hand might freely caress her face as he spoke. "I know how much you love her, how you trained her yourself and care for her. So, what forced you to sell her?"

She shook her head and lowered her eyes, as fresh tears sparkled there. "Oh Ram, I shouldn't burden you with . . . our troubles—"

"No, sweetheart, don't hide from me like that. I would know what's wrong."

The reverend's fate came out in bits and pieces of broken sentences until finally he grasped what happened, letting her know it with sudden vicious curses.

"Oh no." She stopped him in alarm. "Don't be angry with him . . . he had to do it; he was doing it for us." She saw she would have to explain further to justify the reverend's actions. Ram stopped the mount as more of the story came out. He pressed her for all of it, his questions allowed nothing to be kept back. And then he was furious.

Furious with himself. He had kept himself ignorant and away from her family, all to selfishly avoid the damnable and unwanted temptation she presented, only to find this disaster upon those slender shoulders. His only excuse was that while he knew they were poor—one had only to view her clothes or step into their small house to know—he had thought Joshua had a decent enough income.

The whole thing was easy to settle and of no import. What was far harder to dismiss was how it felt to hear of her struggle, to realize she had been begging positions in another man's house, though he didn't wonder why such a valiant attempt at that kind of position failed. She carried the family burden alone and without help. Where the hell was Joshua and— "God girl," he suddenly demanded when she was through, "why didn't you come to me?"

She looked up in shock, then away to shake her head. "Ram, you know I couldn't. I never even thought to appeal—" She stopped and thought to ease his worry. "Please don't worry. It's all over now." She glanced down at the purse. "I can pay the reverend's bail plus the rent, and there's bound to be enough to buy some medicine and food . . ."

They were nearing the outskirts of the city, and again he stopped the horse, alarmed as he saw the drawn and thin features in a new light. She looked all eyes suddenly, large dark blue eyes. It was masochistic to ask, and he was afraid of the answer. "When was the last time you ate?"

She looked away, embarrassed, attempting to dismiss his concern with a wave of hand. "Oh, Cory and I don't need much, and naturally Joshua and Sammy come first—"

"Sweetheart, you're not telling me something. Even if you would not come to me for some mistaken idea of propriety, I

186

know Joshua would, at least before he saw you and Cory go without food."

Then he saw it. Fresh tears filled her eyes, and he knew he had finally reached the real burden she carried. "He doesn't know, does he?"

She shook her head.

"Does he know any of it? Is he that bad?"

Again she shook her head. "Yes, he's worse of late . . . I couldn't tell him . . . I was afraid . . ."

He took her back into his arms and held her tightly again as his lips brushed across her forehead and his hands tenderly ran through her hair. She cried softly against him, her sadness and pain pleading somehow with the very strings of his heart, his response alarming him with its intensity.

"Now though"—she wiped her eyes and pulled away slightly—"I can pay off the pharmacist and get more medicine and, and I haven't checked in a week; but maybe he has something new from the continent and with proper food—"

"Joy sweetheart." He stopped her, cupping her face in his hands, staring at the hope sparkling through the tears in her eyes. He saw now what Joshua had meant. In his past visits with her guardian, he had found much to respect and admire in the man. The quickness and depth of their intimacy sprung from the press of time of a man facing the imminent arrival of his death. Joshua himself had faced the certainty of his death some time ago; his condition was hopeless, the suffering it brought made death welcome. Joshua's only fear—and this was a great one—was for Joy. Joy's future seemed so uncertain; her character and countenance were patently ill-suited for the docility of domestic life of marriage—how Ram knew the truth of this—and despite the benevolence of her motivation, her wildness constantly flirted with danger and certain ruin. What man was strong enough, Joshua had asked him, yet gentle enough to temper those failings by the act of marriage?

187

These worries were secondary, however, to Joshua's primary concern, a concern Ram now faced in the plain hope shining in those eyes. Joshua's main fear was Joy's inability to face his death, this after he, the reverend, Sammy and once at Joshua's coaching, even Cory, had all attempted to prepare her for the inevitable. She steadfastly refused to believe it and in a way that alarmingly portended of her devastation when it finally came.

She waited for what he would say, entertaining an idea he was about to rescue her by adding some happy new hope, some clever doctor he knew or a miracle medicine he had come across in his travels.

"Joy, medicines don't matter anymore." He spoke as gently as he could, "Joshua's not going to be getting well again."

He might have just spoken tongues for the sudden incomprehension lifting on her face. She shook her head, slowly at first, but then violently.

"That's not true! How can you say such a thing?" Pushing from his arms, she slid quickly off his horse onto the ground, then backed away, still shaking her head. "He has to get better! He has to! Joshua's all I have in the world, he's all I—"

"Joy!"

It was too late. She turned and ran from him, disappearing down the dark street into her house. Ram did not pursue her; this was the one thing he could not fix or change. Long after she was gone though, he remained staring after her with the echo of her small running boots ringing in his mind. Thoughts spun in many directions but finally settled on a point of alarm.

This one girl with the long brown hair and eyes like openings to a summer sky, a pretty package of a hundred or so pounds and of nothing but trouble, had worked her way quite easily into his heart.

He had never been a man to entertain a "what if"; he had

always taken what life had given him, working from there with his visions. Not once, he realized, had he ever wasted a moment on a "what if." Until now.

What if he could marry her? Had this passage in life been open to him, no doubt he would have already been married by this point—if not for love, simply to have some woman bear him children. Cold and unfeeling perhaps, but the truth, for in all his years he had never been touched by that one poetic sentiment for a woman. Since the tender age of ten, he had known that love would be a luxury he could never afford, for if he did any one thing in this life, it would be to stop the Barrington name with his death.

After all these years, this young girl slips into his life; and using only the music of her laughter, the wonder of her tears and the maddening tease of her innocence, she merely touches the iron wall surrounding his heart, and like the touch of sun upon morning frost, it starts to melt.

"Joy Claret, you are a grave danger to me," he said out loud as he swung off the horse. He removed his boots and shirt, stuffing these carelessly into his saddle bag and after slapping his mount hard to send him on his way, he started running, running long and hard into the dark that was the night.


Strange dreams visited Joy through the night, dreams of a wise old woman calling to her with silent words. She dreamed of Ram kissing and loving her, gently comforting her with his strength but then suddenly transforming into a dark shape that shouted at her, raising his hand to strike her, and she was running and running from him—she could not let him catch her, but Libertine!

Libertine, Libertine, where are you?

She woke with a start, and upon encountering the morning light, the dream faded into the dark recesses of her mind, though she struggled with long seconds of disorientation. The events of last night came back to her and with them the near debilitating burden of her loss. Grief filled her, overwhelming the queasy gnaw her hunger had lately become, and she rose unsteadily. There was much to be done. She had slept in the study to be near Joshua, and seeing he still slept peacefully enough, she felt ease at having to leave him for a time.

She woke Sammy and Cory and hurriedly went about dressing. It had been arranged last night. Sammy would leave immediately with the bail money. The day from work would cost him an added two weeks of indentured service, but there was nothing to be done about it. She would go to the landlord, pharmacist and market, while Cory stayed to care for Joshua. It would be over today. Over save for the price her heart had paid.

Cory and Joy met Sammy in the small parlor to see him off. Few words were spoken and all looked solemn and weary. "I'se be back on the morrow, but I suppose I'll be goin' straight off to work. So, I don't reckon I see you'se two till night. Take care of Joshua now."

Joy nodded and kissed his cheek, too numb, sad and hungry to say anything, even goodbye. Grabbing her shawl, she followed him outside, bumping right into his huge back as Sammy suddenly stopped dead. There she confronted the surprise, but as it was such a surprise, she couldn't at first make sense of it. Cory stepped outside, too, and had anyone been watching, they would have been three people standing in mute shock at the boxes and boxes of foodstuff piled beneath the awning of their small house, spilling out onto the street.

The golden morning sunlight slanted across the nearly deserted street, and the air was still and quiet, until Sammy's deep laughter sounded. He rubbed his chin with the wonder of it, shaking his head. Cory knelt down to cautiously peep inside a box. Frantically, Joy searched up and down the street for an explanation. A maid pounded a rug with a broom, and turning the corner, an early vendor called out strawberries for sale but that was all.

There were waist-high sacks marked flour, sugar, wheat and corn, enough to last a year! There were boxes and boxes of produce, fresh market vegetables and fruit, two buckets of molasses—a treat they had not had in a year. There was bread already made, and meat: a whole side of bacon, another of beef, two turkeys and one, two three, four chickens, far more than their small cold house out back had ever held! There was all this plus a hundred small, medium and large brown sacks of things yet undiscovered!

Cory picked a plum and bit into the juicy fruit, giggling and ripping open the huge sack of sugar, wetting her finger to taste.

"Cory May!" Joy cried in a whisper, still looking anxiously up and down the street. "That's not ours!"

"Well then, why is it in front of our house? Do you see anyone else's with a porch full of food?"

Grasping the logic of this, Joy abruptly knew their benefactor. "Ram did this," she gasped. "He's responsible!"

"And I'll be a thankin' him as soon as I finish feastin'!" Sammy laughed, already lifting a box and carrying it inside.

It was like a Michaelmas morning, and she was suddenly laughing too, ripping into packages, tasting and eating. Cory threw the first handful of sugar and Joy tossed a sticky clump of molasses and the fight was on.

Cory could have passed for white and Joy looked like a sugared cookie, giving as good as she got. They were covered head to foot in sugar, wrestling now, with Joy laughing so hard she fell to the ground, only to have Cory jump her, stuffing grapes in her mouth amidst her peels of giggles.

Riding up the street, Ram and Sean came upon this happy scene. Sean's laughter rang out as a magnificent sound, but Ram stopped his mount and just stared. Then, without a word of explanation, he turned away and disappeared. Sean understood perfectly; it was too much, but then Joy Claret was always too much.

Cory greeted Sean with a smile of white teeth that perfectly matched her powdered skin, and she rose, pulling Joy to her feet, too. Too giddy and happy to be embarrassed, Joy was just about to run to Sean with gushes of gratitude for Ram when she saw what Sean had in rein.

"Libertine" came as a hushed whisper as her hands covered her mouth. She stood there in shock, staring with wide anxious eyes. Libertine sensed her presence and neighed excitedly, tossing her head high in an obvious willingness to forgive her mistress everything. Libertine's call could not be resisted.

Sean watched as Joy was reunited with her horse. For long tender moments, she kept her face buried in Libertine's neck as she caressed, petted and whispered to her. The young lady's love of animals—her love of all life—had certainly been a deciding factor in his decision, these things second only to Ram's unsurpassed desire. A love for life was the most essential part of femininity; the God-given virtue was especially important when a woman had sons, for masculine aggression was a deadly thing indeed when left untempered by the virtue of caring and respect for life. He and Ram had his own mother to thank for the imparting of this.

Joy Claret had this virtue in proportions so startling that it seemed to define her very person. It was not just her heroic efforts to free people of color, or her desire to save her friends from ruin or indeed any one thing. Rather, it seemed present in everything she touched, everything she was.

The decision was settled one day when Sean had chanced to see her with children. They were out riding and came upon two young boys playing in the woods with slingshots. One of the boys hit a bluebird, injuring it without the mercy of a kill. Joy never scolded; she simply held the suffering creature in her hands and told them, almost word for word, what his mother had told Ram and himself a day long ago, until the horror and sadness in the young lad's eyes told Joy they felt the needless pain and suffering they had caused. Then she gave the two boys the same penalty his mother had given them: They must care for the bird until its wing healed and promise never to kill any creature unless it was to put food on the table.

He had smiled to himself, still remembering King Henry, the pet Ram and he had made of the squirrel.

Still caressing Libertine, Joy tried to understand. Did Sean borrow Libertine from Mr. Baxter to give her a last ride? Could he not guess that it would be crueler, to part twice, rather than once? "I don't understand," she said slowly, turning to him. "Did you borrow her from Mr. Baxter?"

"My dear girl! Ram never borrows, he purchases what he wants."

"Ram bought my horse from Mr. Baxter?"

"Why, of course. You can't imagine Ram would let that undeserving wretch lay hands upon something you love?"

She turned back to Libertine, not quite understanding why Ram would do so but happy he did. She knew Ram owned a fairly renowned stable in England. No doubt he wanted Libertine for breeding, too. She trusted Ram explicitly, and furthermore, she suspected Ram would let her ride Libertine, perhaps often. If she could raise the money before he took Libertine away—perhaps with an agreement that he could take Libertine's first colt—"Oh Sean, do you think that someday, if I were to make the money, Ram and I could reach an agreement—that he might sell her back to me?"

Sean laughed at this. "I can state with authority that Ram would not ever—under any circumstances—sell you this horse."

She was instantly wounded by this.

"Joy," he sighed. Then stated more gently, "You're being rather dense about this. Ram bought Libertine as a present for you; Libertine belongs to you, no one else."

Her eyes widened, then she turned back to Libertine, suddenly speechless. She couldn't believe it! She backed slowly into her creature, needing support.

Sammy stepped alongside Cory and took Cory's hand in his, as they both watched with wide smiles of wonder at the morning's change in the family's fortune. Cory's eyes filled with happy tears, for she better than anyone knew what Libertine meant to Joy.

Gathering her wits, Joy slowly shook her head. She could not accept such a generous gift; there was just no way she could accept. Accepting food when one was hungry was one thing but this quite another. A young lady could not accept such outrageous generosity from a gentleman who claimed no familial relationship.

"I can't accept such a gift; he knows I can't."

"Ah." Sean smiled. "Ram said you would say that. He said to say, if you do not accept the present, he will personally take a pistol to her head and see the hide made into chicken feed."

Sammy suddenly laughed.

"He can't do that!" Joy cried, then changed her mind, "He wouldn't do that!" But she was not sure.

"Ah, but he can, and what's more is I can guarantee he would. In case you doubt it, I might add that making chicken feed of your lovely beast would not even rank in the top five most notorious deeds committed by your benefactor. The choice is yours my dear; I have only laid it at your feet."

He said it with both irony and sarcasm, and Joy spent several minutes weighing the possibilities. He could do the dastardly thing! He would do it! He was just that cruel and mean!

The fierceness of her love for Libertine made her believe Ram capable of it; she had no choice. Who could possibly fault her for the breech of propriety when the alternative was so terrible? Certainly not Sammy or Cory, who stepped forward to share her happiness and tears, all of which was

Sean's pleasure.

Joy immediately began pressing Sammy to let her take the money to Jefferson Parish, enumerating all the benefits such as saving Sammy weeks of his life, the speed with which Libertine could take her—

"I'm afraid you're all too late," Sean interrupted. "Ram sent a man last night with the bail. The reverend should already be making his way home. I should probably explain the rest. Ram, being ever thorough, yet a man of great discretion, has seen all your debts paid and with credit added. It took two men to do it, so I don't imagine any place was missed." He smiled down at Sammy. "This includes your employer, too. I believe your book with that man has been balanced."

They were shocked, dumbstruck, overwhelmed, each in his own way. Cory, young and unaffected, was struck with the wonder of it, suddenly seeing Ram Barrington as a kind of larger than life Saint Nicholas, a man whose kindness and generosity was too huge to fathom. The reality that all their troubles had been banished by a single sweep of Ram Barrington's hand—especially Sammy's sentence!—was plain in her happy heart.

Sammy's head lowered; he could not look up at Sean, whose presence substituted for Ram Barrington's. He didn't know what to say; he didn't know what he could say. Never, with the exception of Joshua, when the doctor had saved him as they had saved Jim Boy from the certain death of the turpentine swamps, had his life met such kindness. The gratitude he felt soaring through him oddly was owed not just to the fact that the family burden had been lifted from his back, but also to the fact that he was no longer alone in his effort to care for those he loved. Another, more capable man was helping now.

Whatever Sammy wanted to express in the form of gratitude was there as he turned his back to wipe the first tears he had shed in many long years.

195

"Sean," Joy whispered, "I don't know what to do . . . I don't know how we can thank him . . . I—"

"My dear." Sean chuckled at this. "Had you an idea of how you might thank him, I dare say he wouldn't have done it."

He saw more had to be said though. Sean tried to put Ram's generosity in perspective, explaining how money had absolutely no meaning to Ram. "I could name the size of his personal income—plus the supplementary income derived from his properties and investments, which are at least a hundred or two times that amount—but the figure would have little meaning to you three, though perhaps this will: Each year Ram gives at least six-tenths of his income to poor houses in England, India and a few in Boston. No money goes to hospitals, but an impressive amount is given to doctors studying medicine. The remainder goes into investment, all to give the world a larger store of charity next year. So what you've received today is—how do you Americans say it? Not—"

"Even a drop in the bucket." Sammy managed to supply.

"Yes." Sean finished his speech, reiterating again that money was of no value to Ram, except when as today it could buy happiness. Then Sean refused to listen to a single protest, and needing to be alone with Cory, he urged Sammy off to work and Joy off to the pharmacist.

"Cory May." He sat her down in the sunshine of the small parlor after all the food stuffs were in. "I need to speak to you about something."

Cory was all happy attention.

"Something unpleasant I'm afraid."

Cory's face dropped in quick alarm. Her happiness was so complete, the thoughts of Sammy, of at least three happy days doing nothing but cooking with Joy and all. She did not want this happiness ruined.

"Oh, nothing that bad," Sean added quickly. He knelt in front of her to be at eye level and took her hands in his. "I just

196

need to caution you and Joy. You see," he feigned solemnity, "there's this disease going around. It only strikes young women, and the first sign of it is that their monthly bleeding stops. When was the last time you and Joy passed it?"

Cory's eyes fell with the shame of a man's mention of the unmentionable.

"Oh come now, Cory May, don't be a ninny. I specifically addressed you with this concern rather than Joy because Joy's sensibilities are too . . . ah, delicate." He bit his lip. "I'm almost a married man," he lied, "and married men know about these things."

She looked up in surprise. "Dey do?" she asked curiously. If Sammy married her, would he guess this secret—would he know, too?

"Ah, this and more." Sean smiled at her. "Now, when was the last?"

"Are you sure I can be tellin'?" she asked shyly, hesitantly.

"It's for your own good, my dear."

Cory wondered if he did know about such secret things, if maybe he could answer a question. "Well, hit's queer, but Joy and I'se wonder each month 'bout it, cause hers and mine come on the 'sact same day. Yes, hit's true, every month, just lak clockwork, and we'se never missed, not once and dis is it: It comes on the first day of the full moon."

"Every month?"

She nodded solemnly.

It made the whole thing too easy, too blessed easy. "So"— he looked away with a smile, a curious arch of his brow—"it shall be the night of the new moon . . ."

Cory looked confused. "No, the full moon."

Sean waived his hand in dismissal, said something nonsensical, then explained that when two female souls touched, it sometimes had this curious effect. "Not to worry," he added, "while the first sign of the disease is a missed bleeding, it never amounts to more than a minor bout with the flu, that is if it is treated in time. I know the cure, so

197

if at anytime you or Joy happen to miss, you come straight to me with the information."

Cory made the promise to do just that.

Sean now had the date; the next moonless night. All that was really left was the fervent hope that Joy Claret's belief in the sanctity of life was strong enough to save Lord Ramsey Edward Barrington III's first child.

# Chapter Seven

Joy rode out to the long narrow path that branched from the main road and eventually led to the open, tree-shaded glen growing out from the mossy banks of her small lake—the lake where she was to meet Sean, a lake with a memory as vivid as the day it happened. Libertine stepped into the open space, and Joy stopped her, dazzled as always by the splendid colors of nature's garden. The air was still fragrant with the scent of wild flowers, though the long hot summer gave way at last. The rainy season would soon be upon them; a chill bit the morning air.

She abruptly spotted Sean, already sitting in wait for her on a dark blue quilt beneath the shade of a willow tree. It surprised her, for she was an hour earlier than the designated time of his note. She slipped from Libertine's back, letting her horse roam and graze with Sean's mount. Greeting him with a warm smile, she first moved to the water, kneeling to splash the cool liquid over her face, neck and hands. As he watched this, it made him remember Ram once saying, "Her every movement causes me agony."

Well, my lord, you shall finally lay your agony to rest, he smiled to himself.

"What is it, Sean?" she said happily, as she sat upon his soft blue blanket. "I came as soon as I could—" She stopped, noticing it then; there was something amiss. It was written on his face; a serious shine showed in his gaze, and she realized with small alarm that this was the first time he neither smiled or laughed at her. "What's wrong?"

"What's wrong?" he seemed to ask himself, glancing briefly away with the question before returning to her. "The time has come my dear. I have a proposition I must put to you. You will find it insulting, no doubt a breech of our trust and friendship. You will likely hate me for making it."

She listened, staring with confusion, then suddenly smiled. "You are teasing me again—"

"I am not."

She remained unconvinced, dismissing him with a wave of her hand and another smile. "How could I ever hate you? What could make me?"

"I must lead up to it with the question," he said, then fell silent for a long moment. Finally she heard: "Do you have any idea of how much Ram wants you?"

The word "want" meant "cared for" in her mind and she blushed. "I think you're very mistaken," she replied softly, sadness plain. "Ram does not want my society. With Joshua so well of late, I've been to see him many times these last weeks to personally thank him. He is always too busy to receive me, either engaged with other company or gone, and once Bart said he was not there, when I overheard him speaking to someone. I think he tries to avoid seeing me altogether."

Sean's smile seemed suddenly gentle. "Joy, he avoids you because he wants you. Don't you see, he cannot resist the temptation you present."

She wanted desperately to deny this. Modesty demanded she deny it, and yet, she knew Ram did try to avoid her. There was no reason for this, except if what Sean said was the truth. "Has he ever told you this?" she asked in a whisper.

"Many times." Sean chuckled, laying down on his side, and rested on an elbow with his booted legs stretched over the blanket. He toyed with a long piece of water reed. "Ram absolutely refuses to take your innocence. You do know what I mean by that?"

She nodded because she did know; she knew from Ram's kisses, the things he said when he stopped, and this easily met the facts she knew about the physical aspect between a man and a woman. What shocked her was Sean's broach of the subject; it was a breech of decency and propriety, surely in want of discretion.

She could never understand exactly how both Ram and Sean, their men as well, made any polite illusions to propriety seem like farce or even a joke, and true, when she was in their company, she often found herself trespassing without thought.

This though was somehow different. Something in the calculation of Sean's stare, even more than his words, bid her to leave quickly. The only thing stopping her was the fact that she trusted Sean's friendship explicitly.

Sean waved a mosquito from her face and said quietly, "If you do understand this, then I can address my proposition directly: I will have you give your innocence to Ram as my gift."

She stared hard with widening eyes. "What can you mean?"

The shock in those eyes told him all; he knew she understood perfectly. "I believe, my dear, your innocence has in fact finally failed you."

Joy wished—oh how she wished—her innocence could shield her from those outrageous words! It did not though; she understood the words perfectly. What she could not understand—not for her life—was how or why he thought she could, or even how Sean thought she would, sit to listen to it! "You go too far, Sean," she said, rising to her feet. "I don't know why, but you have gone much too far."

She started quickly for her horse.

Sean only smiled as he said, "In return for this, I shall buy you the freedom of three people of your choosing at the marketplace tomorrow."

Joy stopped dead in her tracks as her mind encountered, greeted and measured those awful words. The sounds of the forest seemed suddenly loud and shrill: the creek rushing over its muddied gulley to feed the pond, the screech of distant birds, a noisy scramble of a lizard at her feet, even the crackle of bush under Libertine's hooves in the distance. She heard everything, but nothing; her consciousness suddenly exaggerated in a desperate attempt to escape those words.

"Sean" the name was uttered in a whispered plea. "Why are you doing this to me?"

"I cannot tell you now," he replied as he came to stand behind her. "My reason will be discovered in the future, and someday, I hope you will be able to forgive me for it. For now we shall leave it at my desire to give Ram a gift." The gift of his life, he thought.

She turned to him then. She saw immediately he wasn't going to tell her the reason, no matter how she pleaded. It made no sense why he should do this, past wanting to give Ram something he had no right to. Nothing made sense, nothing but the shocking proposition.

The freedom of three human beings in return for her virtue. It was a small price indeed, and as the proposition stood, there existed only one answer. So it was proposition itself that she addressed. "Is there nothing that I can say to make you withdraw this . . . to make you give me those three people without my part?" It was a cry for help, but the very questions answered his. "Oh Sean." Her eyes pleaded desperately. "Please . . . I can't . . . I—"

"What you can't do is refuse; your conscience—ah, what a wonderful thing—will forbid you to refuse. I can add the rest; I won't let you sit with it. For tomorrow, you will pay with tonight. Tonight, my dear—" and now he smiled as he quietly pointed out—"the night of a new moon."

Upon arriving home, she informed them that at the

market she had met Madame Beauchamp, who had reported that a small mishap—a sprained ankle—had confined Katie to bed for a spell. An invitation had been extended in the natural hope Joy's company would ease the tedium of her friend's convalescence.

Cory felt uneasy, even suspicious. Something was wrong; something was just not as it seemed. Joy was not at all herself. She spent nearly two hours just sitting in the wooden basin used for bathing, this after using a whole bottle of lavender water the reverend had given them for Christmas. Then, too, she said nothing, refusing Cory's every attempt to talk.

Cory's discomfort grew as she waited with Joy in the parlor for the Beauchamp's carriage. Joy still stared numbly into space as if . . . as if she saw ghosts dancing in a graveyard! She simply could not attribute Joy's worry to a concern over Katie's mishap. Joshua was not the cause; he was better than he had ever been. Why, he sat up most of the day in the parlor. He ate well, rarely complained and seemed happy, even reading again! So what troubled her so?

The carriage was finally heard, and Joy rose quickly, bid Cory goodbye and left. Left Cory wondering still. Must be something 'bout mister lord high and mighty hisself, for dat's only person who could upset her so much.

Outside, Joy ascended a carriage that was not the Beauchamp's. No one seemed to notice. The door was shut, and she was whisked quickly, noisily away. Sean's presence seemed to consume the carriage; he was too large for the small space, though as always he seemed comfortable and at ease. She wished she could hate him. She wondered if that might make it easier. Yet the only thing that made the night in any way approachable was the solemn thought of three unsuspecting people waiting for tomorrow.

"You're very frightened, my dear. Here—" He handed her a cask. "It might help a bit."

She took a long sip, then coughed as the hot liquid burned

203

and choked, finally bursting like fire in her stomach. Sean chuckled and the familiar laughter affected her at least as much as the spirits.

Sean could never say why, but he noticed her reticule. He lifted it from her lap and opened it to find a night dress and a hair brush. The two items gave him a long moment's pause, and though he couldn't laugh presently, he looked forward to the day when he would tell Ram what she thought necessary on this, the first night in his bed.

He looked forward to the day when Ram, too, would laugh at it.

"Is something amiss?" she asked shyly.

"Nothing my dear." He turned to the reason he was escorting her into this auspicious night. "I didn't want to discuss it earlier; I didn't want to frighten you any more than you so obviously are. I must warn you, though. Ram will not be pleased when he discovers your deception."

Sean had already explained the necessity of her deception, of lying about her innocence, and this was perhaps the worst part. The only reason she could bare deceiving Ram was the idea he would never learn of it. "But how will he know?" She asked with alarm lifting on her face. "Will you tell him?"

A curious brow lifted, but then he realized the trouble. "Ah, it is your ignorance. Joy," he explained, "your innocence will be discovered in the act."

She lifted her eyes, suddenly wide with fear. "But I understood that such is not always the case; that a man can't always know?"

Sean would not explain Ram had more than enough experience to discover the only virgin ever to lay in his bed. "If he does discover it though," he said instead, "he will be angry. And Ram's anger is rather like a large sleeping monster, upon waking it grows and grows, long before it begins to retreat. You, my dear," he said solemnly, "are in no way capable of handling him like that. He would swallow you whole. I want his anger directed at me; I'm the only person who has any chance of handling his anger. So at the very first appearance of it, you are to leave, escape with any pretext—simply run from him. Do you understand?"

Her face paled, and she swallowed hard but nodded. Escape was one thing she was good at. Nothing more was said. The minutes passed uncomfortably as the carriage moved quickly to its destination. To calm herself, Joy forced her thoughts to the three people she would be saving by this night.

Three human beings! Three—her mind stopped at the number—it seemed so arbitrary. It was arbitrary! Just as the carriage came to an abrupt stop at the ship, she grasped her reticule tightly to stop her trembling and blurted the number, "Six! I'll have six."

Sean only chuckled. "Ah, I knew you would try. I was willing to grant you the first number you tried. Six it is, but no more. As comfortably vulgar as my fortune is, I can ill afford freedom for every wretch in Louisiana."

The driver opened the door, and Sean escorted her down then guided her up the plank to the ship, ignorant all the way of the magnitude of her emotions brought on by his words.

All she suddenly knew was a certain horror at the limits of her imagination. Why hadn't she asked for a larger number? Each added number meant one person's freedom, one person's life! Why oh why didn't she say ten or even twenty? Would Sean have agreed? Yes! Sean was quite wealthy, too. He owned three ships, an estate in Ireland, and he had once shown her the pictures he had transported aboard his ship. Just this small representation of his collection was worth a fortune. Oh God, why didn't she say twenty?

If she could only relive those last moments—

Consumed with these thoughts, she never noticed how much Sean had arranged. The *Ram's Head* was all but deserted, only two men remained on guard, and after greeting Sean, their attention returned at once to their dice. Sean led her beneath the quarter deck to the captain's quarters and opened the door, but went no further.

"Ram should be back within the hour." The last thing he said was, "Rest easy, my lady." He kissed her affectionately goodbye and shut the door.

The door shut, closing in on her numbness. She stared at the closed door, forcing herself not to open it and run in panic. She had no idea how long she remained frozen on the spot where Sean had left her, perhaps over half an hour; but abruptly she imagined Ram was already there, watching her, and she spun around with the horror of it.

The spacious and magnificent room greeted her with silence, though Ram's presence showed in every place she looked. She had seen his quarters twice before, and her impression remained, accented by the darkening light. A single lamp glowed from above his enormous rosewood desk, casting the room in a golden color that made the rich shades of maroon and dark blue in the fine tapestry rug, the bed quilt and the drapes, darker, muted, softer. Yet the blatant masculinity of the room seized her, threatening, yet mysterious.

She frantically looked for some single feminine touch, a bouquet of flowers, a sunny shade. Her gaze moved from the long dining table to the bookcase and back to the bed. There was no sign.

For the love of freedom!

She nervously bit her lip, swallowing her fear. What was a solitary night compared to six lives of freedom? Virtue was a small price indeed!

She walked slowly to the oversized bed, staring at the patched-velvet maroon and blue quilt, and for a moment, she tried to imagine the scene that was to happen there. A hand glided over the thickly bound drapes. She touched her mouth, remembering all too well his kisses, that strange surge of warmth rising through her, and she felt her pulse suddenly race, a tingling sensation of nervous anticipation.

Sean's instructions had been explicit. Hands trembling,

she began to remove her clothes, feeling so oddly close to tears.

For the love of freedom . . .

Like dominoes falling, three appointments had been cancelled, and Ram found a long night stretched before him, open, free and waiting to be filled. The unexpectedness of it brought him the familiar restlessness, as if his energies needed a place to be spent, and the idea brought a chuckle. He'd go for a long run and swim, then tackle some of the work on his mechanical device—a mechanism that would greatly help in the iron mills—perhaps finishing the rare evening with a book.

Ram reached his ship, and seeing there was no one about to take his mount, he tied the stallion to a post and followed Rake up the plank. A nearly deserted ship greeted him. He bantered briefly with the two men left on guard, discovering the whole of his crew had been challenged to a drinking match by Seanessy's men at none other than the Red Barn.

Ram laughed, for it had been a very long time since the last match. The two crews, each fiercely competitive with the other, yet loyal to the end—not one man on either side wouldn't lay his life on the line to save another on the other side—worked out their competitive antagonism and aggressions with these match fights.

Sean and he had developed the means of match fighting in order to survive their boyhood. They might be closer than brothers in spirit, but as boys they were so closely cut from the same mold, it had erupted in constant battles—knock down, drag out fights so to speak. The fights kept both of them in bruises, broken noses and jaws, sometimes broken limbs. Poor Mary! She tore out her hair in distress, and more than once—he remembered with a smile—she fell to her knees with tears, begging them to stop before they ended up killing each other. They in turn answered those tears with the

207

masculine amusement and humored condescension natural to men confronting a woman's concern.

Standing there at the ship's rail, watching the river's ceaseless lure through the darkening light, Ram smiled at the memories. Neither Sean nor himself could stop their fighting; it was more fun than riding, shooting or any of their wild boyhood games. Predictably, they developed unnatural fighting skills, skills that grew as they did, and this, taken with both their unusual heights and strength, gave them an advantage in any fighting situation. God knows, there had been many of those.

Trouble had arrived as they reached adolescence. Mary's fears became a reality due to their ever increasing strength. Aye, despite that, no matter how bad the fighting became, Sean and he would inevitably end up rolling on the ground, laughing through their pain. Yet, as they began to reap permanent effects, they gradually started working conditions into the fights.

Now as men, they fought only after drinking to a point where they could hardly stand, let alone harm each other, and then only with their legs tied—a man's legs were at least twice as strong as his arms and fists. Once these weapons were taken out, they could fight in relative safety, till one or the other was taken out. The crews matched up in the same way—roughly based on size and strength—and though he had seen some great fights among their men, none drew the wild excitement and interest as Seanessy's and his own. Thinking on it, realizing it had been almost a year since his last match fight with Sean, he laughed suddenly, deciding to change his night's plans.

"Are ye thinkin' on goin' down there?" his man asked upon hearing Ram's amusement. "If ye are, I'll ask ye to put Rake on guard, 'cause I've not ever—not in five years—missed a match between ye and Seanessy."

"I'm thinking about it," Ram called back as he moved to his cabin. Rake barked excitedly but stayed with the two men, who had a basket of fried chicken between them. Ram opened the door, and still chuckling, he stepped inside. Moving to his desk chair, he removed his boots, then his shirt. He'd go for a short run and see how he felt. Seanessy would have a head start on the drinking and this—

It was in that instant that he glanced up and saw the small figure sitting in his bed. For a blessedly long time, he simply stared because he could not believe the reality of the vision, let alone understand it. He felt as if some malicious god toyed with the long denied fantasy of his mind, spinning the vision of her loveliness in his bed to torment him.

She sat with her legs tucked under her, holding a quilt over her body as though to protect herself. The long unbound hair spilled over the quilt, and her eyes were lowered, as she nervously bit her lip. The soft light illuminated the delicate features of her face, and she looked deceptively angelic and young. God, he thought, she's ever so beautiful.

With an alarming mix of curiosity and amusement, Ram rose slowly and approached the vision his mind had created many times before. Joy was so scared by this point she couldn't have spoken, even if her imagination could guess what it was a woman said to a man after surprising him by appearing unexpectedly in his bed. He remained silent as well as he stood over her staring down. He finally reached a hand to gently brush the long loose hair back over her shoulders.

She made no protest; she still did not look up. He then took the quilt from her, lifting it, removing the obstruction to his view. She wore only a thin cotton night dress, one that teased with the barest hint of transparency. As he stared at the beauty waiting for his touch, and though she tried, she could not stop her response; her arms crossed over herself as her cheeks burned with a maiden's modesty.

This was not lost on him. He spoke with his gaze more than anyone else she knew, but she still could not quite look up to see the flicker of his amusement—amusement resting on the edge of some inexplicable anger. All this was perfectly clear though, as he finally asked, "Just what the hell are you doing here?"

She had imagined many possible responses to her presence but this was not one of them. What could she possibly say? How could she possibly explain? "I assumed you might guess."

His low chuckle startled her, brought her eyes up to him, only to retreat quickly, instantly behind lowered lashes.

"It's not the what, sweetheart. The what is painfully obvious to me. What I cannot guess—though I am trying—is why?"

She remained mute and silent and did not stir, let alone venture a reply. Her fear was plain, but he would have expected that. He watched for a moment longer, the incredulity of it presenting only one conceivable explanation. Somehow he had underestimated her; somehow she understood, grasped the force of their attraction that day at the lake and attempted, operating on some ridiculous school girl fantasy of her own, to set it into play. Of course she had no idea of what that meant. His desire for her was bad enough left alone but now, after this trick—

Ram moved suddenly to the brandy decanter sitting on the table and poured himself an ample shot. Nothing could excite his desire more than her coming to him like this, despite the shield of her innocence, and as he continued to stare at the beckoning loveliness on his bed, he found himself in a furious fight for some semblance of control.

"Joy." He turned suddenly away and swallowed his drink whole. "I can only guess you don't know what you're doing. I am, as I speak, trying to control myself." He almost laughed at how much. "And only because you deserve so much more than I can offer. I will not be your first Joy; I will not take the innocence that belongs to the man you marry."

This was the point Sean coached her on, the point of deception. She could not say it though, not directly, and the words were whispered as they sprang to her mind. "But I do know what I'm doing and—" she paused, then asked in a barely audible whisper, "did you not say to me once that appearances are deceptive?"

He spun around and stared, just stared, the words crashing into his mind with a question. Never had any pairing of words conjured a more potent seductive force, and he wanted to believe them—God, how he wanted to believe them. He came back to her and lifted her face to see the truth of the assertion there. What he saw though, was that she was hiding something in those lovely eyes, something that frightened her. "Are you telling me I am not your first?"

She kept her eyes lowered, so frightened by his touch, the consuming nearness of his bare muscled frame towering over her at the point of her deception. Yet her silence spoke for her.

He stared down at her, waiting for the answer, and when she remained silent, his mind raced where she had led it. Memories of her, the bits and pieces of her diary that he had read were placed against the beauty before him; he thought of the maddening music of her laughter, the tease that could spring in those eyes, the wild flirting with destruction shown in so many of her turns. He suddenly wondered if he might have been misled. While her nature was innocent, and probably always would be, she could easily not be so in fact.

He knew better than to contemplate the next step further, and he did not let himself entertain for a moment who her first lover might have been, or if there had been more than one. It must have been recent or so damn careless to have given him the impression that she knew not a man's passion. No other woman could make him care enough to wonder who. With her he cared, cared far too much, and the question raised unpleasant emotions; anyone of those emotions could easily lead to a murderous rage. It was enough that the blessed fortunate unknown had existed, quite enough.

"Please," she broke their silence with a soft plea. "Don't make this harder for me than it already is."

He stared at the trembling hands, still crossed over her bosom, the plea in her eyes and the effect was felt as a physical unleashing of his long denied desire. He took her small hands in his own, bringing them behind her back and lifting her as he did so, shocking her with the hard warmth of his body against hers. "Ah, my love," he whispered, his lips gently pressing to hers, teased by the barest hint of lavender. "I will make it difficult for you." He chuckled. "I'll have you pay in full for these many months of tormenting me."

She had not time to think of what those words meant, yet she wouldn't have understood even if she had. She knew only the places where his body was touching hers—separated only by the thin cotton of her night dress—that her heart was beating much too fast. There was quiet amusement in his gaze as his hands ran through her hair, then brought her head back for his kiss.

The first kiss was her undoing.

His lips took hers with a gentle, tender insistence, filling her with the heady taste of his brandy. Warmth, a sweet tingling warmth, surged physically through her. Like a finely built crescendo, the kiss deepened slowly, and she couldn't resist or think or breathe. There was no thought past the lips on hers, the heady flavor of his mouth, the sweep of his tongue on hers, the feel of his body pressed to hers, and without knowing it, her arms reached shyly around his neck, her soft form melted by degrees to the demand of the hard muscles of his.

The sweet taste of her was madness itself, but when he felt the beckoning softness of her small body melting against him, it was all he could do to hold back the full force of his desire. The battle was a blessed torment. The only thing stopping him was the very magnitude of his desire, knowing that a sudden unleashing of it would hurt her. He would force himself to have her slow, force her desire to meet his

212

own, all the while enjoying the exquisite pleasure of losing his own battle inch by precious inch.

His lips finally left hers but only to return playfully, teasingly. She was but vaguely aware of her name on his lips as his hands roamed over her form, barely touching through the cotton shift, dancing lightly over the slender curve of her hips, up from her waist, under her arms and stopping there.

The kiss ended as he lifted her from the bed to the floor, standing very close. Her heart still pounded wildly, her pulse racing with the lingering heat of his touch, yet she felt shy and embarrassed, wanting to run and hide from his gaze. The very intensity of it held her perfectly still though, as he slowly unbuttoned the top buttons of her gown. Once parted, his hands slid over her slender shoulders drawing the gown with the movement. The gown dropped to her bent elbows. She felt the heat of his gaze, and she nervously crossed her arms over herself, suddenly afraid.

He drew a sharp breath at the beauty thus revealed to him, but never satisfied with part, he gently brought her arms to her sides and slid the sleeves from each hand. The shift fell to an unnoticed pile at her feet.

"Ah my love," he whispered as he reached his hand along the curve of her waist to the delicious lift of her breasts. "You are indeed more beautiful than Botticelli's Venus."

The words, the rich timbre of his voice paired with the potency of his touch, brought a heated flush, a tremor of physical anticipation.

Beautiful indeed fell short of how he saw her at that moment. The beauty sprang from her startling femininity, an unmasked vulnerability that made him wonder. He had never known a desire like this, a need to claim a woman as no other man had or would, and he decided for this one night he'd allow himself that dangerous illusion.

He lowered his head and his lips met hers, his tongue tracing a circle over her mouth till she trembled. He gently prodded her lips open to kiss her deeply. She felt uncertain

213

and afraid, not like before, and she trembled beneath him with a surge of desire mixed with and inseparable from panic. When his lips finally left hers, she felt fire and fear, and as he stepped away to remove his own clothes, her arms crossed over herself and she turned away.

The extent of her modesty brought a question, then the certainty that she had been used wrongly. Desire quickly overrode the thought and its subsequent fury. He'd deal with that later, and watching her, he reclined on the bed contenting himself for long a moment to study the vision of his dreams: the lovely lines of her long legs; the soft curve of slender hips and small waist, a waist that could easily be encircled by a man's hands, his hands; the trail of thick dark hair cascading down her proud straight back to the perfectly rounded curves of her buttocks.

Beauty indeed fell short.

She felt his gaze as a tingling sensation along her spine, a heat that made her breath come in quick shaky gasps.

"Come here," he finally ordered as his arm reached out to draw her to him.

She turned, not understanding the tumult of her confusion and fear, about to blurt that it was all a mistake, that she couldn't go through with it, when her eyes encountered the magnificence and shock of his unclad masculine body.

She gasped, her hand flew to her mouth and she spun around.

Dark brows drew together, and having never possessed so much as an ounce of self-consciousness, he had no idea what sent her spinning back around, holding herself in such obvious alarm and fear. Then enlightenment dawned with uncontained amusement.

"Oh Ram, I— I—"

He rose and went to her, turning her around, then lifting her face to him. Unmasked fondness shined in his eyes. "Is this my fearless young lady riding wild through the night boldly braving men and pistols?" he asked. And with a warm

214

chuckle, he answered, "I think not."

He swept her to his arms and laid her to the soft cushion of his bed, coming alongside her. She closed her eyes and covered herself yet again, holding her breath as though waiting for the bullets of a firing squad.

"No my love," he laughed, bringing her hands over her head and holding them there. "I know not what rules you have been taught already but get this straight: there is no modesty in my bed." His hands strayed where his gaze lingered. She shivered and tensed. His touch lightly glided over her breasts, drawing small circles there, causing her to gasp. A gasp answered with a kiss as he gathered her to him. It was as though her body leapt to greet his. Wild feelings mounted and grew; she was swimming in a sea of sensations, lost to everything but him, his warmth and his touch, the feel of his body on hers and a kiss lasting minutes or hours, she could not know. She felt the same surge of sensation when Libertine raced to that jump, those tense moments filled with a heady fear, yet a wild excitement as she flew through the air, holding her breath with a rush of heightened suspense. Only this love was not a flash of time but rather a piece of eternity.

Warm languid desire flowed through her. His touch was light, curiously evoking as his warm lips pressed against her forehead, her closed eyes, her mouth. Then he was biting her lips, teasing with his tongue, kissing her long and hard, stopping only to bring her the pleasure of his lips elsewhere, everywhere.

He was a playful lover and she was his toy, and with a childlike fascination that hid the mounting agony of his own desire, he expertly played the music of her form. The first light and curious caress of his evolved into slow caresses of heated passion. She was lost beneath the exquisite pleasure of his hands on her body, the play of his tongue and mouth on her breasts. The long drawn prelude to his lovemaking felt like dying a thousand deaths. Only each one, each moment passed, carried her ever higher to a peak she had not the experience to know, and just when she thought he could carry her no further—

She was like a wild supple creature in his hands, writhing, crying softly, and he moved to answer those cries. She stiffened and gasped as his hand slid between her thighs and he began a slow caressing there. She panicked, not knowing of this and tried to twist away, but he mistook her sudden fear. Holding her still for the pleasure he'd give, he took her mouth in his for a long deep kiss. Drowning beneath his kiss, mindless from his gentle exploration, she felt the knot of heat burst with small ripples of pleasure over and over, and just when she felt on the very edge of that high cliff, he shifted, turned over and brought her on top of him.

She arched her back, unknowingly offering her breasts to him, which were each taken in turn as he slowly slid her over the smooth pressure of him. Wild gushes of heat rushed in her loins, and she was suddenly crying, begging for something she couldn't know. Ram knew his battle was lost.

He turned her unresisting body over again and came over her. A long muscled leg separated her for his entrance. She was too lost in his tightly spun web of desire to know what was happening, though her body knew its role. As he gently kissed her face, sliding back and forth over her sex, she arched with a soft cry, and he answered with a long deep thrust.

He stopped instantly with the shock of this first feel of her, the tearing of a virgin's resistance. He tensed dramatically, lifting partially from her, and stared into the terrified pools of her eyes.

"God damn your lying heart to hell."

Shocking pain ripped through her, and she bit her lip hard to stop the cry, terrified by those words and desperate to get him off. She pushed against the hard muscles of his chest and arms with all her strength, twisting maddeningly. "Please! I—"

"Oh no, Joy." He caught her fists and pinned them to the bed. "I said once before and now it's true, it's too late; it's far too late."

He stopped her cry with a long hard kiss and finally lifted to thrust hungrily into her, only to repeat the measure over and over, sparing her no pain, forcing her body to yield at last to his size.

She could not live with another second of it, and yet she had no fight left. Like a drowning person's final release to the dark powers overwhelming him, she collapsed suddenly. In the moment of succumbing to him, the experience changed. The very next thrust was a shocking stab of hot pleasure. He knew his triumph and slowed just when her body wanted only to feel the force of his passion. Yet all she knew was shocking hot warmth filling her, the merciful answer to the agonizing tension of the night, and she was wild, clinging to him, calling his name over and over as she twisted maddeningly beneath him, unknowingly returning his torment tenfold. Any semblance of control vanished as he yielded to the pace of passion's call, answering her cries with the full force of his ardor until suddenly pleasure exploded deep inside her, sending her for a moment into darkness, only to return to feel sweet ripples drowning her mind, body and soul with him, nothing but him. Her intensity became his, and with a final thrust, he lost himself deep inside her with a force he, too, had never before felt.

She was only vaguely aware of his weight leaving her to turn over, then mercifully drawing her back into his arms against the long length of him. Mercifully, because she needed the feel of his arms around her, his body against hers as she needed her next breath. His hands lovingly stroked through her hair as his lips gently brushed against her forehead. Never had the warmth of his body been so consuming. The tenderness and vulnerability of their profound intimacy overwhelmed her; she never suffered a thought of saving herself from the questions he surely would

217

be asking.

Ram tried to steel his thoughts from her long enough to answer the pressing question of why. Why she had deceived him with that lie that claimed a previous lover; why she had given him this precious gift of her innocence. The obvious answer was blatant and plain. Innocence mattered not, for she might have had ten previous lovers and this one night would still have claimed her as his. He had deceived himself just as surely as she had.

He wanted desperately to believe she had done it because of the simple need of her love. This could not be the case though, for until tonight, she had naught the experience to know what that meant, to know love long enough to desire it.

No, her motivation came from elsewhere.

He could not for a moment entertain the thought that she had offered herself—like so many ladies before her—simply to put herself closer to either his title or fortune or both, in the futile hopes of soliciting his proposal. Even out of love, this was simply not in her character; such a motivation indeed seemed antithetical to her nature.

Yet she had deceived him and with the single intent of losing her innocence to him. Why? What in the name of heaven or hell had made her come to him?

The contemplation of the next path he must choose could hardly be borne. He might have been able to let her go, had he not been forced to taste her love, but where the intensity of his desire had settled before, it now soared. Like an unquenchable thirst, it would have no limits in any near future. He might chain her to his bed for a month and still be hard with want of her.

Yet the idea of making her his mistress was so bitter, so patently unpalatable, it was as he said to Sean: It would be a good deal easier to put a bullet to her head than to destroy her like that. Destroy her not just by removing her from "polite" society into his bed. No, not just that. The women he took as his mistresses endured something that for Joy—and he knew this for a certainty—would be a tragedy of a magnitude she could not survive, would not survive.

As the only future possible spread before him and he felt the force of a regret he had never before felt, never had reason to feel, the question of why became even larger and more important.

Feelings and feelings and feelings welled inside her. She was as lost to the shocking intimacy brought by the intensity of his lovemaking as she was to the wonder of it. Never had she been more vulnerable to anyone or anything, and when Ram kissed her lightly and rose, taking the warmth with him, it was a loss not to be endured.

He disappeared into the adjoining dressing room, and dreamily, still dazed, she gathered the bed sheet around herself and followed him in there. She stopped in the doorway and watched as he swung a black cotton robe over himself.

Ram turned to confront the unexpected sight of her standing there. The vision of her at that moment would haunt his mind for eternity: her startling loveliness, the naked beauty shrouded only in a sheet, her long unbound hair, tousled, cascading wildly over her shoulders, and more than anything the fragility, the plain unmasked love in her eyes, a love he could not allow himself to return, a love he'd see destroyed and now.

Panic instantly shattered the warmth of her emotions as she met his gaze but briefly, then retreated behind closed lids. A hand reached out to her, and with a quick twist, he brought the bed sheet falling to the floor. Without a word, he held her arms to keep her still, then took the cloth in the basin of dressing water. She gasped and bit her lip with humiliation as she felt the cool moist cloth come between her legs and wipe her there.

He did not need to look at the stain on the cloth; his gaze bore intently into her and he asked, "Why Joy? Why?"

She stood for several moments mute and still, not knowing at all what to say. He waited a moment but realized he would not be talking long with her unclad beauty standing before him like an offering. With an exasperated growl, he abruptly released her and grabbed a shirt hanging in the clothes closet.

The cool silk slid over her bare skin. Needless to say, it did not quite fit, and Ram spent several moments rolling up the sleeves, still staring down at her as he waited for the explanation she obviously struggled to make. Then he lifted her into his arms and brought her back to the bed, leaving her there alone as he moved to the crystal brandy decanter setting on the table. He poured a healthy shot into a goblet, consuming it in one swallow. The goblet was set to the table with a loud clink and another poured. "Come on Joy—talk to me."

She finally found the words she sought and said quietly, "It doesn't matter now. I have done it; it is over. The reason no longer exists."

Ram only chuckled. "Not good enough. Not nearly good enough!"

"Oh, Ram," she said emotionally, "you might be angry—" she stopped while thinking out loud—"Sean said—"

"Sean?" he questioned. "What the hell does Sean have to do with it?"

She nervously twisted her hands, still unable to look up, imagining she'd find his amusement. The thought broke her heart. "Sean bid me to . . . to come here tonight."

She didn't know what to make of his long silence, the intensity of his stare until he chuckled. "Seanessy, of course!" His mean laughter felt like a sudden northern snow. "I might have guessed." He sat down in a chair, assuming a casual pose as he poured another brandy. "So sweetheart, just how did my good friend convince you to do this, hmmm? There must have been more than 'Joy, why not go to Ram tonight, lie about your innocence and get ah, bedded good

220

and proper?'"

His sarcasm was plain, springing from his anger. Just how angry, she couldn't know. She met his gaze again, unable to fathom the depth of emotion there. "Yes," she said in a whisper. "There was more."

"Well, I'm waiting."

"He made me a proposition I could not turn from."

"No doubt. And just what exactly was it?"

"Oh Ram." She felt suddenly afraid. "It doesn't matter now; it's over. Please—"

Ram rose, and before she could finish, he swept down upon her, taking her chin in his hand to demand, "What did you trade your virtue for?"

"For freedom. The freedom of six people I will choose at the marketplace on the morrow."

Of all the things he might have imagined, this was not one. Hearing it held him for a moment transfixed with incredulity and disbelief. The bargain seemed at once as absurd as it was poetic. The idea encompassed the whole of her nature, everything from her naive innocence to her ludicrous benevolence and idealism. The girl who loved freedom. He could only wonder that he hadn't guessed the whole ridiculous thing the first moment he laid eyes on her sitting in his bed.

He left her suddenly and chuckled again, shaking his head, as he poured another drink. "Seanessy, I'm going to kill you . . ." he vowed under his breath. "I swear you will pay for this . . ."

His amusement tore swiftly at her heart, though it hid the real threat of his growing fury until the moment he addressed her, raising the crystal goblet to her as though for a toast. "Well, here's to you, Joy, and to your first indoctrination into whoring. What you lack in experience, you more than make up for in enthusiasm."

The words hit her like a hard slap in the face and her hand flew to her mouth with a small, pained gasp. There was a

221

mistake; he didn't say that, he couldn't say that—

"Don't look so shocked, sweetheart. You do know that that's what Sean made you—my whore?"

She paled visibly, still not quite understanding. Her gaze jerked around her, searching for one thing, anything to settle on, until she spotted the neat pile of her clothes. She rose from the bed like a sleepwalker, panic and alarm quickly overriding her shock. "I . . . I better leave now—"

"Leave?" he questioned as he rose, then moved slowly to meet her to stop her, she didn't know. She clutched the pile of clothes tight against her person, backing into the wall as he approached. "Oh no, Joy. You're not leaving. Let's see, Sean will have paid you approximately, oh I guess something over 3000 of your American dollars." A brow lifted. "Quite a sum. Though needless to say I don't keep track of such things; I think the most I've ever paid for the pleasure was a hundred dollars or so, and while I don't remember the lady, I do seem to recall she lasted nearly a week."

She felt a rush of fear as he stopped in front of her, staring down. His huge frame towered over her, threatening and engulfing her with his great strength. Never had she been more his prisoner than at that moment. Calmly taking the pile of clothes from her, he dropped them unceremoniously to the floor. "So I can at least assume you're paid for the night," he said in a frightening whisper. "And I assure you, I'm not through with you yet."

Like a trapped animal, she backed hard into the wall, panicked, shaking her head. He only chuckled, and staring at the beauty silhouetted in the ridiculously large shirt, his hand moved over the delicate lines of her face and down her neck to the buttons there.

"No, please—"

"I don't think you understand. You're not paid to like it. Though," he added cruelly, "the best whores do."

She cried out at this, and desperate, she was suddenly

222

fighting him. Her fist flew to his face, but he allowed her only a brief moment of struggle before catching her small hands in his, forcing her head back and her lips open to him. In that moment a silent scream rose in her body, protesting what she had started, protesting what would not be pleasant and what she was powerless to stop.

Entrapped tightly in his arms, his kiss hungrily devoured her, purposely giving as much pleasure as pain, and she became limp, weak-kneed and senseless. A savage passion radiated from him, at once engulfing and enraging her.

His mouth left hers suddenly and she drew a gasping breath. As he released her arms to remove her shirt, freedom gave rise to survival. She darted quickly away in a surge of defense, out of his reach.

"Nooo . . . please, I—" She stumbled back, but fear threw her off balance and caused her to fall on her hands and knees. Instantly he was there, lifting her from the ground, keeping her backside against him and stopping her flinging arms. "No." She squirmed. "Don't do this to me—"

"Fight me all you want, Joy Claret." He lifted her hair from the sweep of her neck and pressed moist lips there. Chills raced along her spine, and then with his lips on her neck, his hand ripped open the buttons of his shirt. She was crying, the helpless desperate tears spilled down her cheeks as his one arm kept her powerless and his other hand gently, methodically began massaging her breasts to swollen peaks. A fire spread in her loins; she could not stop it—she could not stop him. His hand wandered over her, finally circling her belly, moving lower and lower until she cried out with unwilling, joyless anticipation. He chuckled meanly and the humiliation of it burst in on her. She cried again, squirming in rage, digging her nails into his arm and clamping her legs tightly together, but only to hear another chuckle, a half growl. The force of his body, the threat she squirmed against, his very passion, rose, soared, permitting no struggle. His leg forced hers apart as his hand slipped

223

between her legs with a touch like fire, causing her to cry, tremble, moisten.

He lifted her to the bed, allowing her no choice of position, though she tried desperately to twist around to face him. He held her hips firm, and she closed her eyes, biting her lip till she tasted blood as his hand parted her again, lifting her higher. She felt the length of him slowly caress her sex, opening her for a hard thrust into her.

His huge body pounded into her, forcing her to tighten with each hard thrust, the tension building and building despite the act of violence. And while each movement carried her ever closer and closer, she was hurt by it, praying for an end that finally came. She stiffened and jolted, the tension exploding inside her, washing those ripples of intense pleasure over her, waves that left neither feeling nor strength in their path. His hands tightened around her, holding her to him for his last hard thrust, and his violence exploded with unexpected force.

Mercifully it was over.

She lay there trembling slightly and crying softly, too shaken to notice anything, too shaken to see the emotion blazing in his gaze as he stared down at her, forcing himself to say the last words that would indeed end it all. "The next time I want a whore in my bed, Joy Claret, I'll select her myself." He gently wiped a tear from her flushed face. "And you would be well-advised not to be here when I return."

Over a hundred men waited at the Red Barn for the promised match between Ram and Sean. No one minded the long wait into the early morning hours, and the ever increasing size of the bets that rose in direct proportion to the liberal amount of spirits flowing in the place kept everyone in a rowdy and heightened state of anticipation.

Ram now understood Sean's message: Sean would be waiting at the Red Barn, and there would be no match fights, save one. He tied Rake up, and with no shirt or boots, nothing but fury fueling him, he started running. Running as hard and as fast as the power in his legs could carry him, and though a fresh mount would surely have done better, he forced himself to run in the futile hope that it would vent some of his strength and fury, simply because this—as bad as it was—did not warrant Sean's ultimate end.

Sean waited in fine high spirits, teased by the anticipatory excitement filling the air, wondering, knowing the monster he would be meeting would be bad but not knowing just how bad. When the doors finally burst open and his lordship appeared in all the magnificence of his fury, the clear visible answer to his question brought him to his feet. The noise rose with a loud, long cheer, and a corridor of bodies instantly formed, leading Ram directly to Seanessy.

Ram's each step forward created suspense. As Seanessy's gaze locked with Ram's, a silent solicitous greeting was exchanged. Sean saw it in full. The monster was a good deal more than he had either expected or imagined: Ram would not be letting him last past the half hour mark.

Normally, the much loved matches between Sean and Ram were as colorful as they were exciting. The battle of wits as the two first started drinking was often enjoyed as much as the match, at least by those who themselves owned wits enough to enjoy the clever, cunning and artful exchange, as with lazy indifference, Ram met Seanessy's sardonic humor with his own rarely exercised but considerable ability.

This time however it was different. The difference was immediately apparent in the shocking violence radiating from Ram's frame, a certain wildness glaring from his gaze, the cruel smile he bestowed on Sean—a madman out to kill.

Two fresh bottles were set on the table that separated the two men. In case the difference wasn't perfectly clear, Ram took the neck of the bottle in hand and with his gaze still locked to Sean, he smashed the bottle hard against the table. "I'll not let anything soften my blows this time, Seanessy."

A low murmur rippled through the anxious crowd and bets were abruptly increased, but Sean, seeing the force of Ram's fury—far greater than he had even hoped for—only laughed. Stoically, he met the numbered minutes he had left with amusement, and some small relief. For if he had any doubts about what he had done, they were now gone, banished by the magnitude of Ram's rage. He rose and met Ram's fury directly and with a simple "As you wish, my lord."

A circle was cleared and the two men moved into the middle, each standing perfectly still like caged animals, submitting as Bart bound Sean's feet and Sean's man bound Ram's. A foot and a half for balance was given to each. A man's arms had far less than half the deadly force of a man's legs, but because neither man was drunk, their arms were bound in front as a necessary added precaution.

Sean was still adjusting his weight to the demands of the ropes binding his strength, and his first mistake was in the assumption that Ram would wait for the first signal call. Ram never fought fair though, and moving with a predator's natural grace, he came swiftly upon his unsuspecting victim. With a powerful lift of his bound arms, Ram landed his first blow hard in Seanessy's face.

The crowd roared as Sean was slammed backside against the ground. The blow reminded Sean only of how very long it had been since he had felt Ram's power untempered by drink, and with a quick chuckle and a curse, he came quickly up.

The two men circled each other with a hunter's patient and slow dance. While Ram waited for the opening that would surely come, he asked the same, though now, far more meaningful question, "Why Seanessy? Why?"

Seanessy's eyes blazed with amusement, and he only laughed. "Ah, but my lord, you do know my fondness for your painting—"

The sentence was not complete when Ram, moving with

amazing speed, lifted high in the air and slammed his bound legs into Sean's chest. Sean grunted as the wind was forced from him, and though both men fell with it, Ram came to his feet with a practiced roll in an instant. Mercifully he gave Sean a few precious seconds to get to his feet as well. Only because he wanted an answer. "That's not good enough Sean," he said the exact words he had said to Joy as they circled yet again. "Not nearly good enough."

"Ah, but it's the only explanation I can give you, my lord." Sean's eyes danced with both amusement and mischief, and he stalled for a moment. "I simply discovered she could be bought, and as your ever obsequious servant, I bought her for you."

Sean only chuckled as Ram's anger flared, and with a vicious curse, Ram sprung on him. This time Sean was prepared and Ram's strength met the great wall of Sean's. Their two huge frames locked and clashed, each an unmovable force pitted against an equal. Muscles tensed dramatically until sweat poured, squeezed mercilessly from every rock-hard fiber of their bodies. The crowd held their collective breath waiting for one side to give. Just as Sean thought he would lose it, Ram leaned back a mere inch, suddenly throwing Sean's huge weight off balance. Seizing the victory, Ram swung his bound arms back and round, hard into Sean's jaw.

The force threw Sean hard to the straw covered floor again, and though dazed by it, he managed to roll just a split second before Ram landed another blow with his legs. Sean came up quickly and just in time, for no one found balance as quickly and as easily as Ram.

The two men circled yet again. Ram, knowing only he was not getting the fight he needed from Sean, said with a dangerous chuckle, "It's too bloody easy Sean. I need more Sean, much more."

"I am trying, my lord," Sean replied drily, still with his own laughter.

"No." Ram shook his head, wiping the sweat from his face with bound hands. "Not even close, Seanessy. But I'll have you. All you have to do is think a moment on what your fine present reaped tonight. Think of her, Seanessy."

The first moment of alarm flashed briefly in Sean's gaze but quickly disappeared as he replied, "I rest assured knowing I placed her in ah, capable hands."

"Capable!" Ram laughed cruelly, still circling. "Aye, her innocence was indeed a small obstruction, made even smaller once I discovered you made her my whore."

Amusement vanished from Seanessy's gaze, and the dance slowed.

"Of course," Ram continued, "she had no idea of what you had made her. So I had to make it clear for her Sean," he said slowly. "And I did make it clear, Seanessy, I did."

Just as Ram intended, tension transformed Sean's handsome features as his gaze warned Ram to stop before it was too late.

Ram would show no mercy now. "Do you know Sean, she never did shed a virgin's tears. Tears yes, but not that kind. Oh no." He shook his head. "The unnamed emotion in those lovely eyes kept a virgin's tears at bay. Of course, you know"—he reached the source of his fury—"how I had to destroy that emotion. One has only to look at the patch I wear to know that. Making it clear to her what you had made her—my whore—" he growled, "only provided the means. It's a small wonder she survived—"

"Stop it Ram," Sean said slowly, as anger grew with each word. "I'm warning you—"

"But you must have known Sean," Ram relentlessly continued. "As wonderfully fierce as her mind and spirit are—that small slender form is as delicate and fragile as a porcelain vase, certainly not made to endure a man's abuse. Abuse, Sean," he said the word, "that I can give the cleaner name of rape."

Any anger, particularly a violent fury, was as rare to Sean's nature as an hour passed without laughter; but it filled him now, and the final word brought the hot volatile liquid flowing into his huge frame. "Why you God damn bastard!—"

He was suddenly crazed, crazed with the same violent need to avenge her as Ram. Sean sprung quickly, efficiently, deadly, finally meeting Ram at last on his own ground. As strength and all else was matched, it was a frightening battle of will, sheer brute force of will. Sean gave as good as he got; blow followed blow as their two huge magnificent bodies locked in combat for what seemed an eternity.

The crowd anxiously and alternately roared and groaned in some shared collective exhilaration and pain, all of it wild. Few were able to believe a woman had caused it, but after the longest hour of watching the fiercest battle any had ever witnessed, the first twinges of alarm began to steal into the gazes of many. Both Sean and Ram could barely stand now, and yet the blows continued, each deadly enough to knock a good-sized man out cold, bringing everyone to hold their breath with the certainty that it was the last. But somehow a force fueled Ram and Sean both, bringing them back up again and again.

Seanessy's man put the question to Bart, who alone had the authority to decide. Bart began to watch ever more alarmed, too, knowing the two perfectly matched exercises in masculine strength could not endure much more. Though what alarmed him most was that he had never seen anything of this kind between them. He began to wonder if their great friendship might be at stake. He couldn't bear the thought of a rupture between Sean and his Ram—the idea was unconscionable. It was because of this that Bart decided it was much better to end it in the ring than to let them carry it over one single day.

The unrelenting battle continued. Increasingly uncomfortable with it, Bart began to see more and more evidence that they were both truly out for a kill, and just as he thought to put a merciful stop to it, the end came without interference.

Ram, using what one would swear was the last of his exhausted energy, slammed his clenched bound fists into Sean's face and sent the huge giant back to the ground with the blessed relief of a moment's blackness. Ram stumbled over to him, and gasping for breath, too tired even to wipe the sweat and blood from his face, he stared down at his friend, making certain he was truly gone.

The crowd grew deathly silent. Ram's uneven breathing was the only sound when, with no warning, Sean's legs suddenly lifted up and kicked Ram hard in the chest.

Ram went down hard, and now Sean somehow struggled to his feet and over to Ram's side, dropping his weight to pin Ram against the straw of the floor.

"Seanessy, Seanessy." Ram tried to laugh, but this small effort cost too much. He had finally landed on the sweet shore of utter, complete exhaustion, pain shooting through every inch of his flesh. It was a liberating force that shielded the real pain of having loved and lost her in the single sweep of one blessed night. "It's over Sean. It's over."

"Nay, my lord." Sean fought every bit as hard for these last words. "It's not over . . . No," he gasped, "not . . . unless you say that you do indeed regret it."

Ram understood perfectly that Sean wanted to know only if the whole bloody night had been naught but a futile, senseless exercise in pain. He stared hard for a long moment, then suddenly laughed. Despite the pain of it, he laughed.

"You God damned bloody bastard," Ram finally replied, and taking Sean, indeed the whole room, by surprise, he thrust his legs up over Sean's head. The ropes binding his legs twisted around Sean's neck and threw him off to the side.

The last thing Sean remembered was Ram kneeling at his

side, his laughter as fine and sweet and forgiving as his words. "Seanessy boy, if I regretted it, if I regretted it for a bloody moment, you—my dearest friend in this life—would not now still be breathing." And then Ram struggled to his feet and took two steps. The wild roar of the crowd faded as a vision of sky blue eyes swam in his head—just seconds before darkness claimed him too.

## Chapter Eight

As he walked along the old river road and for no reason he could think of, the reverend felt remarkably happy and oddly carefree. All the aches and pains plaguing his aging frame were gone, suddenly vanished, and there was a light bounce to his step. An old Irish folk song sprang to his mind and he began singing.

The road remained deserted as though there was not another soul in the world, and the sky, while cloudy, seemed unusually light as though the sun burned bright just beyond. He had no thoughts—not even a thought to know there was nothing past the lightness of his heart, a gladness that was not explained.

Then from nowhere Joshua was standing in front of him.

"Joshua!" the reverend exclaimed happily.

"I've come to tell you I must go."

The reverend nodded, not quite understanding, staring at the sadness in Joshua's eyes.

"You, my dearest friend, must care for Joy now." Softly he said, "Tell her she was the best daughter—and she seems like a daughter to me—a man could have; tell her how much I love her."

A warm hand touched the reverend's shoulder; then suddenly Joshua was gone, and the reverend stood alone. He woke with a start. A chill crept into his small dark room and he glanced around, finally resting his gaze on Sammy, still sleeping in the small bed across the room. The old man swung his bare feet on the cold floor. It creaked as he rose, then he fumbled through the darkness to get a candle lit. Candle in hand, he quietly left the room and slowly made his way down the hall, stopping before the door to Joshua's study where Joshua slept. He paused, the chill came not from the cold night air but from within, bringing tears to his eyes already.

Joshua's funeral was a large affair. Most all the close knit and prominent families of Orleans Parish, many beyond, showed up to pay respects. Perhaps a hundred or more townspeople paid due respect as well, many people of color among them. For Joshua, before succumbing completely to the consumption, during days that seemed so long ago, had administered medicine to the rich and poor alike. He alone established the Negro infirmary. He alone called for summer dredging of the sewers, to rid the city of the foul air that brought so much disease and death. Then, too, dozens of women owed the survival of their children to the doctor who brought the European way of medicine to the new country. Though his own convalesence had taken him away these last long years, few people forgot Dr. Joshua Reubens, his kindness, his charity, his skilled art of healing.

Joy Claret would never remember the funeral. She stood surrounded by her family, looking small, frightened and deathly pale. She had been in a state of acute shock and disbelief, until the very moment the dirt was thrown on the casket and the last prayer was said. Tears slowly fell down her cheeks, and once started, the tears were endless while for months all other pain lay buried in the profundity of her grief.

Days passed unbroken by events, unmarked by anything

save the ticking of the downstairs' clock. The rain eventually came with the passing of summer, and the humidity felt all but bearable in the last week. "Hope dose clouds bring us some rain," Cory whispered idly as she lay on her back in the bed, staring at the ceiling through the thin veil of their mosquito net. The room was dark yet she knew Joy was still awake. "Don' you?"

No reply ventured forth but then Cory didn't expect one. Joy rarely spoke; after two and a half months she was still lost in her silent personal grief. All she did was eat and sleep, eat and sleep. The reverend said it would take time, but how much time? Lawd a mercy, she missed Joshua, too. Not an hour passed when she didn't feel dis huge empty missing deep inside, but nows she missed Joy just as much.

A high gentle wind pushed the clouds across the night sky, suddenly bringing the bright light of a full moon shining through the open window, and Cory found herself looking at the bare shelves lining the room. After their dolls had been shoved into the downstairs' closet, Joy had tried to fill the space with a bouquet of flowers in a pretty yellow ceramic vase, a few books here and a few knick-knacks there. It still looked bare to Cory.

Worry suddenly creased Cory's forehead. "I'se got my monthly today, did you'se?"

"Yes."

The lie came without thought; the word yes just suddenly manifest. Joy first tried to ignore it as all other thoughts, but the question refused dismissal.

Why had she lied?

"Well, I'se glad 'cause—well, I ain't never told dis afore—but a whiles back, Mister Seanessy took me aside an' you'se ain't gonna believe hit, but we'se get to talkin' 'bout monthlies. He knows all 'bout hit! He says de reason ours comes together on the full moon day is 'cause our souls is a touchin'! He says de night of de new moon is de one, and

235

when I ask what one, he laughed and said hit was de best night for us 'cause hits a fortnight from de full moon. Lak hits good luck, I suppose. I know hit sounds mighty fanciful but—"

Joy slowly sat up. "What did Sean say to you?"

"Well you see, he says dere's dis disease 'bout. He says de first sign is a missed bleedin', and if'n you or me miss, I'se to come to him, to get de cure. I was goin' to go first and second time you'se miss, but then with all dat happen." She stopped, not wanting to bring Joy back to her grief this first time she managed to engage her. "So well, you'se never seemed sick, 'ceptin' dat once, but I suppose you'se fine now. You don' feel sick, do you?"

Joy fought desperately to control herself enough to understand through the sudden turmoil of her horrified thoughts. Control herself long enough to ask, "When Cory? When did he say this to you?"


The air warmed with the promise of rain, and bursts of light competed with darkness as huge, billowy white clouds moved continually across the moonlit night. The humidity covered Ram with sweat as he ran north toward Orleans from the river road. One of the first things he always did after a voyage was run.

With effort, Seanessy tried to keep his mount to Ram's even pace. Four men rode behind, watchful when neither Seanessy or Ram bothered. Watchful, for word had it that certain parties in England had discovered that Lord Barrington had sold two of his mining interests, and had guessed the rest. Watchful because Ram truly ran on the razor's edge now.

Needing to get away, Ram had left Orleans to see to the purchase of the ships himself. Ships now with crews were docked in the bay. The small fortune was well spent. The ships would soon set sail for the dark continent under the pretense of filling their holds with the valuable and coveted Black Ivory, only to be captured by the Black Ghost sailing the Atlantic winds long before the ships reached the Gold Coast of Africa. Once captured, Seanessy would sell the crews and see minor repairs made to the captured ships, then sell them and no doubt at a sizable profit.

Ram finished the brief list and description of each ship, the repairs he thought should be made, things Seanessy would be seeing to tomorrow. Seanessy finished his own comments and there came a pause, almost awkward as it stretched with time.

They had not seen each other since the fateful night, and though there was no animosity whatsoever remaining between them—if anything, surviving that night only proved the tenacity of their bond—Sean waited for word of the emotional content of Ram's past months away. None came, yet Sean knew it was there. Not only had Ram's men been quick to tell of the wild "Rampages," as they always called them, but Sean saw it in his friend's face. Harder and leaner, with months of a beard's growth on the devilish features, there remained a sharp edge to his face and manner not previously there. Sean also knew of Ram's unkind farewell to one of his mistresses in Boston, then the stop over on Devil's Isle, a place of barbarian cut throats, rot and whores, of Ram's wild tricks there. He knew of the physical toll Ram's men had watched their captain put himself through. Anything and everything to extirpate feelings he did not want.

"Joy's guardian died," Sean said, at last filling the pause with the news.

Ram came to an abrupt halt, and the four men behind them reined in too late, trampling past and around them. With Ram's gaze locked to Sean's, he but motioned to the men to back away. Ram didn't have to say anything, for the message was exchanged wordlessly in the way two who are that close communicate. He didn't have to say he was sorry but not surprised; Sean knew that, just as Ram knew that if she had needed anything, Sean would have seen to it. He didn't have to say the last part either, except he wanted it spelled out.

"I will hear her name no more." His breathing was heavy, his gaze cold. "God's rest, but I want to forget her, Sean. She has brought me enough trouble."

Sean glanced up at the full moon. Clouds suddenly washed them in darkness as Ram started running again. It was not to be, he knew with a certainty he couldn't explain. Ram would be hearing from her soon, perhaps even tonight—the night of a full moon—when she, even in her grief, would not be able to escape what now should be clear. Sean pushed his mount ahead, riding alongside in silence.

Not minutes from this exchange, they were alerted to the sound of a rider ahead. The four men behind them, ever cautious, removed cocked and readied pistols.

Sean and Ram stopped as the night rider came into view down the darkened road. A small cloaked figure rode atop the magnificent horse that all recognized at wind's speed. Her hair and face remained concealed in a hooded cloak that spread like wings with her flight, and Ram drew a sharp breath, quickly stepping back into the shadows as she reined her horse to an abrupt halt upon the unexpected encounter in the road. She turned the nervous horse till she sided and faced Seanessy. The moonlight burst from behind the clouds, and Ram glimpsed the terror raging with tears in her eyes. Eyes, he saw, locked to Seanessy's; she didn't know he was there.

Joy stared at the man who had orchestrated her fate, changing it for life. Tears blinded her, and she trembled with violence as she raised her riding crop and sent it hard against Sean's face.

Ram started with the shock of it and watched the emotion blaze on Sean's face, none of anger, even as the crop raised a second time.

Sean caught her arm, and she twisted with the rage of a wounded creature's last struggle. "I hate you! I hate you!" she cried, fighting the arms now lifting her onto his saddle, then binding her struggle completely. Helplessness bound the surge of violent fury, forcing her to collapse all at once into tears. "Why, oh God, why Sean? Why did you to this to me?"

Incomprehension mixed dangerously with other emotions as Ram watched this drama, and his gaze locked to Sean's. "Trust me," Sean called down to him. "You will know soon enough!"

Ram made no move at first, but then the light disappeared, and with it, rain started falling. Followed by four men, Ram was gone.

The house Ram purchased for his temporary stay rested on the outskirts of Orleans' affluent Garden District. Surrounded by acres of magnificent gardens, the house was built from an architect's encounter with a roman temple at Nimes in southern France. Double, two-story-high houses, were joined by a spacious single story wing. The magnificent house had romanesque pillars, heavy modillions and triangular roofs, all of which generated a powerful ancient and masculine feel. An unusual and magnificent home but one he felt suddenly glad was only temporary. Nothing, certainly not a house in this country, compared to Barrington Hall in England.

Normally, he had no trouble controlling the restlessness and ill-ease brought by the English intrigue, but of late he had begun realizing just how much it took from him, his life. He had thought the voyage—the ceaseless lull of waves, the salty taste of the air, sunsets made of glorious plays of color, light and form too beautiful to be imagined—would help. It had not, and yet as soon as he stepped into this house, dismissed all but one of the servants and dressed, he longed to return to his ship and to the sea. He longed to return to England.

The one place he could not go.

Dressed now after the run, after witnessing the drama of that unfathomable scene, he stood at the mantel of his study, staring into the dancing flames of the fire there. He rarely drank, having learned long ago that drink heightened his emotions rather than stifled them, but as his thoughts travelled in restless turns around the picture that was his life, he was drinking, and heavily.

He heard the heavy iron front gate swing open and stepped to the window to look out into the dark, rain-washed night. Tiers, one of his grooms, stood in the rain holding the gate open to Seanessy, and upon seeing whom Sean still held, he cursed low and passionately. "Nay Sean—'tis madness to bring her to me again!"

He did not want to know what created that scene he had just witnessed. He could not fathom it, and he could not guess. All he knew was that he closed his heart to her; he would not open it again.

Seanessy had explained to Joy only what he knew Ram would not. He had explained his motivation for forcing this fate upon her; he had explained the English intrigue, how what he had made happen would save Ram's very life. Even when she finally understood, Sean never asked her for-giveness, only her understanding of the deed. Once she had understood, words became superficial and none were then offered. Silently, he set her to the ground before dis-mounting himself and handing the reins to the waiting groom.

Joy stood staring at the great house numbly, vaguely aware of Sean escorting her up the stairs. The doors opened and they stepped inside. She saw nothing; she saw not the spacious foyer, the magnificent dark-green landscape paintings adorning the walls, the polished marble floor or the curious look of the maid as she took her wet cloak. She saw only him, for Ram stood in the hall staring back at her.

A wave of Ram's hand dismissed the maid, though his intense and cold gaze never left her. He wore gray English riding pants, a white silk shirt and a gray double-breasted vest carelessly left unbuttoned. With the crown of dark hair, now a beard and the ever so familiar patch, taken with the tailored clothes, he had the air of a ruthless and arrogant aristocrat. A look matched perfectly by the cold light of his gaze.

"I leave her to you," Sean said simply. "I'll wait elsewhere."

It seemed he had no choice. "This way," Ram said, leading her down the darkened hall to the west wing and into his study. She followed him quietly inside. After shutting the door, he left her standing, and he went to the brandy decanter. Their silence sang loud, broken only by the rain falling on the window, the crackle of the fire in the hearth.

So much had been buried in her grief, but upon seeing him again an emotional swell rose through the numbness of her shock and grief. With the scorching memory of their night, she felt her heart pound, the color rise in her cheeks, a tremble start in her hands. Her eyes found the floor as she tried desperately to stifle it, for she could not feel anything until this was done. No matter what, she could not feel anything.

Ram struck a kindling match to the flame and lit a lamp. Gold light filled the large room, and she saw it all in the sweep of her gaze. Like his ship's quarters, the house spoke its owner's name. Dark Dutch landscape paintings hung on the walls. The colors of the parted drapes, drawn by gold ropes, the oversized couch and chairs all matched with a dark forest-green damask. The huge desk was cluttered with open books, drafting paper and piles, a place where he obviously spent much of his time.

Ram waited now, cruelly aiding the silence. The last thing he wanted was a reminder of that night. Yet there she stood before him. Braids crowned her head, and she wore a simple dark skirt and blouse, a black frock over it because she was too poor to even own a mourning dress. He saw the shame color her cheeks, the tremble in her hands. It cost her much, too, and not able to wait any longer he asked, "What in hell's name have you come for?"

She never looked up but said with simply unalterable truth, "You must marry me."

She spoke so softly he almost hadn't heard, and he stared hard, held for but a moment incredulous. "Marry you?" Her silence confirmed what he simply could not believe he heard. "Marry you?" he repeated yet again in a low tone still marked with disbelief as he came to her. He towered over her, his expression one of mocking incredulity she didn't understand. She assumed, was certain in fact, she would not have to say the rest.

"I cannot guess what has prompted this; I thought even you understood that night," he finally said. "Let me make it perfectly clear." He took her face in his hands harshly forcing it up. "Men do not marry their whores. They pay them. And while I had your innocence, this was unknowingly, and I believe you were in fact paid in full."

He would never forget her eyes at that moment. So wide and translucent with unshed tears, filled with a horror each cruel word had brought, yet disbelieving, too. He was not able to meet the depth of emotion there, and he released her abruptly, turning away. "Now, can I assume you understand your position?"

She didn't know she was nodding, or that her legs were backing her away, that she was reaching for the door. She grabbed onto the brass door knob, clutching it tight as though needing something to hang on to. Seconds passed as she stared in horror at her hand that could not turn the knob. With a small gasp and using both hands, she finally managed and it turned.

"No!" He threw the glass hard against the bricks of the

mantel. She pressed herself against the door and bit her hand to stop her cry as he came back to her, stopping, staring at her as before, yet now fear showed where only anger had been. "No Joy." He shook his head, desperately trying to deny the obvious that had finally reached his mind. "Say it isn't so!"

"Yes," she said with her own pain, "I carry your child."

He came upon her, staring at the awful truth in her frightened eyes until they lowered. Time stopped, as he reached back to untie the ribbons of her frock, then lifted it over her head. The frock dropped to the ground. She held perfectly still as he slowly unbuttoned her shirt. Calloused bronze hands parted it, and he stared through the fabric of her chemise at the changed fullness of her breasts. "No," he whispered. "God forbid, we had but one night—"

Joy did not betray Seanessy. Now done, it mattered not. He had told her why and that—even the motive to save Ram's life—mattered not. Pride, the cruel reality of soliciting Ram's loathing, scorn, fury mattered not. Armed only with the simplest, most fundamental code of honor held throughout mankind's history, she knew only that he must marry her.

He turned away to the brandy decanter again. Joy tried to button her blouse but her hands were stiff, still trembling. A silence returned, a silence broken at last by "I cannot marry you, and you cannot have my child."

She stared for a long moment until realization brought her hands to her mouth with a pained gasp. "I never." She shook her head. "Oh Ram, I know what name you call me, but I never . . . you were the only one—"

"You don't know anything," he said meaningfully. "And God knows, girl, I am not questioning your chastity. If only I could."

He turned to the fire, staring at the bright flames, and then the awful truth was said at last. "The child cannot be born. My seed is stained with the madness of my ancestors; the

243

child you carry is cursed with it. It is not the madness of a poor degenerate mumbling to himself on a deserted street— though aye, it has been known at times mercifully decayed to that—but by far it comes as a cruel, calculating and sick madness." He stopped with the horror of it. "One that has spread untold misfortune throughout the many centuries it has survived."

The image of his father's suicide came to his mind. A pistol put to his father's head, mercifully ending the misery in a horrid splattering of blood and flesh. Yet the slain girl who lay at his side, bloody and mutilated . . . God but she could not have been much older than Joy.

"What?" she questioned in a whisper. She heard the words but with dawning confusion. "I don't understand. You are not mad. Nor feeble or witless. Why you are farthest from those maladies of anyone I've ever known."

"I was spared. It has skipped generations before, only to leave the descendants to work their whole life in effort to repair the damage done before them. Then, too, the madness often lives dormant like a caged monster, waiting a chance to spring free."

Ram did not say that Sean was bound by blood oath to take his life should ever it manifest. It was not important; he had known for many years, and he had escaped it. To question one's own sanity was a faulty game, one he quickly learned to give up. The clarity of his thoughts shined as sharp as sunlight upon crystal, while the control he placed upon his emotions left little doubt that he had escaped the curse.

Ram went to his desk, unlocking the bottom compartment, and after searching the piles of old manuscripts, books and records—the written records of the horrors of the Barrington title—he removed a small leather-bound book. He motioned for her to sit before he began, which she did.

"This is the earliest record of it. It dates 1394, during the reign of Richard the III, and was written by the hand of a scribe, one of the religious monks who lived within

Carfortin's Castle, one of the Barrington Estates then. In Latin he describes the castle life; noting deaths, births, marriages, the seasonal changes and harvests, among various other events: hunts, diseases that came and went, celebrations and so on. Of one of my maternal ancestors, married already with a son, he tells how she was bled three times for hysterics, finally exorcised by a priest when it became clear that she was in commune with spirits not seen or heard by anyone else. A period of apparent health followed; another son was born. Soon after though, there came a night when she fell ill with a baffling head pain. And that night as people slept, she stabbed to death three of her womenfolk, two of their children, one of her sons and the Lord Barrington himself, before throwing herself from a tower to her death."

He watched the reaction make its way to her face; she paled and her eyes widened with the natural horror of hearing such a tale. Yet he saw she was still confused. Not for long though.

"The great tragedy of it," he continued, "was that she left one of her sons alive. He in turn passed the madness on to two sons and a daughter, only one of whom though, managed to survive the usual onslaught of childhood diseases and afflictions. By God's curse though, one was enough . . .

"Throughout the generations following, the insanity has reared its head many times. Occasionally, it has been disguised in history. I have one forefather who, besides being known to have been plagued by these horrible headaches, led the attacks in the first of the Irish wars. He is remembered for the devastation of the Irish countryside, for rapes, pillaging and the mutilation of innocent country peasants. He is said to have had the policy of decapitating children, my God, children—" His voice lowered with pain and solemnity as though he alone were responsible. "And as their mothers begged for their lives.

"Tales from years gone by still persist, will always persist. More than one Barrington has had a torture chamber—a thing drawn from ghost stories told around a dying fire, only so much worse, for real and innocent people were forced to play the gruesome and sadistic games till their death. In my own home, as a boy not five yet, twice my father forced me to such a place, this room in the cellar of the basement. God, I remember that smell, that horrible smell of blood! Where was it coming from? There were shackles on the wall and a rack, whips and—"

He stopped, repelled by his own words, the memories that would forever shadow his life, and when he resumed, his voice was filled with the rich timbre of anger, more frightening for the control he placed on it.

"My father . . . the madness was concealed in a deceptive veneer of sanity, and he was at times charming and intelligent, a sought after member of court, known for his benevolence of all things," he said with disgust. "That is when he did not have those headaches that left him bedridden most of the time. It is little wonder that my mother and her family were deceived. She died at my birth. I never knew her, but I have often wondered what she endured left helpless and at his mercy."

He paused with the solemnity of the thought, and she felt his emotions reaching her through the distance and silence, holding her still and mesmerized.

"My father tried to leave me alone; I could tell he tried. I was but three or four years of age then, and already lived for the most part with Sean and Mary in the village. To this day I don't know how that was arranged or why. Aye, but Mary was a good woman," he said with tender feeling. "She loved and cared for me as her own. I would not have survived without her.

"Anyway, I was too small to run away, too young to understand—those few times I was forced to go home—my father's sudden bursts of violence, an unexpected whip

246

across my back or a sudden strike of his hand. I only knew to avoid the man I called my father.

"One day I was playing with a ball in the hallway, not knowing my father had returned from a long absence. I looked up to see him watching me, only he wasn't looking at me but rather at my eyes. His hands held his head to brace the pain, and I knew, I knew . . . I jumped up to run but he caught me. I fought wildly, but I was only a lad of five and he a grown and strong man. He held my arms and took out a knife, wild with sudden agitation and fury, cursing not me but my mother, the pain in his head. He said he would cut the sin of my mother from my face, and he put the knife to my—"

He stopped, not able to finish, and yet when he turned to her, he saw he didn't have to finish. A hand covered her mouth; tears streamed slowly down her face. All the pain and horror of a five-year-old boy were owned in those large eyes staring back at him. He remembered Mary's eyes when she had found him.

Again, there came a silence, one finally broken by the last awful words: "That is why you can't have my child. There will be no more Barringtons; the madness will at last be buried with my grave."

The emotions brought by his story yielded to confusion again. "But it is too late," she whispered, frightened. "The child is already growing inside me, growing . . ."

Ram did not want to contemplate the innocence of her ignorance, the fact he would destroy it with the simple facts. He turned instead and poured another drink.

"Normally," he began, "it is an easy thing to rid a woman of a man's seed. There is a tea but it works only within the first two months." He paused with the concern of it, then swallowed his drink. "You are past that; it will require a surgeon. There is little pain, I'm told, but needless to say, I would not let you be awake throughout."

It was then, the moment he said those words, that she felt a slow tingling heat rising in the palm of her hand. She held it in her other hand, staring at it. "Ram, you wouldn't—" She stopped, hardly able to say the words that would make it perfectly clear. "You would see our child is killed?"

"Yes."

She stared at her palm: *Do not doubt the gift the Lord gives you. Do not doubt . . .* "But you don't know!" she cried suddenly. "You can't know for certain our child would be mad! What if he's not? How can you be sure—"

Anger flashed as his gaze met hers. "How?" he barely managed to control his voice. "I have only to feel my patch and think of my father!" He abruptly spun around, unwilling to release his anger on her. No, he would make her understand; he would make her see that no matter what else he did, he would not leave any offspring after him.

"Imagine Joy, if this child was born," he began in a tone quickly controlled. "Obviously a female child would not be nearly as bad—women are far easier to control. I suppose we could just keep her locked up if . . . when the madness showed. What if it was a male child? Despite the madness, he would be my son and, damn all Joy, look at me! I am taller by a foot than most men, probably five times as strong. I am intelligent as you are, Joy—it is rare that one meets a woman who can sign her name let alone read Aristotle. So," he concluded, "we might reasonably assume that in all likelihood our son would be tall, strong and intelligent. We can add a title and a fortune, two things that would serve to open any and all vistas to him. Joy, it takes this much imagination"—his fingers separated an inch—"to give him ambition. Such qualities in a man breed ambition and aye, Napoleonic ambitions!"

Coming to her, Ram took her by the arms, staring into the wide anxious eyes as he spoke. "And with all that, give him the madness and my father's ability to conceal it. Give him a need, nay a thirst, to hurt people and watch them suffer!"

"No." She shook her head. "No, he wouldn't be like that!

I know—"

"But you don't know! God girl, I have only to imagine his hand to your face, a knife to your throat and I can say yes! Yes, I would kill my own child!"

He released her abruptly and turned away. She was crying again, holding the scorching palm of her hand. Yet the old woman did not have to warn her of what she knew with sudden fierceness; the child she carried would not be mad, and she would see the child born, with or without a father.

"I'm so sorry, Joy," he said in a voice filled with regret. "You, of all women, do not deserve this." He swallowed his drink, staring out the window at the rain-washed night. He'd make the arrangements immediately; the sooner it was over the better now. He turned round, just as she said, "But I won't submit. I want this child. It is my child, too; he's inside me. I . . . I can feel him, I—" Her hands were placed there as she suddenly realized it was true. "Ram please, I could go away, you would never know—"

"With or without me," his voice rose, "the child will be mad; the result is the same. I'd never allow you to bear the responsibility alone—"

"But I shan't be alone! The reverend, Sammy—"

"There will be no child!"

Tears fell down her cheeks, and the palm of her hand felt as though it were held high over the flames of a fire. Desperately she sought the words that would cast doubt upon centuries of history. There were none, though, and all she could think was: "I won't do it," she whispered. "I won't lose my child."

He saw the determination shining in her tear-filled eyes, the tremble of her lips. My God, what did she think? That he was asking for a favor? Didn't she know? "You don't understand, Joy," he pronounced her sentence. "I'm not giving you a choice."

"You can't force me—"

It was as far as she got. With a swift jerk of his arm, the

contents of his glass were flung in the fire, sending flames lashing up and out as he swept upon her. He took her by the arms, threatening her with his height and strength, the intensity of his gaze. "Do not pair off with me, Joy Claret. You are no match. A battle of wills would not be pleasant for you. I will do what I must."

It was too much; a cold dread engulfed her, a dizziness swept through her. She felt herself falling and falling with nothing and no one to catch her. Was that anger still on his face? Alarm? What was happening? "Ram . . ." she tried to speak, "help . . . I'm so afraid—"

Blackness came quickly and she remembered no more.

She woke to a great warmth enveloping her weariness, calling her back from the depth of sleep. She resisted the call; sleep being only an illusion of escape. She lay upon the sofa. A thick quilt covered her. The fire crackled loudly in the hearth; the rain fell steadily against the window, all of this a backdrop for Sean's voice framed in a seriousness she had only once heard in him before.

"It was the only way! God be damned but they know what you're about; the crown prince himself probably signed the edict. The assassins they send will descend like a hungry pack of wolves with you their prey. It is your life now! And the value I assign to your life gives me motivation and justification."

"My life, my life," Ram repeated with cynical harshness, swallowing his drink whole. "You know me well enough to know I am not bait for any man's ambitions. I will fight them to the end; I will no doubt win. A year, maybe two and my affairs will be covered in England—"

"Greed be a truly wicked vice," Sean interrupted heatedly. "There is reason to guess our lords Kingston and Aaron, the others as well, will not let you rest even after you rob them of their motive. They will seek your death for naught but vengeance."

There came a drawn pause, during which she knew Ram

considered the unpleasant possibility.

"You wear your blessed luck like an iron wall," Sean said, "and aye, no doubt you will escape for some time yet. But how long before a coward's bullet finds your back? Besides your death," his voice lowered with cold determination, "there is only one thing that can stop this. I have laid her bare and vulnerable at your feet. And consider, my lord, what if the child doesn't escape the madness? Between you and I, what chance could the child have of playing out the terror of this curse?"

Ram's fist slammed the mantel with rage. "I will not have it! Measure my words Sean; I chose death over the chance. The future is but a darkness ahead, the shape it will take cannot be guessed. I will take no chance; there will be no child!"

"She is not like any other! You can't do this to her!"

Ram's bitter laughter stopped him dead. "No, she is not like the others. That's your mistake and her misfortune."

"We shall see. Fate has been with me thus far—"

"Fate is naught but the will of men, and by God Sean, my will be done!"

"And by God's grace, I pray that you fail." Sean left then; she heard his footsteps, an angry slam of the door. Ram remained at the mantel, she discerned by the clink of his glass.

Do not panic!

She lay perfectly still, stifling tears and trembling. Stifling dizziness and sickness. Stifling the cold terror threatening to reduce her to hysterics.

Do not panic!

If the reverend had taught her only one thing, it was that panic was one's worst enemy in danger. She swallowed it and tried to quiet the pounding of her heart with deep even breaths.

She could not persuade him! She could not fight him! Nay, his will was the monster of his determination, his

251

strength its weapon.

Oh God, what to do? What to do?

*Wits darlin', wits. That's the key to any hopeless situation. All ye got to do is use your head. Ask yourself, what has to happen to get me out of this? Then make it happen. Wits pitted against strength, or pistols even, wins time and again.*

What has to happen to get me out of this? She must escape, put distance and time between them! But how? How to make it happen?

*When nothin' comes to mind quick enough, then you gotta stall. Stall any way you can: Fall on your knees beggin', pretend you're a dog, mad like, start talkin' in tongues to your dear dead aunt—anything! And this darlin', this is the queer thing—so often the solution comes in the stall.*

Stall! She must stall—

She abruptly realized Ram stood over her, and she opened her eyes.

"You fainted. Are you all right now?"

She nodded.

"Can I get you anything? Water? Tea?"

She shook her head and sat up, holding the quilt over herself. "Did you call for the surgeon?"

"Yes. My men are looking for him." He went to the brandy decanter and poured her a healthy portion, handing it to her. "It might help—"

She declined, for if wits were all she had, she would not dull them.

"I heard what Sean said to you," she began quietly in a feigned tone of defeat. "If he cannot dissuade you, then I cannot hope to. I will not fight you. Besides," she said with a disarming sigh, "I am too tired to fight."

Ram was studying her, she knew, but his gaze revealed nothing. How maddening he was! How could that gaze speak streams of poetry, while now, when it was most important, his stare was a silence as stony as a deaf mute.

Minutes ticked away in this silence as she searched

frantically for a stall. The physical elements of panic conspired against her; oddly, all she could think of was Libertine—Libertine, who gave wings to her flight, who always carried her at wind's speed from danger.

"This has happened before? I mean has another woman—"

"Yes, though normally I see that precautions are taken. There have been women, though, who have used it as a ploy to solicit a proposal. When that failed, each ah, 'lady'," he drawled the title with indifferent scorn, "settled easily for financial compensation."

"They lost their child for monies?"

The shock in her voice reminded him of her innocence, the nature of her heart. "Women can be as mercenary as men, Joy. That didn't surprise me. What surprised me was that they were each willing to bear such a child in return for my title and fortune."

The words spun clear in her mind and she knew. Knew, for the heat in her palm—ever present—began pulsating to the pounding of her heart. She turned away, holding the searing palm of her hand.

"Well," she began in a voice barely trembling, "what you call mercenary, I call fair. You insist I do this thing; then I, too, would ask compensation."

She half thought he could hear the throbbing pulsation of her whole being now, it felt so loud in her mind. The silence stretched endlessly. If she had but met his gaze, she might have been cautioned about the wisdom of this ploy, but her back kept to him as she waited. Finally she heard the clink of glass set to table and his strides to his desk. A drawer opened and a pad was removed, a quill dipped.

"Name your price."

Not having anticipated this, she stumbled uncertainly. What sum could she name? "What of the others? What was their compensation?"

"Oh no, Joy. That's not how this game is played. Like the

253

others, you will name your sum, and like the others"—the meaning of his words were plain—"I'll offer the same advice. Whatever sum your small mind conjures, double it, then triple that. For I shall give you what you ask."

It amused him! The whole sordid scene, the petty greed of women's minds, was a source of amusement to him! Oh, how she'd love to slap that look from his face, to spit back at him! To scream that his entire fortune doubled, then multiplied thrice would not be enough!

"Well," she nonetheless proceeded, swallowing the fury that was liberating in its force. "A thousand twice, then thrice is six thousand—enough for my family and I to live in relative prosperity for always."

Amused but with no hesitation, Ram wrote the sum down and raised the bank note to her.

"No," she shook her head, this being her trump card. "I must have bills." She looked away and whispered in a pretense of embarrassment. "A banknote of that sum from you would be awkward to submit, to say the least."

"You should get used to the . . . ah, awkward consequences of accepting a man's money. I'm sure you could do a good deal more than just relative prosperity."

She jumped to her feet and cried, "How dare you? I would remind you it is your child I carry, it is your deed I must do and it is your history that has brought this upon me!"

The lazy indifference of his gaze sent her trembling with fury, pure, liberating and real. She spun away to control herself and said the last: "I know . . . know not to . . . to trust you. I would be paid before I do this. Before, and not afterward."

She waited, her entire being caught up in the prayer that this scheme would work, that he would have to wait until the morrow when the bank opened. Minutes and minutes filled in silence.

"Very well," he said at last. "The sum can be got on my ship. I'll go myself. You will wait until I return and, Joy," he finished as he moved to the door, "as you say you no longer trust me, I no longer trust you."

With that he left, shutting the door behind him, and making his meaning plain, he locked the door. She silently cursed the fortune that would give him access to such a sum, but with luck, it was good enough. She heard him call quick orders to a servant. The front door opened. She ran to the window. Ram waited in the rain until a horse was brought. She watched him mount and leave.

The groom left the heavy iron gate open.

One less passage to worry about.

She ran back to the door, fumbling to remove a hairpin left from her hasty change from night clothes to skirt, though the letter opener on his desk would have done just as well, she realized. It was an ancient means of escape, but the reason hairpins and locks have been closely linked for the ages is that it works; she knew it worked. She stuck it in the lock, jiggling it. The lock clicked and the door opened. She raced down the empty and dark hall, finding the foyer empty. Tiptoeing, she quietly opened the front door, shut it and raced down the stairs into the rain.

There was no thought past running, running from the death of his will. She flew down the lane, her boots splashing in the puddles, holding her sides tight against the sudden cold and rain. Dashing through the gate, she came to a sudden dead stop.

He was waiting for her. Dismounted, with reins held in folded arms and rain falling unnoticed upon his person, he stood there waiting.

She backed away shaking her head, stopped finally by the cold metal of the iron wrought fence. He approached. The rain hammered against the ground, a loud backdrop for the gentleness of his voice as he said, "If only you were like the others." His gaze bore into her. "I never believed it, for I know you, I know you Joy; I have touched your soul."

Her mouth formed the word "no" but no sound came

255

forth as a violent surge of determination sent her suddenly into his arms. He lifted her, holding her instinctively as her thin arms clung tightly to his neck. "No! Don't do this! Please—"

He closed his eyes, and for a long moment he just held her tight. She felt the restraint and rigidity in the hard lean body holding her, the inexplicable warmth enclosing her in a momentary illusion of security and protection. She felt the force of his emotions, so heavily laden with grief and regret. It was a moment of escape, one that with blind desperation she sought to prolong by bringing her head back to touch her lips to his.

It was as if a hot white burst of lightning struck the sky, the unleashing of it, and he lowered her to the ground only to get a better hold on her head as his mouth took hers with unrestrained force. There was no end of it. Her desperation, their violent warring emotions forced him to throw her this one lifeline. The cold sting of rain could not wash the wild ravishment of that kiss, the surge of mindless desire like a rushing onset to obliterate what must come, what would come later.

She still clung to him when his mouth left hers and he bent to lift her to his arms. With a soft vicious curse, he carried her back to the house, kicked the door shut and quickly brought her up the stairs and down the hall to his bed chambers.

Any other time Joy would have found herself beholding the most beautiful room she had ever entered. It was spacious and warm. An enormous fire crackled in the hearth, throwing warmth and dancing shadows about the room. The furnishings were dark, prominent and heavy. The colors were not the muted shades found in most homes but rather the rich and dark shades of green and blue, the colors of the sea that he loved. Dark blue velvet drapes hung on the four poster bed and framed the windows where rain pounded noisily, unceasingly. A magnificent tapestry, depicting Diane's mythological hunt, hung on the wall above the bed. A thick, dark blue and green, patched velvet quilt covered the bed. A bearskin rug spread before the fire.

Yet she noticed none of it, for her heart pounded and her pulse raced with a potent mix of fear, desperation and panic, all of which blended to meet the intense desire in his gaze.

His hands wrung the moisture from her hair as he stared down. She didn't know pain and helplessness marred her features, that his breath caught with the utter vulnerability of her desperation, that she was trembling with it, until he caught her small cold hands in his. "Joy," he whispered passionately, "it will not change anything. I give you less than this night. One night—"

"Please—"

Hesitation flashed in the dark desire of his gaze but only briefly before he lowered his head to take her mouth. She was but a night removed from innocence, and he might have wanted to have her slowly, to lead her gently to desire's call, yet such could not be the case. It was an act of desperation for her and himself as well, and he knew the moment his lips came to hers that he could not stop or even slow the avalanche of hungry, terrible need. It was the same kiss given in the rain, deep, plunging, devouring, as he molded her soft wet form against the swelling hardness of his body.

She wanted the bruising pain of his mouth, that warmth sweeping into the cold dead of her limbs as he lifted her into his arms and brought her to the heat before the fire. They separated only as he left her to remove his own clothes, and she turned toward the flames, hiding her face in her arms, but from what she knew not. She realized he had unlaced her wet boots only as they came off, then her stockings. With that impervious nakedness, he came to lay beside her on the soft fur of the rug, keeping some distance as his hands worked the buttons of her blouse for the second time that night. Color rose on her face as he parted this. She closed her eyes and held still as his hand traced a single line over her breasts beneath the fabric of her chemise, cupping the fullness there, measuring its softness against the hard palm of his hand before reaching behind her to remove the skirt. He pulled these off and tossed them away, returning to unlace, then slip her chemise from her shoulders. This slid off her form but slowly, for the unveiling brought him pleasure and a certain cruel agony as well.

He stared, leaving her untouched, shivering and cold and so obviously afraid. Gone was the girl who had awakened to passion in his arms. The new rounded fullness to her slender form made her a woman and so much more beautiful because of it. His hand strayed to the still flattened stomach, lingering there with a soft curse. A curse because no other words could give meaning to what they were doing.

She opened her eyes as his strong calloused hands cupped her face and he was staring into dark pools of pain, pleading. "Oh yes, my love." He bit her lip, then caught the lone tear on her cheek. "I give you this respite, brief and ill-begotten, it is but one filled only with my love."

He kissed the trembling corners of her mouth, then swept deeply and insistently, filling her with the taste of brandy and desire as he gathered her cold form against his warmth. The shocking heat of him brought her from a cold winter snow to lay against a searing desert sun. His arms crossed over her back to draw her even closer, molding her small form to him. Her body instantly absorbed the life-giving heat of him, as pure sensations chased the dark future far, far away.

Her arms were around his neck, and he broke the kiss to grab a handful of hair, gently forcing her head back to trail his moist lips along the soft curve of her neck to the hollow of her throat, then lower still. She gasped as his mouth took the rosy pink tip of her breast, teasing so lightly as to be torture. Wild shivers raced through her, and she grabbed his head, her fingers combing through the raven black curls, holding him against the rise and fall of her bosom. Then his hands glided over her, kneading her back and shoulders, sliding over the curve of her waist to caress her hips while his mouth and kisses urged with the increasing heat of his desire.

He brought her carefully to the edge of ecstasy, blind exultation, only to stop and slow his pace to start again, stretching passion's sanctuary to its absolute limit over and over again. The urgency remained throughout, growing, mounting with the hungry insistence of his hands, his mouth, as though by this single sweep of passion, he sought to exorcise her place in his heart.

She was flushed, feverish, trembling with languid consuming desire, not knowing she called his name over and over until he answered her cries with a kiss almost savage and the sound abruptly stopped. Coming over her, kissing still, his leg parted her for his entrance, discovering with a husky groan, a shelter, the blessed sweet recess of her body, spreading like warm molten ash to accept him—all of him, mind, body and soul, nothing less—and he thrust deep inside her.

He stopped with the intensity of pleasure so great it bordered on pain. Joined to her in the timeless way of a man and a woman, he brushed her face with kisses and slowly began the journey to passion's ecstasy. Never had he loved a woman as that night. It was slow and timeless, carrying her up to the cliff where his own passion soared, sustaining them both in certain agony. He listened to his name on her lips, watching the sultry darkening of her eyes until finally he sent her into rapture's sweet mercy and followed her there.

Timeless and slow, yet not long enough. Not nearly long enough. The dying light of the fire danced over them as they both lay still entwined in each other's arms. His hands ran over her flushed, love-soaked form as his lips brushed her forehead. He could not stop touching her, yet—

He desperately wanted her to fall into a merciful sleep.

259

Her eyes were closed, her heartbeat spiraling slowly down. Just when he thought she had fallen asleep, he felt a sudden tensing, a slow awakening thud of her heart, ever escalating. She opened her eyes and there lay her plea, a plea ever more desperate now.

He sat up, bringing her with him. He held her face and kissed her one last time. "Forgive me, my love," he whispered. "Forgive me."

The words brought a cry to her lips, one never uttered, for he suddenly snapped his fingers to the side of her head. Her head jerked reflexively, and in that instant, using the lightest force he knew, his elbow, not his hand, struck her head. In the same instant he caught her unconscious form before she fell against the fur.

Ram lifted her into his arms and carried her to the bed. His only hope now was that she remain unconscious until the surgeon came, then throughout. She lay so still, a ghost-like pallor to her skin. He checked her pulse and breathing, both faint and low and distant. She would be out for some time yet. The last thing he did was brush his lips upon her forehead, drinking the sweetness of her, hesitating with the thought that it would be the last time.

If only—

He forced himself away and left the room. Halfway down the stairs, he looked up and saw the old woman standing at the bottom of the stairs, looking up at him. She wore a freshly starched maid's frock and held a tray. A brandy bottle was opened and already poured in a goblet. His servants were still new, and while she was unfamiliar, she could have been hired recently by his housekeeper while he had been away. Though his mind was upstairs, still he noticed something strange. It was not just the woman's age but—

A chill ran up his spine. "I thought I dismissed the servants for the night?"

"I'se told to bring you dis."

Not given to irrational impulses, he dismissed the queer feeling, as he dismissed the maid. "Set it in the study."

She nodded and he came the rest of the way down, following the old woman into the study. She set it on the serving table, while Ram walked to the window and stared out, quickly lost to his troubled thoughts.

"Suh?"

Startled, he turned to see she still stood there, holding a drink out to him.

"Hit'll help ease de pain."

"Is it that obvious?" He took the drink from her, swallowed it whole, adding distractedly, "I dare say, nothing will help me tonight."

"A soul never knows what de very nex' moment brings."

He looked up, hearing the words, innocent yet not, but for some reason his mind focused on the old woman's eyes shining in the darkness. Cat eyes caught in the moonlight. She looked so old, ancient . . . No one would have hired her. Had she come seeking work, destitute and impoverished, the housekeeper would have given her a pocketful of money and sent her on her way. Yet here she was, handing him a drink after he had dismissed everyone . . . dismissed everyone . . . dismissed—

"Who . . . are . . . you?" he asked much too slowly. He raised the glass to examine it, thinking of assassins and plots and intrigues, but his hand felt like lead, lifting much too slowly. "Who . . . are you?" He stumbled to catch her, but the room spun suddenly and he fell. "Nooo—Who? . . ."

"Just a old woman with visions."

Visions, visions, visions, echoed in his mind as he struggled desperately to get up. Darkness burst in his head, and he collapsed, moving no more.

The old woman considered the fallen man. Some mens would o' died of hit! He should be out at least the space of

261

three days; three days, Joy Claret, hit's all I can give you.

The old woman turned away. After she roused the girl and got her on her way, this long day that started with that awful vision was through—finished at last. Three days was plenty, for if anyone knew about escapin', it was the girl, Joy Claret. The girl who loved freedom.

Yes indeed! . . .

*Chapter Nine*

Ram opened his eyes to see a winter's sun streaming through the small portholes aboard Sean's ship, the *St. Mary,* docked in Boston after months of pirating the ill-fated slave ships. Only Sean would keep quarters like this. The good sized room was vaguely reminiscent of an Arab sheik's harem, certainly put to the same purpose. Large and small silk pillows, done in muted tones of orange, pink, maroon, green and splashes of blue, a rainbow of colors filled the entire space. There were no furnishings, save for one long and low table. He became aware of the perfumed scent surrounding him, and he closed his eyes, thinking of another. He could easily sleep another two days after last night, a night spent celebrating the Black Ghost's victories.

"Ah, the sleeping prince has awakened at last."

Ram's gaze drew lazily to Sean, sitting at the table cross-legged like an Indian. The amusement on Sean's face told him there would be no more sleep, though the fresh scent of coffee on the table seemed an adequate reward for the effort of rising.

Sean watched as Ram carefully tried to disentangle himself from the two ladies without waking them. "One wasn't enough, my lord?"

Standing now, Ram gave the ladies a moment's consideration. "I thought you said they were this side of virgins?"

"Obviously a wrong impression."

"Obviously." Ram turned from them and took a seat at the table. "Blast all but I can't remember one of them, let alone the two there. And I don't have drink as an excuse." He had not touched a drop of liquor since the poisoning nearly four months past. "A hundred faceless women save—"

"One." Sean finished for him, pouring the coffee. "No doubt the one will be found any day now."

Sean thought of the assassination attempt Ram had recently survived, thwarted by none other than Rake, who gave warning of the two men hiding in wait for Ram on one of his runs, and just in time too. Then too, while Ram thought the old woman who had poisoned him on the last night anyone, anywhere had seen Joy Claret was of a different thing, he was not convinced. It mattered not though. What mattered was that Ram's uncanny luck simply would not last forever; Joy must be found, forced to marry; the child—God, make that child survive—must be christened and named to the title.

"Yes," Ram whispered, standing with his coffee at the porthole, "she will be found." His motivation for wanting Joy found was entirely different than Sean's. "Well, now that this thing is finally through, and once Joy is found, I can finally return to England." The favor for his uncle was over, or at least the end had begun.

Seanessy had returned yesterday from an absence of many months. Word would soon reach the Orleans' port that the mysterious Black Ghost had captured the first eight of the ships—ships that never even reached the Dark Continent. It was now clear that not only would there be no return on their investment, but the investment itself would be lost. The five investors would be devastated. There would be some selling of property in the desperate preparation to make good the bank notes coming due soon. Only, unbeknownst to them, Ram owned their banknotes.

Ram had also taken an added precaution: he bought up all the excess Georgian and Mississippian cotton, planning to flood the market this season. Additionally, with his connections in England, he had made it almost impossible for any of the five planters to sell. They would not know it was Ram who had ruined them, thinking him a victim of the Black Ghost as well, at least until it was too late.

In another month, maybe sooner, it would be clear though. For as it was he who owned the bank notes, one by one they would discover the fact. Where the banks might have shown leniency, he would show no mercy. Charles Simone might be able to hang on for a while. True, he could sell some acreage and Negroes and probably make the first payment. Yet with no cash from his cotton crop, he too would soon fall. So, the favor neared completion; his agents would see the rest finished.

"I know how close she is to delivery now. Two months . . . the knowledge is agony . . ." Ram's voice was laden with emotion.

Sean had reassuring words on his lips—how a thousand dollar reward would surely bring the information within a day or two—and just as he was about to speak, a knock interrupted. Sean's man Tim entered with an excited Bart, and Sean laughed, for words were not necessary. The gleam in Bart's eyes said it all! Joy had been found at last.

Thomas Speigle, the Reverend Archibald Cox's under-secretary, was unused to running, yet as he had run the two long miles from town to the church, his thin, frail frame drew on stamina he never imagined he owned. He raced up the steps and through the doors, down the aisles of the empty church and finally came to a stop at a far door that marked the reverend's study.

The reverend was in the midst of a conference with Drew Paterson, the famed Negro reverend, outlining the speech to be given before the United States Senate next month. The two men were engrossed; the opportunity the address offered would not be wasted. The abolitionist movement was beginning to swell, a small swell but one that, with God's grace, would burgeon with the passion of the hearts and minds of people across the land. The address was sure to cause an uproar. At a time when many people, most Southern senators included, refused to believe that the mind of a Negro could be uplifted from their imposed ignorance, the Reverend Paterson came as a shock. He appeared mild at first, owning a gentleness and serenity that transcended racial hatred and bigotry time and again. Until he stepped on the pulpit. With words of fiery brilliance and elegance, his God-given gift of oration, the Reverend Drew Paterson swept people to their feet with tears, cheers and impassioned cries for justice and God's will to be done. Subsequently, those souls on the other side of the issue were raised to their feet with fists clenched, waving madly. A Southern newspaper, laying across the Reverend Cox's desk, explained the phenomena of Drew Paterson by claiming that he was a white man disguised as a Negro, and as outrageous as the claim was, it came as no surprise that many people believed it.

When the knock sounded, the very urgency of the rap solicited both men's attention. "Come in," the Reverend Cox said.

Young Speigle opened the door, breathless and appearing afraid. "I came as soon as it was brought to my attention. I saw them myself—the posters."

The reverend's bushy white brows drew together. "Posters?"

"For Joy Claret—Miss Reubens. They ask for information leading to her whereabouts. They describe Reverend Doddered, Mr. Freeman and Cory, even her horse. They're everywhere!"

"A reward?"

"One thousand dollars!" Speigle cried.

"Good Lord," Reverend Cox whispered, as his gaze blankly swept his desk. The Lord Barrington's men had been to see him twice, having traced Joy and her family to Boston. Then Lord Barrington himself had appeared. He had heard so much about Ram from his uncle, Admiral Byron, then much from Doctor Reubens before his death. He knew all about Lord Barrington's bold and courageous scheme that was bringing ruin to the five financiers of those slave ships. He knew so much about the man, and yet nothing could have prepared him for meeting him in person.

As he presented his case, Lord Barrington's calm and civility concealed a dangerous power, and the case was remarkably persuasive. He said it was too late to harm the child she carried and his duty now was to marry Joy and see the child raised. If it was her welfare he was concerned for "then let me assure you, sir, she will see no harm from my hand. Indeed, I would bestow upon my wife the kindness, care and consideration of the most solicitous of husbands. I shall not waste time enumerating the benefits of marrying into either my station or fortune, you can imagine that yourself. . . ."

Yet, he could not betray Joy. He had tried to convince her, but just mentioning Lord Barrington's name brought fear and panic into her eyes. She refused to listen to the arguments, wanting only the secrecy and safety of hiding until he gave her up for lost. This, Lord Barrington said in no uncertain terms, would not happen, and his parting words shocked the reverend, reminding him of what was often said about Lord Barrington—a gentleman until the moment it didn't suit his purposes. "It is a good thing for you, sir, that I will find her with or without your help. For if I could not, the noble and decent cloak worn over your dear soul would not stop me from having the information beaten out of you."

"What shall we do?" Speigle could wait no longer.

"Thank God that Lord Barrington's will is not joined

with the devil's."

The small two-story house, buried in a snow-covered valley and surrounded by a forest of birch and pine was where the Reverend Archibald Cox often retired to write his sermons. The beauty and solitude of the surrounding tree-covered hills provided the necessary quiet to commune with his faith and impart his communion to words. It was in this private hideaway that Cory and her family lived as they worked to build their own home not three miles away on a parcel of land the Reverend Doddered had won in a card game—a card game in which nothing had been left to luck.

Wearing scarves, mittens and hats, bundled against the cold none of them could get used to, Cory, Sammy and the reverend waved goodbye from the cart to Joy standing on the porch seeing them off. The reverend's gaze lingered on the lone figure, waving and smiling, before she finally turned back inside.

"I got a scary feeling shakin' me bones today," the reverend said.

Sammy cast him a sideways glance. "I knows what dat's 'bout. Hit's 'bout a no good thrifty scoundrel dat wants to get out of another day's work."

Cory, cushioned between the two, giggled.

"Our girl's safe," Sammy said with assurance. "No one, not even him's gonna find her out here." There came a contemplative pause filled for the hundredth time with thoughts of the situation. Finally Sammy said the traitorous words out loud: "'Sides"—his voice dropped with seriousness—"I ain't all that certain hit would be dat bad if'n he did find her."

The reverend and Cory looked at him. "I knows she's afraid," he began an explanation, "mighty afraid after what happened, but I knows him; we all do. Hit's too late now; he ain't gonna hurt her—we'se heard what he said to Reverend

268 .

Cox—and well, hell, hit's jest that a woman ought to be married."

"You might be right," the reverend conceded with a sigh.

Cory's face was stern. "Hit don' matter none, right or not, hit's what Joy wants dat counts."

Sammy looked at his new wife, seeing her love and loyalty, and he slashed the backs of the nags. "Women!" Yet he was grinning hugely.

Joy looked upon the changes in her body with certain horror, fascination and plain amazement. She rarely went with the others to the house building simply because she was hopelessly useless these days. She tired so easily and was in a constant state of hunger. A good deal of her time was spent satisfying that hunger, and yet, with the exception of her midsection, she remained as slender as ever, as though the vast quantities of food went straight to the child. Her muscles, though, had at some point turned alarmingly soft, like pudding or mush and just as useless. Oddly, there was one good change: When the others battled against the cold, she was always comfortable with a healthy glow to her cheeks, as though warmed from the inside out.

Most troublesome by far was how the child stole her mind. It took enormous effort to hold serious thoughts. When they had first arrived, before she had been showing too much, the good Reverend Cox had arranged an introduction—a meeting followed with a dinner—with the Reverend Drew Paterson and his wife. How she had idolized the great man for some three years now, ever since Joshua first began talking about him and she began reading about him. He was a true hero of hers, one she was quick to quote, a hero she revered and admired. Yet at the dinner she had found herself far more interested in Mrs. Paterson, the births and upbringing of their three children, than she was in the noble ideas being discussed by the men.

Or, like last night, her mind drifted from the editorial the reverend read to the family around the fire, and without thinking of the ninny she would make of herself, she interrupted to inquire in all seriousness, "What do you think? Another pair of blue booties or white?" They had all looked at her for a moment, stunned, then burst into laughter.

Joy went about her morning chores, musing with a smile over these things. This was not the end of it. She had this queer compulsion to do all those household chores she loathed in the past, a compulsion to keep everything in order and neat. The worst of it was the strange comfort in the stitchery she had always hated, whiling away many hours with needlework. Needlework, of all things!

Most of all, she thought of the child, and as she stepped outside with broom in hand to sweep the porch, she wondered not for the first time if the old woman's prophecy could possibly be true; if her child would be a humanitarian. The old woman had rescued her that awful nightmarish evening, and only the word "miracle" explained the vision that sent the old woman to Ram Barrington's house that night. Every time she thought of it, she met the miracle with increasing wonder.

Sweeping the snow off the porch, a small tingle suddenly ran up her spine and she froze. Anxiously, she looked out over the vista. The profound silence of the snow-covered forest greeted her. All was quiet; no sound save the rush of water in the nearby stream or an occasional slide of snow falling from a branch. She dismissed it, renewing the sweeps of the porch.

These mood swings were another thing! How she could move in the space of a breath from a simpleton's contentment to utter panic and fear that he was near, that he would find her, was beyond her. Hopeless indeed, she could only pray that once the child was born, not only would her strength and mind return but she could put the past

270

behind her.

Which she vowed to do, just as soon as he gave up looking for her.

"Did you see that, my lord?" Sean asked. Mounted and hidden behind a cluster of trees on the upper most incline, they watched as Joy finished her task. "That look. It was as though she sensed you were near."

Ram hardly heard, so taken was he by the first sight of her in so many months. The lurch in his heart took him unawares; he hadn't expected it, though he might have known . . .

Joy finished her task and returned inside. After finishing inside, she enjoyed a mid-morning snack of bread and cheese, washed down with apple cider. Stretching lazily, she thought it time for a nap. She climbed the stairs slowly and slipped into the room with her small cot.

Ram never knocked. Silently he opened the door, stepping from the chilly winter air into the warmth of the house. Wood burned in the potbelly iron stove, with additional heat filling the small space from a fire dancing in the hearth. A sweep of his gaze told him she was upstairs; the quiet told him she was asleep. He removed his cloak and gloves. With his soft-skin moccasin boots, he made no sound as he climbed the narrow staircase and entered the room where she slept.

He did not know how long he stood there staring at the vision before him. She lay on her side. Long lashes brushed the curve of rosy cheeks, and the long hair, tied simply behind her, spilled in rich darkness off the side of the cot. How motherhood rewarded her beauty in kind! She wore a pale blue-gray gown of muslin, gathered beneath the fullness of her bosom where his gaze lingered. The folds of the gown might have hidden the changed shape of her figure; but her small hand gently lay there, outlining it, and the sight of his child growing inside her stirred emotions he never thought he'd feel.

271

There was a possessiveness and protectiveness that was not surprising—except in the matter of degree. Far more surprising was how he found her more beautiful, with her startling femininity more pronounced and accented like it was. This was more than a little disturbing, disturbing because he felt it as the physical force of desire. If he were but any other man, it would be his pleasure to keep her permanently in this condition, to fill their lives with the happy sound of their children.

"If only," he whispered out loud. "God girl, how you bring me regret. The punishment will be mine, too, for you shall be my wife in every way save one." One child of fate was one too many; his vow now was that there'd never be another.

Joy stirred, teased by the whispered timbre of a voice haunting her dreams. She opened her eyes. For a long moment she met the devilishly handsome face with no sign of alarm, knowing it was but another of her endless dreams. When will you stop haunting my dreams? Will I ever be rid of this love so consuming as to fill my each breath, fuel my each heartbeat? Dear God, shall I never be rid of this terrible longing.

Oddly it was an amused glint of someone who knows something another does not that abruptly alarmed her. She reached a hand to touch the warm, living, vital and all too real presence.

She cried in a gasp, lifting up to scramble away, knowing only the instinctual panic to flee, but before she even made it to her feet, Ram rounded the small cot and stopped her with gentle hands.

"Easy Joy, easy," he said, with his hands gently taking firm hold of her arms. The shock of his presence, the reality of his touch, brought a mute horror, a desperate fear twisting her face. "I know you're afraid," he said very slowly. "I do not wonder why. Upon my life, I will not hurt you. I will not hurt our child now."

She stared as the reality came in bits and pieces. He had

found her! He was touching her! She was alone; there was no one who could help her . . . "Oh God, please—"

Ram followed her anxious gaze to his hands. He released her reluctantly, then only to watch her scramble back against the wall, clutching a pillow tight against herself, looking as though she fully expected to draw her last breath. He saw it; the marked difference in her was plain. The child she carried imposed helplessness upon her—a helplessness not new in reality but one she never realized before. He had no doubt that had she had not been with child, he would have been looking down the barrel of her pistol again or felt her nails upon his face as he was forced to subdue her. Gone was the tangermont; here was something else instead.

"Do my words mean nothing?" he asked.

She couldn't understand the masked untenderness in his gaze, mirrored in his voice, all in direct contrast to his formidable, terrifying appearance. He wore tailored gray riding pants, baggy black-dyed suede boots—like a savage but not—a thick black belt and a loose fitting white shirt. Her terrified gaze rested on a double shoulder harness holding two ivory-handled pistols, each weighing—she could guess—nearly twenty pounds. Yet he wore the weapons with ease, as though he no longer even knew the cold metal was there.

The question needed an answer and she slowly shook her head. "How could they?"

"What will convince you I will not hurt you?" His hand brushed her face as he leaned over to whisper. She shied from his touch but he ignored this. "What will take this fear from these eyes—eyes that have haunted my sleep?"

"If you leave me—"

"Leave you? After searching all these past months? After worrying and wondering every blessed hour of my waking day? Don't ask me that." He smiled. "Anything but that."

His smile disarmed her, and she considered the words through the ever increasing turmoil of her panic. "But if you

273

have not come to hurt me or . . . or my child, what then?"

"What then?" he repeated the question. He walked to the window, held up the thin fabric of the yellow curtains and appeared to peer out, searching carefully for something. Finally he returned to her, the all important question. "You've left me no choice, Joy," he said softly as he sat upon the cot. "My child will be born; I'm left now with the task of seeing the child raised, of giving the child every chance I can."

She didn't have to think how she felt about it, for she had thought of it no less than a thousand times. "No!" She shook her head. "I'll not have my child raised with a father who harbors vile suspicions, who thinks his child lays on the brink of some horrible madness!"

"The child will know only a father's love from me," he said with masculine simplicity. "Love"—his voice lowered with regret and pain—"that will be my ruin just as surely as I draw breath—"

A small hand reached up to touch his mouth, stopping the words she refused to hear. "The child will be normal! As everyone else! I know it—"

He grabbed her hand in his.

"God's prayers that it be so," he said with naked feeling. "Though know this—if, when that changes, I will be ready. A father's love will not stop me."

She withdrew in sudden fury. "But I'll never let you!" she cried in a passionate whisper. "Don't you know? You'd have to kill me first before I'd let you—"

"Hush!" he said harshly now. "We shall speak of it no more. The child will never know my fears or worries—"

"He will not know your fear because he will not know his father! I will ask you to go and leave me be, and if or when this would-be madness appears, I will call you to your God-forsaken duty!"

Emotions shined bright in her eyes; her fists were clenched white in an effort to control the violent emotions trembling

274

through her, and Ram saw it all, including the incredible fact that she truly thought he might leave her after all. "Joy, even if not for the curse of my ancestors, I would not leave a girl not yet twenty to raise my child alone and in poverty."

Tears filled her eyes, accenting the emotions there: fear, uncertainty, plain apprehension.

"You don't trust me, this is plain," he said softly. "I can only earn your trust with the evidence that comes with time. In time I will prove that my fears will not shadow our child's life, that my fears will in fact never once touch it. The child will know both parents' love, Joy."

She turned from him, looking down at the pillow she still held over herself. She tried but could not doubt the sincerity of his words. He believed it. He truly thought he could raise the child without the shadow of his ominous, vile suspicions. Was it possible?

She didn't know. What would happen if he failed? How awfully would that affect a child's well being? How could she take the chance?

"We will be married tomorrow. I—" Ram stopped with her half gasp, half cry, her utter shock of it.

"I'll not marry you! Not after what has happened!"

She was clearly aghast, and in other circumstances he would have laughed at the sweet irony of it. After spending a good part of his life escaping the clutches of dozens upon dozens of women's ploys, plots and efforts to get him to marry, the one woman he'd have was truly horrified at the idea.

Ram simply stated the fact. "You will marry me. Whether by force or reason, it matters not."

"Force? You can't force someone to marry—"

"Can't I? There isn't a magistrate in this country or mine that would refuse my bid, not when my paternity is etched into every line of your figure. And by God's will, girl, if I have to drag you kicking and screaming into a court, I will. Though I don't think I will, for while I've long since grown

275

used to scandals following my every movement, I should think a mother would want to spare her child's history from a gossiping public's maliciousness."

She tried to deny it, any one part of it, but this was not possible. He could force her! He would force her!

"I'll run away!" she whispered passionately. "If you force me—"

"Run away?" he questioned and then shook his head. "I don't think so. I'll be damned if I spend so much as another hour looking for you again. So understand this, my love"— he leaned over and took her face in his hand to force her eyes to meet his—"after I find you the first and only time you run away from me again, I will lock you away, never to see the light of day!"

The bars of an iron-tight prison closed around her, though at first she was too shocked to cry. She just sat there staring at him with wide, frightened and still uncertain eyes, not knowing the punishment she dealt him as he stared back.

"Joy." He reached to touch her, to offer some reassurance, but she stiffened, her eyes widened more.

"Please. Don't . . . touch me."

He withdrew his hand again, and as though shocked by her own words, she tried to explain. "I need . . . time. I—"

"Time is the one thing I can't give you. We will be leaving—"

A loud and queer bird's call interrupted him, and she had not taken the next breath before Ram flew into action, instantly lifting her off the bed and into his arms. He held her backside against himself, one hand lightly covered her mouth to stop her scream, while both her hands covered his.

As he brought her quickly to the window, Joy held her breath, seized with panic, yet instinctively cautioned against moving in any way. Ram lifted the window, then pressed against the wall, listening, still holding her with an inexplicable force, so gentle yet firm. With his free hand he removed a long shiny pistol from his shoulder harness.

Against the unnerving quiet of the forest, the shrill call sounded five times in close succession. She heard Ram's soft curse above the pounding of her heart and held perfectly still, as the curse seemed to unleash the terrifying power of his braced body.

"Does that door lock?"

She shook her head.

"Can you fit under the bed, then?"

He asked this as he brought her there, easing her backside to the floor. She slid quickly under, not an inch of room to spare her shape and far too familiar with danger to question him now.

"Do not move again until you hear my voice," he whispered. "Understood?"

She nodded but he could not have seen as he quickly brought the chair from her sitting desk to the door to jam it. She watched the steps of the soft suede boots move from the door to the window. She gasped as they disappeared, Ram jumping the two stories down to the ground. She never heard his fall, for he suddenly moved in the cloak of a predator's silence.

Ram took cover behind a cluster of trees and bush shading the side of the house. Sean had signaled five men approaching, not just any five men but five hired assassins with the single intent of murder. They must have followed Sean and him out. This alone spoke for the assassins' skill, for neither Sean nor himself often let such deadly details go unchecked, let alone unnoticed. Aye, he thought, a considerable cut above average, no doubt.

Ram had fought alongside Sean his whole life, save for his years in India and the dark continent, and he knew well what their game plan was. Sean had slipped into hiding, choosing an advantageous position while waiting for Ram to position himself opposite, with the men in between.

The silence of the forest was complete, save for the rush of water nearby and so quiet. Ram heard snow shifting off the tree limbs. There was no sign of any of the five men. This told him everything. Unlike most encounters, these men were to be taken seriously, very seriously indeed.

A shrill bird's call broke the silence, and Ram's gaze swept the distance in that direction, guessing where Sean hid. The sound came from across the open space in front of the house. Very convenient. Now to see where these would-be threats were hiding and just how good they were.

Ram knelt and picked up a heavy stick. With pistol poised and ready, he threw it hard against the wood beams of the house. It worked instantly; three shots fired in close succession, with both Sean and Ram returning fire so close on top of that as to be inseparable shots. Neither Sean nor Ram oft missed; Sean's man dropped from a tree while Ram's man fell from the upper barn window, draped lifelessly over the ledge. Libertine's startled cry filled the air as Sean and Ram, moving in the exact same moment, aimed at the third of the three; but just as Ram's finger touched the draw, Sean spotted the movement behind Ram and shouted, "Turn!"

An outside observer would have sworn Ram turned before the word was out, so quick were his reflexes. He spun round on a heel as he fell to a roll, and between the two movements his pistol fired into the man's chest. A second too late, the assassin's shot only grazed past Ram's ear.

Simultaneously, Sean and another man fired; Sean's distraction losing him precious seconds of accuracy, his bullet missed the mark. The return fire hit his shoulder but with only a sting of a scratch. Sean jumped ten feet to the ground, swinging quickly behind the cover of the tree's trunk.

"Not bad shots, my lord," he called out.

The fallen man at Ram's feet wore common clothes but had the look of a trained soldier. Not trained well enough, Ram thought as he started to circle around through the cover of the trees. "I've seen better," he said loudly in a tone

278

that shocked all who heard, save Seanessy. "The odds are even now, and the thrill is gone. Let's get the bloody business over."

A shot fired so close to Ram's head, he laughed, and his laughter alarmed one Paul Bates far more than the precision of Lord Barrington's return fire or the speed of his reflexes. My God, he thinks he's playing with fools!

The silence of the next minutes changed everything. Ram was just about to offer impunity as he and Sean both circled around the front of the house from opposite directions, dashing from cover to cover in search of the two remaining men. They finally came within twelve feet of each other, having seen and heard nothing. Just as they started back, a movement off to the side caught their gazes.

"Shall we toss?" Sean asked.

"No, I've one shot left. Go ahead." Ram was already loading his empty pistol.

"Very well" Sean said as he took up aim. The man moved again but with a savage's grace and speed, and wisely Sean did not waste fire. "A savage or a half-breed by the looks of him."

Finished reloading, Ram took aim, too. Both were behind trees for cover now. "Jesus, they're always sending the infidels to do their dirty work." Louder, he offered, "Your life or your weapons. Now man!"

There was no answer but then Ram didn't expect any. The savage darted between trees; Ram fired and hit him in the arm. "Geez, I missed."

"It's your sympathies Ram—always been with the dark-skinned dogs."

The man darted again and Sean fired, missed.

"What goes here?" Ram asked.

"Target practice," Sean replied.

"Sean—"

Sean took one glance at Ram, who was suddenly staring at the house, and in a flash of a second, all was known.

"A setup!"

Ram was already running toward the house. The movement drew the savage out, and Sean aimed, firing a split second before a bullet fired at Ram. The savage dropped dead and Sean was running, too.

Joy Claret held perfectly still underneath the bed. Perhaps owing to the adrenaline pump, the pounding of her heart, or the rush of her blood, the child in her womb was moving as he never had and actually felt as though he turned somersaults. Both her hands pressed hard against the life there, partially to protect and partially with the queer idea of somehow holding him still. All she could think of was that the terror pounding in her temples would cause a two month early birth, one that no child could survive!

She was praying, praying as she never had before.

Her small pistol had not been unloaded since the day she had escaped Orleans. This was but another thing that had changed. It was common knowledge that there were no greater protective instincts than those of a mother—any mother. She was no different. Not only had she loaded her pistol, but she now knew to use it; she knew only that she would do anything—absolutely anything—to protect the life growing inside her.

Moving with quiet grace and skill, Paul Bates had taken advantage of the situation. Lord Barrington had come out here for a woman, a woman he had thought worth at least one thousand American dollars. From that, he had guessed the rest. He wondered how much they would pay for the death of the woman carrying Lord Barrington's child. A good deal, no doubt, especially if her death brought the necessary advantage needed for the Lord Barrington's death. Risky for sure but it just might work if he could take out Barrington's man, too.

With pistol raised and aimed at the front door, he climbed up the stairs, ducking in the cover of the hall. One door was ajar, the other closed in a clear signal that she was behind it.

280

Joy's hands flew to her mouth as he kicked the door open, the chair tumbling in a clamor to the side. She never saw the swing of the man's arm as his pistol instantly swept the room in search of a target. Nothing. Nothing but thin curtains hanging lifelessly from the open window.

Joy watched in mute horror, as the wet black boots approached, step by deadly step. She reached for her pistol, but her hand trembled so! Ram's name was cried over and over in her mind as she desperately tried to get a firm enough grip on the pistol. Was he dead? Dear God, was he dead now?

"Come out, my lady. I shan't hurt you."

The husky promise came in a whispered English voice, but she was so scared by this point she never thought. She pulled the trigger, firing at close range into a boot. The man howled as he jumped, but her next breath brought into her lungs nothing but smoke. She choked, blinded by smoke and fear. With a vicious curse, he kicked the small bed. The force sent it to the wall, and she lay exposed.

Joy screamed as she sat up, bringing her knees against herself and her arms holding tight her head. She never saw the man, for as she braced for death, four shots fired in such close succession as to be indistinguishable. Sean from the doorway; Ram from the window. The man dropped with a heavy thud, and before she knew what had happened, Ram's hands were on her, lifting her upright.

"Joy, oh my love—"

She opened her eyes to see him with a choked gasp of relief, and for the second time in her life, she fainted. Ram caught her effortlessly into his arms. Seeing her for the first time, Sean was taken by her appearance. "My God, she's even more lovely than before."

"I had thought it my imagination."

"I verify the reality," Sean said, but his eyes widened still. "And enormous!"

Ram smiled at this, but then, as he held her in a tender

gaze for a long moment, he said, "That was too damn close Sean."

"Aye," Sean's gaze dropped to the dead man. "We grow too cocksure with age, but the next time—"

"There won't be a next time. We set sail as soon as we reach Boston."

"But the child?" Sean asked in alarm.

"I dare say, it will be easier for her to carry the child safely in her womb than to travel with a newborn. She has two months. We should reach England with plenty of time to see her safely settled at Barrington Hall for the birth."

Sean considered it and had to agree. "Better by far than sitting in wait of the next round of fools they send us."

"Indeed."

Late that night, Joy lay in bed crying. The terror of the afternoon was gone, fading upon waking and the presentation of the news that she would be leaving her family at morning light. Cory and she had spent the entire night crying in each other's arms. Sammy spent the night watching this. He felt guilty because he wasn't willing to give up all that they finally had to travel to some faraway white folks land—where they not only didn't have Negroes to free, but they didn't have Negroes period—for what Ram said would be a year or two. Guilty also because his staying meant Cory stayed as well. Then there was the sorrow that they would miss the birth of Joy's child.

Everything had been settled calmly and rationally in a long talk. Seanessy had made the bargain that she had agreed to, as had Ram. If ever she saw Ram's fears shadowing the child's life or if she ever found fault with the way Ram treated the child, she would be allowed to take the child to another household. Ram swore to the arrangement and thereby, in one sweep, her only fear and uncertainty was wiped away. The simple bargain removed the single awful fear she had lived with for so long.

This was not the problem now. She felt desperate, so desperate, and like anyone who had not a stick to fight with, she flung back the covers. With only a thin cotton night dress, grabbing her shawl against the cold, she finally found herself racing down the stairs. A fire crackled in the hearth, throwing light in the small room where Ram lay on the bedroll spread before the fire. Sean was nowhere in sight. Tomorrow, one night away, she would be leaving all she knew and loved. Tomorrow she would be married.

Upon hearing her footsteps on the stairs, Ram's gaze lifted to her. She stood with her hands clasped nervously, staring, pausing with some unspoken caution he understood well. He expected the tears and desperation. What he was not expecting was the sight of her form silhouetted in the firelight, barely concealed in the fabric of the nightgown, and he chuckled with the quickness of his body's response to the woman haunting his dreams.

"I give fair warning, Joy. Approach and plead at your own risk."

"My own risk?" she questioned in a whisper as she came to him. "My own risk? Upon my life, what more can I lose?" She dropped to her knees; the drama of the move was not lost to him, and a bare hint of a smile crossed the handsome features of his face. "Oh Ram, please! I'll marry you; I'll do anything, but please don't make me leave my family!"

He took her clasped hands in one of his, a gentle yet firm hold, as his other hand brushed a tear from her cheek. "I explained already. We must be in England as soon as possible and well before the birth. I cannot wait for a bullet to find me, let alone you. The journey will not be too trying for you—I will see to it. I no longer nourish any love for my country; eventually we will make our lives elsewhere. It will take a year, two at the most . . ."

"Two years! I can't bear it! What will I do? I've never been without Cory since I was but eight years old. And not

283

now! Sammy and the reverend too! If you make me go, then make them go, too—"

"Why you selfish brat!" he scolded, yet with warm humor. "The reverend made it abundantly plain he would not honor English shores with the bottom of his boots despite his love for you. And Sammy and Cory? Would you have them give up all that they have worked so hard for just to sit with you and keep you company?"

"Yes!" she said as a petulant child, soliciting his warm chuckle in response. Distressed, she put the case to him that she had put to a tearful Cory, Sammy and the reverend hours ago, arguing like any silver-tongued lawyer, covering the issue from all sides. Their house could wait until they returned. The reverend had nothing to fear in England—if only he could for once in his life keep his hands clean. There was plenty of work on the abolitionist cause to be done there, and while that country had no slaves to be freed, they could speak at churches and societies to rouse further British support. Support from that country could perhaps conceivably be an influential factor in swaying congress—

On and on she went, dramatically, the English lilt to the lovely music that was her voice always prominent when she was distressed, upset or emotional. Ram listened without interruption, though he had considerable difficulty in following the words. The effect of being so near to her after all this time was maddening, more so because with all the emotions sparkling in those eyes, there was no longer any fear.

She had already told him of the fear she had lived with these last months or so—"It was constant, like a cloud shadowing my every move and thought—" Yet, it was already gone now, and after only hours. Though of course, it would take time for her to trust him completely again. Time as the child was raised; time for her to see that his fears would not touch their child's life. Then too, the major reason she was not afraid of her future with him was owing to her

284

certainty that the child would be normal. Somehow, almost against his will, her certainty, along with Sean's, reassured him, too. If it be true, that the child was well, then all he had to do was raise him or her with the knowledge that there could be no more children.

So, their first meeting was characterized by relief, a strange welcomed relief for both parties, whether she knew it not. Yet what was he going to do with the restrictions this future fate wove? My God, how could he have her as his wife, yet not ever touch those lips or fell the softness of her body against his? How could he survive that? One child was risk enough; he would never have another. If only she could be made to drink that tea!

A thing he didn't think she would ever do . . .

Ram ran his hand through her hair, staring intently as she spoke, then taking a long strand of the thick tresses to his face, drinking that sweet scent he remembered so well. Yet still distressed, Joy continued the attempt to persuade him, as though he were some capricious God who held her family's fate in his hands. She never noticed the intensity of his stare, the unmasked desire so plain there, the way that same gaze travelled over her kneeling form.

"Don't you see"—fresh tears sparkled like bright gems in her eyes as her voice revealed her emotions with a whispered tremble—"after losing Joshua, I . . . I can't—"

Ram finally heard this. He reached out for her, and gathering her in his arms, he brought her gently against his long length, throwing the quilt over them. The warmth that closed so quickly around her, the feel of those muscled arms and the clean masculine scent were so very much like the dreams haunting her sleep and idle hours, she succumbed without protest. She was only vaguely aware she might want to protest. This vanished completely as her face brushed against the smooth hardness of his bare chest, his lips against her forehead, his hands through her hair, and she nuzzled closer still. Succumbing . . .

She knew not how long she lay entwined in his arms crying, but at some point her emotions quieted. So much had happened; so much was going to happen. Yet all she could think of was this ache in her heart—an ache that she had felt for so terribly long now, this queer empty place in her heart that could bring tears to her eyes for no reason at all—was gone. Banished by his touch. With sudden clarity, she realized the ache had not just been the burden of fear that he would find her, but a fear he would not. It was a longing that knew no other answer but him.

"Being Lady Barrington should not be all bad," he said suddenly with a tender smile. "There are, no doubt, certain benefits."

"Oh?" She looked up. "Like what?"

"Like what?" he seemed to ask himself. "Well, you'll have lots of pretty new dresses—"

"I don't care about pretty dresses," she lied. "What else?"

"What else . . . what else . . . Well, you'll have all the maple syrup you can eat. How's that?"

"Better." She bit her lip to stop her smile. "But what else?"

"Why, you greedy wench! Well"—he tried to resist the tease of those lips—"Barrington Hall always has the tallest Michaelmas tree in all of England."

"Ohhh!" The smile lifted to her eyes and he drew a sharp uneven breath. "That's nice," she said, unaware of the effect she was giving him. "But then again, it is a very long time till Michaelmas . . ."

Ram stared intently, wrapping a loose strand of her long hair around a calloused finger. This was just a game, yet it touched upon the unkind reality of their future which he knew she didn't understand. Here they were playing and teasing; she no doubt was imagining a happy ending to the book that was their lives. She knew he loved her and she was right; he supposed she had captured his heart the very first day. Yet what a poor miserly trophy it was. He could give her his wealth and his title, he would care for her always but there would probably be no more.

Soon after the child was born, he would have to put distance between them. It would hurt her, as it would him. She would understand of course. Joy reached a hand to his face, not understanding the changed emotions there, but then she gasped and took his hand to lay it over the movement. Ram felt a tiny foot, a jump, and he laughed with the pleasure of it. He needed no encouragement for this, and thinking he had at least a few months when he could make her happy, he shifted her so that she was cradled backside against him with both his hands resting upon their child.

"What will you name him?" she asked in a whisper.

"How do you know—"

"I just do," she said simply, thinking of the old woman's prophecy. He did not want a son, she knew, but a son was what she carried.

Ram accepted this and returned to her question. "Not a fourth, that's for certain. How about Joshua?"

He said it for her; the sentiment touched her heart and he barely heard the reply. "No, it's too soon still."

"Well, a child should be named after someone loved, respected and admired. If not Joshua, then—"

"Absolutely not!" came Seanessy's voice from a dark corner. Ram laughed, and Joy gasped surprise but smiled when she heard: "There has never been, nor should there ever be, an English lord with an Irish name! Let alone Seanessy! It's at once absurd—"

"Oh Ram, it's perfect. Lord Seanessy Edward Barrington!"

"Aye, my lady." Ram chuckled. "Sean is, after all, responsible. And since Sean will be his namesake, it is Sean who will be responsible for teaching him to defend the Irish name, which he will no doubt have to do."

"I shan't have a chance to teach the lad!" Sean said. "He'll get too much experience on his own, I'll wager. Well, I can foresee now there will be no dandies raised in the Barrington

287

household. Lord Seanessy—oh, my poor little fellow . . ."

It was with laughter still in her eyes that sometime later she fell into the deepest and longest sleep of her life, wrapped in the warmth of his arms. She woke in the morning in the privacy of her own room, wrapped still in his arms. He did not make love to her, but still, what he taught her was a lesson she would never forget.

Ram was quite drunk. It was after all his wedding day, a day he had never dreamt of seeing. Seanessy followed close behind, drunk as well and for the same reason. The marriage had been simple, short and sweet; it was over. What took half the day was the parting. There was simply no end to the tears, the promises, the sorrow, and when Ram last checked in on Joy, now safely tucked away in the carriage driven by Bart, he couldn't figure what she had been doing. Sitting on the carriage floor and using the seat as a table, an enormous picture book beneath a sheet of paper, she was writing a letter to Cory in the dim light, braced awkwardly for the bumps and jostling. Not three hours had even passed since she waved the final goodbye and she was writing a letter.

The road to Boston was good, one of the best he had seen in this country, and the travelling was smooth. It was dark now. A blanket of snow covered the surrounding woods, gleaming white beneath a moon and starlit night. It was quiet, the trampled layer of snow covering the road cushioned the noise of the carriage wheels and horses hooves.

Ram and Sean rode fast ahead of the carriage, passing a cask back and forth. Their laughter and merriment broke through the quiet that was the night and announced their approach for miles ahead.

"You know, my lord," Sean said with an anticipatory grin. "It will be my great pleasure to see what the voracious appetite of English society makes of the new Lady

Barrington. This will be second only to witnessing what she makes of them."

Ram chuckled. "English society is composed entirely of pretenses. Joy has the patience of a gnat when it comes to pretenses. I can just hear her now addressing our 'good' prince regent: 'Sire, it is an absolute imperative that you act immediately for the American Negro! Sending British troops would be just the message those Southern bigots need! I suggest you address your parliament at first chance!'"

Sean laughed for it was only too possible.

"Or," Ram continued after a long draught, "to a group of ladies: 'A pickaninny farm is a hateful place where—'" He stopped with his laughter, imagining the scene clearly. "God's curse, but I only hope I survive her initial introductions. She is not prepared—"

A pistol shot fired in the dark! Sean and Ram instantly drew readied pistols as their mounts reared and danced. Bart, nearly caught off guard, reined the horses to a quick stop, jolting Joy awake, as she was thrown to the floor. Libertine, tied in back, neighed angrily.

The men emerged from the dark forest like rats, and the carriage and horses were suddenly surrounded. "My God, that was a fright," Ram said, assessing the six, seven, eight men, three pistols and so many drawn knives between them. He took a long swallow of the cask and handed it over to Sean. "I thought at first it was another round of assassins."

"No, not assassins these. What is this man? A robbery?"

"Aye! Drop your pistol and get off ye mounts here and no one will get hurt."

Sean merely laughed, causing his nervous mount to prance.

"Oh, my dear fellow." Ram leaned forward in his mount with a frightening gleam in his gaze. "I beg to differ. Someone here is going to get very hurt."

Bart sighed, rolling his eyes toward the heavens for help.

He could practically repeat the next part word for word.

Sean took out a gold coin and tossed it to Ram, who flipped it in the air. "Heads," Sean called, as his horse danced conveniently around so he was very near the two other raised pistols.

"Tails!" Ram won with a chuckle.

"Curse the luck," Sean said.

"Oh hell, Sean! You won last time, remember?"

"What the bloody—" The leader of the pack was a young fellow, big and stocky, with a beard and dark hair covering round, prominent features. His head had been bouncing back and forth as the two spoke, but his men grumbled nervously around him, and he suddenly snapped, "Hey! I said—"

Sean held up his hand for silence. "Just a moment, my dear fellow." Then to Ram he said, "But last time there were only four."

"Oh, very well. I'll split the prize in half." He took another long draught.

"You're too generous, my lord."

"Well, we're in a hurry anyway."

The pistol was raised higher and through gritted teeth, the leader said, "I said plain: Now drop those pistols and get off!"

"The man means business, Sean."

"Aye. It's your move, my lord."

"So it is." Ram raised his pistol as though to drop it but fired into the ground, as simultaneously he kicked the leader's pistol high in the air, while swinging off the horse. Seanessy was known for a certain eagerness in these situations; he had not the restraint to wait. His booted foot kicked hard into another man's face, and this man fell back with such force, he brought two men down with him. The fight was on.

Then came loud grunts and groans. Three shots fired, but in the sudden blur of fists and feet, of brawling bodies, none

290

of the shots hit anything except—"Jesus!" Bart swore as a man caught it in the dead center of his hand, a split second before Ram's fist mercifully put him out of his pain. Bart bore the interlude with feigned patience. This was not the first time, for God knows, England had more highway robbers than other country had honest citizens, and though he had no doubt of the speed in which it would be over, he was nonetheless careful to keep a shiny pistol aimed and ready just in case.

Sean laughed as he watched the last two men turn and flee for their lives, then called to Bart to help move the bodies off the road. Bart descended with a curse. Ram was examining his hand as Sean opened the door to the carriage.

"The bastard must have had his mouth open when I hit him, and I've got one of his bloody teeth lodged in my hand." Ram pulled it out with a curse. "Geez, but I could get rabies from a lot like this. Where's that rum cask—"

"Ram." Sean stared into the carriage.

Sean's voice warned him, and he just stared, not able to move at first. She was crouched in the far corner on the floor with her arms crossed tightly over herself and her knees pulled up in a ball. Her eyes were wide and enormous and filled with certain terror.

"Oh God," he cursed under his breath. The carriage lowered with Ram's weight as he bent and stepped inside. Sean shut the door. Ram sat on the cushion seat and brought her quickly onto his lap. She was trembling, and he took the comforter from the opposite seat and wrapped it around her.

"You're not going to faint again, are you?"

Joy shook her head uncertainly. "Though I do seem to be making it a habit around you. I hate it, too," she said in a still shaky voice. "I remember when Madame Peters returned from abroad, she told Katie and I at some soiree, 'All the best ladies are doing it! One has only to tighten one's stays till they pinch. Then the slightest distress sends one into a swoon! Oh, it is so *tres jeune fille . . .*'" Ram chuckled affectionately and she said, "I don't mean to be such a simpering ninny, truly, but . . . but—"

"It's different now," he said for her as his hands ran lovingly through her hair.

"Yes. I used to be afraid, of course at different times, but I always felt safe with Libertine. I knew I could escape. Now, I'm so . . . so big and awkward and, and, helpless," she said in a whisper. "I can hardly bend to lace my boots, let alone get away from anyone."

She looked away with an embarrassed blush, not able to say the rest. There was something about carrying a child that made her needy, dependent and ridiculously helpless. She knew no other words. She needed him in a way that frightened her. She hoped fervently the feeling would leave once the child was born . . .

"I will never let anything or anyone harm you, and so you, my love, have the luxury to be helpless." The words drew her eyes to him and he was smiling. "And whereas your helplessness and awkwardness sits uneasily with you, it plays differently with me. I have never found you more beautiful."

He kissed her then, tenderly sweeping a warm rush of desire through her, that different kind of tremor she remembered so well. Just as the kiss would have deepened, she felt a sudden shudder go through his huge body, a tensing. He broke the kiss chastely, looking at her with a question.

How could a single kiss, a relatively chaste taste of those lips, send that force of desire through him, a force that shook him? She was large with his child; her beauty should be shrouded in the halo of the Madonna herself. My God, what did this bode for the not distant future? It would be bad enough just knowing she breathed the air in a distant, far away land, but to have her as his wife spelled certain disaster better named tragedy. What would he do? Would any distance ever be enough? God forbid they ever relive that night!

He could do nothing for now. He could not put distance

between them now. Her condition brought out a tenderness and protectiveness he had never known before, and he simply could not hurt her now . . .

Joy was staring back at him, and he saw the love in her eyes. "God girl," he swore softly and low, "you are indeed my curse."

With confusion and a question in her own eyes, he lifted her off his lap and onto the seat. He gently kissed her forehead, and he clicked open the door, leaving her wondering what curse?

What did he mean by that?

Joy brought the quilt around her, leaned against the side and closed her eyes with a smile. Was it truly possible? After all that's happened, could she possibly hope for a happy ending? Were they to be happily married?

Oh, the agony of imagining she'd never feel his arms, taste his kiss or hear his laughter again! Despite all her fear, despite her determination not to let him see his child, she had always known she loved him, as she knew he loved her. She knew, too, the love was forever; she felt it deeply, playing the innermost strings of her soul. Yet it had hardly a chance to begin . . .

Once the child was born, once he knew the child was healthy and well, once he was certain of it, then all would be well. He would know his children would all be well both in heart and mind. The old woman prophesied it. Yet was it hoping too much to imagine many children from their marriage?

She didn't know but put the happy thought aside, content with the deep and sweet longing she felt now, as she imagined—after the birth of their child and she was recovered—a kiss that would know no restraints.


Dear Diary,
 We have been out to sea four days now, and this is

the first day the seas and weather are calm enough to allow a steady hand put to paper. The storm was fierce indeed the first day of sails, as the rain pounded the deck and the wind blew like blaring trumpets—the howling seemed so ominous, like a warning to me—and well, I've no real excuse for the sudden panic I felt.

I opened the door to this fierce weather and stupidly braving it, I ran out, searching for Ram. By the time I found him on the upper deck, working with his men to get a sail hoisted, I was soaked. He took one look at me and flew into a rage, lifting me where I stood to carry me back to his quarters, cursing all the way—cursing me and my wits, my sex in general and on and on he went, much like a time I remember so well. My, what a temper he has. Though I have learned, like his men, that if his rage explodes in a verbal thrashing, one is far, far safer than if he controls his anger in that deadly calm of his—a calm that signals one's certain demise just as surely as seeing the gates of satan's hell swing open!

Well, I endured his wrath with quiet fortitude and without interruption—this being the best, the only means of handling it. He was wearing only a canvas vest, breeches and boots against this weather, water dripping from his person, the wet clothes and bare skin outlining every carved muscle of him, and I do not pretend to know how he looked so handsome to me then.

Finally, he lost wind, and I was able to ask the question pressing on my mind, the source of my anxiety and panic: "Are you certain we'll reach England in time?"

"Is that what this was about?" he asked calmly enough but while looking as though he might tear his hair out.

I nodded. "My fear came upon my introduction to

the ship's surgeon, Bret Holland. He looked like any of the other sixty or so crew members: huge and fit, half naked like a savage, an unkempt graying beard and hair too long for convention and shiny dark eyes prominently set against tan, weathered skin. He looked like no surgeon to me, and after but a few well-chosen questions, it was immediately clear that Dr. Holland knows everything about scurvy, broken limbs and pulling teeth but as he said to me, 'You'd better hold your horses my lady, for the only birthin' I've witnessed was Missy, the ship's cat!'"

"Joy, Joy." He placed his hands on my shoulders. "We have two months. The longest it has ever taken my ship to reach England is six weeks and that was with the worst imaginable weather. This weather is in our favor! We should reach England in three weeks. I promise to have you in Barrington Hall a month before your time."

I tried to be reassured by his confidence, but I can't explain my apprehension. I just have this awful feeling . . .

Ram had promised to reach England in time. Yet two weeks later, only hours from one of the Caribbean islands' coasts, Bart led Sean and Ram to the crew's quarters where, hanging on a hammock with Bret at his side, a man lay already delirious with fever, and Ram knew the promise would not be fulfilled.

"Black fever," Bret said. "The worst kind."

A memory played in Ram's mind. Less than a week of sails, and Joy, already bored with the tedium of sailing, looked up from her breakfast tray and said: "How I miss the fresh fruit of the Orleans' Market."

That was all she said, all she had to say for him to march outside and give orders to the quartermaster to change the bearings and head for a quick stop to the nearest isle where fruit could be got. He was absolutely confident the week's delay would mean nothing. He had been absolutely wrong.

"God's curse, not now!" Sean was the first and last to speak, because that summed up the situation and the sentiments perfectly.

Dear Diary,

Now I know something is terribly amiss. First Ram tells me I am not to stroll on deck anymore because of the chilly north wind. Yet there is no chill to the air! It is warm and breezy, as though after all this time we have not sailed far from the tropical waters. Now I no longer see Bart or Sean or indeed anyone but Ram. He is waiting on me. He brings me food and fresh water at regular intervals, and my, but I could swear he teeters on the brink of exhaustion. Sharp lines are etched on his face, he seems worried and concerned, and I know he is overworked.

Ram sidesteps my every question and concern, somehow making me feel foolish for all my worrying. I am offered excuse after excuse, but today the quiet haunting the ship is worse. When I looked out, there were but a handful of men—Sean and Ram among three others—minding the sails and the tasks. The ship seems to be hardly moving. It is as though his crew abandoned him and jumped overboard. There is now only two weeks left, and if one judged by my size, the child could come any time!

I asked Ram what the black flag meant, worried that he was planning to do some pirating along the way and with me like this! It is the first time I saw him almost smile in long weeks. He said only, "Nay, my lady, there will be no pirating for us." Then he asked me only those endless questions: "How do you feel? Warm? You ate well?" and so on.

"Ram, tell me what has happened?"

"A setback, that's all. The wind and weather, you know. It's certain to change. Don't worry . . ."

So, still he side-steps my every question. There is another queer thing. He no longer touches me. He never draws near. He sets the tray down, then stands back to stare at me. Now, not with amusement, fondness, desire or any of those things I am used to seeing in him, but with concern. I know what he is afraid of, too; he is afraid he is going to have to deliver his child! I am afraid, too, for at this rate we will never reach England . . .


Three days later, shortly after Joy woke from a particularly long sleep and as she prepared her confrontation with Ram to finally discover what was wrong, a knock came at the door. She opened it to see John, one of the crew members. He held a tray in his hands.

"Where's Ram?"

"Oh . . . ah, he's very busy—what with the queer wind that's turned us back a bit."

This was the newest of the lies they told her—that a queer wind had been turning the ship in circles, and she might have believed it, except "There is no wind!" She felt dangerously close to tears.

"Well, no wind is a problem, too, you know," he said, still standing nervously at the door.

"No I don't know! I don't know anything except that I want to see Ram!"

"Now, now, my lady, 'tisn't—"

Joy pushed past him to the bright sunshine of a beautiful cloudless day. She stopped instantly upon seeing the handful of men milling about in the sun. The men all ceased their activities and stared back at her. She slowly approached one of three men nearest, taking in his ravished frame, his ghostly pallor and she knew.

"What is it?" she asked quietly.

The man looked to the others for help. None was offered. For a long time no one said anything. Finally, John spoke in a solemn voice from behind. "Black fever, my lady. Meself, I've recovered now, while a handful of others—yourself included—are the only ones it hasn't hit yet. We've lost twenty-eight men so far. I dare say, we're safe now but you, what with the child—"

Joy thought of the strange splashes—things dropped overboard—she had heard periodically for the last week. Black fever once swept through Orleans. Many people died. Initially the fever lasted about two weeks. Sometimes it returned after a recovery period, and no one survived that second coming. "Ram?"

"He went down last night, after pretending for days he didn't have it."

"Nooo—" came as a whispered plea, and she started running, running as fast as her condition allowed before any of the men could think to stop her. She nearly stumbled down the galley steps, blinded by the sudden darkness. She covered her mouth and nose against the odor there; a terrible foul smell permeated the space. She forced herself onward and pushed down the dark space to the crew's quarters.

She stood aghast. It was a small space for so many men, nothing but hammocks hanging in a chaotic array, trunks and trunks throughout. Men lay listlessly in the hammocks, each in various states of undress and each in various stages of the fever. Those few men who had recovered, or the fever who had not succumbed, were tending to the dozens and dozens who were in the throes of it. These men were the only ones who noticed her.

"My lady!" One man started toward her. "Leave at once!"

"Where is he?"

"He's in the carpenter's room with Sean, but—"

It was too late. She was off and gone. She managed to find the carpenter's room only because the door was open and she heard Ram's voice. His voice was strong and well, and a small gasp of hope escaped her as she stepped in the room. He lay in a bunk, covered with blankets. His face was flushed with the fever, and as she stood there for a moment in pain, she watched violent chills shake him. Still he was awake and conscious, unlike Sean above him, and he sat up on an elbow, instinctively turning to where she stood and said only, "Get her the hell out of here, Bart!"

"No," she said sternly in a voice that alarmed him far more than the fever stealing his strength and health, leaving him as weak as a kitten.

"Bart, you go help the others. Get those men on deck to start cleaning the filth from that room. I dare say that's half the problem right there. Scrub everything with salt water— we've got plenty of that—the bodies, the pots and the floors—everything. Start washing the blankets, too, alternating them till each has been cleaned. Do you understand?"

Bart had been one of the fortunate few who had not succumbed to the disease, and seeing Joy standing there, so obviously well and in control, tore him between immense relief and more worry. "Yes, my lady, but—"

"Where's our doctor?"

"Sick with the others, but—"

"Is he conscious?"

"Not for some time."

"Are you taking proper measures? The highest fevers need constant dousing and fluids—forced if necessary—while the lower ones need warmth. Is that clear?"

"Yes, but—"

"Bart, you're not moving. Don't worry. I'll take care of these two!"

"Over my dead body!" Ram finally spoke after listening incredulously to the onslaught of her instructions. "I said—"

"We know what you said," Joy interrupted firmly but

quietly. "But you're not giving orders anymore. I am. Now Bart, please!"

"Aye aye, my lady." He left quickly.

Ram lay back. He could not fight her; he had no strength. "Joy, if you get this fever, I'll—"

"If I haven't gotten it yet, I won't. Such is the way with these things. Besides, I never get sick," she informed him. "Joshua always said I owned the constitution of iron."

"But our child—"

"Is perfectly safe inside me." It was amazing he could talk at all, and as she wrung a cloth in water, he collapsed against the bed, yet still watched her through the feverish shine in his gaze. "You know, Joy, as soon as our child is born and you are recovered, I'm going to beat you within an inch of your life."

She smiled as she gently placed the cloth over his forehead. "My heart warms to hear it, for it means you will have to recover, too."

She soon had them moved to the captain's quarters. She never heard Ram swear as he did when she told Bart and John to lay him on the bed, swearing he'd have to be dead before he took the only decent bed from his wife who was ready to give birth at any moment. Tapping some hidden strength to fight the frighteningly high fever, he stood, refusing to lay down until another bed was brought, and when it was, demonstrating how much the show cost him, he slept for the next fourteen hours.

Sean's fever rose dangerously but only for a matter of hours before settling. Like Ram's, his fever was at a place that kept him bedridden but not high enough to be life threatening, as so often was the case with the fever. Over the next few days Joy earned the name Angel Shrew. Angel because her ministrations helped and shrew because it was obvious she enjoyed the upper hand. Joy could only wonder at how they managed to tease and laugh being so sick, but on the eleventh day she understood.

She opened her eyes to see Ram, in all his impervious

nakedness, up and walking around the room looking for something. A hand went to her cheek as she felt the heat rise there. He stretched, then kind of shook, as though to rid himself completely of the disease. There was no sign he had ever been ill, at least not on his muscled frame. She gasped as he jumped up to grab an overhanging bar and started doing pull-ups. The chiseled muscles worked with fluid ease, and the sight was as unnerving as it was patently unbelievable. She was too dumfounded to speak.

Seanessy sat up with a curse. "What the hell is this?" he asked as his hand found the braid she had made of his long hair to keep it from matting. Ram only chuckled, still doing pull-ups. "Ram, toss me that dagger of yours," Sean said. "Quick, before I develop a lisp to go with this braid."

Ram swung down with easy grace to retrieve his dagger. "Hold it up, Sean. I'll do the business."

Sean held his braid to the side and Ram tossed the knife into the air. Joy screamed, but all for naught. Thrown with a light curve, the knife cut the hair at the nape of his neck, then fell point down in the floor boards. Sean held a braid of blond hair.

Joy had the unmistakable idea that they were no longer ill.

"Ram, you should get back in bed. You're—"

"Fine," he said with an easy smile. "A little hung over from it but nothing a swim won't cure."

Rake perked up suddenly.

"A swim! Oh no—"

He was already heading for the door, still with impervious nakedness. "Joy, love, your days of commanding are over. I am no longer the one confined to a bed. So, that bare foot I see there will not touch the floor. Understood?"

Joy could not see her bare foot any longer and when he watched her try, he started chuckling, then laughing, laughing all the way out and to the side of the ship, laughing as he dove thirty feet into the cool blue waters.

*　　*　　*

Two weeks later, Joy lay beneath the afternoon shade of a palm tree on an unnamed tropical island Ram said was about a hundred miles from Spanish Cuba. She lay on a blanket, reading a French translation of Dante's *Inferno,* of all things. This, while polishing off a small mountain of shrimp, a side plate of juicy pears and mango-like melons. Yet, she could not concentrate above her misery.

So much had happened. Ram could not sail the *Ram's Head* with the skeleton crew, at least not over the Atlantic waters to England. Yet supplies had dwindled to nothing but a pile of crusty, rock-hard bread that to Joy's horror was infested with worms. Unlike the other crew members, she could not think of the creatures as nourishment. More dangerous by far was the water supply. Ram had no choice but to try to sail to the nearest island, which was where they presently were stranded. The ship was anchored in a beautiful crystal-clear bay, while the still recovering crew was banished to the other side of the island.

Had Ram any idea of the extra time he had been granted, he would have gotten Joy to civilization and the care of a surgeon or midwife or someone, anyone who knew about delivering children. As it was, this was her first child, and by the closest estimation she was over two weeks late. She was enormous. He never let himself think of his own mother, Joy's mother, the number of wives of his crew members that had died during childbirth. He couldn't, for the thought would have truly driven him mad. Bret Holland was too weak to give anything but advice. With all her experience with Joshua, Joy knew plenty, and though she was uncomfortable in the extreme with the idea that Ram would be there, he pursued the subject relentlessly, prying every last detail of her knowledge from her.

Joy looked up to see Ram and Sean approaching from the beach. Ram carried a bucket of fish, Sean the fishing poles. They were laughing and talking, and she felt a pang of jealousy at their easy movements. They had nothing to

302

worry about!

She squirmed with a queer restless energy that her body's profound lethargy simply refused to accommodate. That was another thing, too, she thought as she plopped another finger-size shrimp into her mouth. She was sick to death of fish.

Ram's gaze turned to her, studying her with unsurpassed scrutiny, and she looked away, irritated. Next he would ask her—

"How do you feel?"

"Ohhh!" she practically screamed, throwing the shrimp down in the sand and, with effort, trying to sit up. "If you ask me that just one more time—"

She tried to get up. No help was extended. She glared at them, daring either to laugh at her. She finally managed to get to her hands and knees but could not seem to get her legs under her. In an effort not to laugh, Ram bit his lip so hard he drew blood, finally losing. The sudden laughter brought her pained humiliation; the more they laughed, the greater her humiliation. She was going to hit him, then she was going to cry.

Still laughing, Ram finally went to her and helped her to her feet. He was just about to hold her face to kiss her, beg a thousand apologies, when she stepped back and sent a small clenched fist hard into his stomach, only to meet a surface that felt far more like a rock than flesh, and with a small cry, pain shot up her arm. Seanessy dropped to the sand, overcome with his laughter now, while Ram grabbed her hurt hand. "Oh love." He laughed. "You must warn me before you take a shot like that." Suddenly though, his laughter died. Color drained from her face, and she gripped his forearms with a shocking strength.

As the first wave of it washed her body, she knew she was in trouble. The pain was not normal. She had walked dozens of women through the first stage of labor. Yet she could not take so much as a step. By the time Ram had carried her to the small hut he had built, the third wave washed over her. She could think of only two possibilities: Either she was truly a weak soul, one who had far less pain tolerance than any other woman she knew and would be unconscious or dead by the time the child actually came, or the child was coming far more quickly than normal.

As it turned out, the latter was true.

The sun just touched the distant horizon, melting into a breathtaking play of light and color that bathed the land and sky in gold, when Ram lay Seanessy Edward Barrington in Joy's arms. Nothing in his twenty-nine years prepared him for the joy surging through him as he took his wife and child against him, cradling them in his arms. Nothing prepared him for the next three hours Joy and he spent staring with profound, quiet marvel and awe at the little face, the dark hair and the bright, amber colored eyes.

Marvel and awe that melted into laughter and tears.

Emotions that would surely be his ruin . . .

Several hours later, Joy woke as though she had never slept, and the lantern Ram kept burning guided her eyes to little Sean's sleeping face, which was tenderly kissed, kissed because seeing was not enough. A new mother's emotions were far too large to be contained in the poor vessel of mere words.

As though nature knew a woman and a child were most vulnerable at this time, she endowed Joy with heightened senses. She heard the distant sounds of Ram's men still celebrating on the other side of the island. The voices coming from somewhere down the beach sounded far away, and she only heard small bits and pieces as Ram's and Sean's voices rose.

Ram seemed to be taking all the credit for little Sean, thinking he missed his calling as a doctor, and for a while she listened to an endless stream of toasts Ram and Sean were giving to the boy.

"And to the mother," Ram finally said. "To a woman whose beauty is delicate and lovely as a blossom, as irresistible as a siren's song but—" he laughed heartily— "who obviously owns the damn facilities of a brood mare."

Sean laughed and Joy blushed unseen, biting her lip with embarrassment.

"Speaking of her beauty though," Sean said. "She seemed to recover as she lay there."

"Aye. I have in fact seen cats have a harder time of it."

"That's not what I meant," Sean said, suddenly serious.

There came a pause broken at last with Ram's seriousness. "I know," he said. "I have no idea what I'm to do with her as my wife. Believe me, it would be bad enough just knowing she drew breath in some far away place like Louisiana."

"Have you asked her yet?"

"No, and I won't either. I don't have to. When I see my son in her arms, the love in her eyes, I know the only answer she could give me." His voice dropped to a whisper. "She would equate the drinking of the tea with the murder of a child. Perhaps not in those words but with the same result. She has no choice but to deny me her bed."

Ram studied the stars in thoughtful silence. "I feel such a queer mix of things," he finally whispered as much to himself as to Sean. He could hardly comprehend how his love grew so in these last months, culminating like a heaven bound Handelian crescendo upon the birth of his son. "When I think of my boy in her arms," he said out loud, "I am overwhelmed with my joy—it's almost a physical pain in my chest. I have cried. Me, a man grown to his twenty-ninth year, cried.

"Of course I will watch this boy of mine but somehow, like Joy, now I feel—nay I know—he will be well in mind and in spirit." He shook his head. "Yet I cannot gamble another," he said in a passionate vow. "And when I think of what that means . . . of never touching that girl again, I—" He stopped, literally unable to face that near future.

Sean in turn, waited patiently through his struggle as any good friend would.

"Sometimes," Ram said in a question, "when I hear her laughing, teasing me, I wonder if she knows ... But of course she must know what this ill-begotten marriage will reap. Yet she seems so happy with me, so confident . . ."

"It is not the same for a woman," Sean ventured. "A man's love is his desire, he wears it as such. Whereas a woman's love sings a different tune entirely."

Intellectually Ram knew this was true. While he had never known a woman whose passion met his like Joy's, she was hardly experienced. She had known love only three times. Three times! Once with a virgin's fear, once by force and once as she tried to save a life far more precious than her own. The experience could not have been pleasant, at the very least. Of course, love would not be the same for her. It made sense why she would not be overburdened with the prospect of not knowing his love again. He would have to put distance between them and soon. How awfully would that affect her? She would try to understand, of course but—

"God's curse Sean, I see the future and it is bleak indeed."

"There is nothing you can do—"

"I know," Ram sighed. "I know I'll be forced to her side for the trip back, the initial rounds of introductions—a couple of months, I suppose—but then after that, it will be a matter of avoiding her and remembering that God awful night. I will not force her, Sean. And God's curse is right!" he swore, knowing the irony was that Joy was every reason why he should never have married. "The agony of it is what I'll never forgive you for . . ."

Joy could make little sense of the bits and pieces of this conversation she was certain she was not meant to hear. What agony? Why was the future bleak? Quite suddenly, as she thought of this, she felt angry. How could he discuss business prospects on this night? Men!

A frown lifted into a smile as she heard Ram's voice raise

and the crash of a bottle as Ram christened the island Little Sean, vowing someday to bring his son back to teach him to swim. That was more like it, she smiled. It was the last thing she remembered on this, the first night of a long journey home again . . .

After giving the final orders of the night to the crew, Ram stood alone on the quarter deck, staring out at the dark depth of the boundless blue ocean. It was the last few moments of the day, long after the sun had set and just before complete darkness swept over the sea and sky. Stars appeared one by one, and as the ship glided gracefully over the swells finally heading to England, his thoughts raced ahead to that distant shore.

In three weeks, he would be home. At his side would be his wife and son, and together, they would finally be able to put a halt to the assassination attempts, the threats to his life. Finally! He knew exactly how he would do it, too; he had lived the moments in his mind many times. No, he would not spill blood in revenge, despite Sean's eagerness to do so, and not from any elevated or noble ideas but simply because revenge seemed more trouble than it was worth. He had had it with trouble; he wanted to get on with life. It would all be over and all because of Joy Claret's precious gift of his son.

His son! He was not imagining it! There was something truly remarkable about the little fellow, something that spoke of health, well being and happiness. Joy and Sean were both absolutely convinced—they knew as fact—that little Sean, like him, had escaped the curse. His enormous love aside, and though little Sean was only six weeks old, did boy sing this blessed song. So one part of his nightmare was dismissed day to day, while the other part grew.

A picture emerged against his will in his mind's eye: On the island shortly after the birth, he had left Joy and little Sean asleep in the small makeshift hut. Upon returning with two fair sized fish, he found the hut empty. He could not explain the irrationality of his sudden fear; they were, after all, alone on the island, no one but his men on the other side and with Sean there, too. Perhaps it was her unmasked vulnerability of those days, the thought of her alone with little Sean, of one of the island's wild boars, a fall or a step onto a rock fish, but a panic fueled his race down the beabh, then on to the only navigable path into the jungle.

He came upon the waterfall, the cool clear pool surrounded by a profusion of ferns and growth, with a sudden stop. Little Sean lay on a blanket at the water's edge. Joy was swimming, gliding gracefully over the water, long hair trailing behind her. He heard the music of her laughter, and watched as she dove in and out. The innocence of an Eve playing in the water of her garden, and he only knew he had been smiling at the enchanting scene when she stepped out of the water and his smile disappeared.

Unknowingly, and with a song to his son, she presented the unclad beauty of her changed shape. Water slid from the white silk of her skin, sliding over the rounder, fuller lines of her slender curves. Curves, he knew, that to touch would render the very word softness. He was shaking, barely perceptible, but felt violently as he stared at what was simply too beautiful to believe—

He stifled the thought and turned toward the wind, striding toward the ladder to descend onto the main deck. Joy and little Sean would be asleep. The time for distance had arrived. He would just gather the necessities and leave.

Ram quietly lifted the latch of the door to his quarters and stepped inside. A moment stretched endlessly as his eyes fell on her sitting in his bed. Little Sean was cradled in her arms. A brush lay to her side; her long dark hair cascaded neatly behind her shoulders, shining as though touched by moonlight. Her eyes were shadowed, lowered as she stared at their son, one hand caressing his face. A thin cotton night dress was unbuttoned to her waist, carelessly hanging on her bent arms.

Peace was shattered in the instant as his gaze lowered from the delicate loveliness of her face to her shoulders and the pearly-white smoothness of her round, full breasts. She, like the time he found her swimming just days earlier, seemed the most beautiful thing he ever beheld. Cold, hard desire shot through him again, and he was held helpless by it, unable to move if his life depended on it.

Joy's eyes lifted to see him standing there, staring like that. She blushed, the rising color not helping him at all, and nervously she tried to straighten her gown. "Oh, I—" She was tongue tied, ridiculously tongue tied as she pulled up one side of her gown but was stopped on the other side by Sean's head resting on the gathered material. He saw she at least comprehended his trouble. With a new mother's caution, she managed to lift little Sean's head and disengage her gown. She looked back up but he was already opening the door.

The time to put distance between them had passed, long past.

"Ram, where are you going?"

He stopped but just for a moment. "Where? Joy"—he almost laughed—"I could no more sleep in this room than I could on a battlefield."

"Battle . . . what?" she asked but was answered with a slam of the door. Within days Joy began to realize something had come between them, and like a slowly lengthening shadow, it was growing, every so slowly; she felt it growing. . . .

# Part II

## Lady Barrington

## Chapter Ten

After writing four pages about little Sean and another ten pages trying to describe London, it was close to midnight when Joy finished the long letter home, concluding with an explanation of the situation. She was at an inn, where the entourage awaited Ram's delayed departure from London before going on to Barrington Hall, the place where she and Sean would live. It was not just the grandeur and unparalleled opulence of Ram's London town home that they had just quit, a place that surely matched the grandeur of any royal dwelling, though this was part of it. Tension and discomfort sprang far more from the uncomfortable position she was placed in regarding the endless stream of servants, servants that included a personal maid whom she neither needed or wanted, and a Madame Bouvia, whose sole occupation was to teach her protocol and the manners of a lady, all of which she loathed and thought ridiculous in the extreme. Thankfully Madame Bouvia would be at Barrington Hall for only one night! All this was in addition to the unendurable and endless sittings with the famous dressmaker.

Joy picked up her letter, and by the light of a bright lantern, she read over the part where she tried to explain what being Lady Barrington was like:

". . . I know that to be rich without cares is a thing every human being seeks; to have plenty of food and nice clothes, to have a pretty home and monies left over for necessities and bills—well, who could not want this?

"I assure you, Sean and I are not in this position. Nay, we fly so far above comfort I am afraid to land for I can no longer see the earth. I cannot so much as lift a teapot before a servant jumps up and does it for me. I sit down to eat with three people standing by to watch me with blank, impassive stares. My chair is held for me, my napkin unfolded and laid upon my lap, my tea is poured, my portions served to my plate and alas, the servants stop only at actually placing the food in my mouth. They are polite and solicitous in the extreme but distant, so distant, my friends, that no attempt on my part has yet been able to bridge the enormous gulfs of the English class system; gulfs that are larger than the distance between a Negro field hand and the planter himself in our country. Why, the twenty or so servants at the townhouse had a hierarchy more stringent than the social stratification found in an ant colony. It goes like this: The butler is absolute monarch in the house, sharing his throne with the queen, the head housekeeper. Beside them, but not beneath them, are Ram's secretaries and the chef. Directly beneath the monarchs are the maids, footmen, grooms and kitchen or scullery help. It goes on from there. For instance the maid's hierarchy goes in rank order: the serving maids, the upstairs maids, the downstairs maids and lowest, the kitchen maids. So it is with the grooms and the footmen and all others. Queer, nonsensical ranks spring in all directions; for instance, a footman can be free with the upstairs maids but must condescend to talk with a downstairs maid or kitchen maid. One downstairs maid, a kindly and simple Mrs. Grose, took me into her guarded confidences—this after a ridiculous amount of prodding on my part—to tell me it is her fondest hope that her daughter aspires to the lofty position of upstairs maid! Because of my look of dumfoundedness upon hearing this confession, the poor woman took fright, looking like she expected me to scream, 'You uppity sod! Off with your head! Off I say!'

"Oh, it is all so awkward; I know not where or how to begin! From my hastily drawn picture you can imagine where I, Lady Barrington, sit in this hierarchy. How can I make a friend of someone whose fondest wish is to polish my boots, so to speak? It is as though I live in a glass cage. I am trapped; I see and hear the people around me but I cannot touch them. If not for the joy of my son, I fear I should be very lonely indeed. I miss you all so much . . .

"I miss you so much . . . so much . . ."

Tears formed against her will as she thought of Cory's smile, the reverend's quick laughter, Sammy's gentle eyes. She thought of a simple life, small pleasures like fixing breakfast in a predawn light with Cory, reading to the family by the firelight, of Sunday church outings and riding Libertine bareback and barefoot into the bayou wildness beneath a hot Louisiana sun . . .

Joy stopped the tears with a deep breath and a quick wipe of her cheeks, and knowing the real conflict of her heart, she opened her diary and tried to confront what had happened.

Dear Diary,

When had it changed? I try to think back over these last months searching for the exact moment that marked the change in his affection, all in the hope that if I found this moment and saw it clearly, I'd understand what caused the distance between us, for if

I could understand the cause, then perhaps I could provide a solution.

There is no single moment though; I can see that now. It seemed to start when we finally left the island of blue lagoons and thick green foliage. His men were recovered from the fever. I was recovered; I felt free again, light of foot and weight, filled with laughter, a previously unimaginable joy, a mother's new love. I never knew such happiness before . . .

There were no more feelings of awkwardness, helplessness or neediness! My joy spilled over into everything I did and was, and that was it; it seemed the better I got, the more he changed.

After the uncomfortable exchange that night he came upon me just after I finished nursing, I remember the afternoon I gave little Sean his first bath on the ship. I was laughing at how wide his enormous eyes were, his excitement registered in wild movements, and as I lifted him up and out, then guided him back, I suddenly realized we were not alone. I looked up to see Ram staring at us. I cannot forget the agony in his gaze, the tension etched into the hard lines of his face, filling me with such quick fear that my hands tightened instinctively on little Sean while my eyes darted to him, expecting to see something hurting him. Yet little Sean was wiggling and happy, and when I looked back at Ram with a question, he was gone.

I don't understand what has happened! A hundred times I turned to him with the question of what has happened only to find myself stammering, the question stopped before being voiced, all because I'm afraid of the answer. He married me for Sean, of course I knew this, but I thought nay. I *knew* he once loved me. Didn't he? Memories are vivid in my mind—memories of his kisses and his touch, of the desire of his gaze that sent me swooning, filled with that wild rush of longing, sweet, warm longing! Memories that spin in my every dream . . .

How life changes unpredictably. I would have sworn my greatest fear would have been Ram's relationship with his son, that despite his efforts, his fear would manifest there. This is not so! I know of no two people who take more delight in each other's company than Ram and little Sean. I know most fathers ignore their children until they start talking, and even then the vast majority of child raising is by the designs of nature delegated to women. But not so with Ram! When Ram's with us, he spends as much time caring for Sean as I do. Little Sean is always in his father's arms. Ram teases and tickles him, sings to him, talks to him like he is a boy of five. Why, he will even tell me how to care for him! Once when Rake accidentally stepped on little Sean as he lay on a blanket and I immediately rushed to comfort his cries, Ram stopped me. "No love, don't fuss over him. Try distracting him first." Sure enough, the second little Sean saw the jeweled belt buckle Ram held in front of him, the capricious little fellow forgot he was hurt. To watch Ram play with little Sean, to see Ram's pride and love is my greatest joy, except—

Lately, he takes little Sean from me, rather than including me in their time together. The distance between us still grows, ever slowly but awfully, and now indifference begins to take turns with the tension. The indifference seems somehow so much worse, too. He is always polite and considerate, too polite, too considerate, for I want none of that.

Once, in the beginning, his feelings for me were shadowed by the madness of his father, the idea he could nevery marry or have children, but now it is not that; I know it is not that. Little Sean's wellness has destroyed that idea; little Sean is absolute proof that the madness exists no more, that it shall play no part in our lives. So, what shadows have come between us now?

Ram, where has your love flown? What is happening? What have I done?

I have never been one to play with the conventions of society and yet, the more I lose him, the harder I find myself struggling to please him, to become the Lady Barrington he must want, to look and act a role most unnatural and uncomfortable to me. I persist in this fool's game, hoping, praying that some flicker of his response will guide my direction. Yet none has come. He leaves me alone in my struggle, leaves me with only hope, hope dying a little each day—

She stopped, standing at the light, her pen suddenly wavering unsteadily. Tears glistened in her eyes and she was lost again. She set the quill down, turned out the light, and not for the first time, tears saw her to sleep.

The two men riding through London's streets looked at first glance like two common travelers, until one noticed the quality of their mounts, their impressive stature and bearing, and on one of the men, the signature of his patch. They rode at a casual lope through Hyde Park, now dark and deserted, buried in the thick mist of a London fog. They came out of the park onto the King's road lined by the magnificent townhouses owned by the world's most elite personage, and they slowed their mounts.

It had been a fine stay so far. The gaming and politics of London were unmatched anywhere else in the world, certainly the politics were of a caliber high enough to keep Ram's interest. He had not realized how much he had missed London's pace. Of course, his affairs were in a shamble, a shamble that would keep him occupied for years and a day. The intrigue though, was almost over; this was the last of three houses he'd visit.

Less than a mile down the famous thoroughfare, they reined their mounts to a stop in front of Lord Guiness's manor. Ram dismounted, handing the reins to Sean, wordlessly moving to the great wall surrounding and protecting the estate. With a catlike grace and agility, he vaulted the wall and disappeared over the side.

Ram moved easily through the dark garden, he might have owned the place. With little effort, he found the right balcony. He jumped up, pulled himself up and grabbing on to the ornate baluster, he vaulted that. With a dagger already in hand, he tapped the glass pane of the locked French doors. It shattered with a light rain of glass. A gloved hand reached through to unlock and open the door.

Lord Barrington stepped silently into the dark chambers of his peer Lord Guiness's bedroom. His gaze immediately came upon the huge four poster bed where the lord and lady of the house slept, only heads showing from beneath the piles of satin quilts. The lord looked ridiculously small and harmless, and yet, he was one of the prime players who reaped hell into Ram's life.

With a deadly calm, Ram stepped over to the bed and placed the point of his dagger at Lord Guiness's throat. "Wake up, my lordship," he beckoned in a low whisper. "'Tis your worst nightmare come to haunt you."

With a slight start, Lord Guiness's eyes opened on command. To say that Lord Barrington, leaning over his bed with a dagger at his throat in the dark dead of night as he slept, was his worst nightmare was an understatement. There might indeed be something more frightening in hell, but Lord Guiness had not yet imagined it.

"My God—"

"Aye, prayers are appropriate at this point." Ram applied some pressure to the knife. "But quiet now, we will not wake the lady for this."

Stark terror engulfed him as he tried to swallow, stopped

319

by the point of the shiny blade, gleaming in the night. "In God's name what do you want?"

"What do I want?" Ram's chuckle was low and mean, somehow more ominously frightening than the dagger at his throat. "Only this. I come bearing news I happen to know of great import to you. My wife has bore me my son. A bright healthy and bonny lad he be; the announcement will be in the morning's paper. I've come also to extend a personal invitation to his christening. You will be there, my lord; I'll insist. Is that understood?"

Prodded by a hard jab of the knife, Lord Guiness managed to nod through his shock of the news, his fear for his life.

"Oh, by and away," Ram added as an after thought, "should anything, natural or not, happen to my boy, you will not live past the night—just so that I might count on your prayers for his continued good health. Hmmm?" He smiled. "Is that, too, understood?"

Rage began to rise over the naked terror gripping Lord Guiness but an impotent rage, and the nod came with no prodding whatsoever.

Ram recognized his enemy's defeat. "Good, now I'll leave you, my lord. Yet I fear not in peace."

Ram's arm raised with the dagger. Terror choked the lord's face. With all his great strength, Ram forced the dagger to its mark. By the time Lord Guiness opened his eyes with the startling revelation he was not dead, that the dagger was stuck in the pillow inches from his head, Lord Barrington was gone, vanished into the dark dead of the night.

Lord Guiness bolted up in bed, staring in shock at the darkness of the room.

A son! Who could have guessed? No doubt if Lord Barrington had one son, a man like that would have ten following. Oh, how he tried to warn the others that Barrington was not to be trifled with! It had all started so innocently, too, the whole plot to get the Barrington fortune growing and burgeoning before anyone really saw—saw what? The wrongness? The evil?

Abruptly, Lord Guiness started praying, and a good part of his prayers were taken up with the fervent hope for a young lordship's continued good health.

By the time Joy Claret finished her song, little Sean's enormous amber eyes closed and he fell asleep. At last! She placed him carefully in the bassinet on the carriage floor, turning from the two ladies across from her to look out the open shutter at the lovely English countryside.

There was no prettier, greener land than England. The sun was shining in a vivid, bright blue sky, broken by cotton-white clouds arranged as though for an easel. Yet it was past noon, they had been traveling since dawn and she felt restless within the small confines of the closed carriage. The footman had said Barrington Hall was only an hour away at last. Ram and his men rode well behind the entourage. She could hear their laughter and bits and pieces of their banter in the distance, behind four other carriages, two carts and so many horses. It was Bart, she knew, who held Libertine on rein.

She was forbidden to ride. "Oh, 'tisn't done, my lady," Clair, her maid, had said aghast.

Madame Bouvia had nodded, then explained, "A lady doesn't descend on her new household mounted. It would appear most un—"

"But I'm wearing a riding habit," she had said, glancing at the dark midnight-blue velvet folds of a perfectly fitted gown. A cumbersome outfit this, she thought, feeling like an overdone Christmas package.

"One I'm sure my lady would hate to have soiled or worse"—the older lady's frail snow-white hand withdrew a delicate lace kerchief from her reticule, which she placed over her nose—"smelling of a beast!"

Joy hadn't said that she loved the scent of horses, that she always had, or that she wouldn't give a hoot if her fine and expensive gown was cut into squares to be used as dust rags. What was the point?

She heard the fine sound of Ram's laughter in the distance, and she tensed with a mean pang of jealousy. He was having a fine time of it, leaving her alone with the company of—

"Please do draw away from that window, my lady," Madame Bouvia presently said. "The breeze threatens your hair."

Joy turned to confront Madame Bouvia and Clair, and had they been Joshua, Ram or anyone who knew her, they would have realized the sudden spark of rebellion.

Madame Bouvia sensed something though. "Is something amiss, my lady?" came her ever obsequious inquiry.

"Yes! I am not your lady. I am not his lady! I will not be put in a glass cage!"

Clair gasped, unable to make sense out of this sudden outburst, while Madame Bouvia grew pale as though to faint. Fainting was very fashionable, and Madame Bouvia held everything fashionable in her esteem. Joy didn't care; she didn't care a whit. "What in heaven's name are you doing, my lady?"

"I'm removing these boots. They pinch my feet."

Joy unlaced the new shiny boots, working frantically, then removed her stockings. Off went the pretty jacket and matching vest. She unbuttoned the top pearl buttons of her blouse so that she might breathe. Then she rolled up her sleeves to her elbows. She felt better already. Finally, she pulled out the pins holding her hair dressing in place. Hair had been the only point of interest Ram had shown in her predicament; passing her dressing room just as the deed was to be done, he forbad so much as an inch of her hair being shorn and to Clair and Madame Bouvia's intense disappointment.

The long locks swung free, and Joy rubbed her scalp to loosen it more. Ignoring the aghast stares, she leaned out the window to shout to a footman to stop the carriage. Instantly, the carriage stopped, the rest of the entourage following like dominoes. A footman jumped to quickly open the door, only to see Lady Barrington put bare feet to the ground.

"I think you win the bet, my lord. She lasted less than a month," Sean said with a grin as the sight of Lady Barrington, marching toward them in all the glory of her bare feet and disheveled appearance. They had a wager going on how long Joy would maintain her docile pretense of being fine and one with Lady Barrington and her trappings.

"I'm surprised it took this long," Ram replied with a crooked grin.

Joy ignored everything and everyone, determined steps taking her directly to Bart. "Give me my horse, please. And where's my saddle?"

"My lady, you can't be thinking of riding now—"

"I'm not thinking of it; I'm going to do it."

"I tell you, my lady—"

"If I hear 'My Lady' one more time, I'll scream, and if you don't get my saddle, I'll mount astride and bareback." She locked her eyes to his. "I swear I will."

"Bart," Ram called out, and had she the courage to turn to him, his amusement would have been the permission she swore she didn't need. "I'm sure you remember Joy is perfectly capable of carrying out that threat." He motioned to the waiting footman. "Find the lady's saddle."

Madame Bouvia and Clair had stepped out of the carriage, watching the proceeding with horror. The saddle appeared in a groom's hands, and shocking everyone watching, perhaps more than any other part of the scene being played, Joy insisted on saddling Libertine herself.

Ram came round on mount to hold Libertine's reins as she pulled the cinch tight. She had no idea of the sight she created. Her face was flushed with anger, her manner set

323

with determination, a hand trembled with the effort to control it. She was beautiful; the thick mass of light brown hair cascading down her back, the lovely flushed face, the round full thrusts of her breasts against the white silk of the blouse, lines tapering to that small waist—a waist bearing no mark now from the birth of his son. The thing most disturbing to him, however, was that the wild young girl who had captured his heart had emerged once again.

Ram's battle raged every moment he was in her presence and often when he was not, as now when pictures taken from the long voyage back to England came unwillingly to his mind: Joy teasing, playing, singing to his son, Joy asleep in his bed, Joy with her gown parted so seductively after nursing, Joy taking a bath with little Sean in his ship's huge brass tub, Joy sitting in a chair as she furiously tried to get the tangles from her hair, Joy, the night Sean got her drunk on but a half cup of rum and she amused them both with a solo performance of Romeo and Juliet, before passing out with girlish giggles in his arms, and God, a hundred other pictures etched in his memory.

Yet, now with rebellion in her eyes and the determined lift of her chin, it would not be a battle but rather a war. A war, he knew he could not win for long, and yet he had to be with her for two more months at least. Two bloody months . . .

Before any of the footmen could step forward, Joy was in the saddle. She could not fathom the depth of emotion in Ram's gaze as he handed her the reins, but by so doing, he handed her freedom. She embraced the freedom instantly, and with a nudge of her feet, she was off.

"My lady forgot her hat" was all Madame Bouvia could think to say as she and Clair turned at last from the shocking sight.

All of Ram's men were grinning. When one of the grooms smiled, all the others followed as they watched Joy ride in the distance. "I fear our lady is not a conventional type," someone said.

"Indeed!" Ram's laughter was the loudest. "Whatever Lady Barrington is to become, I think it assuredly will not be conventional."

They waited as Joy circled back, racing Libertine to a quick stop before the large group. "Oh my, it's so good to be riding her again!" Not one man there doubted the words, for the truth of her assertion appeared in her sudden happiness and smile, the exhilaration of freedom. "How far is the place?"

"A mile farther, then three down the first turn."

"A goodly distance for a race, is it not?" she asked, looking at Ram. "A race to the end; winner take all!"

Instantly cheers went up, Sean's war cry the loudest, and there came a sudden scrambling for mounts, at least from those who had them. Ram did not want to consider what winner take all meant, though he nonetheless kicked spurs to his stallion. She was already galloping in the far distance, never so much as glancing back to see the dozen or so men in chase. For she was the wind. Libertine had not felt her mistress's weight in nearly a year, and she rewarded the long awaited rider by giving the run all she had, leaving the others in dust.

Joy should have been awed by the marble archway marking the entrance to the property, the brass enclave bearing the Barrington arms; but Libertine cut the turn sharp, at a dizzying speed, and the thrill of keeping to the saddle took precedence over what for years had been ogled by sightseers. There was no thrill like racing; she felt happy and alive, at one with her horse galloping over the well-kept road.

The landscape flew past, nothing but green grass-covered hills broken by clusters of birch trees and bush. It was beautiful and breathtaking, this world that was suddenly hers again. Libertine raced down an incline, disappearing into a thick forest. They crossed a well-made wooden bridge, arching over a stream. Hooves thundering against the wood

325

as the road wound with turns now, turns she let Libertine maneuver until finally, they emerged at the other side of the forest, greeted with the greenery of the hills again.

Still she flew with the wind, safer now as Libertine raced up a slight incline. At the top of the incline, the world spread below to a vast flat land, and there, as though brought by a wave of a wand from the worldly place of dreams, Barrington Hall rose before her. She reined Libertine to a quick halt on the hill, and breathless, she stared at it.

Her heart pounded wildly but not from the rigors of the race. Ahead, the road split in the distance to start a large square, each side splitting again to form a pattern through well manicured lawns, flower beds and sculptured gardens, at least a square mile of green upon green. Directly in the center of the squares, a fountain rose prominently, made of three circles with their circumferences touching. The fountain itself seemed big enough to swim in.

The largest house she had ever seen in America could fit in a corner of Barrington Hall. It was three stories high and made of marble, washed gold with the weather of many, many years. The front formed a perfect rectangle, but the great manor was built in a square, with three separate wings surrounding a courtyard. The stables and the servants' quarters, a half mile away, were of the size she imagined the house might be.

The riders at last caught up with her, and upon seeing her stopped on the hill, they knew well what she stared at. Ram signaled the others back and rode to her side. A gloved hand caught Libertine's reins to stop her prancing, and as he looked at her, he thought of a girl dressed in boy's breeches in a tree, aiming a pistol at him. He remembered her wild rides through the night, her quick passion and fury, and all of that temerity was in contrast to the timidity so plain now.

"Why didn't you tell me?" she asked in a pained whisper, watching in the distance as an endless stream of servants poured out from the enormous front doors, lining up like so many busy ants.

Ram thought of her supreme utilitarian ideas and had to stop his smile. "Would it help if I said you'll get used to it?" he asked quietly in turn.

"No," she cried in a whisper, "I could never be used to it!"

She jerked her reins to run away from all of it, from him and a wealth unmatched by many kings, but he suddenly held the reins firm. "There is no running, Joy Claret," he said softly. "Your fate was sealed the night you came to my bed and conceived my son. And this, my lady"—his arm swept the distance—"is your fate." He watched her small hand clutch the riding crop till her knuckles blanched white, and again he had to stop his smile.

Anger melted by degrees as she approached its source, turning from him to the vista of Barrington Hall again. He had indeed sealed her fate, a fate she could only confront with fear and uncertainty. She was not raised for this world; she was certain she could never belong. Yet instinctively she knew it would be so different if—

The question rose in her eyes as she turned back to him. Where has your love fled? Did I ever have it? Could I have been mistaken by memories spun so clear and vivid? How can I accept indifference when once I had—

Ram watched the emotional play in the wide translucent eyes, the slight tremble of her lip, and just as he feared she would trespass where he refused to go, the emotions changed. In their silence as they stared, it changed.

She lifted her chin with sudden, renewed defiance, deciding a number of things in that one moment. Intimidation disappears with familiarity; and she would not only accept her fate, but she would use her lofty position to continue the fight. Likewise, she would raise little Sean with all the noble ideas of social justice, despite the silver spoon thrust in his mouth. She would also make friends of the servants, if she had to order them to do so. Most importantly, somehow, some way, she would try to win the only thing that mattered to her—his love.

Also, if Ram was this wealthy, she would start milking him for every pence she could get.

Joy calmly took the reins from him and asked, "Did you not once say fate was determined by the will of men and women?"

Ram did not remember mentioning women in the statement and he chuckled, relieved as they turned back to join the others.

"So, what do you think of Ram's ah . . . place did you call it?" Sean asked lightly as they joined the others and everyone started forward again.

Joy ignored the appreciative humor in Sean's eyes. "I think it's rather large."

Sean chuckled. "You demonstrate a remarkable flair for the understatement."

"Joy." Ram too, chuckled. "Why have I suddenly got the impression you're looking at Barrington Hall as a larger-than-life Prinkley's Girls' College?"

She smiled, putting him off guard. "But I am," she confessed honestly. "Only, you are its master and yet I shall not be the one to receive the thrashings this time."

"Oh? And how is that?" Ram asked now with dangerous amusement as they descended the incline.

"Well, I've a wager for you and you too, Sean. How many servants are lining up in that receiving line? Over thirty?"

"Over thirty," Ram replied with suspicion.

Joy knew from her past experience to stretch the limits of her imagination, and she braced herself. "I'll wager two hundred American dollars from each of you—to be donated to the American paper, the *Libertine*—that I can go through that receiving line once, hear each person's name once, and can repeat it."

"A fool's wager, Joy," Sean said. "How can you put over thirty new names to over thirty new faces? I'd wager Ram knows less than a third of their names, and that's after living here off and on so many years."

Joy knew a barely containable thrill, for neither man blinked at the outrageously high sum. With feigned calmness "But I wager I can."

"I'm interested in your forfeit," Ram said, still suspicious. "What if you lose?"

"Well, if I lose to you Sean, I will promise not to mention to a certain Lady Francine—whom Clair tells me I'll be meeting soon—the name of Miranda. Not that I would mention Miranda's name, but these things have a way of slipping—"

"What?" Sean interrupted and Ram laughed. Sean's face was an exercise of incredulity as he said, "That is not a wager! That's blackmail!"

With a deceptively sweet smile, she turned to Ram. "And you have said I'll be meeting the Prince Regent next month, and so if I lose to you, I will promise not to mention the abolitionist cause, no matter how difficult I know such restraint would be."

The entourage, a respective distance behind, witnessed Lord Barrington's roar of laughter, marveling at how easily his lady amused and engaged him, wondering too, at the lady's own quiet amusement, especially upon receiving Captain Seanessy's colorful curses.

As they approached ever closer to the anxiously waiting people, neatly forming the receiving line, Joy would have been shocked to hear the murmured round of whispers.

"My 'eavens, she's barefoot and riding like . . . like—"

"A man!"

"Look at my lady's 'air—long and loose like an Irish maid's!"

"She's lovely!"

"Like a storybook princess!"

"Why, she 'asn't the look of a commoner!"

"If she be a commoner, then I be the Duchess of Windsor!"

As they came to a stop, Joy felt nervous flutters being the recipient of so many interested gazes. Ram offered the traditional greetings and received the traditional welcome in turn as he dismounted, handing the reins to a groom without so much as a glance of acknowledgement. With the same indifferent air of aristocratic bearing, he called quick orders to others. She watched with interest, seeing that while she may not have been bred for this, he obviously was.

Ram came to lift her to the ground himself. His hand stayed on her waist a moment too long, and Joy found her small hands braced against the wide stretch of his shoulders. She tried to steer her consciousness from the maleness of him, from the corded muscles of his long arms, bulging beneath the rolled sleeves of his shirt. Yet her eyes fell to the narrow waist, the flat hard stomach and the muscles defining his thighs, straining against the black riding pants. Her eyes shot back to his face, only to find her stare returned with amusement as he warned, "You better pray you're not as smart as you think you are—"

"Aye," Sean said, holding Libertine's reins, still mounted himself. "For if you win this wager, I'd wager Ram would not stop me as I cut out your traitorous tongue."

"Stop you Sean? Hell, I'd provide the dagger."

With that, Ram presented the new Lady Barrington; but before she started through the line, she swallowed her own nervousness, and a melodious voice offered first a shy collective greeting, then explained the situation she created. "I have a wager with my husband and Captain Seanessy. I wagered that I could repeat each one of your names after going through the line once. So, as you tell me your name, could you also say something about yourself that might stay in my mind?"

Whispered murmurs went up and down the line, smiles all around. Ram sighed and Seanessy cursed, as it was obvious the entire household had instantly rallied to her side. Thinking only that Ram and Sean were far easier marks than she had imagined, with a deep breath, Joy started at the beginning.

"Pansie, my lady." A young, dark-haired girl curtsied, and then with a giggle, she withdrew from behind her back a bouquet of flowers freshly picked for the new mistress of the house. A bouquet of flowers dotted with tiny purple pansies. Joy took the flowers with thanks, her eyes filled with laughter.

"Bertha, my lady, and me form will not give me name away."

Bertha was rail thin, and Joy laughed again. In this way, she proceeded through the line. Of course, even with everyone's helpful hints, there was no way to remember all their names, but she didn't have to. She simply enjoyed hearing the names and what each person said about themselves to help her remember, until finally, as she felt Ram's impatience, she came to the last in line. An elder gent, of fine stature and bearing, wearing the unmistakable air of perfect English pretense and civility.

"My lady." He bowed ever so slightly. "Mr. Cutler," and he added with no humor whatsoever, "I am your butler."

She laughed, and with a pretty rush of skirts, she practically skipped back to the front of the line. Ram and Sean were suddenly at her side and, like hungry dogs, ready to devour her first mistake. All waited with excited anticipation and Joy did not delay.

"Pansie, Bertha, Margaret and Mary, Tomas and . . . and—" she stopped at the young footman, stumped.

"Ah huh!" Ram said triumphantly.

Prematurely, for Joy silently mouthed these words: "Help me!"

With a grin, this was mouthed back: "John."

"John!" She laughed and moved on to the next person.

Neither Ram nor Sean moved as she raced quickly through the line, finally ending with "Mr. Cutler, the Butler!" A long and loud cheer and applause rose through the crowd, and Joy curtsied in turn.

"I think we've been had, my lord," Sean said.

"I know we have," Ram replied, and hearing the triumphant sound of her laughter, he knew, too, he would not make it through the day, let alone the next two months. Something would have to be done.

It was like the time before, the night of their reunion and the day of their marriage, when Joy woke in his arms. She felt toasty warm, enfolded in his heat, surrounded by an intoxicating male scent. Abruptly she stiffened, becoming aware. She felt the tickle of his breathing against her ear. A long muscled arm lay across her waist. Her backside pressed against his chest, while her buttocks pressed against the hard pressure of naked male hips. He was hot and hard—

She relaxed, sighing languidly, giving herself over to the sensual feel of his huge body next to hers, the naked feel of him. Pin prickles of pleasure began erupting from everywhere their bodies touched. As though he knew, he shifted slightly, nuzzling her ear with his lips as his hand moved to her bare breasts. The hand only laid still, cupping the soft fullness in his palm until her entire being centered on the heat of his hand there. Her nipples rose to greet the pleasure. Then he slowly began to massage the sensitive mounds. Ripples of sensation raced through her. His lean, calloused fingers tantalizingly probed the anxious tips, lightly pinching, teasing. Fire stirred in her loins, and she arched back, nuzzling closer to the hard, waiting shaft of him. He groaned, rewarding the seductive moment by sliding his other arm under her. One hand continued to massage her breasts while the other ran up and down her bare midsection.

Her nerves went wild. She cried softly as that hand traveled lower still over the softness of her belly, but there he stopped, waiting as the sensations piled up, gathering at the tips of his fingers. The sensations grew to a ferocious need, a pulsating hunger she could not long bare.

"Oh please—" she gasped, writhing slightly.

He chuckled softly and lightly grazed her neck with his lips as his hand finally slid down to the moist recess of her most hidden part. Warm rushes of pleasure escaped from the sweet well of her desire as his fingers played there with exquisite gentleness, sliding over her, boldly slipping in and out, and just as he carried her to the point of ecstasy—

Joy bolted up in the bed, looking dazedly around the empty room. She was panting lightly and tried to catch her breath, to slow the pounding of her heart. Her body had absolutely no inkling she had been dreaming until, slowly, the disappointment grew and intensified; an ache spread where only fire had been.

She fell back against the pillows and stared blankly at the ceiling, feeling dangerously close to tears. How, oh God how, can dreams be so real? So vivid?

She did not wonder long. Yesterday, after the receiving line, Mr. Cutler had shown her to her rooms. Even after seeing the magnificence and grandeur of Barrington Hall, she was not prepared for the fairy-tale beauty of these rooms. The rooms were exquisite. Expensive Louis XIV furnishings were majestically set against soft shades of peach and cream, textures of silk and satin. Everything was colored these shades: the bed clothes and canopy, the drapes, the damask covered chairs and the thick carpets. Lovely French romantic paintings adorned the walls: pictures of pretty milk maids, plump rosy-cheeked children. It was beautiful, but initially, she had seen none of it.

She had walked over to the window, staring down at the hand-carved, round sitting table. Glass covered the mosaic of pearl inlay, gold and other precious stones that created a detailed picture of a man and woman picnicking by a lake. The table was a museum piece, one that no doubt took an artist years and years of intricate and painstaking work to complete. Numbly it occurred to her, the table alone was worth a fortune of a size she could not guess, and yet, as she stared down at it, there was no appreciation in her gaze.

All she could think of was that they were to have separate bedrooms, for no doubt was left by the ornately feminine decor in the room. She tried to tell herself she should not be surprised after the long voyage and the stay in London, but somehow, she had felt a tremor of hope, hope that had died as she was presented these rooms. She had to finally face the fact that he never intended to consummate their marriage, that he didn't want her like that. He had only married her for Sean.

Was there another woman? Could she know him so intimately and not know that? An image of a beautiful woman came to her mind, one witty, intelligent, sophisticated . . .

A lone tear slid down her cheek. She wiped it quickly and rose unsteadily. She would not show her tears; she would hide them behind a façade. A façade of what though? Peace and contentment? Happiness? Could she do that when inside she felt like dying?

It seemed her only choice. She would pretend everything was fine, that this was what she had expected. She would pretend to be gay and carefree; she would involve herself in her work, trying to please him . . . She would be the perfect Lady Barrington. Yes, she thought as she looked to her closets.

Joy felt numb by mid-afternoon, and as Rolph, a footman, threw open the double doors of the last room comprising the east wing gallery, she reached that point of mental exhaustion where it was impossible to separate one room from the other. Each room was becoming but a blur in her dazzled mind, a blur that became a backdrop for a memory of a dream, the sadness in her heart that she tried so desperately to hide. Still, she was determined to see the east wing tour finished, and holding an ever active little Sean in her arms, she swept through the doors behind Mr. Cutler, followed by Pansie and Clair, her two maids.

Hiding his increasingly favorable impression of his ladyship behind his stoic demeanor, Mr. Cutler gave her a moment to take in the spacious high ceiling room in its entirety before proceeding. She looked magnificent and regal both, so markedly different from yesterday. He had been so alarmed yesterday. Of course, he never expected Lord Barrington's new wife to be conventional, but the young lady riding barefoot and disheveled, making a game of his receiving line, far surpassed his gracious allowances for the fact she was a commoner and very nearly an American. Yet he was ever generous. He had to admit her shenanigans yesterday had won her the collective favor of the entire household, and this he knew to be important.

Today she looked stunning, and her manner was . . . well, subdued somewhat. She wore a pale yellow, silk day dress, low cut and with short sleeves, yet covered by a white saffron overdress, this trimmed in lace and dotted with tiny silk daisies. Her hair was dressed properly, too, piled high on her head with thin yellow ribbons woven into it. True, the lady was in need of polishing—her manners were alarmingly provincial—yet he could not dismiss her graciousness and considering her background, her inexplicable bearing that seemed almost regal.

She might do very well after all.

"This room is of particular importance," he said.

"Mr. Cutler," she sighed forcing a smile by sheer will, "that's what you've said about each room, all fifty-three that I've seen today."

They had seen fifty-three rooms, and they still had this whole wing left. This wing had not been opened for eleven years, except for the traditional summer tours of gaping Londoners. Each room was an exercise of elegant and exquisite taste, and it seemed to her a terrible waste that the only people to walk the floors were maids with dust rags in hand.

"Each room is important, my lady."

The only distinguishing mark of this room was that it was the last room she could bear seeing, but before Mr. Cutler could proceed, Sean, every bit as bored as his mother, wiggled impatiently in his mother's arms and with a happy scream, socked her hard in the face, then waited expectantly for her reaction. "Oh darling"—she lifted him high in the air—"we don't hit people! We especially don't hit mothers who love you so much!"

Sean laughed at this and received her kiss as she swung him back down, then laid him on the luxurious maroon carpet, one matching the paler silk of the sofa and chairs. Mr. Cutler provided the little master with the largest key ring in the world, and seeing her son for the moment distracted, Joy fell onto the sofa. "So, what is important about this room?"

"This is the first room of the portrait gallery."

"There are two portrait galleries; I've seen one. What is special about these pictures?"

Mr. Cutler straightened formally. "These, my lady, are Lord Barrington's parents and his maternal grandparents."

Joy's gaze flew to a portrait, and she slowly came to her feet. "This—"

"Is Lady Alisha Barrington, Lord Barrington's mother."

The portrait showed a lady, pretty and delicate, yet regal and possessed. A lace cap, such as they used to wear, covered thick and dark curls, ringlets framed an angular, thin face. A tiny gold cross adorned her neck. Ram inherited his mother's wide forehead, one that spoke of intelligence, and the shape of her sensual mouth. Intelligence also showed in the lady's lovely pale gray eyes, eyes that matched the silver-blue silk of her dress.

Yet a sadness played there, too, she saw.

Joy stared too long. The reason was simple; she was afraid to turn away. She was afraid to see a portrait of a dark, sinister and mad man who would be Ram's father.

"Here is the Lord Barrington the second," Mr. Cutler insisted with a lift of his hand.

Reluctantly, she turned to the portrait indicated. With drawn brows, she stared long and hard at the handsome and distinguished looking gentleman, looking in vain for something that simply was not there. This was not the monster of her imagination!

She approached slowly, staring still, stopping just in front of the mantle over which the picture hung. Lord Barrington the second had light brown, almost blond hair, a slightly round face. A faint smile played on his small mouth. Like Ram, his nose was rather large and prominent, but that was the only resemblance. Bushy eyebrows darted over the features her gaze—indeed anyone's gaze—were drawn to: his magnificent eyes, remarkable for their color of aquamarine stones, a color reminding her of the crystal-blue depths of the lagoon on Little Sean's island.

If madness played there, the artist failed to render it.

Joy stared so long that even Mr. Cutler's enormous well of patience was taxed somewhat. She felt a physical discomfort, one she could hardly explain—as though there was something wrong about the picture, and if only she kept looking, she'd find it. She supposed the feeling owed to having expected a monster and finding instead this mild looking gentleman. Mild looking indeed, he looked absolutely harmless—

Clair and Pansie, playing with little Sean, suddenly laughed and clapped. "Oh, my lady, look at him!" Pansie cried.

Joy turned to see Sean had pulled himself up to stand, smiling triumphantly. She laughed, and with a pretty rush of skirts, she lifted him up into her arms and forgot the disturbing portraits, forgot the tour and Mr. Cutler, forgot everything but little Sean and the sole reason she picked the pretty yellow dress. "Let's go show your father!"

Ram's study was set between an enormous library and a

large hall. The hall was used to receive guests and associates, but as it was used more than any other room by Ram, his favorite pictures adorned the walls. All of these were seascapes, dark and stormy, metaphorically depicting the unrest of the soul. Three of these enormous seascapes hung on the wall opposite three huge picture windows, draped in a light-blue velvet that matched the carpets and the damask covered furnishings. Two large desks were used by his secretaries, Mr. Mitchell and Mr. Linton.

Joy swept into the large room to find Ram doing pull-ups on an overhanging bar in the doorway between his study and the hall, as he dictated a letter to Mr. Mitchell. She had not seen him since arriving. He had not joined her at supper, dinner or breakfast. Sean had joined her, only to tease her about being the mistress of Barrington Hall and to say goodbye, claiming Ram was hospitable only to a point, and since Ram wouldn't allow him access to the maids, Sean thought to find happier hunting grounds elsewhere.

Ram's gaze found them, and he swung down from the bar.

Joy felt suddenly shy and awkward, remembering for the hundredth time her dream upon waking, and she blushed, trembling. "I fear I interrupted . . ."

"No, nothing important," he lied, and watching his son jump up and down with excitement upon seeing him, gurgling wildly, he chuckled and took the boy into his arms. The next minutes passed with Ram twirling, singing, tickling and teasing his son, amusing everyone until little Sean's wild peals of laughter mixed with the entire room. Finally, he rested little Sean in his arms and turned back to his mother.

Joy felt the intensity of his gaze through every fiber of her being, and when she saw his disapproval, she felt a quick certain death. He turned abruptly away. "Finish the letter yourself," he said to Mr. Mitchell. "I'll carry it to London tonight."

Joy missed Mr. Mitchell's surprise, the glance he gave to Mr. Linton, as she missed the nervous glances of Pansie and

Clair. His tone said everything. All Joy saw were the tips of her pale yellow slippers as she interrupted Ram's banter with little Sean to ask, "You're leaving . . . so soon?"

"I'm afraid so."

"When will you be back?"

"Not for some time," he replied, indifferent to her trouble, turning instead to his son, telling the ltitle fellow how much he would be missed. As he spun little Sean in Mr. Mitchell's turn chair, he said, "I'll send for you in a couple of weeks, and besides the social obligations we've discussed, you're a free lady till then."

When he looked up, it was only to see that she was gone, her maids following, leaving him with a soft curse, relieved that there would be real distance between them, if only for a short time.


Joy finished her correspondence: three carefully worded letters to leading members of the United Christian Anti-Slavery League in England, each with an introductory letter obtained from the Reverend Archibald Cox and Ram's uncle, Retired Admiral Byron. She carefully poured wax into a seal that depicted a rose beneath the north star, a gift sent by her family. It was her seal, not the Barrington seal. The other letter on her desk was to her family, at least the twentieth since embarking on the long journey to this new life, and it would go in one of the three trunks Bart promised to be on the next ship sailing to America. In her attempt to share her fortune with those she loved, each trunk held treasures, books and clothes and even jewels.

She leaned back in her chair, watching as the red wax dried. She picked up her diary but felt suddenly exhausted. It was late. Tomorrow she would be traveling to London. The thought filled with a montage of conflicting emotions, none of them pleasant, all of them apprehensive. She needed to sort her feelings out, as only her diary allowed her to do, at least enough to find the composure she desperately sought for her next meeting with Ram.

She wanted to impress him. When she imagined his mistress, she saw a beautiful woman, one intelligent, sophisticated and socially gracious and adept. She wanted to be the same, to manage her introduction to society with grace and charm, two things she felt certain she didn't have. She wanted him to see she accepted their loveless match with calm and composure and dignity, all things in direct opposition to the pain in her heart.

Yet she was tired. It was after one in the morning, and no doubt Sean would be up by the crack of dawn. She blew out the candles and rose to turn out the lantern. Despite the closets full of dresses and gowns, drawers and drawers stuffed with the sheerest silk undergarments and night-clothes, she wore a plain white, cotton night dress, her old worn shawl. Pansie and Clair were shocked; they begged and pleaded but to no avail. She would not wear the trappings of Lady Barrington except when absolutely necessary. Not after seeing his reaction that day he left.

She stood in front of her vanity and picked up her brush to smooth and tie her hair before retiring. The brush had not yet touched her hair when she saw it. Lying innocently upon the smooth polished wood grain was a delicate gold chain with a small gold cross. She picked it up, staring and recognized it instantly as Lady Barrington's.

Who sent it? Ram was not home. Would he have thought to send a note asking that his mother's cross be given to her? No—

Holding the small treasure, she tried to puzzle through these questions. Upon arriving in London, she had been given three boxes of Barrington family jewels, but as they had been given impersonally, the stunning antique collection of gold, pearls, diamonds, rubies and more than a dozen emerald pins, matching necklaces and earrings, meant nothing to her. In fact it hurt when she had asked Ram about them.

"What jewels?" He had been heading out the door with Sean on one of the endless nights he had left her alone in London.

"The family jewels, they're beautiful . . . I hardly—"

"Oh, those jewels. They're yours, love."

Sean had been putting on his boots at the doorway and suddenly laughed. "God, don't say that. Whatever you do, my lord, don't tell her that! The jewels will end up in a swap shop and the money in some abolitionist fund."

Ram's hand was on the door, and he stopped for but a moment, amused. "You weren't planning on selling them, were you?"

She had wanted only to thank him for the gift she couldn't believe, and his disinterest, the present amusement, hurt so much she couldn't speak. She shook her head.

He chuckled. "That would be just like you. I don't give a damn what you do with them, but I've an idea of their worth these days. If you do sell, be sure to get a good price." Still laughing, they had left.

They meant nothing to him; she meant nothing to him. So, she had selected the best pieces and sent them to Cory for keepsakes, trying to find some small sliver of pleasure by imagining the wonder on Cory's face when she opened the package.

The family jewels meant nothing to her, nothing compared to the small gold cross in her hand, which she held in her hand as she slept. A small gold cross that caused a strange dream to visit her sleep that night.

She stood in a familiar room, yet she could not see it to know what room it was. Joshua stood near her, pointing urgently, excited and agitated. "Joy Claret, it is right there before you! Look girl, look!" She felt his urgency, and she looked and looked, straining to see through the darkness.

Then suddenly Lady Barrington was there, saying too, "Don't you see? Don't you see?" All Joy could see was the gold cross on her neck. She reached for it, but suddenly only the darkness remained.

The darkness vanished upon waking but the queer feeling remained. She felt a nodding, a tickle in her brain as though something important lay hidden just beneath her perception. She stared at the small gold cross in her hand, wondering who sent it. It was a mystery, yet she had no time to ponder it now.

For today she was going to London.

# *Chapter Eleven*

Joy could not believe this was happening. She felt the dark impenetrable eyes on her back. A chill raced up her spine and she bit her lip, feeling nervous, so nervous. Where, oh God where, were Admiral Byron and Melissa, his dear wife? Where were the four lads following them? She was alone with him in the spacious, dimly lit room, and he—

Dear God, what was he thinking?

Nervously, her eyes shifted to the small crystal candelabra in the doorway, not fifteen paces away. It held five tiny gas lamps ingeniously shaped like candles, all of which emitted such a dim light she had not a shadow to lean on, let alone enough light to view the El Greco masterpiece before her.

With sick horror she heard her breath come in quick pants, louder than the music drifting from the ballroom downstairs, and she swallowed, focusing again on the painting. She desperately searched for something to say about it, but all she could see in this light was grotesquely stretched flesh against the dark background, a hand reaching for the salvation of the heavens. The pretense was absurd and he knew it. The longer she stared, the more ridiculous—and frightened—she felt.

Minutes gathered in unnerving silence, a silence punctuated by his labored breath pushing against his excessive girth, and just as she was about to scream, faint or run, a thick jeweled hand reached for her shoulder. It might have been a hairy black spider; she jumped, gasped and stammered, "I've not ever seen an El Greco before!"

His Royal Highness, the Prince Regent of England, laughed, a low deep laughter that spelled certain doom. "I dare say, you're not seeing one now."

The enormous man chuckled again. A hot sick wave of panic washed over her as the hand stayed, squeezing slightly. She felt his warm breath, and he was turning her and oh God—

"Jeezus!"

That single loud expletive came from the door, and she gasped, even before she turned to see the towering shape that filled the archway. It was Ram. His tall and imposing figure, outlined in the darkness, looked wicked and threatening, the devil himself emerging from hell to claim his maiden. The jeweled hand reluctantly left. She nearly swooned with relief, until the very moment the violence of Ram's person reached across the distance. She felt the violence radiating from him; she heard it in the hard click of his boots as he quickly crossed the distance to her side.

Ram took her arm just above the elbow, and she trembled beneath the iron grip, suddenly knowing a far worse fear. His fury was palpable, having worked like hot liquid steel into his muscles, fueling the murderous rage in his gaze as he turned to the Prince Regent of England.

The prince, in turn, watched beneath the hooded lids of bemusement. "Your wife, my dear man, showed keen interest in my collection."

"Not," Ram interrupted smoothly, "in becoming part of it."

This was met by light laughter, dying too quickly. "As always, your wit, my lord, is as blunt and sharp as a butcher's knife. Yet wielded unnecessarily, I assure you. To my utter delight, those lovely eyes viewed my prospects with

344

only innocence."

"Indeed!" The murderous rage at last turned to her. "One, I swear to see tainted by the end of the evening. Which is now. You've met your end Joy Claret."

She gasped in a short cry as Ram kicked a slippered foot from under her and she toppled back, only to be caught effortlessly in his arms. He carried her from the room without bothering to beg leave or say goodbye, a formality unnecessary by the sound of royal laughter that followed them. Frightened senseless, she wanted to die, just die. It was a disaster, the magnitude of which she could not guess. She knew only his anger, the rage shining bright and hard in his gaze as he carried her down the darkened hall.

"Please!" she cried in a whisper. "I can walk."

"The hell you can!" Ram carried her swiftly down the darkened staircase, through three anterooms and finally into the wide open space of the magnificent ballroom. She saw a blur of pale silk and black as ladies and gentlemen parted to make way for Lord Barrington carrying Lady Barrington through the room. The sudden roar of whispers, the keen shrewd gaze of every living soul present made her hide her face in Ram's shoulder.

She heard Ram call for their coach, explaining that she had twisted her ankle. A flurry of kind and concerned inquiries followed, hollow and hypocritical, for they all knew, and these were faint above the still loud roar of whispers, as even the music stopped now.

Dear God, how had this happened? How, when all she had wanted so desperately was to please him? Just three hours ago she had been standing in front of the glass. If only she could go back to the beginning. The beginning . . .


"Oh my lady, you're beautiful!"

Pansie pronounced sentence on the reflection Joy watched, staring at it with incredulity and marked disbelief, this riding over nervous butterflies. Tonight was the grand ball to welcome the Prince Regent home from abroad; an event that would serve to introduce her to society as well. Never had she put so much time and effort into her appearance, all in the desperate hopes of pleasing him.

She first chose a pale pink gown, simple but lovely, only to find Pansie and Clair arguing about her selection. "Oh, all the ladies will wear pink. Pink or white, 'tis the fashion, and since most complexions look like death masks in white, the ladies shall all be wearing a shade of pink." Joy had chosen one of her four pink-colored ball gowns for that very reason; the shade was fashionable and for once in her life she wanted to blend and belong. Yet Clair, with an amazing sense of fashion, provided an alternative.

She could hardly believe she was the lady in the glass. Modest and delicate, the full empire gown was made of white silk but with layers of sheer pale lavender gauze over a skirt and bodice of pale green. Silk ropes of white, lavender and green created sleeves draping loosely over her upper arms, leaving her shoulders bare. The colors accented her pale skin and dark hair, which Clair had managed to twist and roll into a pretty crown. To her maid's distress, she refused any jewels, save for her wedding ring worn over lace gloves, but again Clair demonstrated a remarkable genius for transforming Joy's whims and eccentricities into fashion—she simply tied a thin dark-violet, velvet ribbon around Joy's neck. Such a simple thing, yet the effect was stunning; it drew one's gaze to the painfully slender lines of her neck and shoulders while, as if by some trick of magic, the dark violet played with the blue of her eyes.

Joy bit her lip nervously, unable to accept the reality of the picture she presented. She had been raised the charge of a poor country doctor, such a modest position in life. Months ago she struggled with poverty, with the far more pressing matters of finding enough food and medicine, not sparing a thought of worry over the only four worn skirts and dresses to her name.

Now, here before her was a lady of elegance and obvious wealth, surrounded by the walls of one of England's finest houses. She had boxes of jewels, at last count over seventy-three tailored silk dresses. Streams of people—human beings—waited on her, rushing to meet her each and every whim. Tonight a royal prince would take her hand and say ado! She never had such grandiose aspirations. Yet here she stood, a true-to-life Asherella—only minus the happy ending.

What would he think? Would this gown bring that same inexplicable, yet unmistakable disapproval—as though the country girl failed so miserably and completely in the role of Lady Barrington? Or would she meet only his indifference?

Ram, what has happened to you? She closed her eyes, and on demand an image appeared of his bronzed handsome face leaning toward her to take her mouth, his gaze dark with desire, yet softened with love . . .

Clair and Pansie stopped their excited chatter—all of which consisted of predictions that all the ladies would replace their jewels with velvet ribbons at the next gala—and exchanged confused glances upon seeing Joy's pained expression.

"Oh, my lady," Pansie thought to comfort her. "You're going to be a success, I know—"

A servant announced Lord Barrington in the previously unheard of position—he was waiting. Pansie rushed for the matching lavender wrap, and amidst sincere well wishing, Joy walked quietly from her rooms into the bright light of the hall.

While less than a tenth of the size of Barrington Hall, the London townhouse was a stately mansion, one of the many prominently resting on the edge of Hyde Park. Double front doors led to stairs, descending into an enormous entrance hall the size of a ballroom. All the rooms both upstairs and downstairs centered around the square, and from the balcony hall, one had a panoramic view of the downstairs.

Yet Joy was not looking, as with downcast eyes she made her way to the stairs, and lifting her skirts, she descended. The servants stood in gaping awe of the beauty thus appearing. Ram, magnificently clad in formal black evening clothes, took but one brief look before turning and snapping to a footman, "Saddle up Lance. I'll be riding."

Joy's gaze shot up at this and she stopped, her eyes nervously falling to her costume, as though to discover the fault he found there. After but the briefest greetings upon her arrival in London, she now received this rejection, one that felt like a hard slap to her face. Lance was his prized stallion, and ordering him saddled meant she would ride in the carriage alone. He would not even share a carriage ride with her.

When she finally found the courage to lift her eyes and ask what was wrong, Ram was gone, gone without a greeting or word. As she stared at the empty foyer, she felt her heart stop, her hands grow clammy, numb and cold. Even Rolph and Charles, the waiting footmen, seemed shocked by Ram's cold rejection of her. The reasons were unknown, yet the fact was plain—she had failed. The night had yet to start and she had failed already.

Failure pronounced even more, as she was led into the cool, moist night air and ushered into the empty carriage. With Lance's hooves sounding loud in her mind, her apprehensions heightened, intensifying dramatically with each turn of the carriage's wheels. She didn't dare contemplate the rhyme or reason of his rejection. No, not now. That would come later, much later she knew, after this fateful night was written and she was safely returned to the lonely walls of her bed chambers.

For now, her apprehension centered on getting through the evening. Here she was about to be presented to the most elite peerage in the world as Lady Barrington, and yet, her husband could hardly endure the sight of her. What would people think? Would they think he hated her, that there was an awful rupture between them? Then, would they, too, turn from her? She imagined herself standing alone and isolated, watching as handsome gentlemen engaged their lovely ladies, the only attention cast her way in the form of scornful or pitying sideways glances . . .

The picture was in her mind as the carriage came to a slow stop, and with a deep uneven breath, she tried to steady the tremor in her hands, preparing for the worst possibility. The carriage stopped behind a long line of other guests in front of the ancient walls of Windsor Castle.

One by one the carriages moved up as their occupants descended. Each driver, at his turn, handed an engraved card bearing the name and title of the carriage's occupants to a waiting footman. This was raced to the grand hall, where the party was announced as the people unhurriedly descended. It took over half an hour before their driver handed down their card; the wait felt interminable, yet she wished fervently the suspension from time could stretch endlessly—as limbo was preferable to purgatory.

The next hours would forever remain a blur in Joy's mind, hours shadowed by her fear, uncertainty and apprehension, a nervousness unmatched by the wildest ride through a dark night. She was at all times acutely conscious of him and his nearness, the gentle press of his hand on her gloved fingertips as he escorted her up and through the doors, the inexplicable warmth emanated by this small but significant touch. Not comprehending what he was saying with it, she could but grasp this one small lifeline of his touch.

They emerged from the dark night into the blinding light of the palace. She had endured endless coaching on protocol, and it seemed something inside herself snapped as she stood there at Ram's side, listening to the lengthy stream of words comprising Ram's full title as their presence was announced. It was as though she withdrew and fled and a mechanical version of herself took over.

Joy was but vaguely aware that the room seemed to stop as everyone turned to see the Barringtons' much waited for appearance. With the possible exception of the Prince Regent himself, no one solicited as much attention as Lord Ramsey Edward Barrington the Third. As a scrubbing maid wrings laundry through a washboard, every detail of Ram's life was wrung through the gossip grind mill. The dark shadow of the Barrington family history only added another ingredient of illicitness, and then too, this was generally dismissed as exaggerated, especially by the many who knew and remembered Ram's father, his civility, intelligence and charm. Besides, who didn't have embarrassing family skeletons? Certainly not the Prince Regent. If the King of England could be mad, then so could Lord Barrington's father. This was the common wisdom concerning the matter.

The effect of the Barringtons' history on its most noted descendant was far less easily dismissed. Ram Barrington was one of the most eligible men in the world of Great Britain's aristocracy, and he refused to marry and sire an heir, this despite the many ingenious and persistent attempts by nearly every lady. Though no one understood why, everyone saw how this gave him a license to outrage and excite.

One could sum up society's interest in Lord Barrington in three words: envy, admiration, outrage. The stories and anecdotes taken from his life were endless, and somehow the worst outrages were ones even the least generous were forced to forgive if not congratulate him on. First, the unimaginable amount with which he had increased his fortune was as well known as the unimaginable variety of his affairs. He demonstrated a shocking proclivity for large numbers in all things. One simply did not make money for money's sake like a common merchant; it was a vulgar endeavor in the extreme, one wisely relegated to the lower class. Yet, how could one fault him when so much went to charity? Then too, his connections in the House of Commons were well known, as was the social legislation he sponsored. Granted, much of this legislation was offensive and criticized as such, but few could fault the benevolent intentions behind it.

Lord Barrington also held the distinguishing mark of being the sole man to refuse a challenge and not only keep his honor intact, but to have his honor enhanced by the refusal. There had been many challenges, too, mostly due to his well-exercised preference for married women. Yet somehow the contemptuous amusement with which he delivered his refusal always made the challenger look foolish! One simply could not question Lord Barrington's courage or his infamous ability to fight, while his arrogance was such that one always had the unkind suspicion his refusals were as much due to saving himself the small effort acceptance required, as to sparing another man's life.

Considering all this, the question pressing on everyone's mind was how had Lord Barrington finally been caught? The question was answered as Lord Barrington's title was announced and over three hundred interested gazes turned to see the new Lady Barrington. The first sight of her gave rise to another question, though. How had that loveliness emerged from the far and distant corner of the world, France's last and most ridiculous attempt to bring civilization to the new world, a place of swamps, fist-sized insects, dark-skinned Negroes, people who spoke French? It was simply not possible!

Joy's gaze swept across the grand room once, that was all. The single glance took in the gold plated candelabra above a black and white checked marble floor. Like a giant chess board, it was decorated with the pale pastel colors of silk gowns prettily interspersed with the black uniform of the gentlemen's dress, all of which was laced with bright glitter of jewels and acented by the dizzying aroma of too much perfume. She was acutely aware still of his calloused, ungloved hand on her elbow, his height and stature, the warmth emanating from his nearness as he guided her through the receiving line. Yet the moment he stepped into the bright light, something had changed within him, too. She could feel it, a sudden tension and weariness, the shrewdness of a hunter. Why? She could not but wonder, for like a puppet, she smiled, curtsied and spoke, mechanically going through the motions of being real and alive while she felt she floated to the distant ceiling, watching from that safe distance.

All sense heightened as she was presented to the Prince Regent, yet so did the strings mechanically manipulating her, and she would have been hard pressed to repeat a word of the exchange. She listened to the banter between Ram and the famous monarch, seeking a sign of their animosity and hostility, yet finding none—unless one looked beneath the innuendos concerning fathers, health and the expected congratulations on their son. Finally, the Prince Regent's attention fell on her, and as it did, Ram's grip tightened on her elbow perceptibly. He brought her arm behind her back, drawing her closer with a possessive intimacy lost on no one, least of all her. A minute later Joy could not have said what the Prince Regent looked like, past his excessive girth.

The introductions continued and Joy's numbness produced a curious effect on people's impression of her. As Ram watched what was happening, he could have laughed. Her vulnerability in the situation created a mysterious and ever so alluring air of extreme gentleness, while her numbness was misread as shyness. People found Lady Barrington so delicate, so perfectly fragile, the startling gentleness of her person contrasting provocatively with the man at her side. Fault was looked for in vain. The shyness and fragility fooled no one; one had only to gaze into those lovely eyes to discover the intelligence sparkling there, an intelligence revealed further in her clever evasion of inquiries. Many ladies had prepared cunning remarks with which to damn the new Lady Barrington, and yet, as the moments came to deliver their indictments, they found themselves awkwardly silent.

After two short hours, Lady Caroline summed the matter up: "Lady Barrington is an unprecedented success."

"With her horrid background, one could never have imagined," another said.

"It's such a shame, too," still another lady sighed. "I had such high hopes of finally seeing something Lord Barrington was to fail at."

Music played magnificently, dances were danced, champagne drunk and throughout it all, it was a dream and a nightmare in turns. Never, in all the time she had known Ram, had he been this possessive of her. With only the exception of when she danced with another, Ram's touch never once left her. She experienced his possessiveness with conflicting feelings of reassurance and nervousness; reassurance because no one watching could perceive his animosity, nervousness because he was obviously afraid to leave her. Was he afraid she'd embarrass him? Didn't he know she'd rather die than embarrass him?"

"Look there." Ram pointed.

Joy swung around, and there, presented for the enjoyment of the guests, was an enormous grotesque, pink glass swan, the opulent center piece for the buffet tables. Only it wasn't glass, it was carved ice, melting by degrees into a shiny brass bowl of punch, the size of a garden fish pond.

She stared in stunned disbelief, trying to guess where the ice had been found, how the monstrosity was created. Her gaze travelled over the length of the tables, seeing the variety, abundance and artful array of foods. Every imaginable food! She felt an impulse to steal some for Sammy and Cory, and Ram saw her first sincere smile.

Soon after, Ram finally did leave her but only to the familiar company of his uncle Admiral Byron and his wife, Lady Mellisa. No one was more pleased with Lady Barrington than Ram's great uncle and aunt. A practical, straight forward man, he never understood his great nephew's obsession with Barrington history. Upon the death of his sister, then later her husband, he had been Alisha's only surviving relative. After her death, when he had found how her boy was being raised, when Ram had told him about Lord Barrington, he had searched through Alisha's last letters. He looked for signs of her trouble. One might view her appeal for his neglected visit, her repeated request for his company as a plea for help, but then again she might have just been lonely. Of course that was queer business itself, the way her husband had removed her to the lonely, isolated coast of Ireland . . .

Frankly, he never knew what to make of the wretched mess. He felt certain his nephew made too much of it, until he received the letter saying that Ram had married Dr. Reubens's lovely niece, that he at last had a son! Oh, he had celebrated with Mellisa, yes indeed. Not only had Ram finally set aside the past, he had picked the perfect wife—Joy Claret Reubens.

Numbness began a sudden retreat and interest perked as the retired admiral enthusiastically engaged Joy with a detailed description of the last letter he received from their mutual connection, the Reverend Archibald Cox. She did not know how long she engaged the kindly older couple—it could not have been long—when quite suddenly, she felt a chill race up her spine. Instinctively her gaze lifted with a sweep in search of Ram.

She found him, twenty or so paces away, on the outskirts of the circle surrounding the dancing couples. His back was to her and he engaged a lady. Not just any lady, but one of the most beautiful women Joy had ever seen. She was laughing at something Ram said. Joy did not know how she knew, past the natural instincts given to females in all species, but she did; the woman either was his lover or had been at one time.

She watched as Ram led the lady through the doors of the balcony, and the world receded as a roar sounded, growing

354

in her mind. The elderly Lady Byron grabbed her hand. "My darling," she asked, "what's wrong?" Then Joy looked up to discover she was just about to receive the unlikely attention of none other than the Prince Regent himself . . .

Held effortlessly in his arms, Joy bore the rush of hurried fare-thee-wells and regrets as best she could, aware only that Ram's limited civility was taxed to the extreme. Finally, mercifully, the doors opened and he carried her into the dark night of a thick London fog. The Barrington coach waited, with Lance tied in back. Ram wasted no time in bringing her there. With the solicited comments and concern of the footmen, the doors to the coach opened. He set her on the seat, called orders to the driver and climbed in, taking the opposite seat. The carriage lurched forward at the exact moment he demanded: "What the devil did you think you were doing alone with him?"

The last pronoun was drawled with a contempt that sent a wild tremor through her. Never had she seen him so furious! Nervously she twisted her gloves in her hand, not daring to look up to see the anger she felt as a tangible force. "I . . . I didn't know."

"Didn't know what?" he spat with barely contained disgust. "That the Prince Regent was trying to molest my wife?"

She shook her head. "He asked me if I'd like to see the pictures in the gallery and, and . . . I was so flattered . . . I thought—"

"Flattered! What the hell did you think? That the Prince Regent was interested in cultivating your appreciation of art? God girl, you cannot be that naive!" Yet, the tears forming in her eyes told him she was that naive. The fact somehow made it so much worse.

She had no defense but ignorance. The quaint and provincial society of Louisiana, to say the least, could not have prepared her for this. There, if a gentleman kissed a lady's fingertips, it was a source of gossip for weeks. If a chaste kiss was stolen in a garden, it meant an engagement to be announced the next day. There were no plots, intrigues, malicious intents; there were no affairs among married people, at least that she knew of.

What could she say? How could she explain what it felt like for her to have the attention of what was arguably the most powerful man in the world? As the great man engaged her with the most benign subjects, she had been thinking only of children. Thinking of Sean, their Sean, a little boy whom she loved with all the fierceness of her being, and with this new mother's love came the thought of other children; a thousand faceless children who, by any of fate's capricious turns, could have been Sean. Words had been forming in her mind; words to make this man understand he simply could not ignore the abandoned children swarming in London's streets, children so desperate that they were turning to pickpocketing and oh, so much worse, prostitution, in order to survive. She had been in such a panic not to lose this opportunity, that no, she hadn't known his malicious purpose was seduction, until far too late.

Watching her closely, Ram demonstrated how very well he knew her with his next words. "Why, you megalomaniacal little fool."

Joy's gaze shot up, lowered with pain.

"My God girl, did you truly imagine that man's attention had a whit to do with your damnable charms? The limited intelligence and value of your social concerns? Let me make it perfectly clear Joy; that man's sole intent was to show me that while I won the war, he could still increase the casualty count by seducing my wife, which owing to the ludicrous extent of your naivete, he very nearly did!"

The pain of it could not be borne. She felt his disgust and revulsion for her. A trembling hand covered her mouth, desperately attempting to stop the tears that already fell.

Ram encountered the pain in those eyes but briefly, before cursing softly. He tried but his gaze could not leave her—the misty enormous eyes, the tears falling over flushed cheeks, the rapid rise and fall of her breasts barely contained in that gown—and when he felt his hands shake with the effort not to touch her, he knew he had reached the limits of his endurance. After one damn night, he was there.

Ram knocked twice on the wall. The carriage came to an abrupt halt. The door opened to a burst of chilly night air, and he left. Left her mercifully alone.

That night as she lay in the enormous feather bed, crying still, she felt, among a hundred other things, confused, terribly confused. Desperately her mind traveled again over the landscape of her short time with him, searching every dark and hidden recess for what had gone so terribly wrong.

She had first known his desire, so passionate and consuming! The slightest thought of it sent her heart and pulse racing, a blush she felt from the roots of her hair to the very tips of her toes, that sweet warmth sweeping through her limbs. Her dreams were spun from vivid memories of his kisses, the caress of his touch and his lips. Tonight was the first time his touch lingered since—since when?

Since soon after the birth of their son, she realized. Then, she had felt so utterly helpless, ridiculously vulnerable, yet he had matched those feelings with a tenderness and gentleness she could never forget. He had at all times been loving. Yes, he had loved her then! Love had shone in his gaze as he laughed and teased and comforted . . .

Or had she been wrong, misled by what was happening to her?

"God's curse is right Sean, I'll never forgive you the agony of it."

The words he had said to Sean that night on the beach came back to her, and with sudden sick panic, she saw not only that she was wrong but just how wrong she was. She never had his love! His kindness to her had been a natural

357

response to her condition, for he had known then, the night Sean was born, that their marriage would be agony for him. He never wanted to marry her! He resented her that much for forcing him to marry her . . .

Distance, she saw with a pain filled, yet clear vision, had started to come on the voyage back, beginning with his politeness and solicitousness. Teasing stopped, as did the laughter so quick to spring beteen them. He began to be quick about leaving her company. The distance had grown and grown until tonight when she had embarrassed him in front of the worst possible person, and his response showed her what his resentment was becoming. Anger, animosity and—

The very next word her mind produced set her trembling, lost to tears, endless tears that lasted throughout the first long night she met with the dark light of the unbearable future.


Little Sean fell asleep early after an exhausting day with his father, and as Joy lay in her bed, staring at the ceiling, her thoughts centered on her son. She should be getting dressed—the passing minutes vaguely pressed upon her consciousness—but her thoughts weighed heavily on her, keeping her still. She thought of little Sean, of what he meant to her and what his one day's absence from her life had shown her.

Little Sean meant everything to her; she had nothing without him. Her day had been a blank page with nothing to fill it. She felt so strangely empty inside, sad and lonely . . .

She wanted to go home . . .

A light rap sounded on her door, an unknown voice called from behind, "Milady, his lordship awaits!" The footsteps retreated without waiting for a reply.

How was she going to face another night of being Lady Barrington? Throughout the initial whirl comprising her introduction to society, her only thought was to please him. The best response she could hope to solicit from him was indifference, indifference being only slightly less painful than his anger and resentment. Sometimes now, he resented her so much he could hardly bare to look at her . . .

Ram waited impatiently downstairs. Where the hell was she? They were already late, late on one of the few nights it mattered. Correction: the only night it mattered. He had made a mistake, a potentially disastrous mistake but one he might rectify by tonight's dinner party, for one Reginald Kempster would be there.

It had all started long before he arrived home. He had been so bitter and angry over what had happened, fighting assassins sent by his peers, that all he wanted was out. He had wanted out of Britain, the land and country of his ancestors, out and away from the unfathomable depth of the hypocrisy of the court. The price was high: He had to leave London and Barrington Hall behind; he had to sell his holdings which he had worked so long and hard to build.

There lay the problem. The price was too high, too damn high. He didn't know the exact moment it had occurred to him, but as he started to set his affairs in order and confront the chaos created by his brief absence, the thought gradually occurred to him that he could not leave. How does one leave a place like Barrington Hall? A heritage of centuries? A city, nay, a world, like London? For what alternative?

Far more important, only he had realized it too late, were the men and families dependent on him. The selling of his holdings had begun with his three iron mills in South Hampton. Employing over a hundred men, the mills ran smoothly and efficiently at a fair profit. He had thought he exacted a good price from one Mister Reginald Kempster, a merchant with connections with the crown.

Not long ago Joy had brought a woman in to see him. The woman had been hiding on the grounds, trying to escape the servants long enough to get an audience with him. She wisely

359

seized the opportunity Joy presented; her story fell on those ever compassionate ears. He had not understood the accusation in Joy's eyes until the woman, not knowing he no longer owned the mills, was brought to him, and he heard her story himself.

The horror started with a three-fourths reduction in her husband's wages. "Oh, sir, we knew ye were generous afore, we all did, and I kin see if ye cut the wage a bit; but I have six little ones, six," she pleaded softly. "An' now, thar but a hairbreadth from starvin'. The longer hours are killin' our men, too. 'Tis against the lord's will to force men ta work on the Sabbath, 'tis . . ."

He had not been the only one furious upon hearing this. Mr. Wilson and Mr. Linton were in shock. Joy stared first with accusation and shock, too, but then she knew, despite everything, he was not responsible for it. "You didn't know about this, did you?" She had realized.

"No but I should have." He explained what had happened, sent the woman back with a bank note that could hold her family over until he had a chance to buy back the mills from Mister Reginald Kempster. That was what tonight was all about.

Ram's thoughts raced over the various ways he might approach Mr. Kempster. He needed to make a good impression; Joy would help with Kempster's wife of course. He would extend to the Kempsters an invitation to Barrington Hall. Then he'd explain he'd had a change of mind about the mills, wanting to buy them back. Hopefully the meeting would be on amicable and friendly terms, and he could get the mills back without losing a fortune in the transaction . . .

For several precious minutes Ram was lost to his contemplations until abruptly he realized he was still waiting. With a curse, he left his study, made his way up the stairs and down the hall to stop at her room.

Ram opened the door with her name on his lips, a name he

360

never uttered. As his gaze adjusted to the brighter light, he encountered her form lying on the bed. Her long brown hair spread over the coverlet like a fan, and she wore only a white cotton chemise, that was all. This was enough to bring his gaze travelling over the outline of the soft mounds of her breasts, the flattened stomach, a small dark patch of silky fur and the curves of her long legs, all hidden beneath the tease of white cotton.

He was held suspended with the quick, frighteningly potent physical effect of the sight of her like that. Awareness crowded into his mind in a flash of understanding; all the other women he kept in his life served only to provide momentary relief from his desire for her. Aye, he wanted her and at times so desperately, he'd spring from his bed, ready to barge in her room and force her will to his. The only thing stopping him, the only thing that could stop him was the memory of a rain-washed night, the terror in those eyes as she fought to save the life she carried, a life he had given her with but one night of passion. Then too, she would never accept him willingly, knowing well the inevitable consequence should she get with his child again, and he would have to force her. The idea was unpleasant, what followed more so. His desire was then reduced to numbers; he could force her once, twice, three times, conceivably more and still leave her womb barren, but what would he be left with? Only the renewed force of his desire; to take her once was to want her that much more again and again.

Joy never heard the door open, but the sudden sound of his curse brought her bolting up in the bed. Wide misty eyes locked with a cold hard gaze, and she gasped, meeting the cruel burst of naked fury. It held her for a moment transfixed, unable to separate the cold slap of pain from fear. So transfixed, she failed to notice the thin strings of her gown had slipped from one shoulder. Ram noticed though, and when he did, he lost control.

"What game is this? Do you purposely keep me waiting?"

She nervously pulled the coverlet over herself, then shook her head. "No . . . no . . . I'm sorry, I—"

"Where the hell are your maids?"

"I . . . dismissed them . . . I—"

"Then you have a problem—" he was not smiling—"for I'll give you ten minutes to remedy the disaster of your appearance."

The door slammed and she listened to the click of his boots echo down the hall. A furiously pounding heart banished her lethargy, but her hands trembled as she nervously donned the costume of Lady Barrington, murmuring a frantic prayer for the strength to get through the evening.

Please dear God, just one more evening . . .

Not more than ten minutes later she emerged from her room, and as Ram's gaze encountered the beauty of her transformation, he had reason to regret the irony of his words. Disaster indeed! The simple gown of pale blue silk accented the darker emotion in her eyes, emotion also brightening her cheeks. The gown had the fashionably high waist and alarmingly low neckline, a neckline triggering his quick geometric skill by producing the sum of four: only four inches of material allocated to covering the full thrusts of her breast. When he realized he held his breath waiting for her, he silently cursed the dressmaker, Sean, God, the devil, anyone and everyone who had anything to do with bringing her into his life. . . . Just give me the strength to get through this night.


By the preconceived arrangement of the day, an invisible line separated the gentlemen and their politics and business concerns from the ladies and their lighter matters. The ladies all clustered around the duchess as they always had and always would. All comments were addressed to her. The grand dame had just returned from abroad—her home in

Venice—and the ladies eagerly sought her stamp of approval on everything from their new gowns to that recent invitation.

No other family name held the same prominence and distinction as the duchess; her social position was unquestioned, if not unparalleled, and from her lofty position, she single handledly orchestrated the whole of society. While in the earlier days of the older woman's illustrious career, she had savored the power of it, of making or breaking careers on whims, of artfully arranging the hierarchy of society, now she was bored. It was a profound boredom, for that simple word summed up her existence.

Finally, as they waited, Lady Ann, so terribly delicate, afflicted with mild nervous disorders that made her seem all aflutter all the time, gave voice to what everyone pretended not to notice. "The Barringtons are late."

"Lord Barrington is always late," the duchess told them, regally reclining in the chair. "Once last year, I was waiting on Lady Margarite in court, and I recall Lord Barrington kept the entire household from moving to the country for two days. Apparently he had arranged a meeting with the prince, insisting the prince put off the move a day. Then he had the unprecedented gall to keep the prince waiting another. I dare say," she sighed, "if Lord Barrington can keep the Prince Regent waiting, he can keep this company in wait."

The duchess shrewdly watched Madame Merle Kempster blush and knew the woman took this as a slight against her name—Madame Merle having one of the richest, though alas, untitled husbands in England. It was good to keep them uncertain. Just to add to the confusion, she complimented Madame Merle on her jewels.

Madame Merle beamed with false pride and fondling her necklace, she said, "I understand Lady Barrington wears no jewels?" She had yet to meet the most talked of young lady.

"She doesn't have to!" Lady Ann leaned forward, her eye twitching infuriatingly. "Oh, my dear," she told the duchess, "she is lovely beyond belief! Though—" she giggled—"I suppose she'd have to be to capture Lord Barrington."

"Capture?" Lady Catherine questioned. "I believe the word is trapped." Young and beautiful herself, Lady Catherine was not the only lady who had reached for Lord Barrington, only to fall.

"Lady Catherine, tsk . . . tsk—" the grand dame rebuked with a shake of her head yet with a contradicting smile.

"We all know it's true," Catherine said undaunted, too assured of her position with the elderly duchess to be afraid.

"Oh, but did you hear about the Regent's Ball?" Lady Ann asked excitedly. "That other man's attention to Lady Barrington?"

The duchess returned with a sigh, "Capturing the Prince Regent's eye is no feat of distinction, since his eye snares as many flies as butterflies."

The ladies laughed, but Catherine warmed to the subject. "To my eyes, Lady Barrington is absolute proof that one simply cannot hide one's background for any length of time. Oh"—she daintily sipped port from the tiny crystal glass— "I'm not referring to her numerous slips, slips a generous person might forgive, the less generous might dismiss simply for the amusement of it. And while it's true she seems to have swept society off their collective feet, there's something hidden beneath the façade of gentle sweetness."

"Façade?" The duchess showed mild interest.

"Yes, one that drops occasionally. For instance, the other night at my dinner party, Lady Barrington suddenly disappeared, only to be found by Lord Barrington and my husband outside in a circle of our grooms apparently discussing horse breeding!"

"Horse breeding?" Lady Ann paled as she tried to imagine what a lady might know of this subject. "I've seen her show a peculiar interest in politics, especially the House of Commons. Why, I've even heard her express opinions—to my Edward! But horse breeding?"

364

"Opinions that outrage!" Lady Catherine added.

"Well at least there she's matched well with her husband," the duchess observed and the ladies laughed again.

"Yes, I've seen that," Lady Brett joined in, less bold than Catherine, but just as enthusiastic. "As she listens to one politely, one might glimpse her foot tapping impatiently. And she does seem to exercise a preference for men and their politics."

"She also seems to have these . . . ah, queer passions . . ."

"Passions?" The duchess wanted to know about this.

"Why, Negroes, if one can believe what one hears," Lady Brett said.

"Negroes!" Madame Merle now seemed quite shocked.

"Children for another," Catherine added, then said to Lady Brett, "Why, you remember during dinner—"

"Oh yes." Brett laughed. "Lady Barrington made the most outrageous suggestion, a charity ball for homeless children! She was quite enthusiastic, while we were all quite shocked, and it was your long time friend the earl"—she directed this to the grand dame—"who replied, 'For whom?'" Lady Brett humorously mimicked the earl's deep voice, 'You mean those filthy urchins running wild in our streets like rats? Why my dear lady, where do you get such notions? Just the other day, my wife and I were ascending the steps of Saint Paul's when from nowhere this filthy pox-marked little boy broke through my footmen and snatched my wife's brooch. Help them? Hanging them is too good . . .' And well, you know how the earl can rave—"

The conversation abruptly ended then, as the Barringtons' arrival was announced at last.


The duchess peered above her cards to Lady Barrington across the table. No wonder she attracted so much attention! She was lovely; she possessed an alluring beauty, one that drew the eye, then held it. The blue silk dress accented the paleness of her skin—and my, what a flawless complexion—the dark sable color of the artful pile of her hair, making her recall what Lord Marshmaine said about her eyes: ". . . like openings to a summer sky," Lord Barrington's response was "Yes indeed, my mind has conjured those exact words, though in the future Marshmaine, my wife will not be a subject of your poetry!" They had all laughed, though indeed no one missed the warning.

Dinner had gone very smoothly, and presently, three card tables were arranged in the elegant drawing room at Stein Hall, where the ladies had adjourned for cards and music, while the men retired to the study for brandy, politics and business. Chatter abounded, and though Lady Barrington replied politely and smiled occasionally, she remained aloof and quiet. If the duchess's shrewd appraisal wasn't wrong—and heavens but she was never wrong—Lady Barrington operated under restraint, as though the real woman lay hidden beneath the façade of gentle breeding. Façade, yes she thought, remembering the gossip hours earlier in this very room as the party had waited for the Barringtons.

The card game ended at last, and the duchess watched as Joy congratulated the winner, then immediately withdrew behind—yes, they were right—a façade. What are you hiding, my dear girl? Could it truly be my same boredom? It took years for me, yet you're so young! Do you know—have you any idea—that any other young lady with your background would be thrilled to breathe the same air as our servants, let alone be presented as an equal among us!

No, the duchess realized, the reserve hiding Lady Barrington's boredom went deeper. There was more there, perhaps hinted at by those passions mentioned. She smiled faintly to herself, deciding to at last end her boredom by unveiling the real Lady Barrington.

The duchess signaled an end to the card games while their hostess Lady Brett called for aperitifs to be served. Two servants immediately entered carrying trays, and the ladies retired to the sitting chairs and sofa for quite conversation before the men returned.

Joy accepted the crystal goblet, a Kir Royal, and resisted the urge to use a finger to blend the layer of champagne and creme de cassis in her glass. Lady Barrington was all about resisting urges; she resisted the urge to say anything important and to do or be anything she was, anything that might embarrass him. Smile, keep your small finger away from the glass, don't cross your legs, do sit up straight, address a duchess this way, a marquis that way, and on and on it went, this oppressive list of dos and don'ts.

She lived in the glass cage again, and like a porcelain doll, she was left in glass on the top shelf, never taken down to know a child's play, only stared at from a distance for display. She was so tired of Lady Barrington, of these endless teas and parties and dinners. They were all the same, only the color of the gowns changed. The subjects, the people and their pretenses were all the same. She was tired of dressing in nothing but silks and ribbons, looking like an over done Christmas package, tired of smiling and nodding, pretending to care about that guest list, who that lady will marry, lord so-and-so's gaming debts, or how prettily that lady plays the pianoforte. She had quickly grown weary of people telling her how lovely she was, how miraculously she'd overcome the debit of her background. So tired of it all . . .

Throughout dinner, her mind had teeter-tottered: these faces contrasting with those of Cory, reverend, Sammy; the length of the great dining table contrasting with one for four; the delicate Spanish lace over the table cloth contrasting with a red checkered cloth; the engraved silver of the utensils contrasting with the wood ones Cory and she had been so proud to own; the pale blue silk of her dress contrasting with crimson and gold cotton. Joy stifled her homesickness, fighting for composure, a composure she still struggled for as she listened to the chatter around her, wondering how she could love gossiping with Cory so much while this left her empty and cold.

". . . Lady Barrington?"

"Pardon." Joy looked up at the Duchess. "I'm afraid I didn't hear that?"

"Madame Merle had just shared her impressions from her recent trip abroad to the states, where she stayed on her son's plantation in North Carolina. How many slaves did you say he owns again?"

Madame Merle Kempster could hardly believe the duchess would condescend to show interest in her son's plantation. "Over two hundred," she announced proudly. "He's the youngest, of course, and while at first we were naturally displeased by his decision to take his inheritance away from Britain, he's done so well." She smiled broadly. "I'm afraid you must forgive me a mother's pride."

"Slaves! Imagine it in this day and age!" the duchess exclaimed, watching as Joy's fingers tightened noticeably around her glass. Relentlessly she pursued, "I understand that slaves are treated no worse than our own servants? Is that how you found it, Lady Barrington?"

All eyes turned to Joy, watching a magnificent play of emotion in her eyes, but those eyes lowered uncertainly as she seemed to hold her breath.

"Yes indeed," Madame Merle answered for her. "My son treats his Negroes kindly and fair. Why, in my entire stay, I never heard one complaint from a person of color. Not one!" she repeated happily. "The house servants, why they're almost like family, and the colored woman who cares for my grandchildren, even more so. They call her mammy, isn't that just so quaint . . . so provincial!"

"A mammy!" the duchess repeated in a tone dripping with sarcasm. "Lady Barrington, did you know any of these charming American equivalents to our cherished English nannies?"

At first no emotion showed in Joy's eyes as she

encountered the expectant stares of every lady in the room. "Why yes," she said so softly everyone leaned forward expectantly. "I once knew a mammy. Her name was Delilah. Should you like to hear Delilah's story?" she asked the company. "Her story is uncommon only by its ending—that the well-known and prominent family who owned Delilah had her sold, sold with the barest hint of suspicion that it was she, Delilah, the loving family mammy of two generations, who had been putting arsenic in her young master's food."

Shocked gasps came from all around, but she had captured them all, including the men who just threw open the drawing room doors. Once caught, she held them mesmerized as she broke from the glass cage, the façade and its pretense, and with a haunting sadness she told the story of Delilah, almost word for word as she remembered Delilah telling it a long time ago:

"Weren't too bad as a youngin," Delilah had explained. "My mama is de mammy den. I get everthin' de lil master get—food aplenty, a room beneath de stairs, even a genuine fet'er bed. Ain't much work for a house nigger chile, either. Until I was 'bout twelve an' de master starts eyin' me funny lak. First time was on de kitchen table. Never said a word neither, but after, he puts a nickle in my hand. I was cryin' so hard I never even know w'at he gives me till I tries to get up. Den I sees hit—a nickel! He t'inks a nickel even us up! A nickel fer de pain an' hurt, for de scared dat choked my insides fer near a week!

"Well, pretty soon I had 'nuf nickels to buy a white folks bank. I had me three youngins by de time I'se seventeen, and oh lawd but I tell you, dose chilun almost make de nickels worth hit. Two boys an' a girl! De boys is trouble an' de girl is sweet an' pretty!

"De oldest boy gets on to six an' my girl is 'bout four, an' de older dey git, de plainer hit is where I'se gettin' all dose nickels from. I knows de mistress doan lak lookin' at 'em none, an' sos I trys real hard to keep 'em away. But den one day, I'se out pickin' apples an' I get back after de noon sun. I'se look for my chilun but I can't find 'em. 'Mama, where's dose youngins run off to?' But she doan answer none. Weren't till I look everywhere and I'se start screamin' an' hollerin' dat she says dey's been taken to town to get sold. She says de mistress, she sells 'em so she kin get some peace of mind.

"Well, I'se couldn't talk none for near a year, an' I'se take to weepin' most all de time. I'se miss dem chiluns fiercely! De mistress never did say a word 'bout hit—lak my youngins never took breath in her house. Dis, when I'se a carin' for her five youngins lak my own—I feeds 'em, play wid 'em, sing to 'em, nurse 'em. I'se thar mammy since de day thar born. Hit warn't right; she shoulda knows hit warn't right.

"One day I 'member I'se out in de garden pickin', near 'nuf to de house to hear de master speakin' to de oldest lil master—he was oh, 'bout ten an' five den. He says, 'so if'n you gets de urge, pick one of our darkies an' give de girl a nickel. Dey doan mind none for a nickel,' he says. 'Delilah's been servicin' me fine for years.' Den he laughs and I was sick; sick right over de carrots. Not 'nuf dat I get nickels from de master, but now I'se got to get 'em from his boy, too.

"My last babe is born de first day o' summer, and dat's what I name her, Summer. I'se scared right off cause—you ain't gonna believe dis but her eyes is blue. Yes suh! Summer got dese big blue eyes dat never did change. Lawd"—she shook her head—"I trys not to love her. I tries so hard hit hurts, but 'tweren't possible not to love Summer. Even de white folks love her! She ain't lak no one else, you see. First off, she's touched. She never learn to talk. Never, but Lawd, ain't never seen a chile wid so much love an' happiness. She's always a smilin' an' she love everyone an' everythin'—she loves flowers, de ole barnyard dog; she loves cats and mice, bugs and peoples. She were somethin'! Ah Lawd, when dat chile laugh, everybody laugh. Weren't no sound, but her lil body a shake and shake, an' she be grinnin' ear to ear.

"Well, 'bout when my Summer is four an' hits plain she ain't never gonna talk, I'se suddenly see de lawd made her touched so's dat I'se can keep her. Pretty soon I'se knows dat's why! An den hit seems dat all de love for my other youngins is for Summer. I never stop to know dat no one cares if'n a nigger woman can talk or no.

"One day I'se swallow my fear, and I ask de mistress please to let me keep Summer wid me. She says fine, if'n Summer is truly my last chile, if'n I stop she-cattin' hit 'round. She says she hopes hits so 'cause she doan reckon she could part wid Summer neither. Dat what she says. I never knows she been thinkin' hit my doin' an' dat I'se deserve to lose my youngins. To dis day, I'se shock.

"Well, I'se get to feelin' hits all gonna be fine anyway cause de young master marries an' moves, an' de ole' master doan come round no more. But one day de mistress is gone an' I'se upstairs wid a dust rag an' de master comes wid a nickel. I say 'no' an' he says he doan take no from none of his niggers an' he force me. I knows, lawd I knows. She comes home early— doan never know if she saw or heard or w'at. She acks lack nothin' happen. But de next day she says she's goin' to town an' wouldn't hit be nice to take Summer. I'se panic, I say no; I want Summer wid me. She say I'se bein' foolish. I'se start crying but it wer de last day I'se ever saw of my Summer."

The collective group remained trapped long after the last word, held and mesmerized as much by the truth shining in blue eyes as by the words of a story. Silence reigned; reactions were slow in coming. The men waited helplessly, shocked as much by the story as they were that it had been told, not just in front of ladies but by a lady. Lady Brett watched curiously as the room blurred, it being so long since she'd shed an honest tear, she first thought her shock triggered a vision malady. Lady Catherine felt her husband's hands lay across hers and she grasped them fiercely, welcoming his touch for the first time in her three years of marriage. Lady Ann had not in the total of her twenty-six years heard anything like it—the knowledge was bane; after several minutes she realized she was no longer breathing, and with the realization, she swooned. As Lady Ann swooned, Madame Merle conjured horrid visions of her grandchildren at the hands of their mammy, and though her swoon was not nearly as convincing as Lady Ann's, her face paled as she gasped for smelling salts.

Abruptly, chaos reined.

Servants were called for, chairs toppled over in the gentlemen's rush to aid the ladies. Only the duchess remained composed and collected with the result of what she would consider her greatest social triumph: uncovering the real Lady Barrington. Which was not to say she wasn't affected by Delilah's story. Heavens no! She was as moved by the story, as by the real Lady Barrington.

In the midst of the clamor, Joy felt strong hands gently come upon her shoulders. "I think it's time to leave" was all he said, all he had to say. She rose obediently and quietly, though rebellion rose in a potent force through her heart, mind and soul. He might have pulled her initially into the depths of despondency, but no one, not even him, could keep her down. A wise old woman's words rose to echo over and over again in her mind. "You might not be happy, but happiness is but a small price for a good life."

Joy now understood what that meant.

If only she had the courage to meet Ram's gaze then; she would have seen that love was not and never had been the issue. He never once thought of the small fortune Delilah's story cost him. No, not once. It was after all only money, and money was nothing when placed against the emotion in his heart—the tragedy of loving the only woman he could not have.


Joy paused nervously outside the hall, hearing the heated argument inside between Ram, Sean, and eight or nine of their captains inside. She hated to interrupt anything important. She hated to interrupt anything period. Yet, the hours she was home and the hours in which Ram was free had not overlapped for the past three days, days which she had anxiously awaited the right time to make her appeal. If Mr. Cutler was right, he was planning to leave Barrington Hall again on the morrow, and it was now or never.

She had sent Ram a note through his secretary requesting an audience—the painful irony of having to ask an audience with your husband unfortunately did not escape her—and she had been told she might come immediately. Now or never, and since never was unconscionable, she took a deep breath and knocked on the door.

No one answered, the arguing continued, something about Gibraltar, corsairs, the French. Voices were raised and she imagined arms raised wildly, too. There was no more frightening group of men than these captains. One did not reach their lofty position with any trace of meekness; they each had enough strength, ambition and power to lead hundreds of the most ribald and hardened seamen across the seas, often to battle and more often than not, to victory and riches that seemed ever accumulating. The only men she knew more frightening were Ram himself, Sean too, but only if one didn't really know him.

Riches, think of the riches they're arguing over!

She knocked harder, more insistently. Ram's secretary, Mr. Mitchell, finally heard the knock and opened the door. Silence descended as she stepped through the door, uncomfortably aware of ten shrewd and hard gazes, none the least of which was Ram's. With quiet strength and determination she politely apologized, "Gentlemen, please forgive the interruption." She looked to Ram. "You said I might speak with you now?" she questioned uncertainly.

Ram had already opened the adjoining room of his study doors, and with a rustle of skirts, she followed him in. As the door closed, the voices rose again, and she paused for a moment, tensing as she felt his gaze wash over her.

She was acutely conscious of the tumult of confusion his nearness always brought. He was well over a foot taller, now somewhat less as he leaned against the closed door, though the breadth of his powerful shoulders and the length of his muscled legs made him look taller still. The plain white shirt did not hide a chest and arms armored in hard muscle, a lean and flat belly. Do not think of dreams now! She swallowed nervously; the unreadable expression in his gaze, taken with his overwhelming physical presence were the first obstacles she forced herself to overcome.

"I am truly sorry for interrupting you," she began in a soft tone of feigned control.

"It's of no consequence, and besides, I have something to say to you as well." He moved with easy strides to his enormous desk chair. "What is it you want?"

The bland arrogance of his tone sparked a tremor of anger, one instantly suppressed for her purpose, only for her purpose. The result of her endless search for an explanation of the strange and awful thing that he put between them had finally resulted in the single liberating thought that it was not her fault. Sean had made the bargain she could not refuse, but Ram had sealed it. She could no more regret little Sean's birth than her own breath. He had been forced to marry her and she him, but even with that awful realization, she did not deserve either his animosity or the unbearable strain of his resentment of their entwined fates.

It was simply not her fault . . .

She came directly to the point, and from her apron pocket, she removed the folded pages that held the carefully constructed figures and explanations. She set the paper in front of him. "I need more money for a new wing at the Chester House. The numbers of children are growing—there are so many—and this provides the space necessary to accommodate them."

Ram never looked at it. He stared instead at her eyes,

wondering why no one ever warned him what a woman's eyes could do to a man. The emotions he had just watched there had passed, replaced with the determination, warmed it seemed by the small piece of humanity she sought to single-handedly save. When he had not been able to keep the distance between them, he had forced her to. She managed the job fervently, avoiding him with unreasonable lengths. She threw herself into this charity work from dawn to midnight—squeezing the abolitionist cause in between, mostly with speeches at various churches and correspondence. She worked far too hard, and it was beginning to exact a price, a price he was not at all willing to pay.

Ram finally glanced at the bottom line. "A pretty sum," he said, yet with indifference. "I don't recall ever denying you before, and I won't now; but this time I want something in return."

Once upon a time her heart might have leaped at this baiting, a guess of what he might want from her. No such thing happened. He wanted nothing from her, save her natural role as mother to his son. "Your return is knowing you have provided food and shelter for that many children."

"Mr. Wilson and my banker informed me just this morning how many children I am providing for. I want something more."

She braced herself for what she was certain would be a cruel lash. "What?"

"I want my wife to restrict her activities at that orphanage to no more than three mornings a week."

Her eyes widened. "What?" she whispered. He couldn't mean it, he just couldn't. "Ram, you don't mean it, you—"

"I assure you I do and there's more. These speeches you give—I don't like it, the idea of my wife sleeping under another man's roof—"

"Another . . . man? But they're always reverends!"

"I don't give a damn if they're the saints themselves. I don't like it. I also want my wife to stop neglecting her son. He needs you, Joy." His tone changed. "You leave him far too much with Mrs. Thimble and the other caretakers."

"That's not true! I've never, never neglected him! I couldn't if I wanted to, and the only time I ever leave him is when you're here and want to be with him. I almost always bring him with me—"

"Yes, and I don't want my son being raised in an orphanage of all places, and with his mother's attention divided between twenty other children."

"Oh, but Sean loves it there! He's at an age where he loves nothing more than to be surrounded by other children's laughter and games and—"

"Enough!" His tone sliced into her arguments as a blade cuts flesh. "Look at yourself, Joy," he said as he stared at the loveliest woman it was his misfortune to know. In a futile though, what seemed to him, almost desperate attempt to hide her beauty, she wore a plain muslin gown of no adornment, one he knew could not have come from the chiffoniers he had paid, a plain apron over that. Her hair was simply braided and wrapped around her head. What bothered him were the dark circles under her eyes, a slenderness he had last seen when she had been months without proper food. "It is not just that one would think I had trouble clothing my wife, but that I also had trouble feeding her. You are working too hard Joy; it has begun to affect your health, and I'll not have that."

He couldn't do this. She wouldn't let him do this. "No"—she shook her head—"you can't ask me to give it up—"

"I'm not. I'm merely asking for you to restrict it somewhat."

"Somewhat?" she questioned. "Three mornings a week? When there's so much to be done and so little time to do it! What of the empty hours? I'd have nothing—"

"You'd have Sean."

She said then what they both knew was true. "He's not enough. He's the most precious thing in my life, but he's not

376

my life."

Ram absolutely refused to consider how many of her own children it would take to tap her boundless energies. No more dangerous thought could have intruded, and he stifled it instantly.

"You can't ask me to give it up, you just can't," she repeated with conviction. "You don't know what it's like—the children—forty-three of them under five and they're kept in cribs, and with the shortage of caretakers, they hardly ever know a woman's arms, laughter or play. They're just left there ... Every time a simple head cold sweeps through Chester House, three or four children die, despite good food and a doctor's care, and you see, I have this theory about it. This month we started a new program. The older children now help the younger ones—caring for and holding them, playing with them. This plus—"

She stopped abruptly, suddenly fascinated with the pattern on the carpet. She was running on about her concerns, concerns he didn't share and concerns she was certain he didn't want to know about. She was about to tell him how between Clair, Pansie, herself and the older children, the youngest children were finally getting enough love and attention. She felt certain this would make a difference in the mortality rate.

Ram could never meet the fierceness of her spirit and remain unaffected, and watching her struggle with the sudden intimacy between them was as painful for him as it was for her. The hardest thing for him was to meet her passion and turn away; nothing was harder.

Damn your passion, Joy Claret.

"I'm sorry," she said softly. "I got carried away. I'm sure you have more important concerns to think about."

He ignored the self effacement and returned to the point, grateful her eyes were lowered. "Joy, I'll allocate funds to hire more people to replace you. How's that?"

"Fine," she said, a change in her tone as well. "Only I want to be there, too. If I don't have work, I only have Lady Barrington to do, and I don't think I need to remind you what a disaster that is."

Yet he knew Lady Barrington had not been a disaster; quite the contrary. Word of the story she had told spread through London with unprecedented speed and nothing—not even when he had knocked the Prince Regent out cold—incited society's interest more than the apparent contradiction of Lady Barrington. He had a sky-high pile of invitations to prove it. This, however, was not his concern.

The point was she was pushing him and a dangerous game it was. "You misunderstand, Joy Claret. I don't give a damn about Lady Barrington or her social life, though I do care very much about your health and the well-being of my son."

Joy's eyes lifted in sudden rebellion, and he fought the maddening urge to tame it, knowing without a doubt it would take but the slightest touch to end it all, that the last thing he needed to see was this, the little hellion she could be.

"Thank you very much for your concern," she said without feeling, save what tormented him in her eyes. "But my health is fine, and Sean's well-being—I feel foolish to even point out—is a good deal better than hundreds of other children! Children I want to help. You simply ask far too much."

Ram would argue no more, and like the slam of a judge's gavel, he said, "What if I said I was not asking?"

"Then I would tell you to go to hell!"

Ram slowly came to his feet and leaned forward on his great wide desk, his clenched fists braced by the suddenly tensed muscles in his arms, startling her with the indication he physically restrained himself.

"God girl"—something dangerous and deadly came into his gaze—"do not make me start threatening you. Do not make me say that I would without hesitation withdraw my financial support of those children to force you to comply with my will or that, if I had to, I would physically restrain you. Do not make this disaster of a marriage any worse; do not make me hurt you any more than I have."

Tears instantly sprang to her eyes, and he watched her struggle desperately to fight them back. "You have no choice," he said coldly, turning suddenly away. "Do as you're told and get the hell out of here."

Ram heard the door open and shut, the small black boots run from the outer hall, and he cursed. Cursed himself and her, the disaster he simply could not see a way out of. It had been bad enough trying to resist the wounded, fragile creature she had been those first months they tried and tested, then felt the full, awful effects of their marriage. A dozen times he had almost lost, but now, ever since she broke her own restraints with the telling of Delilah's story, the woman staring furiously at him and telling him to go to hell was his Joy Claret, the wild and rebellious girl who rode through the night being chased by men and pistols and dogs. She was a girl with more passion in the small of her hand than the rest of humanity had put together, a passion he still wanted to own with each and every breath, a desire not diminishing with denial but, like some crazed and caged animal, waiting to spring—

He had to get away from her.

The day was overcast, and like so many hundreds of others, a thick mist shrouded the land, a light drizzle fell from the gray sky. She had run and run, ending up nearly two miles away. Seanessy found Joy a half-hour later. She was leaning against a tree, staring at the running water of the stream, and cloakless, she held her sides to keep what small warmth she felt close. She cried softly, looking forlorn and lost. He felt his heart break cleanly in two.

"Joy—" he beckoned softly.

She looked up, then away again. "Seanessy," she asked in a soft voice broken by tears, "why is he so cruel to me?"

As always, Sean's answers were simple, "He can't help it, Joy. I dare say, you're driving him madder than any of his dead ancestors ever hoped to aspire."

She shot him a pained, startled look.

"Well, what did you expect?" he asked softly. "Can't you imagine his agony at being trapped in this marriage to you? You, of all women—"

Her lip trembled in horror, she caught it with a gasp, and Sean stopped, stupefied and confused by the effect he saw of his words. "Joy? Joy!" he called as she turned and ran, shooting through the forest like a frightened doe, and she was gone, long before it ever occurred to him that she, unbelievably, had not a clue as to what was so terribly wrong with her marriage.

# *Chapter Twelve*

Dear Diary,

Little Sean is finally asleep in my bed, and tonight at last I feel I can make an appearance on these pages after such a long absence. I shall confine my thoughts and impressions only to little Sean, for since the night Ram left nearly two weeks ago now, I have enjoyed Sean's company from the moment I wake until the moment I sleep and the hours of night in between. I don't know why hearing words put to what I knew— first by Ram himself and then by Seanessy—affected me so, only that it did, and ever since I have needed little Sean to remind me that my short time with Ram had been worth the pain of having solicited the animosity of the only man I shall ever love. With little Sean I see there exists more than pain; there is our beautiful and remarkable little boy.

Little Sean is so like his father that just seeing the thick raven-dark curls, enormous brown eyes and determined lines of his jaw and mouth brings such a bittersweet mix of joy and pain. He is like his father, too, in that he's a handful: aggressive, determined and my, ever so boisterous! He is a bright boy, that is plain, and though at a year old he manages but a few words, he understands a surprising amount. One cannot turn one's back on him for a minute, a lesson the household learns over and over again. Today, when he was left unattended for just a minute, he worked his way out of the nursery and into a linen closet, to be finally found beneath a mountain of bed sheets and tablecloths, giggling wildly with this jolly game of hide and seek. Then, there was last Sunday. We were in attendance at the village church, and Mrs. Thimble thought I had him and I thought she had him. Suddenly, the sermon was interrupted by blaring organ music, and there he was, sitting on the organ bench, grinning and so obviously pleased with himself—looking as though he fully expected thunderous applause. I still laugh when I think of it, though I should say the reverend was not as easily charmed by the merriment in my son's eyes.

Where he is not like his father is in the realm of affection. Mrs. Thimble, who has raised three of her own boys, says she has never seen such an affectionate or loving child. Here I am reminded of Summer, for like that child, little Sean loves everyone and everything; he is at all times filled with life and happiness.

For Sean I can endure. I can survive, yet I wonder for how long. How long before I lose the strength to rise above my circumstances? My sadness is intense: I feel as though Ram has died, and I grieve as such, yet my grief follows no natural course, one I think that normally leads to acceptance and peace. For each time I see him, it's as though he has been miraculously resurrected, and happiness, joy and hope fill me till I tremble with it, only then to have it wrenched from me as he inevitably turns away!

Death would be a merciful void, as is losing oneself to the needs of others. Yet he took my charity work from me, too. I cannot keep going on like this; I must change my circumstances. This is my plan: As soon as

Ram returns, I will ask to leave for a visit home—a very long and extended visit, though I won't tell him that. Once I am home again and the prearranged time of departure nears, I shall send a letter home asking for a longer visit. Of course he'll say no, but it will take two to three months just for the exchange of posting. Then I'll repeat the measure, and again, and who knows how long I might gain? A year? More?

The thought of going home to Cory, Sammy and the reverend—

Joy could not hold the thought and keep writing. She rose abruptly, with her hands on her cheeks, willing herself not to cry again. Crying did so little good. Turning from her desk, she stopped, seeing a reflection through the doorway in the looking glass. An ancient pair of eyes, the oldest she had ever seen, stared back at her. She gasped, swinging to the door, but the figure was gone. Racing to the doorway, she caught sight of a candle turning down the dark hall.

"Oh, that must 'ave been ole Nanny 'awkins," Pansie told her the next day as they took a picnic basket to a pleasant spot by the stream in the woods.

"Who?" Joy asked as she spread the blanket. Pansie set their things on it, while Joy set little Sean on the loosened moist earth of the bank and, to his delight, presented him wiht a bucket and shovel.

"Ole Nanny 'awkins," Pansie repeated as she sat down. "Lady Barrington's ole maid."

"Lady Barrington's maid! Why, I never knew! She still lives here?"

"Aye. She has 'er own rooms on the third floor of the east wing. 'Ardly comes out. Only person who sees 'er really is Bertha, who brings 'er meals and tidies up. But I don't 'ave a farthing what she was doin' near milady's rooms, I don't."

"Hmmm." Joy's gaze thoughtfully fixed on Pansie. "How very queer. Ram knows, I suppose—"

"Oh, that 'e does. 'Tis only decent to look after dependents, I know, but a lesser man than 'is lordship would 'ave thrown the ole bat out."

"Why do you say that?"

Pansie had learned to be as frank with Joy as she was with her own mother. "Well, 'tis common knowledge that the ole woman was always mean to 'is lordship. Bertha says she blamed 'im for 'er ladyship's passing. There were many a time when she spoke bad about 'im. And 'e so generous with 'er!"

"Oh," Joy murmured watching Sean's industriousness as he filled the bucket, dumped it over, then with a happy cry, socked the neat mound. As always, Rake sat by his side—Rake having aspired to the unlikely and exulted position of little Sean's best friend. Despite Mrs. Thimble's unconventional use of a broom, Rake insisted on sleeping in the nursery, and recently Ram finally gave up coaxing Rake to go with him. "How sad," her thoughts came out loud, "she must have loved Lady Barrington very much."

"That's one way of looking at it," Pansie said, but with clear skepticism.

"I wonder why she was watching me, Pansie." It suddenly occured to her. "Why, you don't suppose 'twas she who gave me Lady Barrington's cross, do you? I mean, if Ram never had it, she probably did!"

"Makes sense, I suppose, save the fact that the ole woman's not sweet enough for such a kind gesture. Though unless there's ghosts, I don't see how else it ended up on your vanity."

Silence came between them as Joy thought of going to meet the old woman. She would ask for an explanation, and no doubt, she'd hear all about Ram's mother. What was she like? How did she survive?

"Milady?"

"Hmmm?"

"You don't imagine I'll ever be old, senile, stuck up in those rooms long after you're gone?"

Joy smiled and nudged Pansie playfully, then dug into the picnic basket. The smile stopped suddenly as she lifted a huge plump orange from the basket. She held it up, staring at the fruit, remembering how he had once stopped a whole ship, nearly eighty men, and changed its course merely to satisfy her whim for fresh fruit. She held the poignant reminder of his tenderness and fought back the familiar swell of sadness. To have once thought she knew his love, to know now its loss . . .

Despite her efforts, the sadness shadowed the rest of the day, though she carefully hid it from Sean. After eating, she took Sean to the stables where they counted the number of kittens in the lofts. Between the picnic of mud pies and the stables, little Sean was happily covered in enough dirt to leave an inch-high layer of mud in the tub. Carrying him back to the great house, her eyes fortuitously came to rest on the fountain, and she smiled, hoping Mr. Cutler didn't catch them in their mischief.

Ram spotted the disaster from the hill, and every forward step of his mount magnified his unease tenfold. He heard her laughter mixed with the wild giggles of his son, as she stood knee deep in the fountain, bending over to hold little Sean up. Little Sean's clothes and Joy's sun hat were discarded carelessly on the ground. She wore a pretty apricot, cotton day dress, the skirts of which were hiked up and wrapped around her legs like boys' breeches. Her long hair, apparently once piled neatly on her head, now fell in chaotic disarray. He tensed with the quick and familiar effect, damning her and his desire, never suspecting it could be worse until suddenly, she stood up, and shielding her eyes from the sun, she looked to see him mounted there.

He couldn't move at first; he just stared. Flirting dangerously with his control, the dress was wet, not only

385

nearly transparent but it clung to those slender curves like an extra layer of skin. Unwilling, he imagined lifting the cloth from her skin . . .

While little Sean splashed wildly, pointing—"Fa! Fa! Fa,"—Joy met Ram's intense disapproval and held her breath. He looked fierce with sudden anger—nay fury—all of which was accented by the three-week growth of beard, an ugly bruise on his cheek and what she always thought of as his pirate clothes; an open vest, breeches, boots, the jeweled dagger. The overwhelming physical presence of him made her breath catch, tension gripped her where only play and laughter had been.

Little Sean tried to climb over the fountain edge to get to his father, and recovering somewhat, Joy managed to lift him up to Ram, before he was trampled under the hooves of that beast of his. As she lifted him over head, her breast rose up from the fabric of the gown, and his swift curse brought her eyes to him. Little Sean jumped excitedly in his arms, yet Ram could not even pass a greeting. "What's wrong?" she asked, trepidation softening her voice. "Are you angry that we're playing in the fountain?"

He looked away, chuckling yet without warmth. "Hardly. What has touched my temper is seeing your charms displayed in a way that's bound to have half my household trying to cuckold me!"

She lowered her eyes to her dress, and he swore when her arms shyly covered herself. "Here," he said removing his vest, handing it to her. "God's curse, girl, don't let me see you like that again." He reined his mount around, and with his son's laughter, he rode away.

A wave of humiliation and embarrassment washed over her, and for a long moment afterward, she stood barefoot and dripping wet in the fountain, numb and chilled by turns. He simply could not bear the sight of her. She met his disapproval at every turn, no matter what or who she was. How much animosity he must nurture if to meet her eyes brought agony.

As Ram could not bear the sight of her, she could not bear the thought, and she stifled it. She wrung out her skirt and climbed out of the fountain, but as she walked back to the great house alone, the irrepressible longing filled her again. How much love she had once had in her life! She had held Joshua's love for as long as he lived, Sammy's, Cory's and the reverend's. True, she now felt a mother's love, and though nature's infinite wisdom made this love greater, it also was not enough. How she longed to be with her family, happy and laughing and . . . loved again!

The longing followed her everywhere; every time she let her thoughts run, they ran home. Home.

Yes, she would ask him tonight.

Joy anxiously waited through dinner with Pansie, Clair and Mrs. Thimble, all of whom had long since stopped protesting the highly unconventional practice of dining with their mistress. She was like no other; they knew that the first day and got used to it every day since. Of course, they cared for her, more than she'd ever guess, and had long since agreed among themselves that to know her was to love her. Only one subject was avoided between them, that of his lordship and the obvious rupture between them. By unspoken agreement it was never mentioned, though on nights like tonight, when he was at Barrington Hall and their mistress dined in the company of her maids, it pressed heavily on everyone's mind.

Ram saw his son to bed, then retired to his study with his secretaries for a long night's work. Joy waited for the chance to speak to him; but she refused to disturb him and besides, she wanted to speak to him alone and uninterrupted, all of which meant she had to wait till he retired. She waited in her rooms, trying to amuse herself with a book. She read the first page a hundred times before giving up. The wait seemed endless; she began pacing the floor, nervously phrasing and rephrasing the simple request, as though she was petitioning the House of Commons for a change of law.

It was after midnight when she finally heard the clink of his silver spurs ruining the polished floor as he walked down the hall to his apartments. A door opened and shut. She raced to her dressing table, splashed water on her face and tossed down the towel. Taking a deep breath, she quietly left her room.

Ram began removing his clothes, thinking not of his day or his work but of the set of seven brawls he had had in these last two weeks. It was an old trick, one he tried the day he left, four times in between, and twice before returning. First, select the tavern, not a seedy place but the next step up, a place where working class stiffs congregated after a long day's hard labor. Walk in, order a cheery wine, ask politely that it be put in a champagne glass, then insult the tavern master when he starts laughing. The better dressed one was, the quicker the brawl. The brawls were not easily won, for the challenge came by balancing force and restraint—the rule being no one could be permanently hurt. Before returning to Barrington Hall, he had closed two such taverns and might have gone for a third if it had had any effect in dissipating the force of his emotions.

Nothing helped; that was it. He felt lost and out of control, a restless ill ease because of it. The last person he wanted to see that night, any night, was Joy Claret. Yet a soft knock sounded on his door.

"Ram . . . it's me. May I come in?"

He heard the trepidation in her voice, and he might have saved her by shouting to get the hell away from his bed chambers, of all places—especially after the two hours it took before the hard press of his groin eased from seeing her in the fountain—but that very trepidation cautioned him. He thought immediately of little Sean, and he moved quickly to the door.

He opened the door, took one look, and his hand tightened on the brass knob. She stood shrouded in the soft light of the hall lantern. The long hair was unbound and brushed smooth, the front ends held back by two thin silver barrettes. She wore only a night dress, no robe, nothing but a single layer of rose silk held on straight shoulders by two thin strings. Every inch of the slender curves was silhouetted in the flickering light . . .

The last thing on Joy's mind was her nightclothes. Long ago her maids had conspired against her by getting rid of her two plain cotton night dresses, leaving her with the two dozen or so silk nightgowns. Each night one was selected, laid out for her, and since she never saw anyone in the hours of night, she never thought about it and could honestly claim she had never viewed the night dress in the looking glass.

Ram's apartments, which included a sitting and dining room, a dressing room and his bed chambers, were the only set of rooms in Barrington Hall she had yet to venture in. Nervously, she briefly cast her gaze behind him to his bed chambers. One glance was enough to tell her it was like no other room in the house. It seemed large enough to hold a small ball, smaller by feet than the downstairs hall. The huge hearth alone, occupying the far corner, could comfortably house three people. The colors were dark: shadows hid the room, for only the light from two lanterns and the fire filled the enormous space. The furnishings were like nothing she had ever seen. They were heavy, polished dark wood and large, though sparsely populated throughout the room. Few things adorned the tops, for there was no space not taken by the piles of books and papers. At a glance, it seemed half of the library was in this room. The one painting she glimpsed was a seascape, a small ship battling an omnipotent raging storm.

Returning her gaze to him, she received the message there. With no explanation given, she felt the violence radiating in his tall muscled frame, somehow accented by the ugly bruise on his cheek, a scrape on his arm, and another, she saw, on his leg, all pronounced by the dark patch, the small scar disappearing into his thick dark curls.

He turned abruptly away and stalked to an open window, where he looked out into the black velvet night. Desire felt like a physical jolt through him, the effort to control it a battle between the will of his mind and the force in his body. Every muscle strained as he forced away images of a rainy night and the terror he had brought to the only woman it was his misfortune to love.

The message rang loud in their silence as she saw the evidence of the agony she brought him. The muscles defining the width of his bare back tensed dramatically, his strong hands clenched tight into fists on the window sill and he seemed to be fighting for control. As she watched, her own eyes filled with his inexplicable pain, and she acted without thought, stumbling forward into his room. "What is wrong? Why do I upset you so?"

He heard the questions but could not for his life answer, as still he refused to turn around. "How can you ask that?" he, too, spoke in questions. "Why would you come to me like this? Do you want me to force you? God girl, do you know how close I am—"

"Force . . . me?" Confused and distressed, her thoughts stumbled stupidly over the idea. "I know you don't want me . . . like . . . that."

Ram stiffened, more so as his mind encountered, greeted, met those words. So unbelievable, he desperately sought an explanation but there was none. She could not have meant that. "My God, Joy," he whispered as he finally turned around. "Tell me you know that's not true."

She stood perfectly still, frightened and nervous by this and confused, just confused. She slowly shook her head. Long minutes passed as she stood there stupidly beneath the heat of his gaze, her confusion growing with this unspoken question, the alarm that something was happening.

Ram knew only to tread carefully before jumping to wild conclusions. He walked to the door, shut it and leaned back against it, studying her small form. "Joy," he finally asked, "what do you imagine is the reason I've—" he searched for the words, finally selecting ones so mild they almost made him laugh—"ah, put distance between us?"

She watched her toes curl into the thick carpet, and with the next breath, she realized she was going to cry.

"No, dear God, don't cry." He fought desperately not to touch her. He would not touch her until he knew for a certainty. "Not until you tell me what you've been thinking these many long months."

"I can't talk of it."

It was a plea, he saw. "Joy, I need to know."

She turned from him, simply unable to face him with this, the matter of her heart.

"At first I didn't know," she began in a distant whisper. "A hundred times I'd tried to think of what I did wrong, why I . . . displease you so much . . . but I couldn't— I didn't know. I would remember when you cared for me, how you teased me and laughed with me, how we would talk as though there was never enough time to say everything, and I'd remember when you used to look at me . . ." Words could not describe how he once looked at her, and she paused in the futile effort. "Then when I carried Sean, you were so gentle and tender . . . when he was born, I thought because I was recovering—" The pain of the words made her pause, fighting to say the last. "Then I could only guess you resented me for a marriage you did not want."

He could not believe it, yet there it was. She didn't know; she had no idea. He was struck with the only possible explanation of her ignorance. Her unconditional love for his son, her complete confidence in his wellness, had made her assume he would want more children, that his life could be normal now, the curse removed with living proof. He wondered if she even questioned this? It was her naivete, the infallibility of her optimism and goodness . . .

Yet if she didn't know, then what? What if he deceived her?

How long would he gain her love? A month? Two? A year? Would it be worth the cost of such a deception?

He felt as if he had spent the last year fighting nothing but his desire for her, a near constant agony of wanting something so desperately, having her so near that the mere reach of his hand would bring her to his arms. When he thought of ending it, of having her love and passion and laughter, the answer was yes. Yes, if it were even only this night . . .

"Don't want you?" he questioned and she spun around, startled by how close he was. Her eyes shot up from the wide expanse of his chest to confront the intensity of his gaze. His strength and power, his warmth threatened to overwhelm her. If she but leaned forward she'd fall in his arms—

"Shall I show you how much I want you?" he asked with a calmness he didn't feel. Not waiting for a response, he took her small hand in his, locking his gaze to the luminous blue eyes. "Do you feel how my hand shakes, my love?"

The only trembling she felt was her own, whether from fear or something else, she knew not.

"Do you know why my hand shakes so?"

She slowly shook her head. His gaze lowered over her form, and with an instinctual urge to protect herself, she forgot to breathe. "It is with the effort not to do this—" His free hand reached to her gown, and with a single tug, the thin straps broke. The gown slid to an unnoticed pile at her feet.

She never knew how long she stood there with her arms folded across herself and her eyes closed, victim to his gaze. The tension built until she felt herself sway with it. Two strong hands caught her, and she opened her eyes to see his nakedness, magnificently bold in its readiness. He brought her arms behind her back, while pulling her gently against the full measure of his desire. She gasped with the feel of it.

His huge body tensed dramatically until he released the sharp intake of breath. With his arms crossed over the small of her back, cupping her buttocks, he lifted her up and over him. Where their flesh touched, fire leaped viciously in force. "This is how much I want you," he said huskily. "I have never wanted anything more."

A question struggled desperately above the onslaught of wild sensations. She could not think to even know her feet had touched ground, for her back was arched and his hands combed through her hair. Two silver barretts tumbled to the carpet. Her head was held back as his mouth blazed a scorching trail from her soft lips, along her neck, over the hollow of her throat and lower still, seeking the thrusts of her breasts, too long resisted. Then she was swooning, nothing but small pants beneath a pleasure too great to describe, as his tongue flicked over and around the straining peaks, swirling and sucking, feasting on the creamy white softness like a starving man.

As a mindless tingling pleasure stole every last sane thought in her mind, her arms were freed to circle his waist, then climb up and down the hard muscles of his back, desperately searching for a lifeline as her knees collapsed. Yet he was holding her as his mouth found hers again, and he was kissing her with all the strength and tenderness of his being.

He broke the kiss only to lift her the short distance to the bed. Though her body was finally lit with the fuel of his desire, confusion, fear and uncertainty crowded into the brief space of the interruption, and she closed her eyes with the anguish of it.

As he lay her gently on the soft folds of a satin comforter, Ram came partially over her. Her dark hair, darker in the night, spilled over the pillows. The firelight danced over the beauty spread before him, and no, he had never wanted anything as much. Yet he saw the cost, a cost he'd not pay. "Look at me, my love."

She opened her eyes, and he saw the fear sparkling with the question.

"Oh no, my love. I had you once with a virgin's fear, once

by force, once as you fought to save our child's life. I'll not have you with fear again."

"Then why? Why would you love me now? After—"

Something dark and awful came into his gaze, leaving before she could name it as deception. "The reason no longer exists; we shall not consult it." That was all he said, all he had to say for his hands brushed through the smooth gloss of her hair, and his lips gently kissed the spot on her neck where her pulse fluttered wildly, then hovered over her mouth as he said the words spun from her dreams: "Know only this! I love you. I have always loved you, and I will always love you."

Tears blinded her. The rage of emotions added to the tumult of desire coursing through her. She could not think, certainly not as he kissed her again, so tenderly at first, his hand playing over her form, brushing her skin with fire. The hot constriction in her chest melted by degrees, but the kiss became wild and hungry, flaring as the enormity of his desire flooded into her. His kiss was devouring her; she was drowning, drowning until she felt the shudder pass through his huge body and he broke the kiss. "Joy, Joy" came his husky whisper. "I want you so much. I'm afraid—"

This was never finished in words, for his hands and mouth moved over her in a crescendo of need that spoke louder than words. His tongue and mouth found her breasts again. She tensed, feeling flushed and feverish as he drew softly and slowly, then urgently. The hot swirling patterns made her breathless, dizzy, helplessly wanton with an agony of yearning. At last he answered her with the searching probe of his hand, a hand seeking, finding the sweet dampness of her desire. The combined assault of his hands and mouth laced her small body with a silken sheen of heat, bringing tiny pulsating ripples of pleasure, a sweet prelude of what was to come.

All she knew was the pleasure spilling into her body, a need for his lips on her mouth. Soft cries escaped her. Her hands grazed the muscle encased back and arms, a touch part clinging, part urging. He felt it, as aware of her untutored touch as he was of the creamy soft breasts swelling with passion beneath the play of his mouth. He thought he would die.

Those small hands circled the thick curls of his head, and she writhed and twisted, finally managing to find his lips, hardly aware of anything but the need for his lips. Softly, shakily, she was kissing him. He was shocked with this play, shocked more as those untutored hands gradually grew bold, learning quickly. He knew he would die.

The kiss ended as he took her hands and shifted to hold her down. She felt his mouth move lower still, across her belly and lower. She tried to twist away, writhing wildly, but he held her still for the lash of his tongue. Hot chills raced over her, washing her in thick pleasure, yet creating a yearning so intense, it pierced her soul; all she wanted was him, all of him. Her body quivered with the need, and his name was called over and over again.

At last he answered the luminous pleasure of her small writhing form with a fierce thrust that drove her arms around his broad shoulders, jolting his entire body with a lightning bolt of pleasure, and he stopped instantly. "Sweet mercy, I have died."

She opened her eyes to see his gaze filled with dark passion, twinged with amusement and joy. He held still for a long moment, and she felt the heat of him melting her insides, then his light kisses on her face. His very next movement seemed to reach her very heart. He was everywhere—inside and outside of her—and that was all she knew.

He simply could not have believed this passion meeting his; each muscle in her small body did its part to make her a supple, agile animal, sending pleasure trembling through him. He was shocked by it, by the passion matching his, and overcoming her was a pleasure he had never known to imagine. With his full length and thickness, he thrust rapidly and forcefully, not sparing her, avidly listening to her cries. Watching as she writhed and winced, finally clinging to him as he brought her to the height of exquisite pleasure, he joined her there in a final culmination of their love.

She lay breathless and still, dazed and humbled, hardly able to feel her love-soaked body as he turned on his back and gathered her in his arms. Consciousness was no place near her; she couldn't even think enough to reach for it. Had she looked at him, she would have found him staring at her with bright unmasked love and plain unmistakable awe.

His warmth consumed her, the hardness of his body felt like a secure fortress surrounding her, and though their bodies touched at all points, she still could not get close enough. His hands ran, lovingly through the tousled mess of her hair, smoothing it, drawing it from her face and back so that he could freely caress her back and tenderly kiss her face.

Words were poor tools this night and none were used as they lay in the warmth of their love. Time passed unnoticed, and just as sleep might have claimed her tenuous grasp of consciousness completely, he moved.

Surprise lifted on her face as he brought her body completely over his length, startling her with the feel of his readied desire. Hands braced on his chest, she lifted partially up, then felt his sharp intake of breath, an answer to the question in her eyes.

"My God, do you have any idea of how beautiful you are?" The renewed desire in his gaze gave her an idea. "All I know is my desire, my love, that I would have you again and again; for as long as I have you, my love will know no limits."

The very choice of words might have warned her, but he pulled her head down for a kiss as he slipped back into her and desire was reborn in the instant. Love sparked anew, quickly filling her, and with a warm chuckle at her gasp of surprise, he taught her the advantages of the position . . .

Daylight stretched long lazy fingers into the room when he finally released his claim on her. Cradled in the warmth of his arms, she felt her heartbeat spiral down, an utter complete exhaustion. From somewhere down the hall she heard little Sean happily informing the world he was awake. For the first time in his life, she would not be there to greet him, but no matter, Mrs. Thimble was the next best thing. She thought she heard herself asking Ram for something, something terribly important, but she never knew for sure, for the light of day was quite suddenly extinguished.

After a hard day of riding, exhausted and tired, yet excited, Seanessy burst through the great front doors of Barrington Hall like an enormous gust of wind. Mr. Cutler rushed to greet him, seeing the wind had muddied feet and certainly no appointment card, much less a dignified wait for the proper announcement. Three of Sean's men followed him in with a noisy clamor of spurs, indecently raw comments and enough mud, Mr. Cutler saw with dismay, to create a swamp.

"Where's our lordship?" Sean demanded, removing his gloves.

Mr. Cutler absolutely refused to contemplate how Barrington Hall's doors looked suddenly small, consumed by his lordship's acquaintances—for he saw these characters as such—and taking first things first, he rather unhurriedly brought the glove box to Sean and opened the lid, presenting the jeweled case. Sean never noticed as he tucked his gloves carelessly into his belt.

The lid shut with a loud slam. "I'm afraid his lordship is unavailable presently."

"Oh? Where's he off to?"

"Lord and Lady Barrington departed recently for Ireland."

"What?" came not as a question but as a demand.

Mr. Cutler watched the unmasked confusion lift on the handsome pirate's face, and after repeating the assertion, he excused himself, smiling at finally gaining the last hand. Abandoned and confused, Sean stood dumfounded in the entrance hall.

He had left on a run to Gibraltar, through the Mediterranean to Egypt, where he negotiated a shipping contract with the reigning Sheik Adol Kabar, one that would potentially land Ram and him a tidy fortune. He had met with considerable success; prices were negotiated and settled upon but with one condition to be met before the contract was theirs. They must rid his highness of some troublesome sea scoundrels operating out of an isolated area of the coast there. This was hardly a problem; he had assured his highness it would be their pleasure to do so, and indeed it would; but as neither his or Ram's ships were rigged for battle, he needed to secure the *Catrina* and *Atlantic Ann* for a couple of months and get the docked ships readied and manned. There was much to discuss with Ram, not the least of which was the hope that Ram would see the task as an interesting divergence and want to come along.

Sean caught sight of Pansie, motioning to him from around the corner. She seemed all smiles, and Sean, recognizing a woman who was anxious to tell all, came quickly to her side to hear what he simply could not believe.

"They came to terms," Pansie said in a rush of whispers. "Oh! 'Twas all so unexpected! Took us by surprise it did, but one day my lady wasn't in 'er rooms anymore. Milord locked 'er in 'is rooms, 'e did, and for a week afterward she never came out, not once. Meals and little Sean were sent in but she never left. And oh, we 'eard nothn' but the 'appy sound of 'er laughter all week long.

"Well, after a week of this, they finally came out, so to speak, with a 'andful of instructions, mostly to Mr. Wilson. Cancel this and cancel that. Then 'is lordship says, 'We're off to Ireland!' They left that day, they did, and this is it—they took only common traveling clothes, their 'orses and the little master, that's all! No maids or footmen, or even Mrs. Thimble, trunks or a carriage. Imagine that! They planned to book passage on a passenger ship for the crossing, just like commoners! And 'is lordship says, 'We're going to camp under the stars,' then 'e kissed 'er in front of everyone. Oh, to see 'er now—my lady was lovely before, but 'twas like she suddenly blossomed, she was so beautiful!"

Seanessy got the point. Turning from Pansie, he made his way into Ram's study and found Mr. Wilson, who confirmed everything. Sean fell into a chair, nodding distantly as Mr. Wilson excused himself and left. He found himself staring blankly out the window onto the gardens.

My God Ram, what are you doing to her?

Joy would not drink the tea, Sean knew just as well as Ram. She probably wouldn't have even before little Sean was born but certainly not after! It was as Ram oft said—Joy would see the act as synonymous with the unconscionable; drinking the tea would be one and the same as taking little Sean's very life. Of all the women he knew, Joy would not be able to drink that tea.

It was conceivable that, in a moment of passion, Joy had thought she could drink the tea. Conceivable but unlikely, and even Ram had thought of it. "I could see her saying yes, even believing she could for me," Ram said once as they talked of it, "until she actually got with child. Once she felt the life within her, it would all change. I know it would, and I'd be put in the same position as that night I'll never live long enough to forget."

If Ram knew this, then what the hell was he doing? How long before she had to drink that tea? Knowing well the magnitude of Ram's desire for her, not long, not long at all. What chance would Joy have of saving her second child's life? None, Sean knew for a certainty, though what concerned him was that a second battle of will with Lord Ramsey Edward Barrington the Third would destroy her like nothing else.

God's curse Ram, what are you doing to her? What have you done to her?

Sean suddenly stood up, and cursing Ram, he slammed his clenched fist into the three-hundred-year-old wall.


Each and every time he loved her it was with the intensity of their first and last time; it was a love that indeed knew no limits, as Ram had said as they first started out on their odyssey: "We are looking for our limits, the limit to our love. We will search under star-filled skies and no doubt some cloudy ones, buried in nothing but a bedroll with our son. We shall wander over the countryside, looking in glens and meadows, forests and villages. We shall look upon the Irish sea and then upon the Irish land."

"And my lord." She laughed. "Do you anticipate finding this limit?"

"My dear girl! If there is any one thing I've learned in my years as an adventurer, it's that the treasure hardly matters; the joy is in the search!"

Ram proved it right there and then, for as little Sean was lulled by the rocking of the traveling sack in which Ram carried him and his eyes were closed before they had even got off Barrington land, Ram had made love to her on the forest floor beneath a blue springtime sky.

They had found no limits the first month and a half it took to cross England, and the happy fact was celebrated with laughter, nothing but laughter and love. They had camped beneath the stars and traveled over the countryside, stopping at inns only for supplies, an occasional meal and to trade the cold spring water baths for a hot one. They finally reached the coast, where they sailed the short distance to Ireland aboard the passenger ship, the *Holland*. They continued their odyssey from Dublin, taking two weeks to finally reach Galoway, then headed north to Kilkorian Castle, where

Ram had been raised, collecting nothing but memories, memories Joy felt certain would last a lifetime.

Joy learned a good deal more about Ram. Though English and non-Catholic, he had a deep affinity for Ireland and her Catholic people, always sympathetic to the oppressed of any land. As they traveled across the gray mist shrouded land, she felt suspended in time, and in a manner she was, for Ram talked at length about the troubled history of the land he knew so well. The history of Ireland was one of his great interests, second only to the history of the Greeks and of course, England. He talked of it all—starting with the Celts, eventually leading to the centuries of strife and bloodshed between England and Ireland, Protestants and Catholics, two opposing forces destined to meet upon this ancient island. He knew everything, not just dates and facts but causes and effects, the historical players and their motivations as well. While in between history lessons, Ram shared the folk tales and songs, songs that made her laugh and cry in turns.

Though the history was troubled and the people poor, it seemed a magical, mysterious land. Mary Seanessy had taught Ram the language, and he spoke it well; a Gallic tongue opened the people's arms to them everywhere they went.

Her fulfillment went beyond happiness, and if not for the unanswered question between them, she would have known only this dreamlike satiation of her love. Many times she pressed him to tell her why he had waited to give his love, but each time he resisted answering, stopping her finally with: "We will not talk of my mistake now. Not now my love. Someday but not now." There were a few times she experienced the rationality necessary to be frightened by the truth hidden from her, and her desperation created many different explanations for the pain that was now so distant; but all of these were eventually abandoned, leaving the question: What did it matter now?

Now, she had his love and it consumed her every moment. His love was all she knew, all he allowed her to know. Passionate and intense, Ram's love was almost savagely physical, and though his love was pure, his intent was malicious. He purposely consumed her in her entirety, leaving no part of her heart, mind or body untouched, leaving no place where the shadow of doubt might grow.

Soon after Galoway, the day came when they rode along the jagged cliffs of the coast, turning onto a road that led through rocky hills to Kilkorian Castle. Against the gray overcast sky, the landscape was desolate, nothing but sparse grass and rocks, a smattering of wind-blown pines. They rounded a bend and stopped, for the castle rose in the distance. It was a small castle, if any castle were truly small, and made of cold gray stone set against the rocky hillside. The castle had been barred and closed, left to ruin the day Ram's father had died, and it looked hauntingly forlorn, isolated and shut up as it was. Even their boisterous son fell silent as they stared at the place.

A strange sadness rose from the sheer desolation of the land, and Joy thought of Barrington Hall, lovely and grand, so close to the frantic pulse and life of London. She thought then of: "Your poor mother, Ram."

"Aye, my poor mother. She growing up amidst the beauty of the lake district. I don't know how she bore this . . . I don't know why my father had her removed here."

"How did you bear it?" she asked in a whisper as she still stared.

"I was hardly ever there. Mary found me and took me away before I remember, and by the time I was five, I lived day in and out with her and Sean in their small cottage. Even the tutors my father sent came to the cottage. The only time I was ever really at the castle were the few times my father returned from abroad and then only briefly."

Their silence was filled with the solemnity of their surroundings. "Let's go see the village," she finally said. "Do you think the cottage will still be there?"

"Oh, I know it is. Sean and I know the tenants; we pay them an outrageous amount to keep fresh flowers on Mary's grave."

"Then, we shall have to make certain those flowers are there, and when I am at that dear woman's grave, I shall give her my thanks and gratitude for raising two such fine men." She brightened with a smile. "Knowing the two of you, it could not have been easy for her."

Ram smiled, and as Joy shared his saddle in front of him, he brushed back her hair, tilted her head and kissed her mouth. Trapped on his father's back, Sean thought this a wonderful idea and wanted his turn, too. He interrupted the kiss with a loud voice; Ram felt a furious pounding on his back, and the kiss broke with laughter. Such was the way they left the dark past of Kilkorian Castle.

They were treated like royalty upon entering the village, and they spent their day there with Ram sharing memory after memory of his boyhood with Sean and these were happy memories indeed. With the surprising well of tenants in the old two room cottage, they dined on a peasant feast of cabbage and ham hocks and spent the night there in a room shared with five children. Joy thought it would be the first night they didn't make love. She was wrong, and finding the control necessary to hold perfectly still in the darkness, not making a sound as he so expertly played her senses, was a maddening torture. Her last words were a promise to pay him in kind.

The next day they set out for Mary's grave, about two miles from the village. A little used, weed-grown road led through the forest pines and oaks, eventually leading to a small clearing. A wood fence surrounded the graves, many of then unmarked—the common pauper's grave. She spotted Mary Seanessy's grave at once, for it was the only well-tended and flower-marked place in the yard, the only resting place marked with a small white marble tombstone.

It was mid-morning and quiet, so quiet. The sun broke through gray clouds, falling in grayer streams to earth. They tied their mounts on the fence. Little Sean was napping, and after Joy carefully spread the bed roll away from the horses, Ram gently laid him down before they walked through the gate and stopped at the tombstone.

Mary Seanessy
May she rest in peace

Ram's sadness and regret were plain when he said, "I wasn't here when she died you know. Sean swore it was an easy death, her influenza, but I'll never know for sure. He would have told me that no matter what."

"I know you loved her as a mother," Joy whispered quietly.

"Aye, and she was." He smiled. "Sean was her son by birth, but I might have been, too. I knew only her kindness and love, the occasional and futile attempt to discipline us."

"Where's Sean's father?" she asked after a thoughtful pause. "Why isn't he here, too?"

"Sean's father? Why isn't he here? Well, nobody knows who the blackguard is, that's why."

"What? Sean told me—"

"That his father was an infamous sea captain?" Ram questioned with a lift of brow.

"Yes, that he died before Sean was born in a horrible ship wreck off the Dover coast."

Ram shook his head with a sad smile. "Nobody knows who Sean's father is or was. Sean's a bastard, as was Mary and her mother before her. The story of the sea captain is the product of Sean's imagination, a fanciful one at that."

"Well, that devil!" Joy felt properly duped.

Ram knelt on a bent knee, idly pulling weeds from the field. "Don't blame him, my love. It would be hard on any man not to know who his father was, where he came from or

404

what he was like."

"Didn't Mary ever say who he was?" she questioned.

"No, though God knows we tried, I don't know how many times, to pry it out of her, for we knew someone had been supporting her all those years. She died over fifteen years ago now, the year before my father. All she would ever tell us was that the affair happened when she was young and that there is no creature on earth more foolish than a girl of fifteen. She always added that God blessed her mistake by giving her Sean, and then said to me, 'in a round about way you, too, Ram.'"

He stared at the grave, remembering how badly Sean wanted to know, the stories he always made up to answer the question of the identity of his father.

"There was a rumor," Ram said in a distant voice, "that Mary Seanessy had a young girl's crush on the village priest, a Father Patrick Shaw, but—" he paused, then shrugged— "Mary was never particularly religious and true. While a few priests inevitably fall from their vows of celibacy, it's hard to imagine Sean coming from anyone so noble."

This story immediately earned Joy's keen romantic fancy. "Do you know this priest? Did he look like Sean?"

Fear came to his expression suddenly, mixed evenly with inexplicable pain. "No," he said softly. "The priest died the year Sean and I were born." She first thought he wasn't going to say more, but with the pain and fear plain in his voice, he said, "He was murdered, stabbed to death, the murderer never named, never known. The villagers thought he fought with the devil that night, and in their peasant wisdom, they burned the church to the ground as sacrament. They say my own mother was known to see this priest, and sometimes I've thought, with my father so close—"

"No," she knelt beside him and took his face in her hands. "No, don't torment yourself. Leave the past behind, Ram; it has no part of us now."

Ram stared at the unmasked love in her eyes and wished,

would give anything, for it to be true. The past would always shadow his life, as the past would soon come between them. The thought brought his lips to her with a kiss brutal in its intensity, as he laid her to the bare ground of the graveyard. "Love me Joy," he whispered. "Love me now as though it is the last time we ever shall."

She felt his pain and fear; it became her own beneath a gray sky in an isolated graveyard, knowing nothing but the desperation of her love for him and his for her as though it was the last time they ever would.

The carriage rolled steadily forward, at last luring little Sean asleep in the bassinet on the floor. Joy sat comfortably on the seat, thinking she knew insanity when she felt it. For the first time in three months, she and Ram had separated. Ram had to go to port for two days, and not having accommodations there for her and little Sean, she had been forced to quit London for Barrington Hall alone. He had trouble getting work done with her near, which was a good deal better off than she, for she had trouble holding a coherent thought in her head when he was near.

After her long absence, she spent yesterday morning at Chester House, where she saw the success of her programs. The last illness to sweep through Chester House cost no lives. The children also seemed happier, more alert, less apathetic. Later, she had afternoon tea with none other than the duchess, that shrewd, irascible old lady who, despite Joy's determined efforts otherwise, was going to cut through Joy's defenses and be her friend. Twice during the day, Joy had a queer impression of viewing herself as others saw her, and she saw a smiling, blushing, giggling young lady, bubbling over with joy and happiness, a happiness that certainly flowed over onto the children at Chester House, a happiness the duchess had questioned repeatedly.

Yet how did one explain the happiness she felt? How did

one explain what his love meant to her? She was not a poet and had not a poet's words, and even if she possessed a poet's expression, she could not describe what passed between them. Words were poor vessels indeed.

Despite Bart's objections, the dark road proved not to hinder their progress, and comfortably seated in the plush, maroon velvet seats, the dim light surrounding her became the backdrop of memories of their time together abroad. She owned a thousand memories now, each a precious treasure that she would guard until the day she died. The memories filled her, forming a swift moving stream of consciousness, and she was lost.

The innocent pictures of Ram, playing with his son, their singing and laughter, their long talks into the night and longer rides, the things they saw and people they met soon gave way to a different kind of memory, erotic memories, memories of his kisses and touch, the ways he loved her and the ways she loved him. How he had loved her! Desire, starting from somewhere deep inside, rose in a blush, a tingling and—

Bart's curse, a crack of the whip jolted her from the very next unchaste thought and threw her from the seat as the carriage lurched forward with sudden speed. She fell to her knees, braced against the opposite seat. The footman, Rolph, shouted against the wind. Bart replied with another curse. Little Sean miraculously continued to sleep undisturbed; and after that quick assessment, Joy grabbed the side rail, bracing againt the jostle, she lifted the shutters too. "Bart!" she called against the wind. "What's happened?"

"Robbers! Comin' from behind! I tol' ye—"

Robbers! Again! Was the rest of the world nothing but thieves? "Faster! Faster!" She panicked.

It was her fault, the whole thing, for she had made Bart pass the inn to press through the night, despite his many reasonable objections. One footman had been ill, leaving her the protection of only two men. Carriage rides through the night were particularly dangerous in these times. Ram and herself had met with robbers twice on their trip abroad, and though he made each encounter a game, one of poor odds for the would-be molesters, Ram was not here now!

She never thought of herself, only little Sean. A pistol quickly emerged from her reticule. She pushed the bassinet against the side, and crouching in front of it, she aimed the pistol at the door. There would be no warning shots this time.

The carriage raced forward at a dizzying speed, yet the hoof beats grew closer and closer! Suddenly Bart cursed viciously, and tension froze her fingers on the trigger as Joy stopped breathing. The carriage abruptly slowed, then dipped slightly with added weight. She heard something— Rolph, the footman! Her mind screamed for someone to shoot—Rolph or Bart, someone—at the exact moment the latch was undone and the door opened with a cold burst of wind and—

"Ram!"

Relief flooded through her in force, relief that her finger had been numbed with tension, for she had come within a hairbreadth of shooting him. "Oh, Ram—"

Ram encountered her position, the narrowed, determined eyes of a murderess, the steady aim of the pistol, and he laughed, contrasting the sight of her now with a similar situation he remembered so well. He swung easily to the soft velvet cushion and shut the door. "Joy, love, is that any way to treat your loving husband?"

His hand came over the pistol, and he gently pried her fingers from the trigger, then placed the pistol in the small traveling compartment beneath the seats. Once safe, he turned his attention back to her.

The small lantern was behind him, and shadows fell over his face, yet she saw that his gaze sparkled with his mischief. "I almost shot you!" she informed him rather breathlessly.

This was not on his mind. "My God"—he reached for her,

bringing her to sit on his lap—"how can you be more beautiful each and every time I see you?"

She ignored the hands as they sought the pins holding her hair up. "Ram," she repeated in a frightened cry, "I almost shot you!"

"So I saw." He chuckled, as her hair swung free, falling in a silken mass of tangles down her back. His hands wove into the tangles, smoothing the rich tresses down her back. "How could you mistake me, your loving husband, for a molester? As though—" his warm lips grazed her forehead, then traveled to a sensitive spot behind her ear—"I might be pernicious enough to demand a reward for my trouble."

Small chills raced up her spine. "Trouble?" she questioned stupidly.

"Indeed, I worked long and hard through the night to finish my work, then raced Lance like a bullet to catch up with the carriage."

"Oh, I see," she said, though all she saw was his skilled fingers on the gold buttons of her neat blue riding jacket. "Just what reward do you seek?"

"Why, what any would-be molester seeks." He chuckled as her jacket came off.

"Ah." She giggled with a different kind of nervousness. "Yet I am determined to resist any and all molesters."

"Oh? Well, by all means, resist me if you can." He drew her head to him for a kiss. Unlike his easy banter, his kiss, fueled by a fierce longing, hungrily devoured her. He found no resistance in the incredibly soft lips yielding to his, lips indeed sweeter than wine and infinitely more potent.

Heat seemed to suddenly fill the small compartment. She flushed as he broke the kiss. The next light caress of his lips, a tease along her ear down to the curve of her neck, sent delicious little shivers through her. "Of course," he said, distractedly, "if I was truly bent on molestation, I'd have to finish with these clothes."

Her arms were around him, toying maddeningly with the

curls at the nape of his neck. "An ambitious task," she observed, seemingly content to passively witness his efforts at the buttons of her blouse.

"Ah, but I am an ambitious man." He chuckled as he slipped the buttons of her shirt free, revealing the beauty of her breasts. Work-calloused hands cupped the creamy white fullness, thumbs brushed the tips. She drew a sharp intake of breath as his hands worked with exquisite gentleness there, his pleasure rewarded by small gasps from moist and parted lips that sought, then found his.

The kiss deepened as he explored her lips and tongue, the delicious heights and hollows of her mouth. His hands opened her blouse further, caressing the mercifully small indentation of her waist, before slipping the buttons of her skirt free. A deft hand explored the beckoning contours of her abdomen and hips, dancing with a feather touch over her thighs, until she broke the kiss, and he heard her soft moan of anticipation.

The movement provided the delicious bud of a breast, which he provoked and teased as his hand slowly stroked the other. She felt an explosion of shivers. That ever tightening pleasure grew, blossoming deep inside her and her hands sought the refuge of his body. The buttons of his shirt were torn apart, and then they were kissing again, reveling in the places where their disheveled clothes allowed the heat of their skin to touch. His mouth molded to hers, his tongue played tantalizingly with hers as he fanned the sweet flames within.

With a low groan, he broke away to twist free of his breeches, then turned her to him again, lifting her over his flank to fit her to him with a long and hard kiss. She clung desperately, washed in the hot sensations of the pleasure. The jostle of the carriage heightened her ecstasy, and she was mindless, crying, soaring toward the bliss of the oh-so-physical aspect of love, until—

Suddenly the carriage hit a hole and bounced, driving her

harder onto his unyielding manhood, and in all eternity, she could not be any closer to him. She heard his warm chuckle; yet he held her to him, and with gathering motion, they took in a wild ride, soaring toward a shared and wondrous bliss . . .

Joy woke maybe an hour later to find herself cradled in his arms much as she might hold little Sean. She was warm, his silk-lined cloak covering them as a blanket, while his body shielded and braced her from the movement of the carriage. A troubled gaze had been and still was upon him. "What's wrong?" she asked in a soft whisper, as a small hand reached to his face to erase the inexplicable pain there. "What troubles you so?"

What troubled him? He was living on the razor's edge again; it seemed his destiny. In order to savor her love today, he had to deny the future, which he somehow managed to do much of the time. Yet there were times like tonight, after loving her like that, holding her close as she slept, that the future not only came to him, but it rushed at him. Like some dark and terrible monster, it was a horror, which he, with all his strength and will, was helpless to stop.

He was afraid, afraid as he never had been before. "I love you," he said simply. "I love you so much that—" He kissed her softly, sensuously, but then withdrew with the knowledge. He had known the first night he felt her love again that to love her once was to want her more. His love for her was like some wondrous winged creature ever seeking higher and higher skies. "Will you always know that, my love? That no matter what happens, I love you."

His words were a warm caress, but one shielded in pain or fear or both, she didn't know. It was, she knew, the unspoken question that still came between them. No matter how she tried to ask it, he resisted answering, keeping the answer hidden beneath their love.

She had always thought happiness was but fleeting moments life served up, moments one grasped but could only hold in memories. Could it be that he, too, was afraid of their happiness? For it was different; their happiness was made from a continuous and consuming expression of love, moments knit so tightly together there was nothing in between but joy and happiness. Was he too afraid of waking from this dream? Was his pain about that? Or was it something else?

"I love you too," she finally said. "And I will always know you love me as I will always love you."

She pressed closer as his arms tightened around her, and he kissed her again as though it was the first and last kiss between them.

## Chapter Thirteen

Little Sean did not want to sit in his chair, not when the tablecloth made the table into a tent. The trouble was he was hungry and the food lay on top of the table.

His mother seemed unusually happy this morning, but this, he knew, could be misleading. As soon as her back was turned though, he grabbed a handful of eggs, giggled with his mischief and shimmied down from the chair, scrambling quickly under the table. Rake whimpered and poked his head under the table. Knowing sharing was a very good thing, Sean offered to Rake a generous handful of eggs.

Joy turned back around to see the abandoned chair. She smiled, knowing this game. "Where's Seanessy? Where's Seanessy?" She ignored the excited giggle that was his reply. "Is he in the drawer?" She opened a drawer of the enormous chest, receiving more giggles in turn. "Is he behind the drapes?" She lifted the heavy drapes. "Oh, I know where he is!" Sean's suspense was unbearable, certainly uncontrollable, and he fell over with laughter when his mother's face popped through the tablecloth with a loud "Boo!"

Joy laughed with pleasure, and after ordering Rake out of the room, knowing tents were the best place to share secrets, she brought the small plate of eggs and the cup of unusual, though ever so delicious, tea beneath the table. Obviously thrilled, Sean began to devour the buttery eggs.

When she finished her tea, she leaned forward conspiratorially. "Tents are the best place for secrets. Would you like to hear my secret?"

Sean nodded enthusiastically, not sure what she said but certain by her excitement it would be fun.

"I'm going to have a baby!"

"Baby!" He giggled. "Me!" He pointed.

She laughed but then shook her head. "You're not a baby. You're a little boy. And not so little at that," she said, lifting him into her arms. "I can't wait." She nuzzled his neck. "Let's go down and tell Mr. Cutler to send a note to your father in London. We can't wait any longer."

"Fa!" He nodded, and with laughter she emerged from under the table. Setting him to his feet, she took his hand and headed out of the nursery, down the hall to the great staircase. Even in the most subdued circumstances, the banister was rarely resisted, but filled with such happiness and excitement, and with no one about, she lifted him securely to her arms and assumed the improper position. Sean's cry of glee stopped half way as his mother's arms abruptly tightened. Joy gasped and stumbled onto the staircase, gripped with a sudden unnatural pain. Miraculously, she managed to set Sean to his feet just as she doubled over with it and felt the first warm, awful rush between her legs.

The strong bronze hand held the brass knob to her bed chambers steady for a long minute before turning it, opening the door to the future he had feared for so long. The peach colored drapes were drawn tight against a rare morning sun, bathing the bed chambers in a warm golden light. The room was empty, save for the small figure laying in the four poster bed, buried beneath a quilt. She had already turned away from him.

She knew by now, knew everything. She knew he had ordered the tea to be given to her, the tea that washed her womb of his seed. Only one question remained between them, and that was why?

Without seeing, Joy knew it was Ram. His footsteps sounded soft on the thick rug, stopping at the bedside. The silence stretched, broken only by the soft labor of her breathing. Sometimes, if she remained very still, she didn't feel anything. Time lost meaning then, granting her a merciful suspension from its passing, until she awoke to the taste of her tears. Such quiet tears, she thought, such a quiet sadness, yet one unfathomable in its depths.

Ram's hand finally reached to touch her. "Joy—"

"No . . . don't touch me. Please." The whisper was like a surface wind rippling over the ocean depths; yet it stopped him cold.

"Why Ram? I just don't understand, why? When the surgeon told me it was the tea, and when Bertha said you told her to give it to me . . . I just can't understand, why? After Sean?"

He sat down on the bed. For a long moment he just stared, resisting the need to touch and hold her, to comfort her as he searched for words that could explain. All he could think of was a question in return.

"Joy, how does anything change with Sean?"

She sat up and turned to him, incredulity on her face. "Sean's normal. He's as everyone else!"

"Aye, my love," he said in a passionate whisper. "Sean is a bright, healthy and happy lad, everything a man could want in a son, but still, the risk! The risk of another!

"That first night you came to my rooms and I saw you didn't understand why I kept you from my bed, I was shocked. Shocked that your love for Sean is so complete and unconditional, you assumed he removed my every fear and doubt of my paternity. You assume he, our boy, plays on my heart as he does on yours. It is different for me, Joy, so

415

different. It is because of little Sean, because I know little Sean, I know a love so fierce that it can make me cry . . ." He stopped in the emotion of his words. "Don't you see"—he took her by the arms—"I would love any child you gave me as much. It's because of Sean that I could never have another!"

"But you did have another!" Tears formed two lines down her pale cheeks, making her eyes large and luminous. "You did! You gave him to me . . . you gave—" Her voice choked with the tears, yet she struggled to explain. "Ram, Ram, it was like taking Sean from me—"

"No! It was not the same!"

"Maybe not to you but to me it was. I felt him, I felt him! I was . . . so . . . happy, I—" She collapsed against him then, and instantly, his arms came around her, holding her so tightly he felt certain he hurt her.

"I'm sorry Joy . . . I'm so sorry . . ."

She pulled away to tell him, "How much better if you had left me believing you didn't want me, that you hated and resented me! But now, after giving me your love, planning the whole time to hurt me, to do this—"

"No!" he said adamantly, refusing to think of it like that.

"You did! You took the most beautiful part of my life and made it vile and ugly! You sent me to heaven, knowing it would become a hell! You used me like a man uses a—"

"No!" He stopped her with force, a hand came over her mouth, but she pulled away, falling back into the pillows with tears.

"I'm leaving." She realized as she said it. "I'm going home."

"Joy—"

"You can't say no," she whispered the simple truth. "Not now."

Ram tried desperately to deny it as he stared, seeing only the long river of hair spread over the pillows, wanting desperately to turn her back and confront the emotion in those eyes now hidden from him. It was too late, far too late. Had he imagined a different ending? Had he been hoping beyond reason she'd find forgiveness in her love, that she'd understand his sins were committed only because he loved and wanted her desperately, beyond all reason?

God's curse, she was the living truth for him. Life had blessed him with every conceivable gift: health, wits, strength and power, a title and a fortune thrown in like icing on a cake. He had everything but the only thing that mattered, the only thing that gave meaning to all other aspects of his life—her love.

Her heart was closed; he had lost her love—

No, he realized as he rose, and with hand on the door, he cast one last look back. He never really had her love; it had been only an illusion, a blessed dream, nothing but a fleeting taste to remind him the rest of his days ahead of what he didn't have—the one and only thing that mattered.

The days warmed by degrees as Sean's great three-masted ship sailed ever closer to America. The time of daylight cushioned between sunrise and sunset, grew mercifully shorter with each day's passing, and for this small favor Joy felt grateful. She stood at the rail of the ship as was her habit at twilight and stared vacantly at the blue water. The wind whipped her unbound hair across her face, but she made no move to tame it, all acts superficial. In the distance she heard her boy's laughter as Sean's men tossed him in a torn canvas. Yet the happy sound seemed distant, pushed to the farthest recess of her mind. The music of laughter could sound no tune on her sadness.

Some found solace and peace with the confrontation of the infinity that was the sea, but she, staring at the endless blue horizon, saw only loneliness. It was a profound and haunting loneliness, one that sealed her heart the day her bedroom door shut, the day he had left her life.

She no longer wrote. The desire to express what she felt and saw died when she felt neither happiness nor hope, when she saw only the dark future she had feared for so long. Nothing changed, not with the monotonous passing of minutes to hours gathering in a collected emptiness of meaningless days.

There was one exception. One thing changed. She forgave him, forgave him everything. Love made it so easy to forgive. Yet the act itself meant nothing, for it changed nothing.

She stared until the empty blue depths changed and became a backdrop for the vision of him. She saw her pain reflected in his gaze; she felt him reach to her, a touch that would give purpose to her next breath. Yet he was so far away, so terribly, terribly far away. She could not reach him. Longing filled her, a yearning so intense that nothing else existed, a yearning for the unobtainable desire. It hurt, washing her in waves of utter hopelessness and despair . . .

She didn't realize Sean stood by her side until his hand reached up and brushed the silent tears from her face. "Oh Sean, dear Sean, tell me it will go away . . . Tell me I'll know hope again . . . Someday, with time . . . when I'm home again."

She turned to him, begging for something Sean could not give. For he knew time changes nothing when nothing changes. He knew, too, she was not going home again. With every passing minute the ship carried her farther and farther from that place in her heart.

He turned suddenly away, knowing a regret few people ever see, leaving her with the sight of the barren blue desert of the sea.

The sun crested the meridian, sinking lazily to the small foothills, pushing against a bright blue sky as Joy and Sean, holding little Sean in the traveling pouch, turned their mounts down a road that she thought promised to bring her home after nearly two long years. Just when she would imagine herself racing ahead, by some unspoken agreement, they kept their mounts at a slow walk. A cloud of dust shaded the landscape gray. The wind rushed through the maple trees lining the road, echoing a lonely song. She couldn't understand why her hands grew suddenly clammy. Emotion welled inside her, constricting her chest. They turned the last bend, and she felt suddenly frightened as the house she had never seen stood before them.

It was far lovelier than the letter had described. The house rose two stories high, with a steeple frame roof like a church. White-washed, with pretty green shutters, it shined beneath the summer sun. A picket fence surrounded the flower garden which Cory worked long and hard to keep. Chickens cluttered the yard. The two familiar bays grazed in the pasture, separated from a cow named Meredith. The cart, with its false bottom and many memories, stood idle alongside the barn. It was lovely and quaint, so perfectly suited to them, but—

It was not her home! This pretty white house would never be her home. Her home lay across three thousand miles of water, on the distant shores of England, where he was . . .

The porch door swung open. Carrying two buckets, Cory emerged in the bright sunlight on her way to the well. With a foot holding the door, she carefully let it swing back so as to avoid waking the reverend napping in the shade of the porch. Half way there, she glanced up. The buckets dropped. Cory thought her mind collapsed; she just wanted to see Joy so desperately, her mind tricked her with some neat sorcerer's trick, conjuring the vision before her. She started running though, running with the fear that the mirage would vanish before she could get there.

Joy's heart-wrenching gasp spurred Sean to sudden movement. Carefully, so as not to disturb little Sean, he leaned over to reach for her, lowering Joy to her feet. He watched Joy run into Cory's wide, outstretched arms and waited patiently through an embrace that seemed to never end. He'd only stay for the homecoming, leaving on the morrow for England. He did not welcome the thought, for Ram would be no better and probably a good deal worse, not owning a woman's emotional ability to grieve.

Joy sat with her arms around the reverend's legs, her head resting lightly on his knees, as she stared into the flames of a fire at the side of his rocking chair. The rest of the household was asleep and it was quiet. The reverend's thin hand stroked her loosened hair, the gesture as loving as their silence.

Things had changed. Sammy had two freed people of color working for him, and though times were hard with the depression, he was managing. She had not been surprised to learn Ram had been supplementing the household's income all along. Sammy still worked from dawn to darkness, but he was happier than Joy had ever known him. The reverend claimed that Sammy's happiness was owing to living in a free state, a place where he was not forced to constantly confront the bondage of his race, and Joy thought this must be true.

Sadly, Cory had had a miscarriage. The reverend claimed this explained Cory's unusual relationship with little Sean. Just when little Sean began to show adverse effects from his mother's despondency and his father's long absence, Cory came into his life. He loved Cory and she him, this was plain. Their relationship was unusual in that it was not adult to child. No, Cory loved and played with little Sean as a child herself. Within these last two months, their love grew, blossoming daily, and Joy, treated to the happy sound of little Sean's laughter again, felt grateful and relieved.

She tried to heal herself, desperately tried to heal the despondency of her heart, but the terrible longing would not abate. Time seemed not her ally. Against her will, she was lost to memories: memories of the time they had together, memories of his love, his touch and kiss, of their laughter, a thousand too many memories.

"I don't know what to do," she suddenly whispered out

loud. The reverend's hand stopped stroking as he saw the familiar tears. One never knew when they would come: in the middle of supper, at church, yesterday as she was milking the cow. "I just can't stop thinking of him!"

There was absolutely nothing he could say, nothing any of them could say that would change what had happened to her. Sammy said it the other morning: "We'se just have to be here for her. She's our Joy, and if'n hit takes our whole life long to see our girl smile again, so be hit."

"I just want to see him again and so badly," she said softly. "This ache inside . . . just to see him, to touch his face—" She hid her face in his knee. "Oh, reverend, what am I to do?"

The reverend leaned over and took her pale face in his old weathered hands. "Darlin', oh my dear, sweet darlin'." Gently his thumbs wiped her tears. "There's nothin' you can do but wait for the slow march of time to pass you by. It's all you have." Her eyes closed to the pain, and he kissed her. "Come now, we'll talk of somethin' else. I'll try to distract you a bit."

She wiped her eyes and drew a shaky breath, returning her gaze to the fire, while the reverend traveled back to days long ago, looking for some momentary distraction. "Hey, did your friend Katie ever write to you?"

Wiping her eyes, Joy nodded, pausing until she could speak. "Yes. I wrote Katie once I arrived in England, and since then I've received three letters. She was quite naturally shocked and thrilled upon learning of my marriage and little Sean's birth, and either she's never been told it was Ram's duplicity that caused her family's ruin or she's simply so . . . very . . . good—"

The reverend nodded, waiting patiently as Joy struggled with small uneven breaths to stop the slight tremble of her lips.

"Well, they lost Shady Glen, you know," she spoke with a soft whisper of a voice, "but she never mentioned how hard that must have been. Apparently Mister Beauchamp finally took employment at the bank. The Beauchamps live in town now, and Katie, she married Tom Henry."

"Tom Henry? Not that shifty fellow who used to steal your kisses at garden parties?"

"He . . . never stole my . . . kisses . . ."

The reverend watched the blue eyes widen, encompassing what she saw in the fire, then her small hand reached to her lips. With a sigh, he saw his poor attempt to tease her had failed.

Tears formed anew, and silence settled between them until a whisper broke it, one so soft he almost didn't hear. "Do you still miss Joshua, too?"

He knew without words from where the question came. In her distress, her thoughts turned to a primary source of comfort she had always known—Joshua. Joshua gave her not just the answers but the solace and peace of love. Things he felt, too, and his own sadness replaced the sympathy in his tired gaze. "Yes." He nodded. "Not a day goes by that I don't think of him, not a day when I don't remember him. It's queer, too, but I have this dream about him that still comes nearly every night."

"I dream about him, too," she said softly. "Why is that odd to you?"

"Oh, old folks don't dream—a body's just too darn tired at this age, I guess. Besides this dream, I don't figure I've dreamed in some twenty-odd years."

Still staring into the fire, she missed the reverend's bewildered expression, but when he ventured no more she asked, "What of your dream? Tell me."

The reverend leaned forward with his elbows on his knees, staring into the fire, too, as with no effort, he recalled the dream. "Oh, you know how dreams are—bits and pieces of madness." He shook his head. "This one, though, is so clear, even when it makes no sense. I'm in this room, you see, a real fine room such as the likes I've never seen. There's Joshua, standin' right in front of me, and he's real agitated and upset

422

'cause I can't make sense out of what he's sayin'. Sometimes there's a lady with him, sometimes not. Never laid eyes on her afore. She's a real lady, you can tell, and she's wearin' an old fashioned dress—you know, silk with lace and things like they used to wear?"

Joy's brows drew together in confusion, but the reverend was suddenly reliving the emotional content of the dream. "Then, this here lady's upset with me, too! I can't tell you the utter frustration and helplessness I feel as Joshua stands there yelling at me—like I'm too dull-witted to know what he's ravin' about!"

"Yelling?" She turned to look at him. "Joshua never yelled—"

"Aye, but he does a fine job in my dreams. He says over and over! 'It's plain to see! Right there in the eyes! Look old man—look!' So I look at his eyes, and I look and look—what's wrong darlin'? Have I done gone an' upset you with my rambling?"

Joy's eyes darted back and forth across his face. "I had the same dream!"

"What?"

"Does this lady have dark hair and blue eyes? Does she wear a cross about her neck?"

"Aye! She has dark hair, and I know her eyes are blue 'cause I'm lookin' at their eyes; and aye, she's got a cross on her neck—"

"She's Lady Barrington!"

"You're Lady Barrington—"

"Ram's mother!" Joy opened her mouth to speak but at first no sound came. "What can it mean?" She finally managed. "In my dream, Joshua said the same, and he was agitated, upset. He kept saying, 'Look! Look at the eyes,' but when I look, I see nothing but darkness. Darkness all around. I can't see through it—"

"Not in my dream," the reverend interrupted. "I see fine in my dream, but it's just this room—"

"What room? Can you describe it?"

"Aye. It's a fine room like I said. Pink sofa and chairs . . . there's this rug—the expensive, imported kind—fancy furnishings . . . I see a gold or bronze gilded clock on the mantle . . . pictures hanging on the walls—"

"The portrait gallery!" she gasped in shock. "It must be! Are the pictures portraits?"

Excitement coursed through them both, but the reverend said, "Can't say for sure—"

"Oh, but there's a maroon damask sofa and chairs, an imported carpet—"

"It matches—"

"Yes! Yes! Is the furnishing Louis IV? French?"

"Wouldn't know that from a cobbler's bench." The reverend never had a mind for such things. "But they're fine— Well, what's this now? What can it mean?"

"I don't know," she said with a shake of her head. She had heard of such things before, and of course the mystery of the old woman's vision would always be fresh in her mind. This was different though, for— "It's like Joshua's trying to tell us something, something about his eyes—"

"But his eyes are fine! That's what I keep seeing when I look."

"Then it's not his eyes but something he sees," she thought out loud.

"Aye, something he sees in that room. He says it's plain to see—"

"What? What is amiss in the gallery?"

There it was, the question spoken out loud. They stared at each other in sudden silence as there was no answer. For two days afterward they talked about it, trying to put the pieces together with wild guesses and leaps of imagination. Upon first hearing about it, Sammy tried to convince them the mystery, like so many others, lay under the great canopy of coincidence. Naturally both Joy and the reverend explored this avenue many times, only to dismiss it with an unmistakable suspicion that rose not from rational thought but rather from feelings.

There was a mystery; she just knew it, and as she lay in bed on the second night after the discovery, turning the pieces over and over again for the hundredth time, quite unexpectedly and without knowing why, she started crying again. Crying not from the utter frustration of it, but rather because somehow, in some way, the mystery of it was connected with him. The mystery of Ram Barrington, the patch and the scar—

Joy sat up abruptly, frightened by her train of thought. Was that it? Was Joshua trying to warn her about little Sean? That Ram was in fact like his father? That he would hurt little Sean as his father had hurt him?

She released her fear in a sudden sigh. She was the one going mad! The dream had nothing to do with little Sean. Ram was absolutely the sanest, most intelligent and clear witted man she knew, and like his son, there was no madness there. The only madness was her emotions.

Her thoughts spun predictably. Emotions manifest in the intense longing that overwhelmed all other emotions and thoughts. Her love was a physical need and passionate. The poet's song was wrong; she could live without him—her existence was proof—but she did not want to live without him. Like that child's fairy tale of the mermaid who fell in love with the prince, the mermaid sacrificed everything to be with her love. She too, would do anything for Ram's love; she would pay any price—her very life. She would pay anything but the one thing more precious than her life—the life of an unborn child. She could not knowingly drink that tea.

She turned on her side, gathering the blankets and pillows tight in her arms, then shut her eyes on the darkness, as two tears slipped from her lashes. Her memories refused their tenacious hold; she remembered falling asleep in his arms, wrapped in his warmth, their bodies entwined as their souls merged to dance in dreams, and then she'd wake to feel his lips . . .

Late fall sunshine filtered through the pretty yellow curtains on the kitchen window. With a smile, Cory watched Joy try to go through the motions of being alive, chasing her gregarious little boy about the kitchen and making a game of getting him dressed. One look at Joy though, and Cory knew what had transpired in the night. Her heart broke yet again.

Sammy came in with his arms full of wood for the stove, a basket of eggs and some pork cuts from the cold house outside. Turning back to the stove, Cory threw a huge slab of fresh butter into the frying pan, just as the reverend ran down the stairs and announced into the busy kitchen, "It happened again! Joshua came in my dream!"

Little Sean grabbed his unlaced boot, as his mother looked up and slowly stood to her feet.

"'Twas the same, only now I tried to speak back, but, oh gawd, I couldn't . . . I choked . . ."

"Lawd a tellin'." Sammy sighed loudly as he sat down. "We ain't goin' through dis again, is we?"

Moving into the kitchen, Joy set the pitcher of milk and the basket of bread on the table. The eggs were done and the smell of bacon frying filled the room. "Oh Sammy," she half pleaded, half scolded, "you just don't know how it feels."

"I knows plenty. One thing I knows, is ain't nothin' queer 'bout hit. Dreams change with de tellin', is all. Sounds lak you'se had de same dream, but dat's hit—jest sounds so."

"Maybe," the reverend admitted as he sat down, and Joy poured coffee in his cup. "But more than anything it's like the lass says—it's the feeling that Joshua's tryin' to tell us something."

"Yes." Joy nodded. "I only had the dream that once, but I had the same desperate feeling; and then too, Sammy, it's not so easy to dismiss the reverend's description of Lady

Barrington and that room."

"Rooms is all alike—chairs, sofa, pictures. Hey, what's dis, Sean?" He grinned.

"Boot!"

"What's a boot sound lak?"

"Moo," he said. "Cow!"

"An' boo!" Sammy scared him into a fit of giggles. "Lak ghosts and goblins and things dat foolish ole women believe in!"

"Sammy," the reverend said irritated. "Just for a moment assume Joshua is tryin' to tell us somethin' important."

Sammy agreed, but reluctantly with a roll of his eyes and another sigh.

"It's something we're to look at in a room that has portraits of Ram's parents," the reverend thought out loud. "What about Ram's parents, though? What's the missing piece?"

Cory set down the food. Joy's brows were drawn together, and she bit her lip in concentration. Now Cory sighed with frustration. "You two is missin' the point."

"What?" Joy asked distractedly.

"You see a puzzle, yet yo'se missin' a piece. You lookin' everywhere for hit but yo'se can't find it. Don't yo' knows why?" This solicited everyone's attention. "'Cause hit ain't here! Hit's in dat room back at your home."

"She's right, Joy. The answer's in the room."

"But what is in there?" Joy cried in abject distress, right back at the starting point.

Cory threw up her hands. "Pictures of Lord and Lady Barrington," she answered. "There's chairs, a sofa, rugs and all, too, but don' yo' folks get the sense hit's dem pictures dat's important?"

"Boo!" Sean said to Cory.

"Boo yo'self!" Cory said back.

The reverend, deep in thought, looked up to agree. "Maybe it is somethin' about those pictures . . ."

"They're just pictures of two people," Joy said.

Sammy gave up trying to fight them. "Well girl, you'se the only one whose seen 'em. You close yo' eyes and tell what you see. Hey Sean." He laughed. "Can you get dat boot on ole Rake?"

She closed her eyes, and with hands on her head, she visualized the portraits. Lady Barrington's picture came to mind with remarkable clarity of detail. "Well, Lady Barrington looks pretty, delicate yet tall and regal, as though one can tell she's a lady of noble birth. She wears a gray silk dress and that cross, all rather austere—almost like a Puritan."

"Dat's de cross you found on your vanity, right?" Cory said.

Joy had told them about the incident, how she never got a chance to ask Nanny Hawkins if it was her doing. When she had mentioned it to Ram, he agreed it must have been the senile old woman's queer way of welcoming her.

"Well, dat's a mystery, ain't it?" Cory asked.

"Yes, kind of, but—"

"Well, go on," the reverend said impatiently.

"She's beautiful, with dark hair like Ram's and Sean's, and her best feature being pale gray eyes, sad eyes—"

"Nothin' thar but dat cross, and dat don' seem to help none."

"Aye and you'll have to ask that old nanny about that. Drat," the reverend sighed, "well, what about the other one."

Joy closed her eyes again. "Lord Barrington's portrait is remarkable only in that it's unremarkable. One sees no madness there; he looks like a jovial good fellow. Save for his long large nose, there's little resemblance between Ram and his father." She closed her eyes again, resting her head in her palms.

Sammy abruptly wondered why no one was eating, then served up healthy portions of the bacon and eggs.

"Lord Barrington is not as clear in my mind." She

realized. "He leans toward corpulent, I remember, and he has blondish brown hair, a faint smile. I remember his eyes—a beautiful color like aquamarine stones—"

Cory interrupted with laughter, despite the serious subject, for little Sean stood by his mother, and thinking this a game, his eyes were closed and he held his head. "Sean, you rascal," she said, "open dem big brown eyes!"

Sammy's fork stopped midair between the plate and his open mouth, and he turned to stare at the boy's enormous brown eyes.

"Oh hell," the reverend cursed, "maybe we are just playin' a fool's game."

"Mayhaps hit's not the pictures?" Cory asked as she lifted little Sean to her lap for breakfast. "Somethin' else in dat room?"

Sammy was shaking his head, but his eyes were fixed on little Sean's big brown eyes. "What does Joshua say in dat dream again?"

"'It's plain to see, look at the eyes,' and oh hell, that's it! Like you say Cory"—the reverend shook his head—"we're goin' to have to go there to see it."

Joy looked at the reverend. "Oh goodness, would you really come back with me?"

Sammy's fork dropped, he no longer listened, and in a whisper he said, "My God!" He stood up. "Don't yo' get hit? Hit is plain to see!" Sammy met three anxious and confused faces, and he said, "'Member, 'member the Flaubert's babe?"

Quite suddenly all four of them were reliving a shared memory. After church one special Sunday morning, Sammy, the reverend, Cory and Joy headed out to Bonapart Street. Monsieur Flaubert's apartments sat atop his prosperous merchandise store and there, sometime during the night, Joshua had attended his wife for the birth of his fifth child. The four Flaubert girls were well known and everyone, especially Mr. Flaubert, was praying for a boy this time.

Cory and Joy sat in the back of the cart with their legs, arms and fingers crossed over each other for luck. Generous beyond belief if Monsieur Flaubert had a boy child, no doubt she and Cory would land a piece of candy from the huge glass jar on the counter. The reverend would get a cigar, which would be split in two for Sammy. True, in the last year Cory and she were acutely conscious of maturing, and though they pretended not to care about the candy, nonetheless as they climbed into the cart and sat down beside each other, their arms, legs and fingers had crossed of their own independent volition. Seeing it caused giggles to interrupt Joy's reading of the psalms in French as they moved along.

"Some mens are just girl makers, is all," Sammy said to the reverend up front in the driver's seat as the cart rolled along.

"Aye." The reverend chuckled, musing; "I once came across this man who had nine daughters, not a single boy, and lord, each one of those girls was not just as homely as they come, but toothless to boot! Imagine tryin' to get all nine of 'em married out."

"Dat would sure give me cold feet headin' to bed!" Sammy laughed.

"Hell, I'd go for castration at that point." The reverend laughed.

Cory and she exchanged confused glances.

"I thought only horses were castrated?" Joy asked with a fourteen-year-old's keen knowledge of the world.

"Never you mind 'bout dat," Sammy said.

Joy started an indignant protest, but the reverend interrupted with a reminiscence about his last cigar, and Cory nudged her side, triggering another eruption of giggles. The cart turned down Bonapart Street, pulling up in front of the wide awning and painted window of Flaubert's Store. The streets bustled with church goers and Negroes, free for the Sabbath to enjoy their music at Congo Square. Yet, with the exception of the marketplace, all stores and shops were closed. Flaubert's was no different, though as the cart came to a complete stop and four gazes greeted the unnatural quiet and dark store, they knew something horrible had happened.

Joy remembered Cory's hand slipping into hers, the solemnity descending upon the four of them. Of course, it was sadly not unheard of, but after four healthy births, one was not prepared to hear of a tragedy. "Something's happened," she said what they all knew.

"Aye," the reverend said. Abruptly he spotted little Michael, the Flauberts' Negro boy, peeping from the alley. "Hey Michael, run up and fetch the doctor. Tell him we're here."

Michael, plainly looking apprehensive, nodded and ran off. Minutes later Joshua appeared. Then they knew something horrible happened. He was coughing, which happened whenever he was upset, a patient died or Joy was trying him. He came briskly to the cart. The reverend inquired what happened. "Madame Flaubert?"

"She's fine; the baby, too. A healthy seven pound boy."

Cory's eyes found Joy's with confusion, the reverend's own, as he asked, "Well, what's wrong, then?"

Joshua coughed into his kerchief but finally said this, "The boy's eyes are . . .". He leaned over and whispered something to the reverend.

She remembered the pause.

"Oh Lord," the reverend muttered at last. "Does she say rape?"

Joshua nodded but cast a glance at Cory and herself. "Mr. Flaubert is quite drunk, and she's quite hysterical now. She won't have anything to do with the child. I've had to call for a nurse from Garden Court. I think it's best if I stay till it settles down."

The reverend nodded and Joshua said he'd send for him when he was ready. The reverend slashed the reins, and the cart jerked forward. Almost in the same instant, Joy demanded, "What's wrong? I don't understand?"

431

Unlike Joshua or Sammy, the reverend could be counted on for answers to any and all questions. Of course one didn't always like his answers; for instance, "The sky is blue darlin', cause once a long time ago when the sky was green, folks didn't know where the grass and trees stopped and the sky began. So, they asked the fairy people to paint it blue, and those little fairies did just that."

This time however, he had told her a fact, such a simple fact; yet one that had the profound power to solve the mystery of Ram Barrington.


Twilight settled into the study where Ram and Sean talked. Sean related at length progress on the ship's repairs—two torn masts were back up, yet with two to go, and the ship siding was being fitted where cross cannon fire placed a fair size hole. Distractedly listening, Ram watched as a maid quietly entered the room to light the lanterns. What was her name? He should know her name. Joy would not only know her name but her family background, the names and ages of her brothers and sisters if any, the girl's hopes and dreams and—

Ram pushed away the thought with a shot of brandy, and relieving Sean's apprehension, he finally reclined in the oversized reading chair. Sean pushed the ottoman to him, and almost as an after thought, Ram lifted up his wounded leg to rest.

"So, what say you?" Sean asked as he finished, pouring more brandy into his goblet, filling Ram's as well. The antique crystal brandy decanter was set unkindly to the sterling silver tray, as though it was made of common brass, but only Pansie, leaving the room, noticed.

"I say we sail in three days."

"What?" Sean's gaze riveted to Ram.

Ram could never say why he loved to hear Sean's

incredulous "what's"; the aristocratic breeding in Sean's pronouncement of that one word was enough to scare the hell out of half the entire English serving class. It made him remember Sean as a boy, a peasant Irish lad, smart as a whip and just as tough, laughter in his eyes and no damn good on his mind. Sean, his dearest friend in life; how many long roads they had traveled, how many places they had seen, people they had met, things they had done! Aye, they had come such a long way together. . . .

Though in a very real sense Sean was responsible for the agony of his days, he could not blame him. Sean's benevolent motivations aside, to blame Sean for forcing his fate to entwine with Joy's, was to regret it. He could find no regret, despite all. He could not regret knowing her love or her laughter, the joy that was her name, even if he had known it for such a blessedly short time.

"What?" Sean repeated again in the same manner. "Three days? Have you lost your wits, my lord? A poor metaphor but apt, I think, for I thought the only reason we returned was to get you proper care and see those wounds healed."

"Ah, these cuts can heal on the way back."

"You mean fester!" Sean returned.

"I know what you're thinking, Sean—"

"Aye! I think you are indeed seeking an early death!"

"Don't be a fool Sean," Ram snapped. "Had I been bent on meeting death, I no doubt would not now be drawing breath." His tone softened, and he added, "Life is too precious, even without her. I will not forsake it."

Sean thoughtfully considered that last, measuring the words against what he had seen. Never had he witnessed fighting like Ram's during the two weeks they attacked the barbarism occupying the coast lands of that God-forsaken land of Egypt. Ram's fighting was magnificent and terrifying both, a dozen times he had braced for Ram's death as he rushed to Ram's side, only to witness, through brute strength and unmatched skill, Ram escape the fatal blow time and time again. The miracle lay in the fact that Ram had only the saber cut on his leg, a broken rib nearly healed already and a lesser chest wound.

Silence had settled between them, finally broken by Ram's husky whisper, "I have to get her out of my head Sean. She lives in my mind. I see her so clearly—I want her so badly . . ." He stared off at the fire in the hearth; the bright blue rim of the flames reminding him, when he needed no reminder, of the color of her eyes. "God's curse," he shook his head, "I've got to get away."

Ram leaned forward, resting his forehead in his hands as though braced with pain. Sean shared his friend's pain in silence, literally willing to do anything if only it might help but knowing nothing could. Nothing could help but the merciless slow march of time and even then—

A commotion sounded from outside, something involving the footmen. Sean listened distractedly until the front doors opened and in the distance, Mr. Cutler exclaimed, "Milady! Oh, milady! That's not you—"

Sean could barely hear the next.

"Is he here? Dear God, tell me he's here!"

Joy? Was that Joy? Sean looked to Ram, but he remained unaware.

Mr. Cutler said, "He's in the study but—"

Sean heard the distant footsteps, light, determined, running. The footsteps stopped at the outer hall, then passed through, and Sean turned to the door just as she burst through.

The sight of her brought Sean an instant comprehension of stoic Cutler's outrage. It was not just that she was supposed to be three thousand miles away across an ocean, or that she appeared so unexpectedly, with neither rhyme nor reason, nor word. No, it was that she looked wild, wild in a way far surpassing the first day that Ram and he had met

434

her so long ago. She wore a poor boy's clothes and was barefoot, hat and coatless, her long hair wrapped tightly in two long braids, and more than anything it was the blue eyes, wild with agitation. Yet all she saw was—

"Ram!"

Ram looked up, shock registered on his face as he confronted the sudden surprise, the vision from his dreams. He didn't have time to react, to guess why she was here or why she was dressed in a boy's clothes, for she ran to him, falling into his arms where he sat. Tension gripped him in the instant, he didn't know what to do until the moment she cried. "No! Don't push me away! Please. Please hold me—hold me."

The soft plea held the desperation of a wounded creature's last cry, breaking his small resistance. All these past long months he had been traveling over a dark and treacherous landscape, knowing only fear and dark and cold until this very moment when his arms came around her tightly. It was like an avalanche. The feel of her small body crying in his arms felt like the blessed touch of the sun, and he lost his pain in the embrace. Now there was no fear or darkness or cold; there was only her.

Sean couldn't decide if he should leave or stay, and his indecision kept his feet firmly planted to hear the frightening thing that happened next.

"Ram, Ram, something has happened!" Joy finally said in a voice touched with her tears, yet excited and agitated. "The reverend and I had this dream, and Sammy guessed what it meant! Sammy solved the mystery, and that day, the reverend, little Sean and I left for Boston where we boarded the first ship sailing home. It wasn't even a passenger ship; it was a merchantman and we all had to sleep together and the captain was so mean and the crew was unpleasant and it was so awful! Awful because the ship was so slow, oh God, the endless hours I spent thinking of it, of you, only you, of telling you and showing you and—"

"Joy!" Ram pushed her back to search her face. "Slow down—"

"No, no, that's the whole thing! How long it took to come home! Until today, a bit before dawn, the ship finally made port, and I ran to the nearest livery stable where I had to bribe the owner with a diamond bracelet in order to get a mount, a Barrington treasure only . . . only that doesn't matter anymore. Nothing matters, nothing but that you're here! You're here . . ."

She collapsed against him again crying, her relief so intense, she was hysterical, and Ram looked up, locking his gaze to Sean's. Fear reflected in both their gazes. All Ram could think was that she had lost her wits. This whole time he had been so consumed with his own pain he could not bear a thought of hers. What depth of despondency had she known?

"Joy, Joy"—he lifted her up again and tried to sound calm—"my love, where is Sean?"

"He's with the reverend. They're taking a coach and should be here by noon on the morrow, but I couldn't wait . . . I had to get here to show you! I have to show you only, only—"

Quite suddenly she was afraid. It never occurred to her until this moment. What if it wasn't there? What if, in her desperation, she had only imagined the unalterable truth of the pictures? Dear God, could she be that desperate? Her eyes filled with the certain terror that she had indeed gone mad, and watching this gripped Ram with the same emotion. "Joy, Joy—"

"No!" she cried, and before he could react, she bolted from his arms and started running. "I'm not mad! It's there, it's there!"

"Joy!" Ram called but it was too late; she dashed from the room. Still stunned, Sean stood in mute horror over what he

436

just witnessed until Ram, getting to his feet, shouted, "Follow her Sean!"

Sean caught sight of her just as she turned the corner into the east wing. He raced after her. Ram's wound hindered his speed, but his fear fueled his pace, his own emotional pain magnified ten fold in light of hers. Both men ran down the long hall, turning the corner just as she snatched the master key from a vase on a hall table, then a lantern from the wall and took off running again.

"Joy!"

She ignored his call, ignored everything but the urgency brought by her sudden fear, an enormous fear that indeed pushed her past the thin line of sanity. The metal key ring clanking against the brass lantern holder as she ran somehow paired rhythmically with the furious pounding of her heart. She turned another corner, and there it was, the door to the portrait gallery.

She ran to it and stopped. She shook badly as she held the brass holder of the lantern in her mouth and one hand held the doorknob. Her free hand fitted the key in the lock. The door opened and she burst inside. She held the lantern up to Lady Barrington's portrait, saw it and fell to her knees, crying.

Ram and Sean raced into the room simultaneously. There they confronted the sight of her kneeling on the floor, her face covered in her hands as she shook softly with tears.

Sean stood frozen in the doorway while Ram stepped to her and knelt down, taking her by the shoulders, but stopped. He was afraid to see her lovely eyes, afraid to see the madness there. He knew not what to do but to love her; it was all he'd ever be able to do. "Joy," he whispered.

Her eyes opened, sparkling like jewels, the tumultuous emotions of her heart. She said the strangest of all imaginable things: "It's like pickles."

Ram froze as if his heart just met with the cold hard lead of a bullet. He, better than anyone, knew the unfathomable face of madness, and this was it.

"It's just like how I was fifteen—fifteen!—before I knew that pickles were cucumbers," she tried to explain through her tears. "I'm not saying I thought pickles grew on pickle trees or anything, it's just that I never thought about it and that's it; some how, some way, the knowledge that pickles are cucumbers escaped me."

Like all people confronted with a distortion of a person, whether it be physical or in the mind, Ram's gaze dashed to the side, for to stare at it proved too painful. Sean likewise. All Ram could think to do was to get her to bed. By God's grace she would be coherent after rest—

"Don't you see?" She stumbled forward. "Here you are: you read and write in four different languages, you have a mathematical gift, you've read all of Greek philosophy and every book written about it and you know every day of English and Irish history—from the Romans, the Gauls and the Celts all the way to Napoleon. You can recite every date, every major and minor historical figure! You're the smartest, most knowledgeable person I've ever known, and oh God, you know so much but the one thing, the only thing that matters—"

"Joy . . . Joy, oh God, my love—"

He was quite desperate by now, but Joy ignored it to say, "It's like me not knowing about pickles. And you Sean." She turned to him with an accusing look. "Don't you know? Look! It's right there! It's always been right there!"

She pointed to the portrait of Lord Barrington continuing, "I knew when I was so young; when the Flauberts had a brown-eyed baby, and the reverend told me what that means! Don't you know?" She grabbed Ram's muscled arms, ridiculously as though she needed more of his attention. "When he put a knife to your eye and said he would wipe the sin of your mother from your face—he knew! He knew the simple fact—"

"Stop! Stop this!" Ram shook her as though to shake the demons seized in her mind.

"No! Wait!" She broke free from his grasp and turned to look up at the portrait, meeting Lord Barrington's magnificent aqua-blue gaze. "The simple fact is, if Lady Barrington with her pale blue eyes is your mother, then Lord Barrington cannot be your father! Don't you know! Two blue-eyed parents cannot have a brown-eyed child!"

# Chapter Fourteen

There, the simple fact was out at last. The simple fact that would change their lives and sweep them from certain hell into certain happiness. For all the magnitude of this truth, neither Ram nor Sean registered a response. Ram's thoughts traveled quickly and in so many various directions he could not keep up. She was insane, going on about his father and eyes and madness, which made twisted sense, for she touched upon the cause of their tragedy, a tragedy she simply could not accept—

Ram didn't notice Sean's bewilderment as Sean stepped slowly to the portraits, for Ram was transfixed by her lovely still wild blue eyes. "Joy, my love—" She opened her mouth to speak but he silenced her. "Shhh . . . enough of this. Please don't speak about this. You're not making any sense and—"

She twisted her head from his hand. "No! No! Listen to me! Listen!" She felt the desperation of a mute trying to communicate. "Sammy knew; he guessed what it was. The reverend, Cory, Joshua, why so many people know! At least in the southern states where business is made of breeding, everyone knows! But you didn't know, nor Sean or Bart, or they would have told you! I came all the way home to you, but then I thought I was imagining it. But it's right there!

They have blue eyes and you have brown. He cannot be your father!"

Ram searched her face frantically. "What?"

She tried to calm down, to explain what the reverend said to her so very long ago, what it meant when the two blue-eyed Flauberts had a brown-eyed baby, but suddenly it was Sean speaking. "Ram, my God Ram," he said, shocked with the discovery. "I've never seen your mother's portrait—I've never been in this room. All this time, I never—she's right; I know she's right! Two brown-eyed parents can have either a blue-eyed or a brown-eyed child; likewise, if one parent has blue eyes and the other brown. Anyone can have anything," he rushed on, at once consumed with her same excitement, "except two blue-eyed parents—they can only have a blue-eyed child. If Lady Barrington is your mother, then Lord Barrington cannot be your father."

"Don't you see Ram?" Tears streamed from her eyes now and she said, "You are a Barrington in name only, not by blood."

Ram's grip on her shoulders tightened dramatically as his mind raced over this last. *You are a Barrington in name only, not by blood. Two blue-eyed parents cannot have a brown-eyed child.* He turned suddenly to the portraits, first his mother, then Lord Barrington. The words he would never forget echoed in his mind, *I will cut the sin of your mother from your face.* It felt as though the knife pierced that most sensitive flesh again; he felt an ugly throbbing there. His hand grasped his patch. The room spun and he grabbed the back of a chair to steady himself.

Silence hung over them all, broken at last as Ram removed his jeweled dagger. With unnerving precision, the dagger spun through the air to land point blank into the heart of Lord Ramsey Edward Barrington the Second. Ram turned and went through the door, where unmindful of his leg, he started running.

Joy started after him but Sean stopped her. "Give him

442

time, Joy." She met his gaze with a question. "A merciful blow it is," he whispered, "but a blow nonetheless. It's a shock; the very premise of his life has just been pulled from under him, and though 'twas an ugly premise, he needs time to assimilate it."

Uncertain, Joy searched the handsome face. "But it shall be all right?"

Sean smiled then, and that one grin spoke louder than words; it was happy and joyful, filled with all the optimism the changed future promised. "Aye, Joy Claret," he said in a whisper, "all shall be well now."

Joy smiled the same smile. A swift surge of joy filled her, and she and Sean laughed with it as suddenly they were like two young children at a maypole; their shared excitement and joy burst into wild laughter as Sean lifted her into the air and spun her round and round and round until they dropped to the floor, dizzy and breathlessly crying and laughing.

She was overwhelmed with all it meant. There would be nothing between them now, no hideous past to shadow their love. They would be free; their love would soar! Heaven could be the only limit, which they would reach for everyday of their life. Tonight, tonight she would lay in his arms, after so long, after thinking she never would again.

They could, God willing, have many children—

She sobered as she thought of the child she lost so unnecessarily. She would always mourn the life that never had a chance, a sadness from the loss. She thought of all they had been through, and this made her look at the portrait of the man responsible for the hell. Shadows played eerily there in the darkness; the shadow of the dagger hid his eyes. She stared for some time, trying to find hate but at last with no success. Hate played no part in her heart on this day. Yet, there was a question there. "Sean, if he was not Ram's father, then who was?"

Sean lay on his side, filled with the same joyful emotions as she, relieved and glad and happy for the bright future

443

exposed this day. He did not want to think about it. "Who knows?" He shrugged. "I've never known who my father was, and I don't think I've suffered overmuch. What can it matter?" he asked rhetorically. "So long as it's not a Barrington!"

"Sean, I'm surprised at you," she scolded gently. "You of all men should know it does matter. I know Ram will want to know, for I remember what he said about it at your mother's grave the day I learned your sea captain father was a lie."

"My dear girl." Sean chuckled affectionately. "That was naught but a child's play. It is easier to claim a dead sea captain as a father than to confess a bastard's status and ignorance."

"But Ram said you always wanted to know."

"Of course, but wanting to know and finding out are two different things. He existed; I am proof. Someone was supporting us all those years, so he must have been around . . ." He seemed thoughtful. "Yet my dear mother died without telling, the knowledge is buried with her. There's only one reason I can think of that a woman wouldn't tell, and that's unpleasant indeed. If I did know my father and the circumstances, I can only imagine I'd be cursing him."

Joy considered his words but felt unsatisfied. She looked to Lady Barrington's portrait. "Perhaps you're right Sean, but surely the circumstances would be different for Ram? And I just know he will want to know . . . after all we've been through—"

"Joy," Sean interrupted, sitting up and exasperated, "it was over thirty years ago now! He might want to know, but who's alive that can tell?"

"Nanny Hawkins!" Joy quite suddenly realized.

"Nanny Hawkins?" he questioned incredulously. "What? She can't still be alive! Why she was an old woman when I was a lad!"

"But she is! Don't you know? Ram still keeps her. She has rooms on the third floor, right above." Joy pointed, already rising. "Come Sean, let's go ask her!"

"I don't know w'at ye could be wanting with that ole woman," Bertha said as she led Joy and Sean through the narrow passageway, leading to the back stairs. Like the rest of the household, Bertha decided it best to pretend nothing was amiss with the queer way her mistress was dressed. La! Boys' breeches! She could not, however, resist sideways glances to confirm the unbelievable. Who could believe it! Wasn't there a law about that? Church law perhaps—

"Is she well enough?" Joy asked as they started up the stairs.

"Well enough I suppose, at least in body. The ole woman's mind, well, that be another matter entirely."

"Is she coherent?" Sean asked, looking for an excuse not to go, feeling foolish, vaguely apprehensive, though he couldn't say why. Unless it was the possibility of discovering something unpleasant that would ruin what was already too wonderful to believe.

"Oh aye, she's coherent, but she talks to spirits, ye know, the dead Lady Barrington."

"Oh my," Joy said.

"Losin' her mind all these last years. I try to tell 'er that 'tisn't right to speak to the netherworld, but she don't seem to listen to the likes of me, she don't. 'Ere we are."

At the top of the stairs, they came to a long hallway, and Bertha had to stop to catch her breath. The only light came from the lanterns Sean and Bertha held, enough though for Joy to examine their surroundings. The hallway was not empty, quite the contrary. Shelves lined both walls, filled with a clutter that could only be accumulated over a long lifetime. There were dolls and toys, stacks and stacks of books, vases, statues, knickknacks, a pile of unframed paintings leaning beneath a window and boxes piled on boxes.

"Oh milady," Bertha said, "please don't mind all the dust. The old woman throws a fit every time we try to clean up 'ere, she does, and since no one ever ventures up 'ere—"

"Bertha!" Joy scolded, "I would never complain about such things, you know that."

Bertha sighed and smiled. "No ye wouldn't, I suppose."

"Joy look," Sean said, having gone to the window to look out. Joy came to his side. The window looked over the inner courtyard. She searched over the darkness below but saw nothing.

"There, by that tree. It's Ram."

Joy made out the darker outline of his shape. He sat on a bench with his head held in his hands. She could feel him struggling with something, with everything. "Sean," she whispered, "why is it so hard? I feel like I should be with him, that we should be laughing, celebrating—"

"You will be, you will," he reassured her. "It's just that it's all so hard to accept, after all these years . . ." He stared for a moment longer. "Do you know what he's thinking?"

She shook her head.

"He's thinking of all the pain and agony, struggling to accept the idea it was all for nothing. Aye, and his thoughts will enter on the worst part—the child he made you lose."

Sean was right, she knew. Ram would know her very own pain, only now it would be worse for him. He would need her help to forgive himself.

"Come." Sean steered her from the window. "Let's get this fool's chase over. I think somebody will be needing you and soon."

Joy nodded, and Bertha, doing a good job of pretending she neither listened to nor understood what was being discussed, quietly led them down the hall to the old woman's rooms. She knocked first and opened the door. "Nanny

446

Hawkins," she said quietly, "I've brought you some company."

Joy and Sean followed Bertha inside the small apartment. Their two lanterns, plus a lantern over the rocking chair, filled the space with bright light. Nanny Hawkins sat in a rocking chair, fast asleep. She looked old beyond belief, every year of eighty etched into the small bony face, Joy thought. She had snow white hair, pulled to a neat bun at the nape of her neck, and she wore a matron's gown of gray, baggy and loose on her thin frame. A knitted cap of dark blue covered her head, matching her mittens, one with the fingers cut out. A colorful afghan covered her lap, and a small fire played in the tiny hearth, warmth being a most precious commodity in advanced years.

The room itself was small and neatly kept, a small cot, the rocking chair and shelves, that was all. Though as Joy's gaze furtively swept across the room, it was obvious that the collection of clutter in the hallway had spilled from the room. Every space was taken by something, something no doubt precious to the old woman, who now had little left except memories and the accompanying memorabilia.

After his own inspection and increasingly uncomfortable in the room that could barely accommodate his height, Sean motioned to Bertha. She stepped forward and gently nudged the old woman awake. "Nanny 'Awkins, I've brought you company."

The old woman's eyes opened. Several long seconds were used to focus, then realize that the person standing there was not a vision. "Who's this now?" a cagey, sexless voice asked. "Good Lord, 'tisn't . . . are ye . . . Mary's boy!"

Joy was just about to introduce herself and Sean and gently approach the subject of their visit, when unmasked alarm, even horror crossed the old woman's weathered face. The old woman came to her feet with a speed that defied her age. She wasn't looking at Joy but rather at Sean when she backed up against the shelves, inching slowly along there, staring with plain fear at Sean.

"I won't give ye the letter!" she cried. "I won't . . . ye can't make me . . . he don't deserve to see it, he don't."

"My dear woman—" Sean stopped abruptly as Joy's arm nudged him hard.

Joy did not know how she knew, only that she did. "It's his letter," she said. "It belongs to him. You must give it over."

The old woman finally noticed her. "Give it to him, give it to him, that's all milady ever says to me now. She even tried to make me give the letter to you," she told Joy. "Over and over milady says, look in her eyes Nanny! Look at her love for my son there! It's the love I never had! Can't you see it? Well, I see it." The old woman's tone became vengeful suddenly. "But he don't deserve your love, he doesn't! That boy cost milady her life! He—"

She stopped alarmed, staring at them. Sean only wanted out, silently swearing he'd make Ram promise to shoot him before he ever got this senile. Bertha was embarrassed by it, wondering if she should take the initiative to lead her mistress and the good captain out. Joy knew however. Her gaze searched the shelves behind the place where the old woman stopped. There was a vase, a jeweled box, books and an arrangement of silk flowers, dusty with neglect. It must be in the box or a book. "You gave me Lady Barrington's cross, did you not?" she asked calmly, trying to distract her. "I've been meaning to thank you—"

"She made me! When I wouldn't give you the letter, she made me give you the cross. She thought you'd run back to her portrait to see if it matched . . ."

Ram had never felt so lost. He could not believe it, let alone accept it. She said it was a fact; Sean said it was a fact, a simple fact that everyone knew. The reverend, Sammy, Cory, Sean and Joy all knew two blue-eyed parents could not have a brown-eyed child. The simple fact had the power to change the entire course of his life and yet, somehow, some way he had never known it.

Like pickles, she said . . .

Indeed like not knowing pickles were cucumbers, it was an absurdly banal fact, but unlike pickles, the simple fact changed all things: Lord Barrington was not his father and there was no madness within him. The madness had died with that man's death. He was free to love Joy. . . . He could love her, wholly and completely, he could love her!

Emotion surged within him, bringing him swiftly to his feet. He knew he should be overjoyed, ecstatic, celebrating, yet these fine emotions were buried in a sick overwhelming feeling of grief and regret. All they had been through! The child, God he had made her lose a child! For nothing? All her suffering, all he had put her through was for nothing. Why? My God, why?

Why had this happened? How had this happened? He suddenly had to know the whole bloody story, and there was only one person left alive who could tell him. Suddenly he started running.

Ram quietly entered the room, just as the old woman turned away and started crying. Joy, Sean and Bertha were held transfixed and unmoving, less by the incoherent rambling and more by the sudden release of a life's emotion.

"Ye know, she always knew, milady did, always . . ." The old woman nodded vigorously, yet in the next instant her voice changed again and her unseen eyes became dreamy and sad. "Alisha was so pretty, ye see—oh, like a spring blossom, delicate and lovely. I remember her first season. She was such a success. She had dozens of offers, dozens. She was so good . . . goodness shined through her heart, and though she was a quick witted girl, her goodness made her simple. She never had an unkind word for anyone or anything, until—

"Until her father agreed to the best, Lord Barrington. The day we were to meet him, Alisha picked her new blue silk, and oh, we fussed and primmed all morning. We were so excited, nervous. . . . We watched the carriage arrive from the upper balcony, and when Lord Barrington stepped out, he looked handsome, young and distinguished to me. I was so pleased until I saw Alisha's face. You see, she knew, knew before he said a word to her, and she looked confused and frightened, suddenly whispering a nursery rhyme that I taught her when she was but knee high to the ground."

The old woman stared at the fire as she mouthed the words "I don't like thee Dr. Fell, the reason why, I cannot tell, yet this I know and know for sure . . . I do not like thee Dr. Fell.

"I scolded her, I did," her voice rose, "not knowing till it was too late that she—by God's warning—felt then what lived and breathed in that man's soul—"

She turned back and saw Ram with a gasp. "He killed her because of you. You, her bastard boy . . . ye don't deserve to know. So many years I waited for the devil to take ye life like he took milady . . . so many years . . . He never did, not even as the madness got worse and worse, and when he finally died and ye still lived, I had to punish ye . . . I had to . . . So, I never gave over Mary's letter . . . I let ye believe ye had that madness in ye . . . Ye had to suffer for being left alive when Alisha, my sweet Alisha died . . ."

The old woman buried her face in her hands, and Joy moved to her with compassion. "Dear old woman, it isn't his fault. It was never his fault. Children are innocent. No one can blame a child when his mother dies upon their birth. It's a sad thing indeed, but it happens—"

The old woman's face frightened Joy to the depths of her soul. "Oh no." She shook her head. "That's not what happened. Oh no, milady didn't die upon the birthin' bed. I was there, I saw the whole thing." She looked to the bed, yet was seeing the scene that had haunted her all these long years. "I just readied the nursery. I came to take the babe from her, to give her some rest. I stopped in the doorway. He was there, speaking to her. I'll never forget his face. It was so calm he might have been passin' orders to a servant or sitting for a pleasant afternoon tea. Alisha was crying, but she was always crying, ye know. He said, 'I made many discreet inquiries to learn that brown eyes do not change color, not that I ever imagined this boy was mine.' He was smiling—smiling!—and he said, still calm, 'I gave the matter some thought. I decided either you or your bastard would live. You must choose Alisha.' Oh, milady fell on her knees, tears, the endless tears fell from her eyes, and she begged, not him, for she knew well there was no mercy there. She was begging God, begging him to let her son live—

"He took it as his answer. He picked up the pillow and pushed her back to the bed. I thought I was dying! I couldn't breathe! I couldn't move! I tried! But I couldn't . . . move! I just stood there and watched as—"

Four stunned people watched as the old woman collapsed, falling to the floor, her numbed and stricken consciousness no longer shielding her from the guilt of not stopping her beloved lady's murder. All these years she had blamed Ram, assigning him the burden of her own guilt, until this very moment of revelation. "Dear God." Sean finally released his breath as Bertha gathered the old woman in her arms, setting her back to the bed, comforting her like someone would a small child.

Joy tore her eyes from the sight and saw Ram standing there, his face an exercise of pain and helplessness; the pain of learning the horrid truth of his mother's murder, the helplessness of not being able to change the tragic story. With love, her own pain and helplessness to protect him, she went to him. His arms came around her, and for several long minutes he held her tightly, burying his pain in her embrace.

Before they left the old woman to Bertha's care, Joy wordlessly, as though it had been mutually decreed by all, found Mary's letter in the box. It was frayed and yellowed, and she clutched it tightly as they left the room, the old woman, the tragedy that was her life.

It wasn't until they had returned to the study that she opened the letter. Knowing it would be a very long time before either of them could lose contact, Ram reclined in the chair, and she sat on his lap, held in his arms. Sean remained with them, not only because the letter was from his mother but because Ram's past was also his, and like all things, he would be there for Ram. No matter what, he would be there.

Joy slowly opened the pages of the letter, numbering ten in all, and in a saddened and quiet voice that reflected the solemnity of their collective consciousness, one that in both men's minds somehow echoed Mary's own, she read out loud:

My dear sons:

My time is at end. Alisha once told me to trust Mistress Hawkins and 'tis upon her word that I bid this good woman to pen my words as I speak them now. I made her swear upon our dear lady's grave that she will place these words in your hands upon the death of Lord Barrington, when at last all will be safe. By God's will, so be it.

Where do I begin? When I search for the beginning as I so often do these last days of my life, I come to the first day Patrick Shaw rode into the bleak hills of Kilterian. I was but a girl of ten and three. My own mother had died two years before as you know, and I lived with the kindly Potters then. I remember that one day as if 'twere yesterday. The day was gray and cold like so many, and as I toiled in the fields, I looked up to see him. Tall and magnificent, he was black against gray, riding a black horse, wearing a dark cape. He had raven black hair, too, the darkest gaze I ever saw. He was more handsome than a mortal man should be.

Yet beneath the black cape was the cloth of a priest. He was sent to replace Father O'Donnell, who we had

recently buried in the church yard. Some said he was
sent to our small parish in these rock laden hills of
Kilterian as punishment, that he upset the church with
his scholarly knowledge and writings. I think this must
have been true, for he didn't belong among us poor
country folks, people who toiled from dawn to sunset
pulling potatoes from an unyielding soil, peole who
knew only poverty and misery, beaten as we were
under the cruel hand of the Protestants. Like a crystal
vase set against the unmolded clay of the earth, he was
far too fine and high for us. His passion was for noble
ideas and thick books, things too far from common
folk's grasp, and though he was good and kind to all,
the intensity in that dark gaze of his was for things we
could neither see or know.

I was one of these people, a simple peasant girl and
he, a man of God, married to the church and far above
me. Yet, with a young girl's foolish idolization, I loved
him fiercely and passionately. I went to every Mass he
gave, yet I remember not a word he said. I saw him
nearly everyday, too, bringing him, as I would, a
handful of wild flowers, a basket of berries and a bowl
of stew when we had it. A few times, when he was not
too busy with his books, he would sit me down to tell
him the village news. How I lived for those times! I
would amuse him with the village gossip, at times
making him laugh with the simple stories of our lives.
Other times he would solemnly ask for my advice on
this matter or that, which I would enthusiastically give
to him. Always he listened with a smile.

Yet, for all of this, I could not know him. One time, I
remember, I had in my way amused him, and he had
laughed, drew near to me and kissed my forehead. "My
dear child"—he smiled—"if only you could know how
you renew my faith in our inherent goodness." He
turned from me and I heard him say, "A faith so tired

453

and tried . . ." I had to ask five people before I understood what inherent goodness meant. Only then did I glimpse the things with which he struggled; it was evil, even then, and in the end, he met face to face with it—

Yet I race ahead of my story. I wish I could tell more about this man, Patrick Shaw, for he was your father, Ram, and your father, too, Sean—

Joy stopped as she reread these last words. She felt the tension filling Ram's body, and she looked up to see Sean staring in shock at her—the deliverer of his mother's words. "Joy—" Ram's pronouncement of her name was a demand that she read on, and she returned at once to the letter:

"Does this surprise you? I think it should not. You two have always been like brothers, in heart as well as in fact, and the two of you are so similar in so many ways, a thousand times I thought you two would guess the secret I kept. It was a secret I had to keep, not just for fear of jeopardizing your inheritance Ram, for I never knew if Lord Barrington knew for a certainty, but by the time you two were of an age to know, you both were of a height, strength and temperament to commit murder. As I knew one murder, I lived in fear of knowing another.

You both will want to know how this came to pass. It is the story of three different loves, none of which could ever be. It is a sad tale that has shaped my life and fate. Yet for all its sadness I cannot regret any one part.

The year after Patrick Shaw was sent to us, Lord Barrington arrived at Kilterian Castle with his young bride, the Lady Alisha. Lord Barrington was not the first nobleman who was known as a good and just man among his peers, yet a cruel and cold man among his underlings. You both well know how the villagers lived in fear of him, his petty tyrannies being too numerous to count, and I think 'twill not be a surprise when I tell that the simple common people of the village pitied Lady Alisha Barrington, a noble, highborn lady. Of course at first I only knew her from afar, yet all saw the terrible sadness that was always with her. The sadness was attributed to her banishment. She was an English woman, a highborn lady, a Protestant at that, forced to reside among poor common folks in Catholic Ireland, separated from friends, family, all things familiar, for no reason anyone could guess. This was not so, for I was to learn her sadness went deeper, much deeper.

Lord Barrington left her alone for months on end, and within that first year, she began seeing Patrick. A secretiveness surrounded their encounters, no one could guess why a Protestant woman sought the comfort of a priest. Folks kept coming across them walking together though, always deep in communion, lost to everything but the words between them. Oh, how envy consumed me then! I envied her, not her silk gowns or maids or any of her finery. Nay, to this very day, despite all that's past, I envy Alisha her words, words that allowed her to know him as I never could.

It came to pass just before nightfall one day when Mistress Potter sent me out to chase her youngest home for supper. 'Tis a fool's game I play when I ask what if I found the lad that day so long ago? Would Patrick still be alive? Would he have saved Alisha her fate? Would Alisha still live? Would I not now know you, Sean? Alas, it never came to pass, for I searched for the lad in vain, fatefully wandering farther into the forest. I was chilly, a cool sea mist rose over the land, darkness fell fast, and as I came across them there, curiosity made me move closer. I just wanted to know what she said to him, foolishly thinking I would know the right words then. Yet what I heard as Alisha turned

455

to him and clutched at the folds of his cloak was not what I was expecting. "Evil does exist!" she cried. "I live with it, I live with it!"

She dropped to her knees before him, tears streamed down her face. "Help me Patrick . . . dear Patrick, help me!" I shall never forget his pain as he stared down at her, helpless as no man should be. It was his moment of struggle, one he lost, for he took her face in his hands, dropping beside her, and he kissed her.

I wanted to die. I turned away and ran. The next hours are but a blur in my mind, and if I did not have you Sean, I should never know it really happened. I remember running, running until I, too, fell to my knees crying. I remember a despair and pain and cold such as I never felt since. When hours later I finally returned to the cottage all were asleep. I let myself in and lay down upon my cot, crying still. Perhaps I slept, or perhaps I just dreamt that I was Lady Alisha and it was me he was kissing.

So it came to pass. For at some point I could bare it no more. I rose and wandered out. It was dark, and as I made my way to his room behind the church, I saw nothing and no one. To this day my purpose eludes me. Would I confront him? Threaten him? Was I only planning to show him my tears and ask for comfort? I don't know, I don't know.

The door was unbarred and I did not knock. The fire had died to red embers, and as I stepped toward the cot where he slept, glass crackled beneath my worn slippers. I could only guess he had thrown an emptied bottle of rum against the hearth. It frightened me that he might be drunk, yet now I see the fear as a virgin's fear, for I knew, I knew even before he woke and saw the vision of his dreams.

"Alisha, Alisha," he said, "you've come back." He reached for me, drawing me down to the cot. I uttered not a word, for while 'twas Alisha's name he called, 'twas me he loved that night.

The hardest thing I ever did was leave his arms that night, but my fear that he would wake to discover his mistake was great indeed. It pushed me to my feet, made me tremble as I gathered my poor clothes. He woke to see me there, and whether he still saw Alisha or me, the girl Mary, I never knew, for his last words said were: "God have mercy upon our souls."

It frightened me more, those last words, as though he knew the devil waited there in the room. My fear must distort my memory, for I felt him standing there before I turned to see the dark shape of a man. The scream stopped in my throat. I don't remember running; but I must have, for I, with my peasant ideas, my youth and my lost innocence, knew that demons oft took the shape of men to celebrate our sins. I don't remember anything else, but the next day, as I pulled the glass from my feet, the news came that Father Patrick Shaw was found murdered, stabbed many times unto death.

You both have been told the story of what followed. The villagers believe to this day Patrick Shaw fought the devil that night and lost. They burned his church to the ground. Yet I cannot say for certain who the devil was or that the murder was committed in vengeance for a name called in passion. If your mother, Ram, suffered the same terrible suspicion, she never voiced it, at least to me as we came together, drawn as we both were to the ruins and desolation of his church.

You must know I was lost and hopeless and had not a soul to turn to with my grief or fear. It will seem strange as I tell the rest, for any other woman would have hated me when I told that I had lain with her lover as he called her name. Yet not Alisha. My story came out, and when she cried, it was not for Patrick Shaw or

457

herself, but for me. She cried for me! She was a highborn lady and I a poor peasant girl, and yet we shared a fate, a fate as well as a loss, and as we met nearly every day by the ruins of the church, we came to know a different kind of love. Aye, 'twas a simple and good love, peaceful and filled with solace. Oh, the hours we spent holding each other, crying, talking in whispers, mourning our loss! And when my condition became apparent and the Potters abandoned me for not naming the father, 'twas your mother, Ram, whose monies supported me all these long years.

Of course, the shadow of Lord Barrington always hovered near us. When he learned Alisha was with child, Alisha said, "I don't think he knows Mary, for all he said was, 'Ah good, an heir at last. Let us pray mother and child survive the deliverance.' Then something about Eve . . ." She couldn't remember.

Alisha and I willfully ignored the portent of those words, and as he was away the whole time after that, we eventually came to know laughter again, laughter at the strangeness of it, the joy and wonder of the lives he left each of us with. "We shall raise our children together, my sweet Mary," Alisha would say, "and they shall be siblings in heart, before they know it as fact. When at last our secret is safe to share, we shall sit them down and tell them. I suspect at first they shall be very angry with us . . ." Such was how we talked and planned, as any two young mothers, and for those last long months, we knew only the wonder of the miracles taking shape within us, the contentment in each other's company.

The time of your births, as you know, is separated by four days. When you were born, Ram, your mother sent me a note, read to me by the messenger—this good lady here, herself—and it said: "Mary, my sweet Mary, the joy of it! In my arms I hold my son, large and healthy, and you would say a bonny fine lad indeed. The midwife claims 'twas one of the easiest first births she ever partook, but I do not know if this is so. I only know that as I hold him to my breast the love in my heart is truly God's own gift to me. And now, my sweet Mary, 'tis your turn, and I await anxiously!"

I still hear her voice saying this, so gentle and dear, as I cry now. 'Twas claimed she died upon the birthin' bed, yet I know 'tis not so! The suspicion, so much worse than my other, sits upon my heart like a cold winter frost. Did he take Alisha from me, too? Alisha, who to this day was dearer to me than any other living soul before or since—dearer even than him . . .

Alas, I had you Sean, and eventually you, too, Ram. Alisha's dream came to pass, and you two were raised together, brothers at heart as well as in fact. I love you both dearly, as I know Alisha would have, and I leave you with this love, our secret finally shared."

The letter dropped to Joy's lap as she turned with her tears to Ram's shoulder, filled with the sadness and surprise of Mary's story, of knowing love, the shape and meaning it gave to life, the devastation of its loss. Ram's arms came around her, and he held her tightly, though his gaze locked with Sean's, his brother in heart as well as in fact. He wanted to laugh or cry, he truly didn't know which, for the tragedy of their mothers' shared past, at last revealed, mixed with a wide, clear path that led to a bright and joyful future indeed.

# Epilogue

"'Twas a fool's task," Sean said bluntly, following Ram up to the deck. He played the devil's advocate; the real fool's task was his effort to outwit Ram. The *Ram's Head,* as well as the *St. Marys,* sailing off her starboard, were supposed to be bound for the port of Boston, bringing Joy and the reverend to the small white house in the woods for the birth of Sammy's and Cory's first child due in four months time. There was plenty of time for a side trip, which they were taking, only Ram didn't know it. All navigational tools were rigged, as were the sails. Sean also had planted a conspiracy among Ram's men, a conspiracy many would call mutiny.

Ram knew something was wrong, he just didn't know what—past the infuriatingly sluggish response of his ship. Today, he, Sean and a handful of men labored arduously to shift the weight of the cargo, hoping the shift would help increase speed, and this was what Sean referred to.

"Perhaps," Ram replied noncommittally as they stepped over to the rail. The last rays of the sun slanted across the deck. The blue canopy of the sky darkened to a soft violet color, shading the darker sea as well. "Curse all Sean." Ram felt truly perplexed, irritated because of it. "But even the colors are wrong! I've never seen this weather so far north. O'Flattery, Michaels, Tod, none of them have either. I'd

461

swear we were two hundred miles off course if the damn sextant didn't say otherwise."

Sean bit his lips, his gaze resting upon the sea to shield his amusement. They were two hundred miles off course!

Ram shook his head. "I just have this gut instinct something is wrong."

Sean abruptly changed the subject.

The two captains conferring at the rail solicited a comment from a new crew member to which Bart, working the ropes behind them, replied, "Oh aye. Now that everyone knows they're blood brothers, everyone sees a likeness. 'Course, I always suspected." He had convinced everyone. "'Tisn't just their height or their uncommon strength, but Seanessy looks like a blond version of Ram. Some say it the other way around—that Ram looks a darker version of Sean—but all that depends on who's butterin' ye bread . . ."

Sean's talk absorbed Ram's thoughts for a spell, until Ram found his own ever-present distraction. The darkening colors reminded him of her eyes darkening with passion, which in turn reminded him of last night . . .

Sean watched the boyish grin transform Ram's face, a grin of a man pleased with something, pleased with everything. Everything came down to the one name, Joy, and Sean thought not for the first time, he could never have gotten away with his shenanigans if Joy had not been on board. Ram had changed much since the night of Mary's letter, though the most important change of course, was freedom, the freedom to love from which all joy, passion, and happiness sprung.

"She has changed you," he said out loud with his own smile and this, not for the first time either. "She has captured your heart and soul and—" he laughed—"there are times when I think she has stolen your wits as well."

Misunderstanding Sean's remark, Ram assumed he referred to a recent conversation where he had lamented at length over his infuriating inability to deny Joy anything,

462

realizing it when Joy had asked for her third fresh-water bath. He had stared at the lovely sky-blue eyes, and when any right-minded captain would have laughed at the outrageous request, he found himself going to the door and shouting the order out, daring any of his men to say a word. His men might go thirsty, but Joy would be happy.

That was hardly the extent of it, and he chuckled suddenly, remembering how Joy had come into his study with Cory's letter in hand to announce she must go back for the birth of Cory's and Sammy's first child. That he had understood, and besides, the reverend was ever anxious to quit English soil. Yet before they had departed, Joy insisted on personally visiting nine different orphanages to discuss her programs with the matrons. "I know how terribly busy you are," she had said, "but just think if it saves but one child's life . . ."

Again, he could not refuse her.

"Aye," Ram said as he stared at the darkening color of the water. "She has snared me tightly in her spell, and I am lost. Yet"—he chuckled warmly—"I do not think I suffer over much because of it." Thinking of changing sky-blue eyes, of long brown hair, a smile that affected him physically, thinking of what he had been thinking of all day since he had forced himself to leave her sleeping in the morning, he grabbed a line and vaulted the side, dropping a good thirty feet into the water. It was a cleansing plunge before seeing her.

"'E's like a long-tailed cat in a room o' rocking chairs," Derrick came up behind Sean, watching Ram in the water below.

"Aye!" Sean laughed. "And if it weren't for the lady sitting behind that door—"

"Your soul wouldn't be worth a bloody farthing," Derrick finished.

Ram climbed back up the rope and disappeared into his quarters. Nearly fifteen hands immediately went about changing the sails. The wind slapped the sails into place, and once done, Sean looked back to Derrick. "What news have you man?"

"Should be there by morning light."

"Good. Now all I need is six or seven men to go against him."

"Don't look at me!" Derrick said in true alarm. "Me knees are quakin' just thinkin' about it! Ye won't get anyone on this ship to do the dastardly deed, ye won't. Unlike ye, Seanessy"—he grinned wickedly—"Ram weeds out the witless and the fools before hiring 'em on."

"As well as the courageous," Sean observed. Yet Derrick was right. He'd have to get his own men to go against Ram, paying them a pretty bonus, too.

"Then too, Seanessy," Derrick had one last bit of advice, "ye, of all men, should know 'twill take more than six or seven men to take Ram out."

Sean's eyes filled with merriment, and he laughed. "Not if one of them is me!"

Normally Ram, usually working with Sean, took on the task of exhausting little Sean to sleep. Today though, Ram and Sean had been working all day and early evening on the ship, and the task fell on the less sturdy shoulders of Joy, the reverend, Polly and Mrs. Thimble. All of them spent the last four hours feeding, bathing, chasing, playing hide and seek, blocks, the jumping game, touch the sky and catch—this last was important, for Ram and Sean were both convinced little Sean would soon be named Cambridge's greatest cricket player, and by masculine wisdom they thought to get him on his way with practice. Yet little Sean exhausted everyone long before himself, and Joy watched the reverend, Mrs. Thimble and Polly abandon ship like so many rats in a fire, leaving her alone with the task and a good deal of laughter. She finally managed to trap the irascible lad in a corner, coaxed him still in her arms with a song and at last he fell asleep.

Joy nearly collapsed on top of him. She simply did not understand how mothers of two, three and more children managed, especially when most women did not have wealthy husbands and a string of helpers. It was Ram's fault though, she was certain of it. Most people kept children happily tucked away in an attic nursery with their nannies until they were of a height and manner of a miniature adult, at least until they could clearly enunciate the word enunciate. Not so with Ram. He insisted they be little Sean's caretakers and playmates as well as parents, and while in principal she agreed whole-heartedly, would not in fact have it otherwise, in practice she was simply exhausted.

Yet, once she was alone and free, staring at the empty quarters—save for Rake, sleeping alongside the cradle—she felt a burst of renewed energy. Alone and free at last! There was much to do. She lit a lamp, immediately assumed the wide comfortable chair behind Ram's huge desk, and for the tenth time, she carefully unfolded the Reverend Cox's letter. The letter contained William Lloyd Garrison's last and most poignant address to the New England Chapter. He was a founder of the American Anti-slavery Society, the leader of the movement for immediate and unconditional emancipation, and his speeches were largely responsible for the burgeoning numbers of abolitionists. So profoundly moving, she had cried the first time she read the speech while each time afterward, she wanted to jump to her feet, pound her fist deploring people to act, to do something!

She had been waiting for the right time to share it with Ram. This had much to do with a hope that the address would persuade him to write an even larger bank note to the Abolitionist Lobbying Fund. Unfortunately, Ram was absolutely convinced nothing short of war would ever end slavery in the states, and though they argued often and passionately on the subject, nothing so far had persuaded him that if everyone acted now and did all one could—such as write larger bank notes—this war could be averted.

William Lloyd Garrison's address would surely do the trick!
Perhaps tonight, she thought.

The door opened at last and mendacious blue eyes lifted to see Ram's tall frame silhouetted in the impending darkness. The last play of light made Ram's already imposing height seem even taller. Like a vision from her dreams, she could not see his face, only the outline of his rough black curls, the wide breadth of his shoulders and arms, a clear definition of his long, well muscled legs.

Rake thumped his tail and didn't bother rising. Joy knew better. Butter him up, she knew, jumping to her feet with a smile to greet him.

The door shut; Ram was more than ready to receive her. Strong arms slipped round the incredible smallness of her waist, bringing her hard against the broad chest, and before she could say anything, his mouth lowered to hers. He tasted lavender and spices and thought wildly he'd devour her then and there. The kiss deepened as he pressed her lips harder and more passionately, starving for the taste of her mouth. She felt that swift wondrous melting feeling and . . . something else. Something that made her pull back with a gasp. "You're all wet!"

Salty beads of moisture slid from the hard muscles of his body. A huge wet stain covered her blue cotton dress. "Aye!" He chuckled, amusement warm and lively in his gaze. "We worked up quite a sweat, and I thought it best to bathe before coming here. Now my love"—he bent and kissed her mouth again—"you are wet as well."

Adding insult to injury, he shook his hair all over her. Chills raced from each drop, but her cry of protest mixed with laughter as she jumped back safely from his reach. Ram watched the gentle sway of her hips as she retreated to the dressing room to fetch a towel and a change of clothes. Two long ropes of her hair swung with the movement as well, and he could not say exactly why he liked her hair braided so much, except that Mary had always worn her hair that way.

Joy fetched a towel and a night gown, chatting the whole way. "Sean's asleep," she first whispered, pointing to the cradle, proceeding to tell him about that. Ram was only too glad to hear it, for he had plans for the boy's mother. She then seemed particularly interested in how he felt, if he felt tired or no, and Ram smiled at her interest, pleased with her like mind.

He hardly listened though, as she presented him with her back, a long row of buttons. He forgot the towel. The day had been unusually warm—the damnable queer weather again—and she wore only a chemise beneath the dress. He tackled the task, acutely conscious of this, for from his viewpoint above, the rosy tips of her breasts were barely covered in the white cotton chemise, teasing, begging for his touch—

"Thank goodness, he is sleeping early for once," she finished, acutely conscious of the warmth of his fingertips brushing her bare skin. "Of course, I always think he should be sleeping more, but he's always thinking something else. He is so like you!"

Ram pushed the undergarment from her shoulders. Small shivers raced through her as his lips replaced his hands. She closed her eyes to the pleasure of it. He was just about to lift her to the bed, wet or no, when she stepped from the pile of clothes.

"I'm glad though, for tonight is very special."

"Ah, every night is special," he agreed wholeheartedly. Every night was special when a man felt the force of unlimited desire, a desire that poetically might spring from his heart and mind but one he felt physically centered in his groin. The thought made him smile, one short lived as he had trouble concentrating past the beauty of her naked backside.

What was she going on about?

He didn't know, didn't care, not with the vision of those straight slender shoulders, the curves of that waist, the long lines of her legs. Never had a woman's backside been so erotic to him! With her name on his lips, he reached for her just as she turned back to him and shyly, holding her nightgown in front of herself, said, "I've waited for the perfect time. A night when we're alone and unhurried, just you and I."

Her words and manner spoke the very word seduction, and a tender smile lifted on his handsome face. "This night is special to you." He realized, willing to let her have her way—to a point. She looked startlingly lovely, standing there, her unclad beauty partially shielded by the folds of white silk.

"Yes, it is," she said earnestly. "Oh Ram, I just know you'll be unspeakably moved!"

"Unspeakably moved?" he questioned, then laughed, "Well, I suppose . . ."

"I promise!"

"Indeed!"

He felt suddenly on the edge of his seat. He certainly did not need a seductive game, but the fact that she not only wanted to play one but was initiating one brought amusement, delight and admittedly interest. No doubt it would be tame by any standards, for she was still and always would be the innocent in so many respects, at least until the moment he touched her. Then an entirely different woman emerged . . .

She lifted the night dress over her head. Smooth folds of white silk slid over her skin. He suffered a moment's confusion but reasoned undressing must be part of her game. He dropped his wet breeches and quickly donned his black cotton robe.

Joy pointed to the desk chair. "Why don't you sit there and get comfortable, while I pour you a brandy."

Smiling, Ram assumed his desk chair, watching as she moved about the room. She was such a constant surprise and delight, and the way his heart beat he might have just finished a run! How perfect she was for him!

She returned with a brandy, set carefully to the table.

468

Ram's brow rose as she knelt at his feet, looking up at him with wide innocent eyes, a deceptively angelic appearance in white silk. He was not going to last—

"Before I start, I want you to imagine something."

His imagination ran rampant with patently unchaste thoughts and amusement sprang in his gaze, but a thick velvet voice answered, "Believe me, I can imagine anything at this point."

"Good." She smiled, somewhat surprised by how well her plans were going. "Imagine, if you will," she stopped abruptly, "why are you looking at me like that?"

"Because love"—he chuckled—"anticipation has simply never been so sweet. I am in fact on the edge of my seat."

"And I have not even begun!" She could hardly believe his interest. "Oh just wait, just wait."

His smile grew.

Joy cleared her throat. "Shall we begin?"

"By all means!"

"All right. Now imagine if you will that you are a northern abolitionist, yet only in principal. By day you are moved by the greatest evil of apathy. In other words," she said meaningfully, "you don't do absolutely everything you can for the cause."

So set was his mind on something entirely different, he didn't think he heard right. "What?"

"I just know Garrison's address will be more meaningful that way."

"Garrison's address?" he repeated but for a moment absolutely dumbfounded. He stared for a moment more in shock.

She took the letter in hand. "It's quite long—ten pages—" she began, "and if at any time you'd like to finish reading it yourself, just tell me. We can discuss it afterward."

"Can we now?" his voice dripped with sarcasm, barely contained, for the only thing he was willing to discuss was getting his head examined. He should be strung up for being such a fool! He should string her up for playing him so! Yes, revenge—

"Oh yes!" she smiled, completely missing his tone. "Are you ready? Are you imagining you're a northern abolitionist?"

"Oh, I'm imagining things all right!" He swallowed the drink whole, like revenge . . .

"Good. I shall begin." She cleared her throat once again, and with a pretty smile, she began to read, "'It may be inquired of me why I seek to agitate the subject of slavery in New England, where we all acknowledge . . .'"

Her passion, that was the damn trouble, he thought. She had two separate and distinct passions, and he wondered if passion were measured like gold on a scale, which of hers would be greater?

He listened for a moment. The musical lift to her voice alone would have sold him the package, he realized as his lascivious gaze rested on the package itself, wrapped in white silk and kneeling before him. "Joy love," he abruptly interrupted, "come sit on my lap. The light's better up here."

"So it is." Obediently she rose and sat comfortably on his lap. He smiled. Immediately she realized it was a mistake. His great warmth flowed like a current through her. He smelled deliciously of the salty taste of the sea. The rough hairs of his thighs tickled her bottom through the flimsy cloth of her gown.

"Go on, love."

"Yes." She forced her consciousness away from the hard lean body beneath her. "I shall try to do it justice."

"Justice . . . by all means."

"This evil has preyed upon the very vitals—"

"What?"

She blushed. "Vitals," she repeated.

"Vitals." He nodded.

"Vitals of the Union, and has . . ." As the words sounded in the quiet room, Ram caressed a braid of her hair, casually as though he wasn't aware of doing so. Yet as he stroked her braid, his thumb, just his thumb, lightly stroked under her arm on her side, inches from her breast. At first she was only vaguely aware of it, but the sensation mounted, growing. A pleasant tingling sensation spread from the spot and she squirmed. Somehow the squirm brought the heat of his fingertips closer to a place she simply couldn't think about and keep on reading. She stumbled, stopped, and looked at him. Only then she saw what he had been staring at. "Ram." Her arms partially crossed over her bosom. "What are you staring at?"

He seemed only then to realize it. "Oh . . . well, you know how one stares at a spot while listening to another read? Well, there's my spot." He pointed to a small red jam stain on her gown, just over the tip of her breast. She looked down, but all she could see was the shocking transparency of the white silk. She blushed, looked back at his face, but saw only innocence.

"Sorry love," he smiled. "I distracted you. Go on. This is just getting interesting."

Flustered somewhat, she cleared her throat and resumed, "But it may be said the miserable victims of the system have . . ." As she resumed reading, he resumed the caressing of her braid, the movement of his thumb. The maddening tingling sensation returned, somehow increased by the brief absence. A not unpleasant kind of congestion grew in her chest, growing until—

Her nipples tightened like tiny buds beneath a spring rain. She stopped abruptly.

"What's wrong?" he asked. "You're blushing love," he noticed. "Are you warm?"

"Yes," she said too quickly.

"Here, I'll get you a glass of water." He reached for the pitcher of water, set on the desk with two glasses, and the movement brushed his arm across her breast. A lick of fire shot through her. Her breasts, as though called to attention, rose like erect toy soldiers.

He seemed not to notice as he handed her the glass. She took a sip, shocked at her wantonness in the face of something so terribly important. More determined than ever, she took his hand and laid it safely across her lap before resuming. "No! Let the truth on this subject, undisguised, naked, terrible as it is, come, come before us—"

"Naked truth," he interrupted, "now there's a pretty metaphor." He seemed to be contemplating the poetry of the words, yet his unwavering gaze remained firmly fixed on a spot.

She bit her lip, looking up at him, wondering how those words could remind her of the night they spent at the Marquis de la Vern's great house in a bedroom that had gilt framed mirrors over the enormous feather bed, and when he had made love to her—

She squirmed in discomfort again, her heart beating much too fast and her voice curiously shaky as she forced herself to continue. For a paragraph, things—with the noted exception of her heart beat—seemed to settle down. Just when she thought herself all right, clearly owning his undivided attention and moving along fine, his hand resting over her lap stirred. She felt his fingertips moving ever so slightly just above her thigh, on her hip.

So slight, yet she felt heat rising in her abdomen as she mechanically mouthed the words that suddenly had no meaning. She could not steer her mind from those fingertips, caressing so softly, surely. A soft throbbing grew at her most secret point, and she felt an urge to twist, moving those fingers a few precious inches over—

She shifted again, squirming like a small child in the pews of a church. The mischievous fingertips moved a good inch closer to that precious point of need. The paper suddenly trembled, and she stopped briefly to clear her throat, resuming quickly, only to realize the tingling in her breasts continued, a jealous demand for equal attention. She

472

flushed, feeling warm, so warm, and she felt herself losing it, her voice quivering with the paper as she forced herself to read on.

Heat kept rising. She felt tiny beads of perspiration line her upper lip. Those fingertips were maddening! With some horror, she felt herself moistening, and her voice quivered. She shifted again, only to bring her thigh against hard hot pressure of him—

"Now what?"

She looked at him with what could only be described as alarm, a question as she looked down at the subject of her thoughts. The magnificent sight was shielded in black cotton, though she felt its heat in force. "Ram . . . I—"

"Joy." He chuckled. "I cannot even think of you without wanting you, let alone have you sit on my lap. Just ignore my state of affairs. I know I am," he lied outright. "Go on. This becomes more interesting by the minute."

She nodded, blushed profusely, feeling foolish and embarrassed both. He obviously had no trouble separating base physical needs from the exalted moral purpose. How could she? Again, she resumed. "Why are we this willing to believe a lie? Bound by the United States Constitution . . ."

The trouble was she could not ignore it. She felt him! Thoughts intruded. How eagerly she learned the pleasure of roaming her hands over the hard, lean body, kissing, touching, playing, of taking and holding that hard, hot part of him—

She stopped. "More water please."

Ram handed her the glass.

She took a sip, struggling to compose herself. "Where was I?" She stared blankly at the paper.

"Bondage," he replied immediately. "You were just after his poignant reminder that we can never know the agony of bondage."

"Bondage," she repeated, the word triggering another erotic memory. She had overheard one of Ram's men telling

473

another about this woman he had been with the night before, and when she had asked Ram what that word meant in the context, the very devil had sprung in his gaze. All he said was that the principal was best demonstrated, and before she understood, he had lifted her to the bed, gently pinning her arms with one hand and her legs with one of his. She first thought it was funny and had tried to fight him, only to discover the futility of it. Once she was still, held helpless to his will, she felt a twinge of fear, until he kissed her in a way he never had before. The kiss was hard and hot but with a slow lazy quality to it that made her writhe, made her want more. Only she couldn't move—

She wanted him to kiss her like that.

She licked her lips. Distressed, confused, her hands lifted to brush stray wisps of hair from her flushed face. He never wasted an opportunity and his hands came under her arms as though to hold her balanced, lending his support, yet his thumbs slowly began to caress the beckoning mounds of her breasts. Then she knew she would die—

"Kiss me," she didn't know what she was saying. "Please, kiss me."

Ram allowed the laughter in his heart a brief moment's triumph over the desire coursing through him. She no longer cared. All she knew was that she would die if she didn't feel his lips on hers, and with that knowledge, her arms went around his neck and she found his lips. Softly, shakily, seeking, she kissed him, and in that kiss his question of passion was answered.

The kiss broke as the thin strings of her gown were pushed around her waist and his hands brushed over the sensitive bare peaks. Shuddering little shocks bolted through her.

"I was testing you, you know," he told her.

She didn't care what he was doing so long as it was to her. All she knew was that she wanted him, all of him. She wanted to feel him everywhere and all at once. She wanted him to love her until she begged him to stop. Yet it occurred to her to ask, "Did I fail?"

"Quite the contrary love!" He chuckled, as his calloused hands covered her breasts, measuring their softness against the hard palm, massaging gently until her breath came in shaky uneven gasps and waves of pleasure washed over her. "You passed with flying colors."

Her reward was his love, played out endlessly that night. Gently and tenderly, then fiercely and passionately, his love brought her soaring to passion's ultimate height where he followed her with the wondrous winged creature he knew as his love.

Yet, as they finally lay exhausted and spent, wrapped in the warm afterglow of their love's expression, she felt a familiar sadness fill her. "I love you so much," she whispered into the darkness. "Sometimes after you love me like this, I remember when fate separated us . . ."

"Shhh." His lips gently brushed her closed eyes. He knew what she felt, for he often felt the same. Even now, with the privacy and leisure of the ship's voyage, he sometimes felt he could not get enough of her. He wanted to take her away to some far away place where they could be alone, laughing beneath the warmth of the sun. "The past is behind us, over and through," he said. "Joy, my love—" he kissed her tenderly—"we have only just found the beginning of the book that will be our lives." The thought let her drift into a deep dream-filled sleep, where together they danced and laughed and loved the night away.

The first golden kiss of the sun touched the far eastern horizon as a large excited crowd gathered outside the captain's quarters. Seanessy, followed by eight well-chosen men, moved theatrically to the door of the captain's quarters. Sean motioned for absolute silence, and taking a long draught from a rum bottle, he bowed, then gave the signal. With a huge grin, a good hard kick, the door burst open, and Seanessy stepped boldly in the room, the men behind him.

They found Ram already on his feet, his fists clenched, long before Joy, holding little Sean at her side in the huge bed, even managed to dazedly sit up. Thankfully Rake had been let out in the middle of the night when little Sean had sought the warmth of his parents' bed. The dog was now tied to the raft of the main sail, barking nonetheless.

"What the hell is this?"

There was no doubt who asked the question or who would answer. Seanessy stepped forward, laughter bright and menacing in his eyes. "I am sorry for waking you like this, my lord," he had the unprecedented gall to say, as he bowed formally. "There was no other way."

Ram decided he would kill Sean, brother or no, just as soon as he discovered what this was about. "No other way for what?"

"Why, to bring you your wedding present!"

Joy giggled suddenly from the bed. Little Sean watched with wide enormous eyes, yet Ram was not nearly as amused. "My what?" he demanded.

"Your wedding present!" Sean repeated and took what he knew would be his last draught before explaining: "It's long overdue but here at last. Your crew has mutinied, my lord, and your ship has for several days sailed off course. Right now we're two miles from Little Sean's island—which, surprise, surprise!—is your wedding present, a week or two of uninterrupted pleasure with Joy on the island! I and the men here are going to drop you over the side. How do you like that, my lord?"

Apparently not much, for Ram's fist connected hard with Sean's jaw. The giant was knocked into two others. Joy screamed. Little Sean clapped, peels of excited giggles pouring from his mouth. Never had he seen so much fun so early in the morning. Just when he would have scrambled

476

into the now furious battle, Bart appeared and scooped up Joy and the boy into his arms, carrying them quickly from the violence of that room.

Little Sean's scream of protest was met by the loud cheers of the crowd, all of which drowned out Bart's explanation as he carried her to the waiting lifeboat. "Sean arranged everything. The island is divided in half. The crew and the women—don't tell Ram about the women on Sean's ship till he cools a bit, 'cause he don't like lasses taken on voyages at all—anyway, we'll all be on the other half of the island. Your women will take little Sean, and when the two of you want to see the boy, you'll find a flag on your side. Just raise it and he'll be brought to ya. Other than that, Sean says if ye see anyone, 'twill be their head, and he means it, too! There's food and wine and oh, he made it real nice for ye!"

Joy heard only bits and pieces of this over the loudly cheering crowd, the furious clamor coming from Ram's quarters. Yet the excitement on Polly's, Mrs. Thimble's and the reverend's faces, standing near the lifeboat, said all, and she was laughing as the reverend took little Sean from her arms. She kissed them goodbye, then kissed Polly and Mrs. Thimble, too. Bart set her carefully in the empty lifeboat. She waved to all as it was lowered slowly into the water.

The roar of the crowd rose as Ram, carried by six men, was brought to the side, and with a curse rendered mercifully inaudible, he fell thirty or so feet into the cool water. It was the only ungraceful movement she had ever seen from him. He surfaced quickly, searching the crowded deck for Sean, who now held his son.

"You will pay for this Seanessy. I swear I will have your hide!"

Little Sean clapped wildly at his father's show. The other Sean seemed only too unalarmed and called down, "I'll be sure to mark my calendar, my lord!"

Joy could not let Ram suffer alone. She slipped into the

cool water, only then dropping the bed covers. Swimming underwater, she emerged directly in front of him, entwining her body to his. She heard his laughter just as his lips met hers. To the wild cheers of the crowd, he kissed her. Long and sweet, he kissed her in the middle of the cool blue ocean water beneath the warm promise of a new day's sun.